Revenge and Machinery

I am so grateful for your support!
Victoria L Szulc

Victoria L. Szulc

 Although there are references to actual historic events, places, and people, all of the characters, places, and dialogue in this book and its related stories, are fictitious, and any resemblance to any person living or dead is coincidental.

Editor: Debbie Manber Kupfer

Logo design: Becky Hansen

Cover illustration: Victoria L. Szulc

ISBN-10: 1533164517
ISBN-13: 978-1533164513

FOR THE BELIEVERS.

For those who have very little to sustain them but have the strongest of faith against insurmountable odds.

ACKNOWLEDGMENTS

Special thanks to my friends and beta readers: Amy Herrmann, Dana Catalano, and Ann Huber, editor Debbie Manber Kupfer, to friends and screenwriters/directors, Gena Ellis and Chelsea Zotta, supporters Kim Bess Kittrell and Melissa Boyer-Horan, to Jackie James and the staff at The London Tea Room for their support and the best tea on earth, to Morris I. Sless for being the first donor to my GoFundMe which allowed the printing of this book, to Jodie and Joshua Timbrook and the crew at The Heavy Anchor for their support, to Barbara MacRobie of the Missouri Arts Council for your beta reading, insight, enthusiasm, and friendship, to Janel Dahm-Tegtmeier, her family, and the staff of 1900 Park Creative Space gallery for their help in all my artistic endeavors and to my growing group of fans worldwide, I thank you, I am truly grateful.

PROLOGUE-REVENGE

Raterville, Texas, Early November 1895

A slight wind teased the tresses of Kate Church as she stood in the wilderness, a couple miles outside of a small town in Texas. Raterville was much like Iris, from which she'd evacuated just a few weeks prior: barren, broken, and dying.

In the dry heat of the mid-morning sun, Kate spied a small cloud of dust kicked up from the shadow of a single horse and rider. Her heartbeat increased ever so slightly at the sight of her expected guest, sending blood pulsing through her veins. She exhaled and clutched her parasol more closely to her side as if the cool steel of the handle provided her comfort.

Kate knew that Drasco would show; he was now a desperate money-grubbing bastard after his folly in Iris. She'd taken away his livelihood and managed to kill most of his men. Drasco was terribly wounded in the blast at the warehouse that had held his prize stash of mysterious volatile liquids. She licked her lips in the anticipation of his final decimation.

Only a few days before, back in St. Louis, Mr. Bartlett mentioned that the rotten cowboy was still alive. His words left a horrible pang in Kate's gut. She could barely contain her disappointment at the news and bit the inside of her cheek so that she tasted the metallic flavor of her blood. She had hoped to rid the world of all that evil.

Oh and Mr. Bartlett—how he had kissed and confused her. Just the brief memory brought unusual warmth to her heart. Despite the conflict, Kate decided she would join him. But there was business to attend to first.

After that tumultuous meeting, Kate went directly to the nearest train station with his news echoing in her head. She furiously rubbed her temple trying to ease the pain away. As she purchased a round trip ticket back to Texas for the very next day, her hands shook in anger, but she still managed to feign a smile to the clerk.

By the time Kate returned home from her secret afternoon errands, there was no doubt in her mind that Drasco would die and she would do almost anything to make that happen including lying to her family.

She explained to Abby and Ferris that she had been called by her potential new employer to make a quick trip out of town.

"Abby, I just have to go, dear. Don't fret, please. It'll just be a few more days." Ferris looked more than worried, but Kate managed to carefully fudge about where she was going. "I've just got to make a quick stop to a branch office to check on a few things. I won't be long." Kate slowly grazed her sister's upturned cheek with tender strokes of her fingertips.

"Sister, you just returned after being away so long." Abby pouted like a child while her gaze drifted down. But inside she was no longer overtly worried. She was ready to start her new life with Ferris. He was the man she'd always dreamed of finding—tender, but hard working and driven. Abby was done struggling. She didn't want to be bothered with the affairs of working women any longer. She was prepared to be a wife and a mother, God willing.

"Well, surely you must go then." Ferris smiled a bit, and tried to not betray his new bride. A tiny part of him still cared for Kate more than he liked. "I'm sure it's for the best." He put a trusting arm around Abby.

"It most certainly is. Now I must go." Kate twittered sweetly and sashayed up the stairs.

Satisfied that she'd soothed their mild protests, Kate swiftly packed a single satchel and left on the first train out the morning after. As she boarded, Kate marveled at how accustomed she'd become to keeping secrets. How easy it was to assure those closest to her, with a gentle stroke of a hand and a tender eye, that she would only be gone for a few days. Underneath the surface of her emotions, this craftiness disturbed her a bit. Her shoulders stiffened; her mouth dried.

Once seated on her passage, Kate tried to relax, letting her hands fall daintily into her lap for a brief moment. But when the train pulled slowly away from St. Louis, her blood nearly boiled yet again with the familiar sounds of the car clicking along on the rails. An old anger rose inside her as she formulated a plot to kill her once ruthless nemesis. To the casual passenger, Kate may have appeared to be daydreaming, allowing her eyes to drift along the rural landscape. This would be a poor observance on their part. Kate was preparing herself for a simple, yet devastating revenge as her hands tightened around the handles of her bag.

I'll have to be very discreet and quick; in and out, Kate mused. She didn't have a conductor or contact to help her this time. She wore a very modest brown gingham dress and bonnet, in order to hide in plain sight. A change of clothes and her usual weapons were securely packed. She released her grip as she calmed with the steady sway of the train. Her fingers flickered over the simple fabric as her mind rehearsed the urgently crafted plan.

Iris was no longer a stop on the line, but Kate figured that the town just East of it, Raterville, was close enough. Years of working for the rail had paid off. She knew that the line followed the creek. This rendezvous location was perfect, not too close or too far from town. The terrain was a little rougher here; the cliffs steeper along the banks. Another stream merged into the creek just north of the town. It made the water deeper, so cattle drives or prospectors didn't come through too often. But hunters liked it because the game wasn't scared away by ranchers.

Kate had wired ahead to check on the availability of a horse to rent. Once she arrived, she made a beeline for the general store, and paid handsomely for the loan of her steed. And as she had hoped, Raterville was quickly becoming like Iris. More people were passing through than staying. It wouldn't be too unusual for someone like her to make a quick stop here or for outlaws to relocate temporarily.

Her lender, the owner of the store, was grateful for her generosity and even offered her some information on where it was safe to reside for a few days. "Well, Miss, you may want to stay at the Carson, 'cause the Mattson Hotel is rumored to house an unsightly group of cowboys." His kind eyes looked around in a protective glance to check if anyone in the store was listening.

Kate continued to surprise herself, as she feigned ignorance as to why it wasn't safe. "Oh do tell, Sir." She battered her lashes and leaned ever so slightly in the owner's direction as if to hear a delicious morsel of gossip.

The store's proprietor was eager to inform her that Iris had been vacated only a few weeks earlier due to some odd explosion. "A small band of maimed fellas rode in shortly thereafter." He smoothed his goatee in a suave motion. So Kate was assured that the remaining rascals from the now deserted Iris were lying low in town, but most of the people there were uneasy at their presence. "People 'round here weren't too happy when they showed up. It's bad enough that they took over Iris."

Kate played gracious and genteel, taking quick mental notes of the little nuggets she'd been given so freely. She held her gloves as if they were a small child and thanked her unintentional informant as her pleasant grin flirted with him. The owner's eyes followed her as she exited until he realized that Kate had left a ten dollar tip on the counter. He glanced round, snatched the money, tucked it neatly into his pocket and set about his work. The payment had sufficiently distracted him from her departure.

Once outside, Kate made quick work of loading her small stash of supplies on to her ride. She was delighted to find that the Carson was a perfect post from which to observe Drasco's new hiding place. She smiled at the clear view of all the comings and goings in front of the Mattson. And fool Drasco was already making his presence known around town. His boasting hadn't ceased, even after near death.

Drasco had also kept the habit of gambling and drinking at dusk. As the sun set, he and two others headed for the local saloon, just a few buildings away. Kate gleefully noted that he walked with an altered gait, one leg almost dragging behind the other. She had hoped for this very situation. While watching the Mattson Hotel, she'd penned a short but tempting letter:

"Dear Mr. Drasco:

I have heard that you recently lost a large shipment of your "special" explosives. However, I also understand that you know the direct source from which to procure them. I would be most generous in gathering this information from you. Perhaps for a cash sum of $10,000?

Please meet me at 11 a.m. where the creek forks just north of town and come alone. If you arrive with anyone else, any possible deal is off.

Sincerely,

Maggie Barnes"

Kate could almost read Drasco's mind. He had severely disappointed whoever was supposed to receive the liquids. He'd lost a lot of money and was not looking forward to having to harvest more of the cacti with a depleted group of men. He may have even permanently lost the buyer. In any event, she was certain that he needed money. A simple, but large amount could surely buy the location from him. And he wouldn't be threatened by a woman.

Kate was correct on all accounts. She left her note addressed to Drasco with the clerk at the Mattson while the cowboys played cards. A little monetary tip to the night desk personnel guaranteed that her rival would receive the note when he returned from the saloon that evening. His comrades were too drunk to care about some slip of paper and they went straight to their rooms as Drasco scanned the note with interest.

A well prepared Kate set out early the next morning with her weapons triple checked and her ride rested and fed. Her hands held the reigns loosely as her steed took on the desert with a steady gait.

About a half mile from the meeting site, Kate found a small group of trees where she could hitch her horse and change clothes. Within a few moments, the Widow had arrived back in Texas. Kate stood taller as her confidence grew. She walked in long, straight strides towards her destination and arrived with plenty of time to spare. At precisely 11 a.m., Kate saw Drasco emerge from the dusty horizon. Under the Widow's veils, she smiled.

As Drasco approached and dismounted quickly, Kate could see that he recognized her disguise immediately from the wicked grin on his face. "Well now Widow, or should I call you Maggie? You didn't need to meet all the way out here to pay me you know. Heck, a saloon would've been nice."

"Mr. Drasco, surely you must know that I value my privacy." Kate spoke sweetly, trying to sound as feminine as possible.

"I have no beef with you Widow," Drasco growled. He hoped he hadn't ridden almost halfway back to Iris with a bum leg for nothing.

"Oh, Mr. Drasco, I think you're wrong on that account." Kate slowly lifted the heavy veils while sneering at her old adversary.

Drasco squinted as seeing a mirage. A puzzled look on his face soon turned to rage. His cheeks turned a fiery red. Even with her dark hair, he recognized Kate. "Aw, you bitch!" he sputtered.

"Well, that isn't quite what I expected." Kate grimaced. "But it doesn't matter now. I'm here to rid you of your last few moments on earth." She was completely unafraid of him as she haughtily lifted her chin in confidence.

"You can't kill me," he chortled. "You won't. But hah, then again, you're no lady!" Drasco reached for his gun.

As he prepared to fire, Kate fully opened her parasol for the first time. It was the one she'd purchased with the dress, and then made special modifications with Riley's help long ago. The top of the shade wasn't the usual spike. Instead Drasco saw the tip of a narrow shotgun barrel explode with a mighty flash, even in the blinding sun.

The unexpected force of Kate's inconspicuous weapon threw off her aim, but succeeded in blowing off Drasco's right arm. The limb dangled gruesomely by the thread of only his shirt seam. She missed her intended target, his heart, but the wicked man collapsed to the ground in agony with a hysterical cry.

Kate blew the gun smoke from the parasol, placed it on the desert floor and twittered, "Hmm, I guess that will need a little more work." Her eyes never left Drasco as he writhed in pain like the snake that he was.

Kate daintily pulled up the skirt of her dress, unhooked her whip from her garter and stepped forward to finish off her last demon of Iris. She snapped the tool that was the only token she had left of Michael Parker. The whip that had once tortured her had now become a means to her revenge. Kate cracked it with amazing skill and caught Drasco's right ankle. She had no desire to physically touch the filthy criminal.

Drasco moaned and gasped as Kate dragged him by the tightened whip. "Oh, did that hurt?" Kate laughed. "Please, shut up you lousy bastard." She lost patience as his guttural groans continued. It was time to be done with him. A scarlet trail of blood painted the desert as Kate pulled him to the very edge of the steep creek ravine.

Kate then stooped at his side, ignoring his pleas while she emptied his saddle pouch and detached her whip from his ankle. She skillfully coiled it as Drasco babbled empty promises of wealth and power. "I can give you whatever you want. Please. Money, more than you can imagine." He lay on his side, panting and grasping his shoulder. The blood oozed through his fingers.

Kate finally stood over him; her dark shadow appeared like a grim reaper ready to pull him to his last end.

"You are a pitiful liar, thief and murderer. You shan't be allowed to live." Kate's voice came in a low, almost catlike growl. And with that, she kicked his dying body over the side of the cliff. His bloody left hand caught a last bit of hard earth as his legs struggled to find traction.

Kate looked down at him mercilessly, her lips tightening in a firm line. For the first time Drasco looked genuinely terrified as he perilously clung to the edge. "Please, please Kate."

"I think a lady should be addressed properly." Kate's words were filled with scorn as she eyed her former tyrant.

"Please Miss Church. Please, I'm so sorry. I can get you

money, riches, the source of the explosives, whatever you want." The desperate marauder begged.

"So I am a lady?" A grim smile covered Kate's face. "Would you like a hand then?" She barely extended her fingers to him in jest.

But before Drasco could answer, Kate, with a mighty heel, stomped on his left fingers. He howled like a dying wolf and let go. As her worst enemy fell to a certain death, Kate walked straight away from the cliff edge without looking back.

"I think that it would be rude to watch him fall," Kate sneered to herself. She dusted off her black gloved hands with polite precision. With a quick snatch of her parasol, she prepared to mount Drasco's horse. She closed her eyes as an odd satisfaction filled her now that Drasco was dead.

But Kate's pleasant relief was interrupted by what she thought was a metallic clanking sound. Her eyes popped open with alarm. She turned to see a glimmer of light fast approaching behind her. Drasco had come alone. *Who or what could this be?*

There was no time to find out if it was friend or foe. Kate hopped onto Drasco's horse and broke into a full gallop with the wind blasting through her veils. She had to hide and do it fast; there was no time to make it back to her rented stallion. The black of her dress stood out far too much against the landscape. She bolted for a large collage of desert shrubbery and boulders. Once behind some minimal coverage, with hurried hands, Kate tied the stolen beast, offed her dress and hat, stuffed the clothing in her satchel and slid down. Her bosom heaved as she clutched her weaponry in anticipation.

The clanking of metal grew louder as the thing approached. Wearing only her undergarments, Kate peered through the tops of the vegetation at the oddest contraption.

The machine was the height of two men, mounted onto four large sturdy wagon wheels. Although it had a body like an engine locomotive, it was unique in that there was a pair of pincers, much like a crab, mounted on the front. A large smoke stack at the rear end hissed as the machine paused right at the site of Drasco's demise. The steady roar of an engine drowned out the sounds of nature around them.

With another rattle, a sectioned metal tube popped up from the top of the machine and writhed as if it were a snake emerging from the grass. It uncoiled while appearing to scan its surroundings. When it turned in Kate's direction, she saw a large unblinking cat-like eye mounted in the tube's end. Without warning, it retracted into the vehicle with a clang.

Can they see me? Anxiety ripped through Kate's limbs as she dropped to the desert floor all a tremble and tried to soothe Drasco's horse with some apples she'd stashed.

Kate continued to spy as a hatch clattered open on the side of the vehicle. Two men, wearing full brown leather protective gear and goggles, jumped out. They followed Drasco's blood trail and peered over the cliff. She could see them nodding and talking to one another, but with the machine noise, couldn't hear what they were saying. They returned to their odd coach, and opened a few panels in precise succession. One of the men pulled out a thick chain. The other prepped a hook and latches from the machine, and then assisted attaching them to his companion.

Once properly equipped, the first man rappelled over the side of the cliff. Kate could not see over the edge. *Did they come to get Drasco's body?*

No, the mysterious man returned with only Drasco's empty satchel after his partner had pulled a lever that drew the chain in with steady clicks from the machine. They thoroughly inspected the bag, nodded furiously, tossed the satchel back over the ledge and packed up their equipment. Like a pair of ants, they soldiered into the machine and closed the hatch. With another clatter and sounds of steam, the machine turned briskly round and left as quickly as it had arrived. When it finally disappeared over the horizon, Kate stood, dusted herself off, and small flecks of dirt flew lazily into the wind. *Stop shaking, you are strong,* she reprimanded herself.

Kate shook with the realization that they had wanted something in Drasco's bag. Her hands flew into her satchel, deftly sorting through his items that she had procured. There was some money, a few odd gambling receipts and one special item that clearly stood apart; an ornate gold key with a blue gem embedded at the top. As she pulled it into the sunlight, it cast its brilliant reflection on the trees and boulders. Fearing its sparkle would attract attention, Kate stashed it away, pushing it deep into the bottom of the bag. Someone needed this key badly enough to kill for it. She would hide the precious piece until she could find out more.

Kate rode to the same grove of trees, her heart racing. She was still wearing only her underthings, so she stopped to put the simple gingham dress on, and then blazed into Raterville with Drasco's horse in tow. While she was satisfied with Drasco's demise, a piece of Kate's mind would not quiet as she questioned her safety. *Who were those men?*

Soon she had tethered Drasco's beast to the back side of the Mattson Hotel, returned her horse to the general store and was on her way back to St. Louis by late afternoon. All the while Kate had no idea how well she had timed her mission.

About the same time Kate had boarded her train in Raterville, an elegant stagecoach arrived in Iris. Its robust wheels raised a dry flurry of dirt in the deserted town. The passengers had already seen

Drasco's dead body, arriving only a half hour after Kate and the mysterious men had left. They had also visited Iris' little church and its graveyard on their way to the now vacant town. None of the locations revealed what the small group of people was looking for, much to their disappointment.

Inside the coach, a woman and her three adult sons discussed some salacious business. The mother was in her early sixties, with white and blue streaked hair pulled into a neat bun topped with a mini bowler. She had a long, gaunt face and a lacy patch over her left eye which had been lost in a violent accident long ago. She was dressed almost completely in black save for a red ruby ring on her wedded finger that she gently polished with her other velvet gloved hand.

"How could he have failed so miserably? We provided him with money, men, and tools, even poison." The woman complained to her children in a clipped British accent. The young men were all in their thirties, very tall, of slight build, with dark curly hair and light eyes. Each wore fine tailored dark suits and top hats.

"Inexcusable," bemoaned the oldest, as a look of distain crossed his face.

"Horrendous," smirked the middle child.

"Terrible. What a pity," sighed the youngest. "So much work wasted."

"Oh, so much more than a pity, absolutely ludicrous, it is. He should have never been trusted to hold on to so much. Look at this devastation." Her gloved hand waved towards the window at the remains. "Oh driver, stop here," she demanded with a tap of her parasol to the roof of the carriage. The four gazed upon the crumbled and burnt out shells that had once been Iris. "Boys, go have a quick look around. Perhaps the fool lost it somewhere," she commanded her sons.

She too departed the vehicle, opened her hand bag with a crisp pull and proffered a case that held mini papers and tobacco. She deftly rolled herself a cigarette and pulled out a clear miniature canister filled with the mysterious green liquid. A flick of a small switch on the side of the tube caused the fluid to bubble for a brief moment and a small flame emitted from its brass topper. Mrs. Ellis, as she was called, lit her cigarette from the device then dropped it back into her bag. She took slow, long drags as her sons gathered briefly in the street.

Each pulled a small copper box from their pocket. The containers were identical, with miniature clear domes that gave off a yellow glow when turned on via a small handle at the end. They emitted a muted hum.

"Like finding a needle in a haystack," the eldest moaned. He was used to hunting people, not things.

"Hmm, but most everything's destroyed. This shouldn't take too long." The middle child remained optimistic.

"Well, let's get on with it then." The youngest bolstered, trying to sound determined.

The three then separated. The eldest went directly to the saloon, his coat flapping in the breeze. As he entered, shards of glass and broken wood crunched under his feet. The windows of the once lively establishment had blown through with the explosion. He walked to the bar with careful steps and peered around. His angular jaw tensed as his eyes adjusted to the dim light of the now decrepit dance hall.

He wrinkled his nose at the stench in the air. He knew what the smell or rather who the wretched air was, but regretted having to check it out any way. The dead saloon owner may have had the key somehow. He pulled a kerchief from his pocket and covered his nose. He pulled open the door to the closet under the stairwell. He resisted the tendency to gag as the rotted body of Ellie rested before him. She had been picked clean by vermin, and the remaining skin had pulled tightly over her skeleton. But his box crackled to life with a red glow. Beneath the proprietor's dried dead hand was a set of keys.

With one swift glance, the eldest Ellis son knew that they were not what he was searching for. But it did give him an idea. He ran up to the boudoirs of the dancing girls, the saloon steps groaning below his feet. Two of the ladies' rooms had brothel safes. However, each had long been emptied of their contents, left completely open with wispy cobwebs strung from their edges. The box in his hand had returned to its yellow haze. He swiftly checked all the rooms including the one belonging to Miss Church. With a thin layer of dust everywhere and scattered window bits on the floor, it was obvious that no one had been there for a long time.

He walked down the outer steps from Miss Church's room with steady clacks on the weather beaten boards. He lifted his chin as he looked outside. The horse trough was bone dry. He tried the handle of the water pump and it snapped off. He flicked it aside. There was a good-sized hole in the ash pit and a pile of dirt nearby. Perhaps someone had tried to find more water? He wondered. But again, nothing was left at the saloon.

Mother will not be pleased, he thought as he tucked his device into his coat pocket.

Meanwhile, the middle Ellis son searched through the hotel at breakneck speed. He carried an unusually long cane and used it to pop open doors and peer into the long-emptied rooms. He made his way to the clerk's desk. There, his box glowed red, but like his brother, the only keys he found belonged to rooms of the hotel. It was of greater importance to check the orphanage. At one time,

Sister Theresa was supposed to have had possession of a very particular key. Drasco had claimed he had retrieved it from her. The key had cost the nun her life.

Upon arriving in the dead Sister's room, the middle child viewed the damage that Drasco had left behind. Her quarters had been completely ransacked, clothing and toiletries scattered about. His copper box remained quiet. He twirled his cane through his long elegant fingers as he made his way back. *Ah, no such luck,* he pondered.

The third child of Mrs. Ellis stepped into the black shell of what had once been the explosive warehouse. He explored the ashes to no avail, the black dust whirling away in his wake. He then stepped outside to scan the surrounding grounds, crinkles forming around his eyes as he perused. Droplets of perspiration trickled down from his temples and creeped into the silken collar of his cravat, whilst the afternoon sun beat down. He held out his black box at arm's length and walked round in circles, slowly increasing the parameter of his search. Once he'd reached the outer most limits of where the debris had fallen, a stubborn finger turned off his copper box. He gave the crafty tool a light toss in the air and caught it in his outer suit pocket. It had never turned red. He hated to go back to mum empty handed, but it was no use. The key would've survived an explosion. It just wasn't there.

The three men begrudgingly returned to their mother. By the looks of their faces, she knew that the precious item had been lost.

"Hmmph." The mother groaned upon their approach to the coach. "Well then, we'll just have to find this young woman." She again ruefully rubbed her ring. Mrs. Ellis did not like the Americas. Everything seemed so uncivilized. And she didn't have fond memories of the country. The loss of the key would be cause for her family to remain here. Her husband had already been dispatched to another American city on a similar mission. "The others will not like this. They will not like this at all. I believe that they will want some revenge."

"Certainly," quipped the eldest with a sadistic grin. He hoped that he may be put in charge of what he did best.

"Most truly," the second son chimed in. He again playfully turned his cane and climbed into the coach. He was hopeful that he'd be able to trade it for his favorite sabre soon.

"Absolutely." The third child of Mrs. Ellis agreed as he assisted his mother. "We'll find it, for certain." His loquacious tone rolled over his lips in genteel tenderness. For the youngest Ellis son, his greatest weapons were seduction and sleight of hand.

"Back to Raterville then and onwards to St. Louis. We'll send the remaining cohorts of Mr. Drasco to harvest what they can." Their driver closed the door shut and hastily took to the reigns. The despondent characters of the carriage rode off as the sun headed towards a cool desert evening in the western horizon.

CONTENTS

1 JOINING THE GREATER GOOD

Kate fell into a restful sleep on the ride home with the gentle sway of the train. She arrived in St. Louis satisfied that Drasco was gone for good. Now all that was left of him were fading memories. Killing him was most unpleasant business; the image of his almost detached bloody arm wouldn't quite leave her mind at first. But as the train pulled into the station, the relief she felt was almost spiritual in nature. Kate's heart was light and her mind clear when she hailed a carriage bound for home.

As she skipped up the stairs to the Church residence, an excited Abby met her at the door, her voice squealing with delight.

"Kate, I'm so glad you're home," she exclaimed. "Look who's here!" Abby grasped her hand and led her inside.

The elder Church sister could not believe her eyes. Standing in the parlor with Ferris and Martha, was the long departed Silas. "Oh Silas!" Kate cried.

She dropped her bag with a thud and ran to the man that had rescued her so long ago. The pairs of siblings hugged each other and laughed wildly as the sweet sounds echoed against the storied walls of the old home. Kate's heart leapt to her throat in excitement.

"Oh Miss Kate, it's so good to see you!" Silas' voice boomed through the house. He looked the same, still well-dressed and groomed, only now completely bald. "I've been living and working with a family in Boston. When we received word that Mr. Church and Mr. Parker had both passed, I had to come straight away to see my sister." He glowed with happiness. Martha was smiling ear to ear and still clutched her brother's hand. "I don't think I can ever let her out of my sight again."

"I don't either," Martha smiled contentedly.

"I am so glad to see that everyone is safe." Kate burst, her face flushed with joy. Ferris was smiling too, although for a different reason.

"Kate, we have more good news!" Abby laughed. "Ferris received a most excellent employment offer!"

"From a very good investment firm back East." Ferris chimed in. "They've already offered moving expenses and what looks to be a fairly decent home from the picture they provided." He handed the photo to Kate. It was indeed a beautiful mansion. Her body started to quake as she realized that Mr. Bartlett had come through with her requests.

"Oh my." Kate had to sit. The room seemed to twirl around her. Abby moved in next to her on the sofa after witnessing her sister's stunned expression.

"Are you alright Kate?" Abby inquired, suddenly realizing that if she, Ferris, Silas and Martha all went East, Kate would be alone. But that wasn't what had upset Kate, and she couldn't dare let anyone know her new secrets.

"Yes, yes. In fact, I have a job offer here in St. Louis," Kate spoke. "I'm expecting word any day now with the details. They liked how I handled my trip." Kate tried to remain calm. Again the scope of her situation had hit her hard. This world of home was ending. There was no going back.

"Oh my, how the Lord does provide," Martha chirped. "Let's

celebrate!" She beamed at her brother as they went to the kitchen to prepare some refreshments.

"They may have sent something already." Abby jumped up, pulled a familiar looking envelope from the table drawer and handed it to Kate. "This came two days ago. Is that it?"

Kate tried to hide her over excitement. The Invitation had come early. She swallowed hard and faked pleasantries. "Why yes, I think it is."

Ferris crossed the room to look over his new spouse's shoulder in curiosity. Kate could feel too many eyes on the Invitation.

"Um, yes. Excuse me for just a moment; I need to check on the details." The letter's confidential nature had to be protected. She felt incredibly hot as she attempted to conceal the note. "I'll be back in a bit." She hurried to her bedroom, pressed the door shut with her fingertips and immediately opened the letter from her Benefactor.

"Dear Miss Church:

I must trust that you have had enough time to make a decision. We did not want to rush you, but a situation has arisen in which your services would be well applied. I hope that you will be able to meet with Mr. Bartlett on Tuesday at 2:30 p.m. at the gravesite of your father, Mr. Henry Church, in Calvary Cemetery, to discuss further details. Please come alone, dressed in mourning.

I hope that you have decided to join us and look forward to meeting you.

Sincerely,

W."

Kate cringed as she tucked the invite into her bag. Today was Tuesday and it was already 11:30 a.m. She was worried. She had to hurry. Kate leapt the stairs and startled the rejoined families. "I am so sorry. I can't stay," she spoke breathlessly. "I need to meet with my new employer today and I'd like to stop by the cemetery on the way." Kate hoped her bluff would satisfy them.

"Oh, I'd like to visit Papa too," Abby whimpered. Shock covered the faces of the Church clan.

"No, no, I'd like to visit him alone." Kate paused solemnly and brushed her sister's hand with a light touch. "We'll go together another time. My meeting is nearby and it'd be better if I went by myself." She was grateful her younger sister hadn't noticed that she was already dressed in black. The Widow had returned again.

"I'll bring my horse and buggy around Miss Kate." Silas offered. Kate hated how the wrinkles on his face betrayed his concern. She didn't want to be followed or worried about.

"Of course, we can't all go to your interview," Abby laughed. But Kate couldn't help but notice that Abby wrung her hands in disappointment.

"I'll be back as soon as I can," Kate assured them. It had been unusually warm for a late October day. The Indian summer sky had started to fill with rolling, grey clouds.

Silas had secured a simple, covered two-seater buggy with a light brown mare for the remainder of his journey to St. Louis from Boston. He was more than happy to offer it to Kate for her appointment. "Be careful, looks like a storm's coming in." He warned.

"I will, Silas, and thank you!" Kate was grateful in not having to procure transportation at the last minute and gave a hurried wave as she headed to the cemetery. She was almost there when the skies unleashed a torrent of heavy cold rain that felt like a whipping from a wet blanket. As she passed through the main gates, the wind had picked up, scattering brown dead leaves everywhere and stripping the trees of the last of their autumn glory. Mourners were exiting with shrieks of disappointment as Kate pushed on further into the grounds of the departed souls.

By the time she reached the plot where her father was buried, the small thunderstorm was reaching its peak. Kate stepped out to tether the horse and was completely soaked in seconds. Her parasol did little to shield her from the rain, and Kate decided to fold it. She approached the plot for the first time since the funeral and was shocked to see it was already marked with a tombstone. A marble slab with an engraved angel that was more expensive than the one she'd purchased. Kate brushed aside an errant wet tendril to inspect it more closely. *Had W. substituted it?* She shivered. Abby hadn't contributed to the arrangements, and Kate hadn't expected her to help. Kate's spine tingled and she gazed over the monuments of the deceased but couldn't see anything in the driving rain. Anxiety crawled over her skin. *Am I being watched?*

And indeed she was. Mr. Bartlett had stopped his horse under a large oak behind a small burial chapel several minutes before Kate had arrived. He observed her quick approach, was certain she was alone, and had checked that his pistol was tucked securely into his waistcoat. He hoped to make this quick, he did not want any unpleasantness.

Kate tromped through the wet grass to take cover under the entryway of a nearby mausoleum as the rain continued to pour mercilessly. She sighed deeply, checked her father's pocket watch and tried to relax on a cold marble bench. She was relieved to have arrived a bit early. Impressions were important to her new employer and she was hell bent to leave her past behind. She looked up from the timepiece to see Mr. Bartlett arriving in a small buggy not unlike hers. He jauntily stepped out, opened a huge umbrella and approached Kate with a steely gaze. He wore a black suit with a wool bowler and pinstriped ascot.

At last, Kate thought, it was time to move on. "May I join you?" he inquired, his eyes steady.

"Yes, of course," she replied, wondering how terrible she must look; probably like a drowned rat. She tried to sit up straight and offered a kind smile.

"I am afraid I have some unfortunate news Miss Church." He was solemn and his British lilt had taken on a proper tone. He snapped the umbrella shut and remained standing. "Your sudden departure put our business in jeopardy. You have disrupted your Benefactor's future plans." Mr. Bartlett's ferocity made Kate's heart sink. "I must withdraw your Benefactor's employment offer immediately." His voice was harsh and tinged with bitterness. "I have never known you and you are never to speak of our previous work. I advise you to tread lightly, Miss Church. As I have said before, I cannot protect you from those you have crossed. God speed." He popped the umbrella open and walked crisply to his carriage. Inside he was broiling with conflict. *This had not gone as planned.* He clutched the handle of the umbrella as if he wished to snap it into bits.

"Nooo," Kate whined like a child. "Please, I had to finish what I had started. Mr. Bartlett, please." She followed him into the downpour. Mr. Bartlett wasn't stopping and Kate trotted to catch up with him. She felt oddly sick, her insides clenched in knots. "Please sir, please."

He stopped abruptly, turned while dropping his umbrella, and put his hands on her shoulders. His eyes were like beams of steel that bore into her thoughts. "You! You do NOT know me." He hissed and continued sharply, "Don't you understand the peril you put yourself in? The trouble you've caused? Surely you know that your Benefactor knows of Drasco's end?" Kate felt the weight of his hands dragging on her, pushing her down. Her chest felt heavy as her muscles started to ache and give way to the pressure.

"I, I am so sorry," Kate stammered. "I needed…I thought I had to finish what I had started." The rain combined with tears that drenched her face.

"You're sorry? What on God's earth were you thinking? After all that was done for you. You thought you had to finish what? You thought wrong! Well our business is finished. I'd warned you before!" He shoved her rudely and she plopped backwards, flat on her bottom in the mud with a nasty splat. He started towards his buggy again, scooping up his umbrella on the way.

Kate was shattered. She scrambled up on all fours, slipping in the muck and stumbled forward only to land on her knees again. "Please, please, Sir. I have nowhere else to go." Her body racked with sobs. She grasped a tombstone with a muddy glove and yanked herself up. *You are strong Kate*, Chin's voice whispered in her mind. She pursued him, tumbling past the graves and finally caught up with Mr. Bartlett at his horse and buggy. She summoned every bit of courage to speak. "Please, listen, just for a moment. I made an awful mistake. And..and I understand it's over. That you don't need me, but if you would please, I beg of you. I have something, something that might be of use, though I don't know what it's for." Kate paused and was relieved that Mr. Bartlett had stopped as well.

Mr. Bartlett could not believe that Kate had dared to follow him. He looked at her plainly, hiding the turmoil that made his heart burn.

At least the angry face was gone, Kate thought and continued. She lifted her right boot, now filthy with wet earth splattered everywhere, turned the heel aside to reveal a secret compartment and produced the odd key that she had pulled from Drasco's dying body. She created the hiding spot after realizing that there were those willing to kill for it.

Even in the thick rain and rising fog the large key and its

mysterious blue stone shone brightly, its radiance alighting their faces.

Mr. Bartlett could not hide his curiosity. "You found this on him?" he inquired while pulling the umbrella over both of them. His heart relaxed at the sight of the treasure. He took the key and examined it, running his finger over the jeweled top.

"Yes," Kate whispered and wiped soaked hairs from her face.

"Did he say anything about it?" Mr. Bartlett knew what this was. It was important; he just hadn't expected that Drasco still had one of these very special keys. This was very, very good news indeed.

"No Sir," Kate mumbled meekly. "I am so sorry. He was already passed." The rain slowed to a gentle pitter patter. It was eerily quiet. She held her tongue about the men in the strange metal coach. At this point she'd made him so angry, she didn't want to create another argument. "May I go now, Sir?" Kate asked hoarsely. *How had he reduced me to feeling like a sullen child?*

"No, follow me." He replied quietly. He grabbed a blanket from the buggy and started towards a small water pump and well outside the chapel. "Come along now." His voice became almost chipper as he led her through the soaked lawn. He pulled a bucket from the well and pumped it full. Kate stood quietly by, puzzled by his change in behavior. *What was he going to do now?* "Here stand on this slab." He pointed, she did as asked and suddenly he flung the whole bucket of water over her.

"Ahhhh! What the hell?" Kate shrieked. "It's freezing." Goosebumps spread over her. The harsh chill slapped her and awoke her resolve.

"Shhh, a couple more, you're filthy." He pumped two more buckets and repeated the splashing until she was only wet, no longer muddy. "That mouth is dirty too. Quick cursing and act like a lady."

"Do you intend to kill me? You know there are other ways." Kate smirked.

"No, and yes there are other ways, but we don't have time for that now. Back to that mausoleum." Mr. Bartlett commanded. *If she'd only known I was supposed to kill her,* but he just couldn't do it. He had been only moments from drawing his pistol, when he had remembered how perfect she was, the face of an angel that made both his heart and loins ache. *She could turn deadly in an instant. She could've killed me too, right then,* he mused, while blinded by her beauty. She looked ravishing, even in a soaked mourning gown. He briskly broke off his hesitance as he tossed the bucket aside.

"Shake out your clothing on the way," Mr. Bartlett barked as they strode through the wet grasses to the safe marble structure. They needed to be away from possible prying eyes.

Kate dutifully followed the man who would be her leader in all things. She pouted and wrung out her gloves in silence until they reached cover.

"Here now, sit on this bench." He motioned to a marble seat in the entryway where she'd waited to meet him only moments earlier. He wrapped the blanket around her with sturdy hands. The urge to protect her rose. He again tried to ignore the warm feelings that singed his heart. "Let's dry off a bit and we'll discuss."

Kate could see he was troubled. She hadn't expected him to bellow and rant so profusely. "I am truly sorry." She still felt like a child who'd just been caught with a hand in the cookie jar. She'd wanted so much to please him.

"Miss Church," he paused trying to collect his thoughts, "I know that the Benefactor was incredibly disappointed. But with what you've given me, well, I suppose I might be able to persuade him to keep you aboard."

"Yes sir?" She pined aloud. Kate's mind relaxed and she enjoyed the feeling of his arm around her.

"Your Invitation was sent earlier because we have a situation in Chicago. One for which you are well suited. Our previous contact could not make the Engagement. We need a female replacement immediately." Mr. Bartlett could see that she was again eager to please. Her body had eased under his protection.

"I would still like for you to complete this Engagement with me, but we need to leave tomorrow. There must be no second thoughts, no delay. If you have any interest in further business with your Benefactor, this will be your only opportunity to prove yourself. There will be no other chances." He grasped her hand and looked upon her with eyes of steel. "You must give me an answer now."

Kate gazed at him almost adoringly, relieved that she'd appeased him. "Yes, yes I will go."

"Very well then. You will return home at once. Pack your things and be prepared to say goodbye." His strict words crackled through the cool air. He watched Kate's confusion; her brow furrowed, her hands clutched the blanket more closely to her chest. Her chin turned up to his face. Her breath teased his skin. If anyone had been watching in the cemetery, they would have appeared to be lovers, deep in passionate discourse.

He ignored his desire to pull her closer still and continued. This Recruitment and Termination had already been a failure. "You asked me to assist your sister, Ferris, and Silas. I have kept that promise as you requested. Mr. Tomley has received word that they are to leave for Boston tomorrow and that he is welcome to bring his help. You will let him know that you will handle the sale of the house as you will have a permanent residence with your new employer. Understand that this will be the last time you will be able to see your family. You mustn't hesitate; your Benefactor went to great lengths to make this possible. Our train will leave a few hours after theirs, so you will have only a little time to collect your belongings. You will need to leave any personal effects with your sister or they will be destroyed." Mr. Bartlett did not waver in his seriousness. "Do you understand, Miss Church?"

"Yes, yes," she murmured. Again, Kate realized that she was becoming part of something much more than the worlds she'd known in Iris and St. Louis. Her heart quickened.

"I will pick you up at 10 a.m. Our train will leave at 11. You must rest and be ready. You are to say nothing to anyone. Understood?" He was frighteningly direct. Kate wasn't sure if the chill she felt was from the weather or the ferocity of his words.

"May I bring my whip and my pistol?" She asked meekly.

"Yes, of course. You will be allowed what's already in your bag and of course the clothing you were provided with. Although," he paused with a genuine smile, "I think this dress has seen the last of its better days."

Kate blushed. "Thank you sir, again, I am sorry."

"Don't be sorry because the next time you may not have an opportunity to be regretful." He was stern again. "We should be off then. The weather has seemed to lighten." As he turned to look to the skies, Kate finally got a good look at his profile. He was handsome. She oddly wondered if he had ever been married, then warmed with embarrassment at how her mind had wandered.

The rain finally stopped and a light grey mist weaved among the graves. "Come now." He stood, offered his hand and assisted Kate to her buggy. "Be careful Miss Church, do not look back." His face turned up to hers as she slid into the seat, and again Kate felt distracted. Her fingers curled around the reins while wishing they were his hands instead.

"You also Sir, thank you." Kate started off. *What insanity did I just agree to?* Her mind questioned as reality set back in and she set out to focus on the tasks at hand. Kate would soon find out just exactly what strange world would envelope her, mind, body, and soul.

"Don't be so hard Miss Church." Lord Wilson mumbled to himself as he drove away. Thoughts of how appealing Kate was and how eager she was to appease him teased his mind. He exhaled deeply as his steed seemed grateful to leave the cemetery, its hooves clattering across the cobblestones and out the gate with a quickened pace. The key that had killed so many had just saved Kate's life. Some serious discussions with his superior over this matter were eminent, that was for certain.

He hurried back to the Society grounds, the carriage making good time as his horse trotted with a steady gait. Lord Wilson struggled to register what had just happened. Mr. Roth would not be pleased, but fortunately he was on an Engagement of his own for the next few days. Miss Church's arrival to the Society would be unexpected.

If she'd only known how close she was to getting Terminated, Lord Wilson was disturbed. Miss Church wasn't supposed to leave the cemetery alive, but he couldn't bear to kill her. *Why did she have to be so beautiful, even sullied like a wet cat?*

But he was glad she had persisted. He needed her; there was no time to find another female Member for this next Engagement. Besides, he reasoned, she'd had one of three special keys that had been missing for a while now. One of a set, that when combined, could control or destroy a city. Mr. Roth would be very happy with that key.

Lord Wilson deeply regretted pushing her down. His lips

pursed as remembered his callousness. It was all he could do to keep from assassinating her. *A shove was better than a kill,* he reasoned. *But God knows she'd been beaten to a pulp enough already.* He had not acted like a gentleman and in his frustration had abused her. *This could not happen again. This would not happen again,* Lord Wilson promised himself as he pulled onto the Society Grounds. *I must focus,* he chided himself. He removed his bowler as he pulled up to the main building of the Society and ran his fingers through his damp hair. He tipped his hat to his groomsman, replaced his bowler, dismounted from the carriage and sauntered up the steps to the foyer of the Main Hall. Tomorrow would be a true test for Miss Church; one that he so badly wanted her to pass. And until then, he could not reveal his true identity.

2 CHICAGO

Kate and Mr. Bartlett sipped on freshly poured tea as their train left the Eads Bridge Station at 2p.m. sharp. Its woodsy aroma filled the luxury car, while the two read vastly different documents. Mr. Bartlett researched new secret information with such intensity that his eyes misted from the strain. Their porter had just forwarded the papers before leaving to check the train for spies. Kate did not have the same focus. She allowed her thoughts to wander from her newspaper as it flopped lazily in her hands.

As she gazed out onto the foggy, cold station platform with saddened eyes, she remembered yesterday's events and wistfully played with a tendril of her still darkened hair. Upon her return from the cemetery, she'd told the family about her need to leave. It was simply awful; her heart still ached from the sudden departure. But Mr. Bartlett had implemented the arrangements as W had promised. She had to follow through.

While she'd been out that foul-weathered afternoon, a messenger had arrived with train tickets for Ferris, Abby, Martha, and Silas. Ferris' new employer had demanded he start immediately. They were already packing every available trunk and bag in the house when Kate walked in. They were so busy scurrying about that they didn't notice her disheveled appearance.

"What so soon?" Abby cried as she wrapped some last bits of china. She didn't even have time to look up at her sibling.

"Yes, tomorrow." Kate whispered, the words catching in her throat at the sight of crates piled high with clothes and random items from throughout the house. Footsteps clattered on the soon to be bare floors. Select pieces of furniture were marked as most precious cargo while Kate viewed the last remnants of her childhood memories. She clutched her bag and tried to ignore the hollow feeling that washed over her like the cold lake water on the Parker's property. She shuddered as memories of McKendrick and his dirty deeds floated to the surface. Those had been the catalyst for all this drama. *How strange life was to change so fast*, she reminisced.

"Ferris, Kate's leaving tomorrow!" Abby yelled and then was distracted by Martha bringing a few more kitchen items to pack.

"What?" Ferris hollered from the parlor. Kate peered in on him, unnoticed. He and Silas were packing the last of the books and papers from Henry Church. Kate was grateful that Abby would be taking these things with her, for she could not.

"I have to pack too." Kate mumbled as she slipped away upstairs. When she shut the door of her childhood bedroom, the dark enveloped her and mirrored the melancholy she experienced inside. She approached the window and watched the sun drop below the horizon behind a thin veil of fall clouds. Her mind tumbled so much that her temples ached. *Have I really just given up everything?*

Her family, her home and any possibility of a husband, children, and a normal life, was not to be hers. But Mr. Bartlett said there would be rewards, incredible things. She hoped to God that this was true.

Kate's fingers slipped over the buttons of her dress as her thoughts continued their conflicted dance. There was something about Mr. Bartlett; she couldn't quite understand it. *He wants me, but why?*

She was talented and determined, but could she really be what he needed? She remembered his kiss in Lafayette Park. How it had stunned her, yet warmed and stilled her. His lips had been kind but firm. As Kate closed her eyes for a second, she could almost feel them again. She wanted to sense that soothing pressure again. He shouldn't have taken such liberties with her, she felt, even if he'd done it to quiet her. And he'd just pushed her down in the cemetery. But still, it had felt so good to have his strong hands on her. It had awakened the woman in her and Kate flushed with embarrassment. She hadn't felt that power since she'd been with Michael Parker.

Now, I'm almost a spinster, she laughed at herself. She traced over her lips with her fingertips one last time. *Oh to feel that way again, was it possible?*

Kate started a last fire, slithered out of the Widow's dress and hung it to dry. *Time to stop this silliness,* she reprimanded herself. Tomorrow she would start working for Mr. Bartlett and for her Benefactor. She would need to be on her best behavior.

The Church family's last evening at home was spent drinking wine and reminiscing. Silas shared stories of what it was like to work as a free man in Boston. Ferris talked about his proper upbringing and how much of a scandal it was that he'd left a decent family to go out West. Kate kept quiet for the most part, enjoyed everyone else's tales, and was relieved that Ferris had kept their adventures in Iris a secret. Finally the lamps burnt low and the realization that rest was needed enveloped the Church family.

At bedtime, Abby finally cornered her older sister. "Kate, are you sure you're doing the right thing? I mean, it's so odd how you found this employer?" The younger Church sister cocked an eyebrow.

"You needn't worry," Kate tried to soothe. "They are very generous. I'll have everything I need. And the gentleman I will be working for is very kind."

"Is he married?" Abby giggled. Kate was thrown completely off-guard and she blushed crimson.

"No, um, he's a good man. I haven't learned much else yet." Kate wanted to tell her sister everything, but knew it would only put her sibling in danger. And thinking of the handsome Mr. Bartlett had awakened some odd desire in her, but not without disruption. *I want to please him, but is he always going to be so pushy?* She didn't like being anyone's chattel.

"So there are possibilities, eh?" Abby teased.

"Now little sister, you need to get those naughty thoughts out of your head and into bed with your husband where you belong," Kate bantered sweetly. She was truly grateful that her sister and Ferris were joyfully espoused. With all the tragedy each had suffered, they all deserved happiness. As the sisters hugged and parted, Kate cherished the warmth between them. *This was one of the last times we'll be together,* she reminded herself. Kate would hold that in her heart forever.

The Church household was peaceful for the night, but Kate didn't sleep well. The light of a lazy half-moon broke through the early evening clouds, rose over her window sill and gave her bedroom a cool blue glow. An autumn breeze caught the fallen leaves. They danced in languid circles around the trees outside much like the thoughts in Kate's mind.

The morning came far too quick. With first light, the house came to life one last time. Kate awoke to the familiar aromas of Martha's cooking. How she would miss it, the savory eggs and sausages. She had forgotten how good it was; so tasty that her stomach growled in anticipation. *I will need to forget again,* Kate bolstered and pushed herself out of bed.

She dressed efficiently, putting on the green gown that Mr. Bartlett had purchased for her in a flash. As Kate passed by a large mirror she'd decided to leave behind, her eye caught her reflection in the large wooden oval frame. It had a slight crack on the bottom and probably wouldn't survive a trip anyway. Kate pulled her hair up in a neat bun while watching in the mirror. She barely recognized the woman looking back at her and Kate resisted the rising urge to break the looking glass entirely. Instead she went down for a last meal in the home she'd been raised.

Unlike the night before, most of the Church family was quiet in the break of day. The only words spoken were grace and the politeness of please and thank you's, as food was passed. They ate on the last of the unpacked dishes, which Martha promptly cleaned and stowed afterwards. The remaining good linens, almost still warm from the bodies that had slept on them the night before, were also finally packed. A sharp knock on the door suddenly brought everyone to a moment they both welcomed and dreaded.

"It appears our driver is here." Ferris opened the door and greeted their coachman.

The carriage had indeed arrived for them to leave. Kate bit her lip to keep from crying. The driver worked quickly, in and out, taking trunks and bags to the large coach with two horses. There were long hugs and kisses for and from everyone. Kate stood on the walk as they were helped in their ride. Abby burst into tears which made Kate and Martha cry too. The gentleman cooed to their ladies.

Silas and Martha were beaming. "Oh Miss Kate, we are grateful for all you've done!" Martha grasped her hand. Silas whispered a gentle "Take care and God bless you Miss Kate." Kate held them both tightly for a few last seconds. She consoled the pain in her chest with the reminder that they now had each other for the rest of their lives.

Ferris gave a quieted last hug. "Kate you are the strongest woman I have ever known. It has been a true pleasure." His face turned stoically white.

Kate pulled back with a deep breath, "Thank you Ferris, it has been mine as well. Please continue to take care of Abby."

Lastly, Abby held Kate for what seemed like eternity. Everyone had stilled. The sisters wiped each other's cheeks. "I love you sister." Kate spoke gently. A tinge of regret whirled in her mind. She'd not really even begun to know Abby as an adult. And this was truly good bye.

"Oh, I love you too. Surely you'll come to visit?" Abby questioned one last time.

"Yes, indeed." Kate's heart felt suddenly empty. "I will." She hated lying but somehow she'd pulled it off with some sincerity. "Take care."

Their fully loaded carriage rolled off with the passengers waving while the morning sun beamed down. Kate stayed at the curb until they turned out of their street. Her feet dreaded each step as she entered the Church home for the last time. Her single, lonely trunk was at the door. She toured the old place one last time, hearing the long gone echoes of both happy and sad memories. The left over furnishings had been covered, like odd-shaped ghosts. The curtains were drawn in each room giving the house a haunted darkness. Kate sat on her trunk and finally let the true tears fall. She exhaled as the sound of a different carriage arrived out front. *There is nothing left here, the past is the past.*

She dried her moistened cheeks with an elegant glove. Again, it was time to move on.

Chicago, IL

The sky was filled with light snowflakes when the train pulled into the station. It was so much different from the departure from St. Louis, where the sun had warmed the autumn morning.

The ride to Chicago had been filled with information and specifics. Mr. Bartlett had been pure business. Any flirtation was long forgotten as he explained Kate's role to her. She listened with rapt attention, sitting stiffly in her chair as her new employer instructed her on how she would complete this most important task.

As a light meal was served, the two ate in silence. Mr. Bartlett observed his new Member carefully. She was collected and intelligent. He measured that she was up to the task. Her success would be his as well. Failure was not an option.

Kate had managed to put all feelings of the past aside. She was ready to make a good impression. Her future depended on it.

The train slowed and its steam entered the frosty air with a misty shadow. "We have arrived Miss Church." Mr. Bartlett stood and helped Kate into her coat. Their coachman whispered something to him, and left. Kate politely pretended not to notice. Instead she double checked the contents of her bag. "Alright then, let's proceed," Mr. Bartlett commanded and ushered Kate off the train. A part of him felt a bit like an executioner, taking a lamb to slaughter. He tried to ignore that thought and reassured himself that this one was different. Kate was made of sterner stuff.

An early lake effect snow had moved in and chilled the city. A brisk wind blew harshly against Lord Wilson and his new Member, Miss Kate Church. A sturdy black sleigh carriage waited for them. Mr. Bartlett, as Kate still knew him, touched his top hat as customary.

"Good Afternoon, Mr. Bartlett, so sorry about the weather." The driver spoke politely to his passengers.

"Thank you," Mr. Bartlett responded as they entered the sleigh. The driver tucked them into their seats with warm woolen blankets. The horses started with a steady trot. "We have a few moments to review," he turned to Kate. "You are to enter the café as quietly as possible. The contact, Mr. Reed, will be sitting at a table at the window. If he is not at the window you are not to go further in, simply wait at the door. He should come to you."

"At the table, he will stand to greet you and immediately comment on the weather. If he does not, you need to cough incessantly to cause disruption. This public display could save your life by causing unwanted attention. He will want to test your reserve. Otherwise, you will simply reply 'indeed' to his comment and order black tea with sugar as soon as the server arrives. Say nothing while the server is gone and try not to take your eyes off of him. If Mr. Reed speaks during this time, simply nod. When the server returns with the tea, do not drink it. Wait for the server to leave, then hand Mr. Reed the package and smile. Upon his thank you, he will in turn give you his. Exchange good-byes and let him leave first. I'll be waiting about a half block away in the carriage. We will pull up upon your exit. Are you ready?" He looked at Kate somewhat anxiously, a slight furrow crossing his brow.

"Yes, I'm ready." Kate tucked her bag and parasol into her lap as they pulled aside a row of handsome buildings in a quiet neighborhood. The snow had thickened as the sky turned a deeper grey. The driver helped her out and Kate strode quickly to the café. Despite the daytime, the gas lamps remained lit and covered the small establishment in a golden glow. Wisps of snow tickled her ankles as she made her way to the appointment. There was no return. Kate pulled every inch of resolve in her to the very front of her soul.

A host opened the door for her upon her approach and she

declined to remove her coat. *This should be quick,* she unbuttoned her cover in a flurry of fingers.

As planned, Mr. Reed was seated directly at the window. Kate reminded herself that Mr. Bartlett had warned that Mr. Reed would have the advantage of seeing her arrive. She tried to look as confident as possible, standing tall and upturning her chin. He stood and greeted her, "Hello Miss. What a surprise with the snow today." His words were eloquent, with a hint of a British accent. He was a tall thick man, wearing a dark navy suit. He had greying dark brown hair and a short mustache. His sharp blue eyes looked over her. Kate dared to stare back.

"Indeed." Kate replied while fulfilling her role, sitting into her chair with grace and ease. She was calm as the host pushed in her chair. All was going as planned. The server arrived and Mr. Reed ordered his tea.

"And for the lady?" the server inquired.

"Black tea with sugar please." Kate responded politely then said nothing. Mr. Reed cleared his throat and she smiled plainly in return. The server came back, set the teapot and cups down, nodded to his patrons and left. As soon as Mr. Reed poured his tea and started to sip, Kate pulled the package from her bag. She could do this; it was a simple enough task. Her confidence grew and she sat well poised in her chair.

When Kate looked down, she hadn't noticed that Mr. Reed had deftly returned his right hand into his lap. Kate slowly slid the envelope filled with money across the table. There was a sudden odd vibration of the table as her hand drew back. She felt a stab of pain in her right side. Mr. Reed looked at her without expression. Just as quickly, it happened again. This time Kate felt a burning sensation and the warmth of her own blood oozing. To a person outside, the small flashes under the table may have looked like falling silverware.

What just happened? Kate's mind reeled as pain spread through her body.

Mr. Reed was still motionless; his eyes staring as if they were made of the strongest steel. He didn't even blink. The scents of pastries and warm liquids covered the acrid hint of a gun recently fired.

Kate remained in an upright fashion, *"you are strong now"* echoing in her head. Mr. Reed had used some sort of silencer. *Clever bastard*, she grimaced. Her gloved hands slid from the table and pulled her coat shut.

"It was a pleasure" he smiled wickedly and got up without making the appropriate exchange. It was far too late to clear her throat. This was clearly unexpected.

"Mine as well." Kate replied as calmly as possible considering she'd just been shot twice under the table. The crowded café was completely oblivious to the violent event. Dishes clattered and conversations continued unabated.

Mr. Reed turned to leave but suddenly bent down, whispering coldly in her ear, "What a shame for such a lovely lady." The warmth of his breath tickled her ear. Kate resisted the temptation to shudder. He threw on his coat and then casually stepped out the door as if nothing had happened.

Bastard! Kate winced as her head started to spin. *Focus, be strong, pull it together,* she tried to cheer herself to action. Unexpectedly the server approached her table. "Ma'am, your gentleman left his hat."

"Well yes indeed. I'll take care of that thank you. I must catch up with him," Kate spoke in clipped tone laced with confidence. She faked a smile and left payment for the tea on the table. Deftly grabbing her parasol, she discreetly used it like a cane to push herself up. Despite her massive pain, she exited the café as quickly as possible; Kate knew she must stop him. He had just turned the corner into an alley, only seconds ahead.

The snow was now falling heavily as Kate tried not to stumble. She looked round with great care and followed Mr. Reed into the alley. Her corrupt contact was directly ahead, his hair and coat whipping in the wind. Kate was starting to perspire despite the bitter cold. The mini beads of sweat froze on her skin. She gathered as much strength as she could muster to yell. "Sir, you forgot your hat!"

Mr. Reed turned around in time just to see Kate's shotgun parasol open with a bright flash. She had placed his bowler over the tip. The force of the blast blew the hat right through his body with a loud pop. He fell to the snow instantly. Blood poured rapidly from the gaping hole. The smell of burnt flesh assaulted her nostrils. The traitor was shaking, gasping for air. Kate again steadied herself with the parasol, dropped to her knees and effectively cleaned out his pockets. She dumped his pocket watch, gun, and the packages into her bag. His package contained the second of the strange keys; she had to retrieve it at all costs. She stood wearily over him, becoming increasingly nauseated.

Mr. Reed was audibly groaning, dying directly in front of her. "Mercy, please." He whispered while his eyelids fluttered.

"No, no mercy," she replied stiffly. "So you say that I am a lovely lady, but I have no mercy for the wicked." She rebuked him. His eyes rolled back as he expired. The walls of the alley seemed to move. Kate heard footsteps despite a profound ringing in her ears. The searing ache in her side increased as if all her insides were set ablaze.

"Miss Church!" Mr. Bartlett cried, as he burst into the alley, their driver not far behind. Kate steadied herself against a wall and attempted to limp towards him. They had seen her leave the café and run into the alley. For a moment he had wondered if she had duped him again, and refused to follow orders. But then, he heard the shot echo against the cold brick walls, and felt his heart stop with the sounds that were amiss. He was grateful that it was Kate who was trying to stand before him and not the treacherous Mr. Reed. As they approached, Mr. Bartlett motioned to the driver.

The driver dumped Mr. Reed's body into an ash pit with a dull thud, ran back for the carriage and then pulled it into the alley. Lord Wilson could see Kate wavering, barely able to stand. He pulled her aside, scooping her cold body into his arms as he knelt down.

"He shot me." She whispered as her face became ghostly white. "Twice." She whimpered in extreme agony.

"Driver!" Mr. Bartlett ordered with a bark. The coachman hurried to his charges. "We need to go, now. Help me." Guilt rumbled in his gut. She wasn't supposed to be hurt.

They lifted her into the carriage sleigh and started off with the vehicle's blades leaving long narrow trails in the snow. "Miss Kate, are you alright?" Lord Wilson attempted to keep his charge awake.

She moaned pitifully in reply. He opened her coat to see that blood had seeped heavily through her corset and dress. He felt her slipping away, her pulse slowing. He quickly pulled a small bottle from his pocket. "Drink, please." He put it to her lips and she sipped it. "More, open." He urged, propped her mouth with his fingertips and poured about half of the odd drink in. She coughed a bit, but there was no blood. Mr. Bartlett was relieved as he felt the drink do its work as her body started to warm. "To the Museum of Sciences", he bellowed to the driver. He covered Kate with the blankets, holding her tightly while putting pressure on the wound. He listened to her breathing as it steadied. Her eyes were closed and snowflakes had coated her lashes as if Jack Frost has kissed them. She looked like a gentle snow angel. He tenderly brushed them away. "Hang on Miss Kate, we're almost there." He cooed to her as if she were a sleepy little girl. His heart thumped wildly. He did not want to lose another Member. It had been far too long and hard of a search to find Miss Church.

The driver urged their steed along as the blizzard erupted just when the night had fallen. After they frantically drove several blocks, the driver pulled round the back entrance of a large marble building to a small dimly lit doorway. The horses whinnied and steam purged from their nostrils in the chill. The driver descended from his perch, ran to the door and knocked three times. A pleasant woman with dark hair and eyes answered and motioned them in. Mr. Bartlett pulled Kate from the sleigh and carried her inside. "Sorry to interrupt your work, Dr. Finch," he spoke haltingly to the woman who answered the door.

"No mind Sir, let us hurry. In here." Dr. Finch directed them down a short hall into a large room with dinosaur bones placed on immense wooden tables. She immediately cleared one of the remains and replaced them with a crisp white sheet. Mr. Bartlett set Kate down on the fresh linens in haste, while Dr. Finch retrieved a fresh lab coat. Mr. Bartlett motioned to the driver, who scurried off to stand guard outside the door.

Mr. Bartlett and Mrs. Finch pulled off Kate's coat as her eyes flickered and she writhed in pain. Mrs. Finch proffered some ether and gently rubbed a bit on Kate's nostrils. She went limp instantly. "Oh Lord Wilson, what do have we here? Is this your new recruit?" Dr. Finch inquired as she grabbed scissors and cut open Kate's bloodied dress.

"Yes, as I'm sure you gathered something went horribly wrong," he replied with sadness catching in his throat. "She said she was shot twice. I'm so glad that the doctor is in today."

"Hmmm, did you give her the serum?" Mrs. Finch questioned. Mr. Bartlett, known as Lord Wilson to the doctor, nodded. "Well let's see here. I'll have to cut her corset too. Look, a bullet got caught in the boning." She plucked the first one out efficiently with tweezers. "Alright then Sir, help me turn her over. We'll have to find the other one." They rolled a sedated Kate on her side. The doctor snipped the corset lacings within seconds, peeled it off and lifted her blouse up to the underside of her breast.

"Oh my, what do we have here? This is not right." Mrs. Finch was stunned, her eyes and mouth wide open. Lord Wilson thought perhaps the bullet made it through her body, but upon closer inspection, he gazed upon what had shocked Mrs. Finch. More than several deep lash marks crossed Kate's back in a haphazard fashion.

"What the hell?" Lord Wilson exclaimed aloud.

"I gather you didn't know about these," the Doctor grimaced. "And look, it appears she's marked with some sort of tattoo?"

"I had no idea." He was perplexed. "It looks like she's been whipped." Lord Wilson was taken aback; a small pit ached in his stomach. He felt even guiltier than before. Kate Church had clearly already been through hell and now he'd brought her right back to its doorstep.

"Um, indeed. But they look to be old scars; let's find that bullet for now. We don't need her bleeding out." They put Kate on her back. Dr. Finch set about her work, cleaned the wound and skillfully pulled out the offending metal which had gone in about an inch deep. "She's a lucky girl, just missed her liver." Blood still trickled from Kate's side. "Serum, Sir?" she requested. Lord Wilson again proffered his bottle and she poured its liquid directly on the wound. There was a sizzle and some steam. Then, as if by magic, the bleeding ceased and the skin started to seal itself. Kate moaned softly in response. "Oh what mysterious potion you do carry." Mrs. Finch smiled while knowing that only certain Members had information on the serum. He returned her grin, his eyes dancing with relief. She placed a patch over the quickly healing spot.

"Well done Dr. Finch. Always can count on you in a pinch." Lord Wilson was consoled. Kate Church needed to be alive; he had many plans for her.

"Thank you Sir. You know the procedure as well as I. She should come round in about an hour. If she's in any pain, another dose of serum internally and externally as well. Make sure she rests and gets plenty of fluids. Let her eat if she's hungry." Mrs. Finch instructed then looked at Lord Wilson as Kate slumbered under the ether. "You like her don't you? What's her name?" Dr. Finch gave a friendly smirk. "She's lovely and strong to have taken two bullets like that."

"Miss Katherine Church, if you must know. You know you'd find out later anyway." His eyes continued to twinkle merrily. "You are transferring to St. Louis then?"

"Yes, we will be there in about two days. Then we can see about treating those God awful marks on her back. Who in the devil would have done such a thing?" Dr. Finch looked over Kate sympathetically.

"I'm certain to find out," Lord Wilson replied protectively. He would know. There would be hell to pay for whoever had done this.

"Now then Lord Wilson, if you'd please be a gentleman. I will redress this fine lady for you and you can take her home." Dr. Finch smiled. This young woman might be exactly what Lord Wilson needed.

"Indeed." Lord Wilson stepped out with the driver. Dr. Finch crossed the room to a large cabinet filled with both men and women's clothing, selected a dark grey coat, and a warm woolen nightgown. The doctor had Kate redressed in only a few moments. She was very adept in handling emergencies of this nature. Upon finishing, Dr. Finch called the gentlemen in. They wrapped Kate in several fresh blankets and left in a hurry. They had a train to catch and couldn't miss it.

"We'll see you and Mr. Finch in a bit then." Lord Wilson smiled as they boarded the carriage with Kate still under sedation.

"Indeed." Mrs. Finch smiled. "Godspeed Lord Wilson." The doctor was impressed with Lord Wilson's new charge. "She's lovely, don't be too hard on her." She whispered as they drove off into the heavy snow.

Kate awoke slowly in the fabulous bed of a luxury train car headed back to St. Louis. She coughed and sat up with a startled expression, unsure of where she was. Lord Wilson had pulled a chair up to the bed and watched her rest. He patted her back as her eyes blinked. "You're safe, shhh," he cooed to her. "Thirsty?" She nodded and he poured her a fresh glass of water from the nightstand. "Small sips now." He helped her hold the glass as she drank what tasted like pure heaven as her mouth was so parched. "You remember what happened?" he inquired.

"Yes, I was shot." She paused. "And he had another key?" Kate raised her brows. She wasn't sure what really had happened. The fog in her mind was still lingering.

"Yes, yes he did. We have it." Mr. Bartlett confirmed. "Anything else?" He tilted his head ever so slightly. Any information on the demise of Mr. Reed was of the utmost importance.

"No, it's fuzzy from there. Only snow." She wished she could remember more. Mr. Bartlett seemed very concerned. She appreciated his help and for once didn't mind being cared for.

"That's perfect. How do you feel? Are you in any pain?" he ran his hand along her back and she flinched awkwardly. Suddenly he was aware he'd touched her scars. He would not question her about them now.

"I'm just, really sleepy." She replied sheepishly, wishing he hadn't grazed the horrible marks. *Did he know about them?* The thought floated like a wispy dream in her head.

"Alright then, not to worry. No other questions now. The doctor said you'll be just fine, but you need more rest. Let me tuck you in?" His lilting accent was at its sweetest. Kate leaned back in the comforts of the plush bed as he pulled the blankets around her. "Good night then. I'll wake you when we arrive." He smiled and shut the bed curtains. He had succeeded in making her feel like a child again; only this time it was a much more pleasant situation.

Kate closed her eyes for a bit, but then opened them to peek under the blanket. She felt around her side to the small bandage. She peeled it back with just the slightest pinch. There were no bullet holes, only two very light pink spots.

"You should have shot her Lord Wilson!" Director Roth bellowed. "And you took her on an Engagement!"

"She was already shot twice. And how was I to get another female Member in time?" Lord Wilson replied, his voice tensed with nastiness. "Besides, we've now secured two of the keys."

Director Roth bore a stunned expression as Lord Wilson pulled out the most important pieces. As the Director of the Society, he had thought he'd seen everything. Their talk quieted a bit, although it remained still stern in nature.

Kate sat outside Mr. Roth's office as the two men argued, her body leaning to the side of a plush leather sofa. She was too tired to be nervous, but tried to eavesdrop on their conversation. Suddenly her mind cleared and she straightened. *W. is the first letter of Wilson*, she thought. *Didn't Director Roth just call him Lord Wilson? Mr. Bartlett was Lord Wilson. Oh my, he's the Benefactor.* He'd known her all along. Kate inhaled sharply as she listened more intently.

Their voices became louder as their footsteps reached the door of the office. Mr. Bartlett opened it and beckoned Kate inside. "Director Roth, our newest Member, Miss Kate Church." Kate was surprised and humbled by the tall sturdy man before her. Mr. Bartlett squeezed her shoulder and spurred her to politeness.

"Very pleased to meet you Sir." Kate spoke quietly, still in awe of the spacious office and its owner. Several odd contraptions decorated the space. Kate, still in her recovery, absently wondered what their purposes were.

Director Roth shook her hand firmly but a look of kindness crossed his face. "And I as well. Lord Wilson has convinced me that you would make a most excellent addition to our business." The two men, although friends, exchanged somewhat tense glances. Kate tried to take it all in, but her sleepy mind was betraying her.

"He is our Director, over all Members here. I'll explain later." Lord Wilson smiled as he noticed how Director Roth examined the disheveled beauty before him. *Lovely and deadly, a dangerous combination,* Lord Wilson reminded himself. "It's late and we need to get Miss Kate settled in."

"Well, yes indeed. Thank you again Miss Church for stopping by. I'm certain Lord Wilson will fill you in. Have a good evening." Kate felt the oddness of their conversation. *Didn't he say he was supposed to shoot me? Or am I just tired and hearing things?*

"Thank you sir." Kate replied, still in wonderment of where she'd landed. Getting from the train to inside the building had been a complete blur.

"A lovely evening to you as well, Sir." Lord Wilson nodded. The gentlemen shook hands and Lord Wilson guided his new charge out. As he shut the door he leaned to Kate, "I will explain more, I will tell you more about myself, as Lord Wilson, here at the Society. I am certain you will have many questions, but let's find you a bit to eat. You must be famished." His kind eyes lingered over her. Lord Wilson had dodged a very big bullet. One that had allowed Kate to continue living.

Kate smiled politely. "Yes that would be lovely." She was definitely hungry and it was for more than just food. Her curiosity was piqued.

Director Roth leaned back in his desk chair while holding two spectacular keys. Both bejeweled, they reflected off his desk lamp light with an intense brilliance. He moved forward with a grin, pulled a magnifying glass from a desk drawer and examined them more closely. The blue one radiated a deep purple. The second key was topped with a similar green gem with a stunning aqua center. He pulled a velvet bag from another drawer, wrapped them in some of his stationery and placed them inside the elegant pouch.

As he stood up, he pulled a latch hidden underneath one of several paper weights on his desk, one that was engraved with a curio of his long departed wife. A bookshelf behind the desk rumbled and opened to reveal a secret set of compartments complete with a steel safe about the size of a bread box. He pressed a small red button on the safe and with a whisper of steam, it opened. As he focused on securing these most important tools, the Director's mind wandered to thoughts of his alliance and friendship with Lord Wilson.

They'd both been alone too long. Director Roth had managed to find temporary companionship with more than several ladies in the years that he'd been single. He now had one regular female visitor that very few knew about. But Lord Wilson was different.

Although cunning, intelligent, and a blue blood, Lord Wilson had passed over the countless women that swooned for him in and outside the Society's walls. He even ignored the ones who openly threw themselves at him. As long as Director Roth had known him, it seemed that Lord Wilson had always craved the sanctity of a committed female relationship, but hadn't had success in finding that one special lady. Perhaps it was his past that had kept him from choosing another for so long.

Director Roth closed the safe and the bookshelf. He sat back down at his desk and again reviewed the file of Miss Katherine Church, flicking through the papers slowly to catch any trace of impropriety he might have missed. After an hour, and assured he'd done everything he could to protect his friend, the Director of the Society waved his hand over the lamp, effectively shutting it off with a hiss, and left his office to retire for the evening.

Mrs. Ellis was freshly widowed, her husband dispensed of in a terrible trade gone wrong. She gazed upon the dark night rolling by outside her train. A crumpled telegram of the horrific news rested under her gloved hand. She had opened it to read it one last time. She decided that tomorrow, she would tell her three sons that their father had perished and the attempt to assassinate Kate Church had failed. They'd lost another key to boot. Her adult children were fast asleep in a neighboring car. The train was on a rendezvous trip to St. Louis. Only Mr. Ellis would not be meeting them in the largest Midwest city of the United States. His body had been burnt to a crisp in Chicago.

No trace of him would ever be found.

Mr. Ellis, posing as Mr. Reed, was initially only to collect the monies agreed upon in trade for a key. They would easily get it back from a mole soon to be imbedded in their adversary's structure and will have secured the cash as well. But there had been word that the woman who'd killed Drasco would indeed be his contact for the trade. The plan was changed and Miss Church was to die. Instead, he lost his life and the trade of thousands of dollars. They had underestimated Miss Church. Superiors were already disappointed.

Mrs. Ellis swore it would not happen again as she rolled a cigarette with the telegram and smoked it. "Ashes to ashes, dust to dust." She mumbled. She brushed a single tear aside from her cheek, with the hand that wore her ruby ring. It sparkled from the glow of her cigarette and reflected off the window, much like the glow from the two keys already in Mr. Roth's possession.

3 ROOM AND BOARD

The Society Grounds, St. Louis, MO

Kate looked around the dining hall in amazement, her mouth agape. The ornate room was quiet except for the clatter of dishes that escaped from the kitchen in the back. It was quite large, with high ceilings and windows covered in plush dark wine colored curtains that cascaded to the floor. Exquisite paintings lined the walls in between each gilded portal.

She felt completely under-dressed in such a lovely place, as she was still wearing her coat with the woolen nightdress underneath. Kate pulled it tightly around her to hide her embarrassment. But if their host thought less of her for wearing a coat in the dining room, it certainly didn't show when he escorted them inside.

"Welcome to the dining hall." The greeter didn't look a bit tired considering the late hour. In fact their host was quick with a smile and brisk in pace as he seated his guests.

They were placed at an expertly set table surrounded by equally embellished chairs with fabric matching the red shade of the curtains.

Lord Wilson and Kate were alone. In fact, the building felt almost empty as their footsteps echoed off the walls. They had taken a lift down and walked through several long corridors after leaving Mr. Roth's office. They passed many closed doors and only a couple of gentleman. If they had looked at Kate, she hadn't noticed. She was still astounded at the size of the building, her eyes widening at the realization that her world had indeed expanded.

Their host placed their napkins and then motioned to a server who immediately brought them water. "Please drink," Lord Wilson urged. Kate took a gentle sip. It tasted cool and freshly culled from a spring.

"Sir, may I offer you a stronger drink?" their host inquired.

"Yes, a scotch please," Wilson replied with a gentlemanly ease. He leaned back, his stature relaxed in an elegant chair.

"And for the Lady?" Before Kate could speak, Lord Wilson ordered for her.

"Chamomile tea please, with sugar." He gave Kate a delightful smile as their host left for a moment. She was a bit perplexed. "This will be your new life Miss Church. You will act like and be treated like a lady at all times. I know you've been away from civilized life for a while but you will grow accustomed to it." Their host came back with their beverages and warm rolls with sweet cream butter.

"And what would you like to eat, Sir?" the host asked as he poured Kate's tea.

"Duck should be in season, should it not?" Lord Wilson replied.

"Yes Sir. Served with greens and roasted potatoes. And for the lady?" Wilson gauged Kate's needs. She needed to eat, but nothing too heavy.

"Chicken soup with additional roasted chicken aside. Roasted potatoes as well."

"Very good Sir." He trotted off to the kitchen with their order. Kate looked at the large assortment of dinner-ware and had no idea how to start. She began to reach for a plate but then let her hands drift slowly into her lap instead. Even after working for the Parkers, she'd never seen such cutlery.

"Let me serve you a bit." Wilson grinned at her befuddlement and buttered the flaky bread for her. "When looking at your silverware, you'll work from the outside in for different courses. But don't worry about that now. You'll have plenty of time to learn later." He handed her an appetizer plate. "Eat this in small bits."

"Thank you." Kate was truly grateful. The bread tasted like heaven, the warm morsels melted in her mouth. She'd tried to hide her hunger, but she was famished and the audible growling of her stomach gave her away. Lord Wilson watched her eat and waited for her questions to come. He didn't have to wait long.

Kate finished her appetizer and looked at him while leaning in ever so slightly. "So, um…" she started awkwardly. "May I ask why did you bring me here? And where or what is here exactly?" The last part of her question came out as a squeak.

"Welcome to the Society, Miss Kate." He was delighted with her curiosity. "You will learn more about the organization as we go along. We are here to serve others for the benefit of all. Everyone here has a task, a purpose, to continue the greater good." His grandiose statement startled Kate. Her gut feeling of something much larger at hand had been correct. "Everyone has a title and role. There is a pecking order that is strictly followed. We have the most advanced sciences and knowledge. Things that are not known to the world outside these walls. Again, you will be taught everything you need to know and you'll be handsomely compensated. The Society chooses only the best. You are uniquely talented and I am pleased that you have chosen to join us."

His cool demeanor was interrupted as the host and server arrived with their food. Lord Wilson paused for a moment as the deliciously fragrant meals were served. He gestured to her plate and they began to eat. Kate had to refrain for sighing aloud. The food was simply the best she'd ever had. Better than anything she and Martha had cooked for the Parkers long ago. The flavors ran over her tongue with pleasure.

"And how is your meal Miss Kate?" Lord Wilson asked with a laugh. She finished her soup in minutes and was almost half way through her poultry and potatoes.

"Delicious. Fantastic really, thank you." She paused, suddenly realizing she was eating too fast and elegantly muffled a burp in her napkin.

"Would you like another roll?" Lord Wilson offered, his voice full of warmth. It tickled him to see her so satisfied. A faint smile played across his face.

"Oh yes please," she said with the enthusiasm of a child on Christmas Day. He again buttered it for her, all the while watching her enjoy the small feast.

He spoke again as he handed her the tasty bread. "Surely you have more questions." He gently opened the conversation again, his words languished in the air between them.

"You called me Miss Kate in Mr. Roth's office. Why? And when was I going to learn your real name?" she inquired.

"The Society is built of Members. You'll soon see that as your Senior Member, I am the only one allowed to call you by your first name. It is a subtle way of differentiating the Senior Members from the Members beneath them. Besides a sign of respect, it is also code for others to know who belongs to whom. Other Members and even other Senior Members will call you Miss Church, a simple semblance of order." Lord Wilson was very serious. "You should always call me Lord Wilson here on the grounds. It is only here that we use our real names. That is why I used an alias until now. I want you to understand how important secrecy is here." Kate nodded and he continued. "There will be no secrets between us. Honesty is of the utmost importance. Although other Members also work for the Society, take great caution in what you say to them. Greet others warmly but never expose details of current Engagements or your life before the Society." He stopped long enough to see that she grasped the seriousness of the situation. "Any more questions?" He looked at Kate directly and it put her on edge.

"I—I, well, I overheard something about shooting? In Mr. Roth's office?" Kate stammered as she attempted to straighten up in her chair. She had to know. *Did I really hear that? Or was I sleepy from the trip?*

Lord Wilson cleared his throat and measured his words for their greatest impact. "At the cemetery you were given a second chance. It was a foolish episode and should never be spoken of again." He looked distant for a moment. It was very clear that the subject was closed and she was lucky to be alive.

Kate had stopped eating. With all the day's activities, she was starting to feel overwhelmed. Lord Wilson could see her exhaustion; she'd grown pale and dark circles had formed under her eyes. In a gesture of comfort, he reached across the table, touched her hand and spoke softly.

"You'll need further schooling and physical education. Manners will be of the utmost importance. But for the next few days I want you to become acquainted with the Society. Get plenty of rest. Tomorrow morning you'll meet with Dr. Finch for a full examination. One of the Society's rules is 'a weak person cannot complete strong work'. Everyone should be in the best possible condition physically and emotionally to handle the tasks they are given. She will need to know every inch of you in order to keep you in good health." Kate blushed for a moment, her embarrassment obvious. He held her hand a little tighter while he continued his speech with a genteel strength to his words.

"Miss Kate, I know of your scars. You needn't worry. We will discuss the story behind them tomorrow and Dr. Finch will assist in their healing. But remember, there are to be no secrets between us, ever." He was caring but stern. Kate breathed a deep sigh of relief. "Everything will be tailored just for you. You'll have your own attendant available to you at all times. She will help you bathe, dress, and will care for the upkeep of your room." He sipped the last bit of his scotch then continued.

"After lunch I will meet you in the parlor for a small tour of the grounds; your attendant will remind you. Later I will take you to Wilson Manor for tea. Remember, Miss Kate, you were chosen for your strength and abilities. I want you to feel welcome here. You are to come to me with any needs." He smiled and Kate became visibly more relaxed.

"Thank you. I'm very excited to learn more." Kate tried to sound enthused but the very long day and last few weeks had clearly caught up with her.

"Very well, are you finished? Perhaps it's time for bed then? It is very late, after eleven." He spoke much more casually.

"Yes, I'm ready to retire for the evening."

Lord Wilson motioned to the server then stood and assisted Kate from the table. She was a bit wobbly at first but gained strength as they travelled down a long hall. They approached the grand foyer and entry way where they had come earlier before going to Mr. Roth's office. A black marble fountain gurgled in the center of the room. It echoed off the well-adorned walls that led into the main parlor.

Within moments, a woman, plainly dressed in a grey dress and long white apron, entered. She wore her brown hair in a neatly braided bun. She had perfect carriage and manners.

"Miss?" Lord Wilson greeted.

"Yes Sir, I've come to collect Miss Church."

"Miss Kate, this is your attendant." Wilson introduced Kate's assistant then turned to her. "Your things will be waiting for you in your room. Rest well, I will see you tomorrow." A male attendant approached with his coat and top hat. Wilson quickly slipped on his things.

"Thank you and good night." Kate smiled sleepily.

"Good night Miss Kate." He kissed her hand, his lips lingering, and then swiftly stepped out a set of French doors on the other side of the entry way.

Lord Wilson was cheery despite the crisp midnight air that slapped him awake. He couldn't wait to introduce Kate to Wilson Manor. He had several surprises waiting for her.

Kate followed her attendant in near slumber. They walked to a lift that took her again to the third floor of the expansive building. They entered a hall that had a different smell; a waft of florals teased her. Her attendant looked briefly over her shoulder. "Welcome to the Ladies Wing, Miss Church. I am Miss Beatrice." Kate could smell perfumes and bath salts. Even the paintings and statues were feminine. As they passed some of the other rooms, Kate heard the rustling of papers, the distant sounds of music and muffled voices. They walked to the very end to Kate's new home, Room #30. Her attendant opened the door to a room of spectacular splendor.

As Miss Beatrice waved over a small box near the door frame, the gas lamps came on. Fine furniture and rich trimmings came aglow with beauty. To the left, there was a poster bed adorned with large fluffy pillows and plush coverings with matching bed curtains in pinks and golds. Fine carved oak nightstands were on both sides of the bed. Straight ahead were two floor to ceiling windows, their rich velvet curtains drawn. The window, closer to the bed, had a set of chairs and a small, doily covered table in front of it. Just to the right of the other window was a desk and a shelf filled with books. To the far right was a closed door. Next to that, a privacy screen, a bureau, and a lovely vanity trimmed with perfumes and make up.

There were several odd things she didn't recognize. A long clear tube dropped from the ceiling and ended in a small basket at her desk. There was a heavy metal box with narrow slits between the two windows that hummed lightly. And a few things were missing. *Where was her bag?*

"Let me take your coat Miss," Miss Beatrice piped up. She promptly took it from Kate and placed the coat in a large wardrobe. "In here are some of your things. I took the liberty of having your other items cleaned."

"The white nightgown?" It was all Kate had left of Ming and Chin. She couldn't bear to separate with it. Her heart fluttered at the thought of her dearly departed friends.

"I lightly pressed it Miss. It was very delicate. It's here in a drawer of your bureau with your other undergarments. You'll be receiving more clothes as your measurements are taken, and as seasons and fashions change."

"And my other things?" Kate's voice emitted in a high pitched squeal.

"Your weaponry is in the desk drawers." The attendant waved to the desk. Kate quickly crossed the room to check. Her hands trembled as she touched the knobs of her new furniture. The Bibles were in the top drawer. She was relieved to find her whip and gun in the drawers below.

Suddenly Kate had nature's call, but didn't see a pot. *Was there an outhouse on the grounds? Or a water closet?* Her thoughts were interrupted again by her astute help.

"Do you need to relieve yourself, Miss? Let's go into the small room here." Kate's attendant took her by the hand and led her into a washroom like she'd never seen. It was twenty times the size of a good sized outhouse.

The toilet looked like some she'd seen in newspapers, the tub was immense, and the basin was connected to some elegant looking pipes. "It's a proper water closet. But different than what you're used to I'm certain. When you're finished, just press the black button. Your remnants will simply disappear with a flash of steam. Some of the ladies like it to cleanse themselves as well. But there is a small stack of cloths to use if you prefer to wipe, Miss. They too can be disposed of with the button. The wash basin has two small knobs, red for hot and blue for cold water. Both come out the small ceramic tube in the center." Her attendant showed her how the sink worked by turning the knobs to and fro. The mechanical progress of simply relieving oneself astonished Kate. "Then rest your hands in the center and you'll feel some air come on to dry you. See, like this." Miss Beatrice demonstrated by washing her hands, turning off the water then holding them steady. In seconds they were bone dry. "We have the best of everything here, the most modern advances." Her help smiled.

She opened a large cabinet which contained fluffy robes, lavender scented soaps, and various lotions. "Miss Church, please use as much of these as you like. I leave you for a moment and then I'll help you wash before bed." The attendant smiled and shut the door.

Kate lifted her nightgown and sat on the newfangled toilet. The room was so large that her urination echoed. When she was finished, she pressed the button. She relaxed a moment until a sudden whiff of warm mist tickled her. Kate almost fell over in surprise, grabbing at the wash stand to balance. All evidence of a passing anything had vanished. She giggled at her silliness and cleansed her hands, the warm water feeling delicious on her skin. What amazing things and gadgets, she marveled. She opened the door to her eagerly waiting attendant.

"Everything all right Miss?"

"Yes, thank you." Kate blushed.

"Would you like a quick wipe down Miss?"

"Um yes." Kate stuttered not quite knowing what her assistant meant.

"Alright then." As the Miss Beatrice took down her hair, it unfurled in a lopsided mess. She helped her undress with a quick lift of the nightgown and offered Kate her hand as she stepped into the large tub. "Just stand in the center for a bit. I'll do this by hand so as not to affect your bandage." Kate had completely forgotten about her shooting and her scars. There hadn't been any pain since she'd awakened in the train. She was grateful the assistant said nothing of her whip marks.

Her attendant again explained the workings of the various knobs and buttons on a small copper panel adjoined to the tub. As she turned on the water, the plain wall morphed into a full mirror with a small blast of steam. Kate gasped aloud; she didn't even recognize herself. "Oh so sorry Miss, you can turn it off if you like, with this piece here." The attendant turned a pale knob and it reverted back to the cream colored wall. Water gently sprayed up from several openings as Kate stood. Her attendant deftly wiped her down with a soft wet cloth and soap. *It's so odd to be touched,* Kate thought. She was blushing from head to toe, but her attendant was discreet and silent during her shower.

After just a few minutes, the wash was finished. With the press of another button, warm air from above dried Kate like a gentle summer wind. The attendant helped her out and pulled some items from the cabinet. "Well Miss, you have a fresh gown here. If you're ready, I'll turn down your bed while you dress?"

"Yes, that would be lovely." Kate stood in astonishment as the attendant left. After the door closed, she stepped over to the tub side, briefly turned the mirror knob on with a deep inhale and mentally prepared to take a good look at herself. The girl that had left St. Louis more than twenty years ago was long gone. So too was the young woman who'd worked so hard in a rail town in the middle of nowhere. A raven haired lady with an hourglass figure stared back at her. Kate wanted to cry at the unfamiliarity, but stopped herself. It was time to quit pouting. She pulled on a lovely yellow lacy silk gown that teased her skin with softness and stepped out into her new bedroom.

Lord Wilson's butler met him at the rear door to Wilson Manor. "Welcome home Sir."

"Thank you Leeds." Lord Wilson smiled wearily. It had been an extremely long day out in the field. He had appeased Mr. Roth and secured Miss Church. A wave of exhaustion came over him as he stumbled into his library and the butler took his coat.

"I trust your new Member was delivered safely?"

"Yes, yes indeed. She should be settling in right now. Is everything prepared for tomorrow? Privacy and the canine secured?" *A few minor details must be taken care of*, the thought came forward to Lord Wilson.

"Yes Sir. Is there anything I can get for you Lord Wilson?" his faithful butler replied. His master had waited a long time for this event. All plans had been set into motion with utmost precision.

"Just some water at the night stand. Thank you Leeds." Wilson strode down a long corridor to a grand staircase. He passed priceless pieces of art and furnishings. He went upstairs and down another long hall to his bedroom, his footsteps leaving light echoes along the way. Leeds had stoked a fire even though the room had its own mechanical heating system. The burning wood gave the immense bedroom an enchanting, woodsy smell. As Wilson undressed, Leeds brought in a glass and empty pitcher. He turned to a large metal container near the window and with a few turns of a small crank, filled them with water.

"Good night Sir," he bade his master and took up the discarded clothing.

"Thank you and good night Leeds." Wilson nodded to Leeds as he pulled out a long night shirt from his bureau. He slipped it on, sat upon the plush bed with a grunt and examined his right calf which was throbbing. Only a small latch and well-stitched seams of his skin revealed an old injury that had long been repaired. He popped it open and observed the small cogs and pulleys that had replaced his calf muscle. He pulled a small oil canister from his nightstand and with some quick clicks, anointed a few squeaky parts. Satisfied with their lubrication, he clicked the latch shut, waved his hand over the night stand lamp effectively dousing it and climbed into bed easily with happy thoughts. As Lord Wilson slipped into slumber, he pulled an extra pillow close to him like a child with a favorite toy.

Kate awoke to chattering, happy birds. For a moment she thought she was back at the home she grew up in and dreamed the previous day. As her eyes adjusted to the light, she sat up with the exquisite sheets rustling beneath her and looked around the expansive room.

How extraordinary, she wondered. She remembered to press the attendant's bell and sat on the edge of the bed. After a brief few moments and a knock on the door, her attendant entered.

"Good Morning Miss. And how did you sleep?" Miss Beatrice opened the curtains to full sun that radiated through the room.

"Oh very well, thank you. Um, what time is it?" Kate inquired with a sleepy drawl as her arms stretched to the ornate ceiling.

"10:45 a.m. Miss."

"Isn't that a bit late?" Kate looked around with a furrowed brow. "Will I have a clock in here?"

"Oh no, Miss. Your instructions were to get plenty of sleep. You will get a timepiece later. I will bring you some breakfast and then we will go to your examination. Would eggs, sausage and biscuits be satisfactory Miss?" Her attendant opened her wardrobe and pulled out a very simple dress and underthings.

"Yes, oh yes." Kate suddenly felt absolutely lost. Lord Wilson hadn't lied. Everything was given or brought to her.

"Very well then Miss. I've pulled some simple clothes for your exam today. I will be back with your breakfast shortly." As her attendant left the room with crisp steps, Kate washed up and dressed.

She paused at the window, amazed at what she saw. She was quite high up on the third floor of the Main Building of the Society compound. The window opened to a small balcony where a few tendrils of ivy dared to grip along its edge. The trees had lost a good portion of their leaves, but they were still the thick sturdy guards of the grounds. Gentle rolling hills and groups of hedges dotted the landscape. Several large exquisite manor homes could be seen in the distance. A large black iron arbor and fencing led into what appeared to be a vast garden about thirty yards away from the building. A few people walked some of the paths. A knock from her attendant startled Kate away from the window. "Here is your breakfast Miss. Would you like to sit here at the window? It is a lovely day, isn't it?"

"Mmm, yes it is." The delicious smell awakened her hunger. Just as the attendant put her tray down, a soft whoosh from the tube above her desk distracted them. A small envelope landed in the little basket.

The attendant smiled. "Miss Church, that is the delivery system. I'm certain your Senior has left you a message. May I get that for you?"

"Yes." Kate wondered if she'd already have an Engagement. Her heart leapt at the thought of being put to work so soon. The attendant handed her the envelope and then went about setting the table. Kate stood away from her, smiled at the familiar red wax stamped "W", and opened it. A simple card was enclosed:

"Dear Miss Kate:

I hope you have slept well. Please enjoy your breakfast and do not fret over your exam this morning. I will see you for tea this afternoon. If at any moment you do not feel well, please notify your attendant.

Good day,

W."

Kate grinned. She couldn't wait until 4 p.m.

The doctor in the exam room seemed oddly familiar to Kate for some reason; the déjà vu playing in her mind. She would soon know why.

Kate sat on a long exam table while the physician, Dr. Finch, adjusted some strange bits of equipment on a counter. An assortment of metallic boxes with windows and meters glowed and hummed at their user's touch.

After breakfast, her attendant had walked her to the doctor's office. Again, the halls were somewhat quiet, their footsteps easily heard through the corridor. There was a small, non-descript door through which they entered. A parlor in the front had four teal, plush velvet chairs, but Kate was her only patient. She would learn later that this would almost always be the case unless some emergency arose. Each Member's medical history was strictly guarded.

"I will come for you once your appointment has concluded." Kate's attendant excused herself.

After a few moments, Dr. Finch had opened the door. "Hello, Miss Church. Welcome to the infirmary." She was a striking woman with shiny coal dark hair, deep brown eyes and arched brows that contrasted sharply with her alabaster skin. "Do come in." She had a warm but practical tone as she helped Kate into the room and onto the table. "Please sit."

The coolness of the table shocked Kate's skin, even through her day dress. She tried to calm the overwhelming sense of the unknown by scanning the walls of the exam room. It was lined with cabinets and shelves. Colorful apothecary bottles and containers stood ready for use. There were no windows. All light came from two elegant chandeliers above.

Dr. Finch finished her tinkering and pulled up a rolling chair. Her expression seemed gravely serious and with good reason. It was the physician's task to further install the need for privacy and discretion among the Members.

"Well Miss Church, before we begin the examination, we'll talk for a while and I will explain everything to you. Every visit from this one out will be to insure your well-being and treatment should you be injured. You must answer all questions truthfully for your protection. Any lies could be used against you later should someone discover your faulty secrets. After the exam, you can ask me any questions. Shall we begin then?" Dr. Finch asked.

"Yes." Kate was suddenly nervous. She'd never seen a doctor for herself. Dr. Finch started with a quick battery of simple yes or no questions about her and her family's general health. Then she quickly turned to several very personal inquiries.

"Do you have any children or have you ever been pregnant?" Dr. Finch asked in a quiet tone, taking notes with a curved shaped pen that didn't need an inkwell.

"No." Kate answered with such certainty that Dr. Finch looked up from her writing.

"Have you had any lovers, and if so how many?" The physician looked unflinchingly at her.

"One," Kate almost whispered. Her heart panged a bit at the thought of Michael Parker.

"Just one, Miss Church?" The doctor pressed.

"Yes," Kate stammered. *Should I have had more?* She wasn't a whore. But hadn't been wed either.

"And did you love him?" Kate was blown back at this question; she gripped the table. *Didn't everyone love?*

"Yes, I did."

"And where is he now? Or do you not know?"

"He's been dead a long time now." Kate's voice rang hollow in the office. Dr. Finch had to know more. She hated to pry, but she wanted her new patient to put her past behind her and move forward for duty's sake.

"How long ago were you with him? How old were you?"

"Over twenty years ago, I was almost sixteen." Dr. Finch scribbled a few notes as Kate pursed her lips. Memories of Michael rushed through her like the fire that engulfed the Parker's barn.

"How did he die, or do you not know?" the doctor pressed on. As much as she tried, Kate couldn't hide her sadness. A rush of tears poured down. Dr. Finch grabbed some cloths and consoled her with a gentle touch to her shoulder. "Go on, please tell me everything." Kate then relayed the whole story of the day Michael had died; the hard work, the swim, the lovemaking, the whipping and the fire. Dr. Finch held her hand and looked Kate keenly in the eye. "Miss Church, from this day forward, you are never to speak of this again. Lord Wilson may inquire this afternoon. You will give him the same brief details, but only if he asks. Remember this always," Dr. Finch paused with great care, "every Member had a life before the Society. Once you have passed these walls, that life is over and should not be mentioned to anyone but your Senior going forward. Have I made myself clear?" The physician was stern.

"Yes." Kate nodded, but was quite relieved.

"Good then. I will help you undress for your physical." Kate looked around for a dressing panel. Dr. Finch twittered, then attempted to be polite. "Dear Miss Church, I attended to your wounds in Chicago. There is no need for modesty. I am certain you don't remember, but I promise to take good care of you now, as I did then."

Kate still reddened as her simple gown, bloomers and corset fell to the floor.

"You won't need that bandage any more either." The physician whisked off the protective gauze with a nimble flick of her fingers and indeed any signs of the shooting were gone.

"Now stand for a moment. I am going to pass this wand over you. Just relax." Dr. Finch picked up a copper tube attached to the odd machinery and floated it over every inch of Kate's skin. The machine clicked and whirred as data was gathered. Several images popped up on a small screen on the main instrument. "I see the rug does not match the curtains." The doctor commented with a wry smile.

"Um, what?" Kate stuttered.

"Oh Miss Church," the doctor smiled. "You've dyed your hair is what I meant. I believe that Lord Wilson would like you fair haired again. That will be easily fixed at the ladies salon when we are done here." Dr. Finch turned back to the machine. She read a few of its stats and changed the wand to another copper piece, this time only solid and smaller. "Come up to the table dear and do not be shy. I need to examine your lady parts for a moment." Kate's mouth fell open. "It will not hurt, but we need to make sure you are healthy there too. Just relax and try to breathe." Kate was stunned as she lay back on the table. The doctor gently opened her legs and inserted the probe. "Just a few more seconds." The machine popped a few odd noises and Dr. Finch made a click of her tongue. Kate was curious at the procedure, but had no idea of what to even ask. The doctor unlocked a sturdy cabinet, pulled out a small tube and held it before Kate.

"This vial contains a rare treatment. There are not many here approved to receive this medication. And very few know of its existence. Lord Wilson has granted permission of its use for treating your whip marks. You are to tell no one of it, ever. Your attendant will not question their disappearance. If she does, say nothing and tell your Senior immediately. Do you understand Miss Church?" Kate was perplexed at this mysterious cure for her old wounds, but was eager to see if it worked.

"Yes, I understand," Kate replied quietly. "Will it really heal my scars?"

"Yes. But again let me be clear. Only Lord Wilson and I know of your care. I will apply this serum every other day for the next week or two during regular appointments here. It may bubble a bit, but will stabilize after a few moments and dry. Now just lay face down on the table for a moment for your first treatment." Dr. Finch helped her turn over onto her belly. "Just relax, it will not hurt."

The doctor poured a bit of the purple gel onto Kate's back. It did gurgle for a time as Dr. Finch gently massaged it into the old wounds. Kate relaxed and smiled. *Could this be true? Would the scars really heal?*

"Now then, I can already see some progress." Dr. Finch said with satisfaction as she helped Kate sit up. "Let's get you dressed then. I have one more brief discussion before you leave." There was a serious tone to her voice. When she was fully clothed, the physician held Kate's hands in her own. "Miss Church, I must tell you something quite serious. I do not want you to be concerned but it is something you must know. From your internal exam, I can determine that some of your female organs did not quite develop completely for reasons unknown. And at your age, I would sincerely suspect that you would not be able to have children." The doctor measured Kate's reaction carefully. The new Member was hurt, moistness in her eyes, but rapt with attention. The good doctor continued.

"This will in no way affect your position here. In fact the Society prefers that women do not bear children within its compound. You will never see a child here on the grounds unless it is an emergency. The Society believes that young ones should be protected. They have no part in our organization." Kate was starting to wonder at all the odd rules and contraptions. *What have I fallen into?*

"I must be explicit on this point. Which also means you must not have any sexual relations with men unless you are chosen to be a mate of a Senior Member." Kate's somber expression spurred the doctor forward in her speech. "You will notice that men far outnumber the females here. There is an active recruitment of women; however, there is the challenge of finding those who will give up their lives to serve and yet are talented enough to carry out our Engagements. The Ladies have their own wing and accoutrements here. You should feel honored to have been chosen." Dr. Finch was almost cold in demeanor. "Do you understand the seriousness and complexity of this rule?"

"Yes, yes I do," Kate stuttered, still in a bit of shock. But quickly realized why she'd been chosen. She'd been alone for so long.

"Good. Having said that, with such few women here, there is quite a good chance that you could be paired with a decent gentleman. And should you be partnered with one, you could be courted and certainly married. We do have those marrieds on the grounds, even some of the same sex. We must appeal to every niche of the outside world and its underbellies. And there are other ways of satisfying desires which we will speak of at another visit. However, for now, you have Lord Wilson as your Senior. Remember, he is your trainer, not your lover. Later, you will complete Engagements with him. You may act as a couple in the world outside, but here you will be strictly regarded as a Member. Understood?" The good doctor was completely serene.

"Yes." Kate took the information seriously, straining forward to catch every word.

"Let's take you to the salon now Miss Church." Dr. Finch was calm. She leaned in slightly as she helped Kate to the door and whispered in her ear. "Do not be afraid. This is a world unimagined and the possibilities are endless for the greater good and happiness." As the physician opened the door, there was a flash from her hand. Kate was amazed at the size of an exotic stone set in a large gold wedding band on the hand of her doctor. Happiness indeed.

Lord Wilson had been in a spectacular mood that morning. After a hearty breakfast, he walked with a jaunty spring in his step around the outside of Wilson Manor. Lord Wilson was one of the highest ranked Senior Members of the Society. And having such rank entitled him to his own property on the grounds.

The Manor was stunning. It was built of impressive limestone and brick. It rested on a small but sturdy hill and was trimmed with its own decorative hedges and a wrought iron fence. A lush greenhouse, built of shimmering glass and iron like a gilded cage, was on the southwest side of the home. The front side faced away from the other buildings and grounds and overlooked the lush forested land of the Society Grounds.

It was three stories with an expansive dining room, parlor, and servants' quarters downstairs. Fine furniture and art filled the whole home. The upstairs contained an incredible master bedroom and bath with an attached lady's quarters that, unfortunately, had never been used. There were several guest bedrooms and an immense attic. The Society leader, Director Roth, had once stayed for a while long ago and several young male Members had visited during their training. It looked like a typical stoic mansion to those who had strolled the grounds' paths.

The backside of the Manor however was far from typical. It was a large opulent elevated structure held up by thick metal supports of French Gothic architectural style. Made almost entirely of glass and iron framework, it resembled a precious jewel. When lighted from the inside, it glowed a brilliant orange. This portion of the Manor was most valuable to Lord Wilson as it contained his personal library, study, and a small adjoining laboratory.

A doorway led to a spiral staircase that ended in a choice for the descendant. To the left was a sitting garden; to the right stone steps embedded into the ground that led to a finished cellar that housed a scientific lab with additional living quarters of another young male Member, Dr. Harrington.

It was so good to be home, Wilson thought as the sun warmed the fall flowers. He thought of Miss Kate Church and smiled. If she could obey the rules of the Society, he was certain she'd be extremely happy.

After some brief study and preparations for Miss Church's arrival, he headed about a quarter mile across the grounds to the Main Hall for a pleasant lunch with Director Roth. In his office, they briefly went over the details of Miss Church's upcoming training.

"So Miss Church is settled in then?" The Director edged his spoon into a bowl of steaming hot soup.

"Yes, and quite well so far. I think she'll be ready for study after a few days of rest. But of course I'll know more after a complete evaluation this afternoon." Lord Wilson stirred a lump of sugar into his tea with a subtle grin.

"I am certain you'll let me know of the results. We cannot afford to take on a hysterical woman. I think some etiquette will help," the Director warned.

"But we don't want to break that spirited nature either. And I don't think we've ever had any female with her set of survival skills," Lord Wilson countered. "I look forward to what other mechanical ideas she might have."

"You have complete faith in her then?" Lord Wilson's Senior put down his spoon and bit into a thickly layered sandwich of meats and cheeses. His eyes narrowed with a concerned look as he chewed.

"Yes, yes, I do." Lord Wilson's smile hadn't left his face. He too began to eat his meal.

The Director swallowed and took a deep breath. "I say this as a friend to you, Christopher, she is lovely. Talented. But don't be fooled by her looks. She has killed, more than once now."

"Although not without guilt," Lord Wilson again defended his new Member, the grin erased from his face.

"Still, she is yours to train, to earn, and I know what you most hope for, to keep. Know that I only wish you the best on this endeavor. Please don't make it your last one." Director Roth finished his sandwich with a raised brow and sat back in his chair. His friend had been wronged before. He didn't want the worst to happen again. He pulled cigars from an ornate tin box on his desk and handed one to his best Member.

"I know." Lord Wilson turned in for a light, and the two gentlemen smoked. Director Roth had his past with ladies as well. Lord Wilson had always wanted his friend to have that desire for permanent female companionship again, but it seemed that it was for naught.

"I can't imagine what she'll be like, well, once you have relations." the Director bantered. "You think you can tame all of that?"

"Maybe I won't want to." Lord Wilson laughed as he stumped his cigar and stood to leave.

Director Roth rose to meet him and slapped a hand to his shoulder. "Be careful my friend. I—"

"I know, you don't want me to be forced into complying." Lord Wilson gathered his bowler. "Good day Director."

"Good day, Lord Wilson."

Lord Wilson made a brief stop at the mail room. Despite the flurry of activity of mail stewards rushing about, one of the attendants instantly came to the window and confirmed Lord Wilson's inquiry. His message had been delivered. As he strode back to Wilson Manor with the pleasant October sun bearing down, Lord Wilson suddenly felt more alive than he'd been in years.

"Elixir number five please." The salon attendant commanded her assistant. Kate was leaning over a basin with her head tilted forward. She heard a small hiss behind her. The ladies put on some fitted brown leather gloves.

"Miss Church, the discomfort will be short. I will apply the elixir with some hot steam and you will be back to honey haired in moments." The assistant quickly took a small round copper can with several holes at the end, poured the requested elixir inside its lid, and turned a small knob on its attached pump. She handed it to the salon attendant. A warm fluid emitted from the pump through some tubing and finally a gentle steam pulsed from the contraption. The attendant wafted it carefully over Kate's head. Black droplets fell into the basin and vanished almost on impact. "Turn over please." The attendant commanded. The assistant helped Kate flip her hair and lean backwards. The steam was again applied liberally over Kate's scalp. The warmth was almost a bit too much to take, but felt so refreshingly clean to Kate afterwards. "Elixir number ten please." The attendant ordered. "Now we'll just run this through for a moment. Kate closed her eyes as the loveliest smelling potion was spread through her locks. "Hold still one last time." A waft a warm air dried her hair in just a few brief moments. "All done now, let's take a look, shall we?"

Both ladies of the salon helped Kate towards a mirror. Her hair was indeed restored, the blond curls had returned, shiny and luxurious. "All right then, let's apply a bit of color now, for your afternoon event, Miss Church." The attendant smiled warmly while guiding her to a large vanity. The ladies of the salon proffered several small tubes that gently spritzed makeup colors about Kate's face as she relaxed and closed her eyes. She felt gentle wisps of air and a pulling of her skin as the women of the salon worked their magic. After a short while the attendant almost whispered, "Now open your eyes."

Kate was pleasantly surprised at her image. She was fully made up, but not overly so. Her skin, although now porcelain, was radiant. Some bronze shadow had brought out the blue in her eyes. A light rouge gave color to her cheeks and lips. "Lovely, just lovely Miss Church." The assistants applauded their handiwork.

"Bronze palette packet number six." The attendant ordered. The assistant jotted down a few notes and left. "You look wonderful Miss Church. Your personal attendant will have your regular makeup for you shortly and will apply as needed. However, for special events, you will always be welcomed back at the salon. Your attendant should be here at any moment to take you back to your room in preparation for your meeting." Just then there was a polite knock on the door and Miss Beatrice was there. "It was a pleasure to serve you Miss Church."

"Thank you, thank you so much." Kate was grateful. As the salon attendant took off her gloves to shake hands, Kate noticed another large bejeweled wedding ring. Apparently women were an incredibly precious commodity here.

4 TEA AND TIMEPIECES

It was precisely 2:55 p.m. when Kate's attendant led her from her room to the lift and down to the main foyer. It seemed as if the building was alive with unique people everywhere, buzzing along like bees in a hive. Some appeared in strange costumes or carried odd looking bits of equipment. No one seemed to notice the strangeness surrounding them.

The Society's newest Member drew quite a bit of attention, but if the gentlemen noticed the latest female, they could not show their interest, at least not yet.

"He should be here any moment now, Miss Church. I will see you later this evening." Miss Beatrice smiled and trotted off to other business. By 2:59 p.m., Lord Wilson entered the French doors to meet his new Member. What he saw took his breath away.

The parlor and foyer were filled with Members and attendants preparing for various duties. But to Lord Wilson, it was as if the world had stopped and left only him and his new charge to move freely. Kate stood near the fountain. Her eyes wide in wonderment of all the activity around her. She wore a light blue dress with black velvet cuffs and a high collar. Three large black velvet military style stripes trimmed with gold buttons covered the front torso. The skirt was also trimmed in a black velvet block and bustle. Her hair was bound into a neat bun tucked into a ladies top hat with a light netted veil. She held her bag and a small parasol. Wilson swallowed hard and approached his Member. "Miss Kate, are you ready?" He certainly was.

"Yes, oh hello," she stuttered, still a bit surprised at the traffic of Members.

Lord Wilson smiled at her astonishment. "You will soon get used to the activity and not question it. Let us go for a tour then." He took her arm and they left out through the French doors to a small promenade. There were several Members sitting at marbled tables enjoying the late afternoon sun. Some were reading, some talking, some alone, and still others in pairs. Most were male. "Right now is an open period when Members can walk freely amongst others. It's a good sign. It means there's peace right now. But please note, it could change at a moment's notice," Lord Wilson explained as they passed through and onto the open field.

"Miss Kate, this is the general Society grounds. You can enjoy a walk when you have free time, but note that you should not linger at the individual homes nearby. They belong to other Senior Members. Their residences are private and should not be disturbed." Lord Wilson spoke firmly, but his lightness in steps almost gave away his happiness. He was more than thrilled that she had come to the Society.

Kate was in awe of the size of the grounds as her eyes darted about. The attention to detail was astounding. Every blade of grass, every shrub and tree was well trimmed. Autumn leaves were cleaned up almost as soon as they fell. There were white fountains with lovely sculptures of animals and classic figures amongst the bubbling water. Intricate wrought iron gates ran along several of the private mansions.

They passed the magnificent fenced in garden she could see from her window. Flowers bloomed in the autumn sun. Vines and their tendrils caressed the closed black iron gate that marked the entryway. Vegetation peeked over the tops of the decorative black fencing.

There were a few other buildings of various shapes and sizes. Some were obviously made as utility sheds. One looked like a small church. And one, far off and away from most others, was slightly taller and nondescript. Its windows were heavily curtained. The brick and stone were uniform compared to the elegance of the other buildings. A couple of gentlemen exited with smiles on their faces. Lord Wilson noticed Kate's interest.

"You see the different types of buildings. We have them for groundskeepers and repair men, that cream-colored one with the steeple is a chapel. All faiths can be practiced here. But non-believers are welcome as well. It is important that all kinds of people are represented. The Society is not exclusive to who you are, but is inclusive to what its Members can do. Everyone here has a talent or passion that makes them invaluable to how we operate, from the attendants to the most Senior Members," Lord Wilson explained crisply.

"And that plain building?" Kate asked.

"That well, that is where the gentlemen can be, ahem, men." Lord Wilson coughed as Kate raised an eyebrow. "It has a pub like atmosphere and there is entertainment." He suddenly increased his stride pulling Kate along with him.

"It's a whorehouse?" Kate whispered, almost giggling.

"I said, Miss Kate, that there is entertainment. The gentlemen go there to be entertained."

"I'll bet they do," she twittered.

Lord Wilson stopped suddenly and peered around before he spoke in a stern tone. He looked Kate squarely in the eye. "Miss Kate, you must know that these men have given up their freedom of the outside world to be here. They deserve to have their needs fulfilled as promised, just as you were. And so you know and never ask, some men are entertained by other men as well. Again it's the talent of the individual that counts. Everyone is rewarded for their service."

"Oh, indeed they are." Kate had to suppress a guffaw.

"Miss Kate? Did you understand the levity of what I just told you?" Lord Wilson chided her as Kate stiffened.

"Yes Sir. I'm sorry." Kate tried to sound serious.

"Remember, I promised you that there would be rewards. There are ones for the ladies as well." Kate instantly wondered what he meant as a puzzled furrow crossed her brow. "Dr. Finch will apprise you of this later. Let's carry on to Wilson Manor." They continued down a narrow path, through some thicker trees and over some small hills. Kate shook her head. *Surely there wouldn't be gigolos?*

The trees thinned out and a genteel gated garden was before them. Lord Wilson's office shone in the daylight like a gothic gilded gem. As they approached the home, Lord Wilson escorted Kate around the side path to the front entrance.

The red brick and yellow plastered Manor rose up out of a small hill. It had tall rounded topped windows that were trimmed with blue wood. Some on the upper floor had small balconies with black iron décor. There was a short set of stairs with heavy double doors at the top.

"Ladies first." Lord Wilson smiled. Kate climbed slowly while looking at the elegant foliage that surrounded the home. She paused at the top of the porch. As she turned around to take in the grandeur, Kate let out an audible "Oh."

"Lovely isn't it?" Lord Wilson commented.

"Yes." She could barely be heard. Kate marveled at the beauty of Wilson Manor.

"Let's come inside now, shall we?" Lord Wilson pulled out some keys, unlocked and opened the door. A tall sturdy butler greeted them inside. He was a balding older gentleman with a ruddy complexion. They stood in a dimly lit narrow entryway. A carpeted set of stairs went up to their left, a narrow hallway straight ahead.

"Welcome to Wilson Manor, Miss Church." The serviceman bowed slightly.

"Miss Kate, this is Leeds, my butler." Lord Wilson introduced.

A light voice echoed from behind Leeds. "Is she here?" A pleasant faced plump woman came around a corner from under the stairs and approached.

"And this is Mrs. Leeds, my cook and the new spouse of Leeds." Leeds smiled. Apparently recently-wedded status agreed with him.

"How do you do?" Kate smiled. They looked incredibly happy for servants. She briefly wondered if their rewards included each other.

"Very well Miss Church, please come in." Leeds led them down the hall and into a good-sized parlor to the right of the entryway. He waved his hand along a small box along the side door trim and the lights came up in the fancy sitting room. Kate hadn't seen such elegance since she'd been at the Parker's. The remembrance of Michael suddenly made her heart drop unexpectedly.

There was an empty fireplace with a fine wood-trim mantle. A plush sofa and two chairs were upholstered with a rosy pink fabric. The gas lamps were decorated with painted pink roses. An elegant chandelier reigned over a center table trimmed with a delicate doily. A light blue Asian vase held a bouquet of white and pink roses. The room was fragrant with their scent. A few well selected paintings and trinkets lined the room. They stepped onto thick oriental rugs. Kate's heart again panged for a moment as it reminded her of Ming and Chin. How long ago it seemed already.

"Let's let some sunshine in, eh? Pretty soon it'll be winter and we'll have less daylight," Mrs. Leeds chirped as she pulled back the curtains.

"Leave them open, but we'll proceed to the dining room, then onto the study." Lord Wilson smiled at Kate. She looked happy at first, but now seemed a trifle unsteady since they'd entered the Manor. He made a mental note to pick her brain about what she was thinking. He needed for her to feel welcomed here. This was not the moment to pry. There would be plenty of time for questions later.

They moved into the dining room. Again, there were haughty furnishings. The immense table was prepped for twelve with full place settings. An extraordinary hutch held more fine china. A serving table had its proper accoutrements. A large vase and centerpiece held more pink and white roses under yet another striking chandelier.

"What do you think Miss Kate?" Lord Wilson laughed as Kate's face glowed from the lamps and her mouth popped open.

"It's grandiose. Really beautiful." Kate was truly impressed. *Rewards, rewards,* the promise tumbled in her head.

"Tea will be ready in a moment Sir," Leeds piped up.

"Come now." Lord Wilson took Kate's hand and led her out to the hallway. Kate thought she heard some odd footsteps upstairs, but was redirected by Lord Wilson's kind lilt. "The kitchen is here." He pointed across from the dining room. "There are some steps down from inside for the Leeds's quarters and a laboratory workshop. And this-" he smiled as they paused at a large door at the end of the hall. "is my study, my library." Lord Wilson opened the door and Kate was immediately bathed in light. The outside wall was made completely of curved windows with French-styled ornamental iron trim. "Go ahead, step in," Lord Wilson coaxed.

Kate entered the room which was about two stories tall. The solid house wall was lined with rows of books. An expansive desk was placed just in front of them. There were a few curious instruments that shone in the freckled sunlight that filtered through the tall oaks outside. Lord Wilson had a most spectacular view of the grounds.

To the left of the desk was another table with more gadgets and several beakers of liquids. Along the windows were two chairs, a small table, a couple of large plants, several short bureaus, and a lounger. Kate thought that surely this is what it was like to live in a genie's bottle.

"I have all kinds of books." Lord Wilson gestured. "There is a library in the Main Hall, but you are always welcome to read what I have here. Go on, take a look."

Kate's fingers gently brushed the bindings of the fine tomes. Most titles were embossed and printed in gold. She'd loved to read before she'd gone to Iris. The only things she'd read in Texas were letters, the newspapers, and the Bible.

"You don't have to choose anything now. And there is a list of things I want you to study, but we can talk about that later." Lord Wilson was beaming. Kate looked like a child in a candy store. It amazed him that the same woman before him had killed a wicked cowboy just the week before. She was the perfect balance of dark and light.

Leeds knocked and brought in the tea service. The tray not only had tea but some blueberry muffins and chocolates as well.

"Let's sit here at the window then." Lord Wilson guided Kate to the table. Leeds seated her, poured their tea, and left without a sound. "And what do you think of the Manor?"

"It's beautiful, really lovely." Kate removed her gloves and added sugar and milk to her warm drink. Lord Wilson watched as she stirred her tea and then he began to sip his own. The Manor had lacked a female presence for a long time. Now Mrs. Leeds and Kate were both welcome additions, although Miss Kate would only be a visitor, at least for now.

"Try the muffins, I think you'll like them." Lord Wilson encouraged. He suddenly remembered her body on the examiner's table in Chicago. She was a bit thin and wounded. She needed nourishment.

Kate spread the soft churned butter onto a morsel, took a bite and let out a little moan. "Oh, it's wonderful." The warm snack oozed blueberry flavor onto her tongue.

"Eat as much as you like, but you might want to try some of the chocolates as well." He liked to see her happy. Kate's face was relaxed. The sun gave her face a rosy glow. He almost regretted the next part of the conversation, but it had to be done.

"Miss Kate, I must ask you now about certain things. I want your answers to be honest. You do not have to go into details. But I want to know where we are starting from in order to move forward. Is that clear?" He was gentle in his probing. One of the reasons Lord Wilson was retained in the Society was due to high interrogation skills.

"Of course." Kate replied. She tried to relax but felt a series of painful questions coming on. She nibbled on a dark chocolate filled with orange cream. The tangy burst of sweetness nearly distracted her from the conversation.

"First and foremost, what we are doing now is having a Discussion. I will send you Invitations to your room much like I did in Iris. Invitations will either guide you to a Discussion or an Engagement, a task to complete as you did before. Going forward, you and I will have these Discussions in that opulent garden we passed. But for today, we'll start here. Each time we meet, I will give you strict instructions. You are to follow them to the letter. That is all you need to know at this time. You'll be trained and allowed to sharpen the skills you already have before you are be sent out. But first I want you to heal." The last sentence was said with such tenderness that Kate was again surprised. "You understand?"

"Yes." Kate sipped as Lord Wilson relaxed back in his chair. And so the Discussion began.

"Some simple things first. We already addressed the explosion. You know that precision is important on Engagements and you can't let personal feelings get in the way of our tasks?" He watched as Kate's face clouded a bit.

"Well, yes of course."

"Drasco was a despicable human being, but we needed him for a few more days." He sipped his tea casually. To act nonchalant was one of the best ways to question someone. A relaxed atmosphere almost always revealed truth.

"Do you mean he worked for the Society?" Kate looked troubled, her eyes clouded.

"No." Lord Wilson shook his head. "We were preparing to take the liquids he had stored. They are quite powerful."

"Oh, I am so sorry." Kate apologized and shifted uncomfortably in her chair.

"No matter." Lord Wilson waved his hand loosely as if brushing off the comments. "We've secured some of the strange cacti. We'll be able to grow and use it here. Without you, we wouldn't have found the source." He sipped his tea and then poured another cup for each of them.

"Oh thank you." Kate blushed.

"I was harsh with you Miss Kate, but you succeeded on several of your missions. I was impressed with how you handled yourself on most of your tasks. I want to compliment you and hope that you will keep that spirited nature in all your Engagements." Wilson gently praised her, for the next several questions would be difficult.

"I will try my best." Kate smiled and looked down at her tea. The warmth and the food almost made her sleepy.

"Miss Kate, did you enjoy killing Mr. Drasco?" The question was purposefully sudden and direct. He succeeded in catching her off guard.

Kate looked up from her plate. "Uh, no. I mean, I was satisfied that he was gone. I guess." She shrugged and hoped she'd given her Senior the correct answer. She'd never given it much thought other than he had haunted her.

"And why did you? Why did you kill him?"

Kate paused and pondered the question carefully. "I was scared. Afraid he'd come back somehow." She bit her lip as she was reminded of the havoc Drasco had caused. Lord Wilson waited and let her finish knowing that there was more to come. "And I was angry. He'd taken away so much from me." Kate's voice had lowered. Her face had gone white. It pained him to see her emotions, but it was so necessary to reveal them.

"We have to be careful with revenge, Miss Kate. It's not good to act in such haste. Besides," he paused and buttered a scone, "we have Members here who specialize in this. It's to protect the others who do the groundwork, so to speak. Are you well with this?"

"Oh yes," Kate replied eagerly.

Lord Wilson was enthused to see her reaction. He agreed with Mr. Roth, the Society didn't want Kate to be an assassin. She had other more promising skills.

"And you like building, tinkering with things?" Wilson took a lighter tack for a moment.

"Yes, yes I do." Kate visibly brightened.

"I'm impressed with the gun, well I should say guns. The parasol is, well fantastic, yet deadly. We may make it standard issue for the Lady Members with some modifications." He smiled again. "You'll be allowed access to a work house and my lab here. You are welcome to share your ideas with me and a select few others. Inventions and secrets are precious here. To remain ahead of the competition is of the utmost importance. Surely you understand this?" His voice was kind, almost pleasurable.

"Yes, of course. I would love to do it." Kate felt appreciated. It was exactly how Lord Wilson wanted her to feel at that moment.

"Those items were imperative to our receiving two special keys that are most important to our mission here. I cannot say more about this now, but know that your work was stellar in this manner." Lord Wilson was building her up to a crescendo of pride.

"Thank you again Sir." Kate couldn't believe what she was hearing.

"You're a strong woman Miss Kate. It must have taken some ungodly power to make it through a whipping," Lord Wilson stated in a quiet fashion. The question was asked so lightly that he yet again startled her.

"Um, yes." Again she flushed. Kate had forgotten that he'd most likely seen the scars.

"Would you like to tell me a bit about it?" he pried softly.

Kate remembered Dr. Finch's warning. "Well, um." She stopped, wondering what to say.

"Only the basics Miss Kate, nothing more." He leaned forward and touched her hand.

Kate swallowed hard. She had remembered that Dr. Finch had said that the basic information was able to be relayed, so she proceeded. "I was whipped after a man I worked with discovered me with, my, uh first gentlemen. My first love. He was jealous. He killed the man that would've been my fiancé, and then he whipped me. I had to run, that's why I went to Iris." Kate simplified it as much as possible, leaving out Silas, the fire and McKendrick's death. She coughed as the memory almost overwhelmed her. A single tear escaped her eye and plopped into her tea.

"There now Miss Kate, I don't want you to relive it, I want you to forget it." His face was somber. Kate tried to stifle her tears to no avail. Lord Wilson got up, stood behind her and let his hand graze onto her shoulder. His voice was delightful and coaxing as he turned towards her ear.

"I want you to cry one last time Miss Kate, then never again for this. You must understand me. Your past can be used against you. No one should know. I will have to pretend that I've never heard it. That is why I did not ask for details. I should never want to know particulars that could put you in jeopardy should I be restrained for any reason. I know this is upsetting. Come here and relax on this lounger." He came from behind her chair, took Kate's hand and helped her to the comfortable furnishing. He gave her a handkerchief.

Kate lifted the veil of her mini topper and gently dabbed at her eyes. Sadness overwhelmed her.

Secretly, Lord Wilson liked to see her so delicate. He pulled off her hat and set it aside. She was primed for the next task at hand. "Are you alright, Miss Kate?"

"Oh yes, thank you," Kate whimpered.

"There, there now. Take some deep breaths," Lord Wilson cooed. "Why don't you look up at the sky? See how lovely the shadows of the autumn leaves dance on the glass? See how every once in a while, one falls and drifts so slowly?" His voice soothed. "Is that better?"

Kate relaxed. "Oh yes, much."

"See how the wind shifts the leaves side to side? Why don't you just focus on that for a while, then I'll ask you some easier questions? Yes?"

"Hmm, yes." Kate's head grew heavy. The shadows started to turn and blur.

"Go ahead, close your eyes for a bit. I'll shake your right shoulder when you need to awake." Lord Wilson whispered as he hypnotized her. Lie he must, but he wanted to know everything about the whipping. And he didn't want word getting back to Dr. Finch. He liked and respected the good doctor, but Miss Kate was his Member. Her secrets were his to keep.

Slowly he questioned Kate. Her answers were methodical and clear as her subconscious mind revealed her past to Lord Wilson. He heard every detail of the whipping and was horrified, yet pleased at how strong Kate was. She unknowingly told him the complete story of the fire and Silas' escape. She recanted the tale of Ming and Chin when he asked about her tattoo. And how she planned and completed her exodus from Iris. Lastly, he asked how she felt about him.

"Miss Kate, how do you think of me, your Senior, Lord Wilson?" A slow, dreamy smile crept across Kate's face.

"I think you're lovely," Kate murmured. Lord Wilson grinned. *Shame on me for such silliness*, he chided himself. Sadly the inquisition was over. He could handle her past and would be able to help her deal with it as well. He resisted the temptation to stroke her face.

"So now Miss Kate, you've had a very good nap. You won't fret about these things much anymore. Will you?"

"No. No." Kate sighed, her eyes still closed under his mental sedation.

"Alright then, I'm going to gently shake your shoulder and you'll wake, just as I told you before?" He teased in her ear while taking in her lavender scent.

"Um, yes."

"Here we go." And with Lord Wilson's gentle shake, Kate's eyes popped open.

She had been under for about thirty minutes, but to Kate it had seemed like it had only been seconds. "I'm so sorry, I must've drifted off." The room suddenly came into crystal clear focus. She sat up and peered around trying to remember how she had come here.

"There, there now. I didn't mean to upset you Miss Kate." Lord Wilson encouraged as he massaged her shoulder. "I want to assure you that the treatment you're receiving will make your scars vanish."

"But, my, uh, tattoo? I mean, I have one, it was given to me. It's very special." Kate whined a bit as she came round. She clearly didn't remember her questioning under hypnosis.

"We'd prefer you'd not have it, however, we'll allow it as it has a gifted meaning. Someone believed in your strength." Lord Wilson had done his research on the marking. If she felt it gave her more power, even if it was a mental illusion, he should allow it. He never questioned mysticism in any form.

"Thank you so much. For everything really." Kate blushed.

"Come, I want to show you the greenhouse." Lord Wilson smiled coyly as he helped her collect herself. They stepped out of the study via a spiral staircase. They walked along the private sitting garden and over to his prized home for plants. It resembled a beautiful gilded aviary. Several exotic birds and insects flew amongst the foliage. At the far end, a large engine pumped in the necessary heat and moisture to keep the plants healthy year round. He unlocked the gate and allowed Kate to enter first.

"This is fantastic." Kate walked amidst several dozen of plants. Some were familiar, others incredibly odd looking.

"I have a few rare specimens. Many of these have important properties that help us in our research. Come this way to my work bench." He led her to a corner of the building where there was a water pump, several buckets, different soils, and gardening tools. A large sturdy table held several short round plump-leaved plants.

"And what are these?" Kate asked pleasantly. The greenhouse was lush and fragrant. Some birds chirped as if they were welcoming her. She felt as if she were on an exotic trip to a foreign land she'd only read about in books.

"Well, I must talk of a few things first." Lord Wilson looked at Kate unflinchingly. "I have many secrets in the greenhouse. You will not have regular access to it without my permission. Is that understood?"

"Yes." Kate again realized that she was now involved in a world richly filled with well-held power.

"And as we discussed and Dr. Finch has also expressed to you, I am your Senior Member. I am to direct you in everything in regards to your life here. The Engagements you'll go on, the rewards you'll receive. Miss Kate, I have selected you myself because of your skills, and then fought for your entrance here after you had made some hasty decisions. I, in turn, must trust you as well. We must have a bond that cannot ever be broken. You will tell me every detail when it comes to any aspect of your life here. Having said this, do you trust me Miss Kate?" Lord Wilson was stoic.

Kate was overcome by his tenacity. She could feel the strength of his masculinity; a sense of odd power casting a strong shadow. "Yes, I trust you."

"Are you certain?" He turned his head slightly, yet his eyes did not leave her face.

"Yes, absolutely." Kate was steady in her response.

"You'll trust me completely and will not waver?" Lord Wilson asked one more time.

"Yes, yes, I will." Kate used all her muster to dare to stare back him. She did mean it. She felt safe with him here. And that is exactly what Lord Wilson was counting on.

"Alright then, give me your right hand, palm up please." His tone changed to one of pleasantries.

"Yes Sir, or course." Kate offered and Lord Wilson took it gingerly. Suddenly there was a flash of light as he, in one fell swoop, picked a knife from the table and sliced open the meat of her palm under her thumb.

"Ahhh, ouch, oh!!!" Kate screeched as blood poured from the freshly cut wound. She instantly tried to withdraw her hand, but Lord Wilson had tightened his grip around her wrist.

But just a quickly he tore one of the plump leaves from one of the plants on the table. He gave it a tart squeeze and poured its rich purple juices onto the gash. "Wait, Miss Kate, hold still." Lord Wilson ordered.

Kate shuddered as the mysterious plant excretion stung her skin a bit, sizzled and then returned her hand to normal. "Oh my, it, it-" She was in such awe that she couldn't finish her sentence.

"It's a rare healing plant." Lord Wilson explained as he gently wiped the excess blood away with a soft cloth he pulled from one of the table's vast drawers. "Very, very rare." He took care in examining her repaired hand. He looked at her face; Kate was still aghast. "Not everyone has access to this treatment, the Serum. I want you to understand that not even most Senior Members know of this. So you are to tell no one, understood?"

"Why, um, yes," Kate stuttered. "Is this what is curing my scars?" She inquired politely, finally coming round to what had just transpired.

"Precisely. It's a serum that can be used in a wide variety of ways. It saved your life in Chicago. And because you are under my care, I will do things for you, provided you do as you're told. You should feel privileged to have access to this treatment." He gazed into her eyes as he softly stroked her palm. "Remember, the secrets between us, the trust we have, is vital. Do not assume anyone else knows anything. Understood?" Lord Wilson continued to offer a kind grin and kissed her palm.

Kate reddened again at the warmth of his lips as they brushed her hand. He then placed both hands over hers. "Thank you for trusting me, Miss Kate."

"You're most welcome." Again she felt so oddly childish in his presence.

"Hmm, you say that now." Lord Wilson gave an odd snicker. "But for your good behavior, I do have something for you. Let's go back inside, shall we?" He took her arm and then let her go up the staircase to the library.

Once they'd returned, Lord Wilson encouraged Kate to sit, and then summoned Leeds. "Please bring in our guest." Leeds smiled and left.

There was a slight rumble from inside and a clatter of what sounded like an animal running. Suddenly Strax burst forth from the doorway, planted his paws on Kate's dress and licked her face eagerly.

"What? Oh my! Strax!" Kate giggled and cried with happiness. "But how? He was dead."

"Well, Miss Kate, I happened to be very lucky to have seen him poisoned that night in Iris. I was able to medicate him into a deep slumber before the poison took complete control. However, I didn't plan on you burying him so quickly. Fortunately, the ground was cool and further helped his sleep. I was able to reanimate him after you'd gone upstairs," Lord Wilson explained.

Kate petted her long-lost friend feverishly. "Thank you, thank you so much." Leeds handed her some bones from the kitchen. The canine finally calmed as Kate gifted him with the treats. "Did you fix his ear?" The contraption that Kate had constructed was gone.

"Yes. We only improved upon what you had done. Go ahead, take a look," he urged. Kate gingerly lifted his ear to peer in. Deep inside, she could see a miniature cone with a few tiny gears turning. "He just needs a little oil every few days."

"I, I am so grateful. I have no idea how to thank you." Kate suddenly felt light-headed. She'd been given so much by a man she hardly knew in a place so other-worldly.

"Now, he must stay here Miss Kate, but you can visit whenever it's convenient," Lord Wilson offered. "Remember I promised you rewards. This could be one of many." He watched the sunset's shadows play across her face. His mission had been almost accomplished for now.

"Yes, thank you, this is so lovely, so fantastic." Kate sighed as she stroked Strax's soft fur and noticed the wretched mark of Drasco had been cured as well.

"Well now, Leeds will take him. We need to return you to the Hall." Leeds led Strax back inside the stately Wilson Manor. He whimpered a bit, but Kate didn't fret. He was in excellent hands and was assured she would see him again.

Lord Wilson took her hand, helped his new Member with her hat, and they again departed via the spiral staircase.

They walked the grounds in silence as the sky burnt with oranges and yellows. A few high thin clouds turned pink and purple.

"We have one more stop to make, here in the Garden." Lord Wilson's tone turned serious again. He lifted the latch to the gate and they walked inside. "Watch where we're going, remember markers like the sculptures and stepping stones." He led her around several corners as they passed lush seasonal flowers, towering trees, and well-spaced park benches. "This one, here." He motioned to a good-sized seat under an immense oak. He allowed Kate to sit.

"May I join you, Miss Kate?" He asked.

"Well of course." Kate tilted her head in befuddlement.

"I want you to know that I will always ask you this for several reasons. One, if I don't ask, it could be a sign that something is seriously wrong. Two, if you refuse, you are in turn letting me know that it is not safe for us to meet here. Always remember this. Subtleties are of utmost importance in hiding information." Lord Wilson then sat next to Kate.

She noticed a few other couples sat on similar benches in various other parts of the Garden. All seemed rapt with attention. "Please don't stare at them Miss Kate, I need your full attention here. This is the most important part of our Discussion today." And so the Discussion began again.

"Memorize this location; it belongs to us and no one else. This is where we will meet for Discussions, where I will give you instructions. And this." Lord Wilson pulled a shiny pocket watch from his coat and handed it to Kate. "This is yours and only yours. No one else should ever possess it. It should be on your person or within your reach at all times."

"This is gorgeous." *More gifts*, Kate brightened and brushed a delicate hand over its ornate cover. The backside was engraved with "For the greater good. KC".

"It is much more than a trinket. The timepieces are individualized to your person, your touch, your blood flow. Go ahead, remove your gloves, I'll hold it." Kate did as she was told.

He opened the pocket watch and replaced it in her palm. The hands were set at midnight for a brief moment. Suddenly the face lit up and the time piece vibrated in her hand. The hands moved to the current time, 5:45 p.m. "There now, it is set to your body coordinates. It will buzz to remind you of appointments, Engagements. Most importantly, if it ever stops," Lord Wilson paused and stared into Kate's eyes, "it will let me know that you've died."

"What?" Kate cried in astonishment.

"Shhh. Always low voices in the Garden, Miss Kate." He hushed her. "Yes. Our time-pieces are connected. They will glow different colors and vibrate at different intervals. You will learn what each one means." He closed her hand over it. "Take care with it; I should not want to lose you Miss Kate."

She nodded solemnly. "I will."

"And if for any reason it stops after glowing red, and you're alive, you will know that I have passed. You will go to Mr. Roth directly. He will reassign you to a new Senior." Lord Wilson's face was like stone. "You understand?"

"Yes, yes." Kate had gone a bit pale.

"Now going forward, know that you have been given special privileges. Not everyone receives a timepiece here. Another example of your status, is that you've been given lodging on the third floor.

The third floor is usually reserved for those higher tenured members and some Seniors. You will learn more about this practice later. But for now, when we are in the presence of others in the Hall or outside the grounds, you are to address me as Sir. You can address me as Lord Wilson at Wilson Manor. We do not use Christian or first names until you are at some of the highest levels. It also demonstrates manners. You understand this?" he questioned.

"Yes,." Kate responded.

"Yes?" Lord Wilson cocked an eyebrow.

"Oh, yes Sir." Kate smiled coquettishly.

"So we have one last thing to discuss, the weather." His tone turned to one of kindness.

"The weather, Sir?" Kate asked. Lord Wilson liked that she'd addressed him properly.

"Yes, the weather is code for the mood or temperature of the Society. No matter what the actual climate is outside, if someone refers to a storm blowing in, for example, they are speaking of trouble. Again not everyone knows this. But if you hear reference to it, know that there could be issues and you should be aware of sudden changes, even if it's sunny and pleasant outside. It's very simple, you understand this?"

"Yes Sir." Kate nodded.

As darkness enveloped them, gas lights in the Garden and on the grounds suddenly brightened.

"Well, that would be our cue to return you to the Hall. Your attendant should be waiting for you." Just then the pocket watch buzzed in Kate's palm. "She'll help you get settled in and order dinner in your room. Tomorrow you will start dining with the others, but remember to make acquaintances, not friends. You are Miss

Church to everyone here, except me. In between meals you'll receive more treatments for your wounds, some light materials and plenty of time to rest over the next week. Your attendant will help you with your schedule. In a few days we'll prepare for your training. I'd like for you to start Engagements in the next couple weeks. Are you ready Miss Kate?"

"Yes, I am, Sir." Kate felt oddly relaxed as Lord Wilson took her arm and guided her back out to the grounds.

"Well then, it looks to be a lovely evening Miss Kate. Remember what I've told you today. And don't worry about being overwhelmed. You'll have time to process this all. Good night Miss Kate." Lord Wilson took her hand in a slow, intimate fashion and kissed it.

"Thank you Sir." Kate smiled. For someone who had just agreed to join a most dangerous Society, she was strangely at ease. She walked straight to the Hall and remembered not to look back as was customary.

As Kate turned away, Lord Wilson was content. She'd been almost a bit too soft today, but he had her trust. And he knew her secrets. He liked that Kate had acted the most lady-like he'd seen so far. He hoped everything would continue to go as smoothly, although in his heart he knew it wouldn't. He had tamed her for now, but there would be challenges. There always were.

A chilly autumn breeze gave Lord Wilson cause to shudder as he headed off to Wilson Manor. He could not wait for the future evenings of warmth he would spend with Miss Kate. Hopefully his heart wouldn't ever be that cold again.

5 A WORD ABOUT THE SOCIETY

The origins of the Society were clouded in mystery. Old rumors claimed that one of the Knights Templar had started an organization to act "for the greater good". This could not be verified in any files or libraries on any Society Grounds. Its beginnings were probably the best kept secret of all.

The Society acted almost as a parallel universe to the world outside its gates, only was much more sophisticated. The majority of its Members had permanently given up their previous lives to join. In turn, they were given the best of everything from around the globe: food, clothing, education, and medicine. It was a well-oiled machine that ran on endless supplies of money from its mysterious benefactors.

Secrets were the key to the Society's existence and security. Anyone who knew anything about the Society was sworn to silence and dedicated to protecting it. Breaking the code would usually result in Termination. Like other institutions in the outside world, there were rules. These were intensely adhered to by its Members due to possible serious consequences. The Society was not bound by governments or religion, but instead could be called upon by these pillars to serve "for the greater good". These tenants were taught to each Member upon initiation and were posted in the Main Hall should anyone need a reminder. They read as follows:

1. Do not draw attention to oneself.

2. Never speak of one's past before the Society.

3. Follow all directions given by Senior Members.

4. Dress and act properly at all times; etiquette is key.

5. Complete each Engagement as requested and on cue; time is of the essence.

6. Be prompt, but do not act in haste.

7. Engagements are distributed only by Senior Members via Invitations and Discussions.

8. Show no emotion in completing Engagements.

9. Do not question any instruction or giver or receiver of information; discretion is key.

10. Never look back after an Engagement is completed.

11. Avoid violence unless your own life is in danger.

12. Should an Engagement end badly and a Member is exposed, the Society will have no recognition of it.

13. Any treason is grounds for Termination.

14. Balance is important in all things; do not be too hard, do not be too soft.

The Society had its hierarchy of Members. The Director of each location was ultimately responsible for all Members under his tutelage. The Director earned his position after years of service and was somewhat familiar with other Directors and locations. The Director also answered to a higher authority, but these persons were usually not known to the Directors themselves.

Beneath the Director were the Senior Members. Senior Members were usually a bit older than the other standard Members, at least in their late thirties. They were experienced in their fields of study which could be anything from botany to weaponry. They were expected to keep the Members under them in check. They could also be expected to recruit other Members if necessary.

Recruitment could be a sticky wicket for the Society, as the male Members outnumbered females by ten to one. The Society needed to have Members from every level of the outside. They had infiltrated every possible business and government in the dignified and unrefined worlds. There was always a need for more ladies. Many women would not have the toughness to work in the field, but could be used on the inside in various roles. Almost all would be paired with a male after their initiation and education needs had been suitably fulfilled by a Senior female. It was rare for a new female Member to be paired with a Senior male.

Senior Members would have their pick of the litter, so to speak, but not without approval of the Director. The Seniors would be allowed to recruit if necessary; in fact recruiting was highly encouraged. Scouts were continually out seeking new prospects. Members could marry but never divorce, and there were absolutely no children allowed on the Grounds, except in cases of extreme emergency. Rare was the occasion that a female was impregnated and returned to the outside. Once outside the walls of the Grounds, the Society could never guarantee the safety of its Members. To prevent jealous competition between male members, a gentlemen's club with entertainment on the Society Grounds was made available to those unattached male Members. Unattached ladies were given access to the Hysteria Room if recommended by a doctor.

The next level of Membership, was the Specialists. These recruits were selected for their unique skills whether they were mathematicians, artists, teachers, doctors, military, scientists, or linguists. Of the Specialists, the most deadly were the Assassins.

The Assassins were the most frightening group of the Society. They were prepared to kill anyone at anytime, anywhere upon orders from the Director. Some of these Members had troublesome pasts in the outside world, but had been swayed to do their duty in exchange for the sweet comforts of the Society. They did not often associate with the others and had their own quarters in the Hall. The Society was willing to turn a blind eye to their previous shady deeds in order to retain them.

A rare group of Members held positions of such vast importance that they operated fully on the outside of the Society grounds. These Members were referred to as Fixtures. There were many doctors, attorneys, businessmen, journalists, even politicians and royalty who were Fixtures. Because of their access to technology and information, their role in the Society was in high demand. In severe emergencies, their residences could be used as safe houses.

The Assistants were the last level of the Society, but by no means the least important. They included attendants, gardeners, the post workers, tailors, cooks, and porters. These folk were the lifeblood of the Society. They knew some of the most intimate secrets of the Members; their clothing sizes, food preferences, and eventually where their ashes would be scattered.

As Members were pulled from field work or their Society tasks, they could become teachers to the newly inducted apprentices. Members could retire upon the onset of either incurable disease or being elderly. They were cared for in a highly guarded separate facility on the Society grounds.

Each Member understood that once they joined the Society, they could never, ever leave. And that is precisely why Lord Wilson had been so careful in his recruitment of Kate Church.

6 MANNERS, MIND, AND PHYSIQUE

"Open your manual to the next chapter. And Miss Church, please sit up straight. I shouldn't have to remind you again." Madame Prix corrected her new student. Madame was the etiquette authority at the Society. "If this is a challenge, cross your legs at your ankles, and place them underneath your chair. It will help you sit taller." Her voice commanded in a cool French elegance that mirrored her beauty. Her heels clicked lightly on the floor as she glided to her desk and sat down.

Kate and her new instructor were sitting in a large room with ten simple wooden tables and matching chairs. It had the same high ceilings, large windows and chandeliers as most of the other rooms Kate had seen so far. But it was surprisingly spare in décor. A few ordinary shelves and cabinets lined the walls that were without windows. A table, with complete place settings for four, seemed to be the only furnishing out of place.

Madame Prix had the loveliest piece of furniture, an ornately carved desk with scroll trim details. Two ceramic lamps, hand painted with delicate floral designs, stood on both ends of the desk.

Madame was said to be in her sixties, but it certainly didn't show. Her golden mane was pulled into a high pompadour. Perhaps she had a few wrinkles, but her eyes were solid brown pools. She wore an elegant jacquard print bronze gown with puffy upper sleeves and a tremendous bustle. Madame opened a thick manual with precise flicks of her manicured hands. She too wore an ostentatious wedding ring with a black stone. It made Kate want to look at her fingernails. They were finally starting to grow after years of hard work in the outdoors.

"Miss Church, please focus on the task at hand." Madame Prix had put on rosy-colored spectacles. She looked over them at her only Member in class, and then glanced back through the lenses. They were a special pair. They allowed her to see certain things, faux fabrics, artificial colors. Their primary use was determining fakes of antiquities. But most of the Society did not know this. On this occasion it allowed her to see that the boning in Kate's corset was indeed bone and not metal. "Oh and Miss Church, why are you not wearing your waist trainer today?"

Kate stammered. "I'm sorry. I have another few days of treatment before I can wear one." Kate spoke the truth. She was still receiving treatments of the secret Serum from Dr. Finch. Kate was not to wear any restrictive clothing until the scars were gone.

"Hmm. Is that so?" Madame Prix again studied her pupil over her eye wear and decided to test her. New Members sometimes had issues that were being corrected in their first week of attendance. Worries that weren't any of the tutor's business.

"I had a life before here, but that was then and this is now." Kate looked up with a defiant lift of her chin. Lord Wilson had warned her of revealing her past to anyone. The answer Kate gave was the appropriate response.

Madame Prix was satisfied. Her student was older than most of the gentlemen and ladies that had entered her class. And certainly wiser, but was a bit rough around the edges. She was learning quickly, which was the most important task at hand. Miss Church needed to be field-ready as soon as possible.

"Very well then. I'd like you to read this bit of poetry. Remember, think clear, yet smooth," Madame urged.

Kate cleared her throat and opened her mouth, but was stopped.

"Non, no, Miss Church. If your throat is dry, make sure you moisten it before you are to read anything aloud. Coughing can send odd signals to your audience. Are you ill? Are you making a rude statement of some sort? And remember, sometimes coughing is done on purpose as a signal to another Member. In this case, coughing can be catastrophic. Now, pour yourself a drink and let's try this again."

"Yes Madame." Kate rose and crossed over to the table that was set for a dinner. A silver pitcher was at the center. Kate reached for it, but almost knocked over a glass. She caught it before it fell to the floor.

"Tsk, tsk, Miss Church. Although I am impressed by your reflexes, you should know to move items out of the way when reaching for other things. You wouldn't want your sleeve to catch fire on fine tapers now, would you?"

"Of course not, Madame." Kate gritted her teeth. She hated this, the constant scrutiny. Every move, every word, everything was criticized. Nothing escaped the gaze of Madame. Kate pushed a few pieces of the place settings aside and poured half a glass of water. *I thought I had manners*, Kate grumbled in her head. She had seemed to do well at the Parker's many years ago, but maybe they had not bothered to notice her ignorance? Kate lifted the glass to her lips and met the disapproving glare of her teacher.

"Now Miss Church, we do not stand while we eat or drink unless it is a casual setting. Like a picnic or buffet. For all practical purposes, we pretend that this is formal dining. So take your drink to your seat. Walk with a steady gait so it does not spill. And for heaven's sake, roll your shoulders back. One's bosom is a gift. You must carry it with grace," Madame chided.

"Yes Madame." Kate obeyed and set the drink down on her desk with great care.

"Well done Miss Church. As always, put things down lightly, with ease. Now you may sit."

"Yes Madame." Kate tried to sound polite, but the repetitiveness of the exercises bored her. She slid sideways into the hard wooden chair, then lifted her legs together and brought them under the desk. Her hands fell to her lap.

"Now that is lady like." Madame Prix nodded with approval. "You may drink."

"Thank you Madame." Kate remembered to hold the glass lightly and to sip. No gulping was allowed. She'd already been reprimanded for having a death grip during a previous drinking debacle. With the glass safely returned to the table, Kate pulled a handkerchief from her dress pocket and daintily patted the corners of her mouth.

"Well done Miss Church." Madame gave a sly smile.

"Thank you Madame." Kate tried to remain pleasant but she wanted to slap her trainer, hard.

"Now you may read. Begin," Madame ordered.

Kate started, "As the heavens opened—"

"No Miss Church, in proper English." Madame corrected. "You sound like a drunken ruffian." Kate had retained much of her rough Texas drawl. "Light and sweet. Try again."

Kate swallowed. "As the heavens opened, and the rain began to fall—" Kate paused.

"Go on." Miss Prix encouraged.

Kate continued and read the entire passage without mispronouncing a word or stumbling over sentence phrasing.

"That was delightful. Pleasant. Much better. And you've practiced, magnifique." Madame Prix's native tongue rolled out from her mouth like velvet. "I would like you to work on the next chapter for tomorrow. Now, I want for you to walk again. Stand." Madame raised her hand, palm up, as if she were to lead a group of angels to heaven.

"Yes Madame." Kate again turned out properly from her chair. She stood while trying not to make a sound. Too much noise was not polite. It could also draw attention in an event of subterfuge.

"Book," Madame encouraged.

Kate picked up a larger, but thinner tome from her desk and placed it flat on top of her head.

"Walk. Glide as if you were walking through the gardens of Eden," Madame Prix chirped.

"Yes Madame." Kate stepped forward, *heel to toe*, she remembered.

"Don't stomp, tread lightly, Miss Church. Oh, and eyes forward. Think pleasant thoughts. Roses, fine silk. Comfort. You look far too serious," her tutor continued. Kate almost made it three quarters of the way through the room before the book fell.

"Try again, Miss Church," Madame urged.

Inside Kate refrained from punching her teacher in the way that Chin had taught her, and complied. “Yes Madame.”

“Hint of a smile, Miss Church.” Madame Prix crossed her arms in front of her.

“Yes Madame.” This time Kate let herself dream. She thought of walking the grounds with Lord Wilson. With the hint of a grin, Kate floated across the room.

“And be seated.” Madame approved.

Kate again sat, only this time with the book still in place. It didn’t move an inch. Madame Prix sat back at her desk. “Well done, Miss Church, take down your book.”

Just when Kate thought she could relax, Madame spoke again. “Now for something completely different.” Her teacher opened a desk drawer and pulled out a single piece of parchment and two fans. The first was a large, elegant black lace fan that Madame kept for herself. “A lady should always be prepared for the heat.” She stood and brought a second plain cream-colored fan to Kate while giving a wink. “Or how to get oneself out of it.”

Kate wasn’t used to this kind of behavior from her instructor; her confusion showed in the narrowing of her eyes. Madame Prix gave a haughty laugh.

“First, I’d like for you to read the paper in front of you.”

Kate glanced down. It was a set of cues on how to use a fan. She had heard of this method of flirtation before, but not to this extent.

“I will expect you to know all of these, but for right now remember numbers one, five, twelve, thirteen, fourteen, and twenty.” This is how they appeared:

The Language of the Fan – A Ladies' Primer

1. *Carrying fan in right hand & in front of face – Follow me.*
5. *Twirling in left hand – We are being watched.*
12. *Closing the fan – We need to speak immediately.*
13. *Let the fan rest on the right cheek – Yes.*
14. *Let the fan rest on the left cheek – No.*
20. *Opening the fan wide – Wait for me.*

"Miss Church, I have been appraised that you knew of wealthy people in your upbringing. But I assure you, the level of etiquette you need now is far above your childhood experience. To learn to speak in cues could very well save your life. You will also learn handkerchief and window signaling. They are tools, and yes, weaponry." A wicked smirk played on the teacher's face. Kate had seen women slap with their fans, but she was still perplexed.

"Lord Wilson has assured me that you are quite adept at mechanical things. Thus I will show you why you must be so careful with my fan. Let me demonstrate. Number one, follow." Madame placed her open fan in her right hand and in front of her face. She turned and started to walk towards her desk. "Number twelve, close it; we must speak." She snapped her lovely prop shut with a pop, and looked coyly over her left shoulder. "Now if my contact did as if he understood my cues, he would be somewhat close to me. And this would happen." In one swift sway, she stepped aside to the left and from a bend at the elbow, flicked her fan open with a snap. A brief hint of taps were heard near the window, as if the tiniest woodpecker was present. Then silence.

Kate was still uncertain of what had just happened. "Miss Church, please stand and look at the trim of the window. Kate approached slowly. "Go closer, now. Closer, Miss Church." With a narrow gleam in the sunlight, Kate finally saw them. Four darts, each the size of an inch long needle, which bore into the wood frame in a neat perfectly straight line. "They can be set with a poison that will kill someone in thirty seconds." Kate turned to her instructor as Madame Prix continued her grin.

Suddenly Kate had a much greater appreciation for the woman who would teach her to be a lady. She smiled in return as another weapon idea popped into her head.

Kate's quadriceps were on fire. The tops of her thighs burned from her knees to her groin. Her shoulders and buttocks ached with tension after holding fencing positions for extended periods of time.

"Now Miss Church, in this stance turn your left foot out to the West, your right foot to the front of the room, your feet forming a corner. Step forward with your right. Balance your weight between your feet." The smooth British accent of Master Julian Richards sternly echoed in Kate's ears.

He stood behind Kate and at just over six feet tall, towered above her. His lanky frame brushed against her as he guided her arms. "Left arm behind your back for now. Right elbow bent and push back to your ribs." His fingertips grazed her arm into place. "A slight bend of the knee."

He came from behind her and observed her posture. "Lift your chin. Hold your grip tightly, but not so much that you cannot move your arm. Turn the tip of the blade up at my head."

Kate looked into his face, trying not to let the agony show. Master Richards wore tight, spanking white trousers and a fencing jacket which enhanced his bright blue eyes and curly black locks. To Kate he seemed to be an angel of pain.

"Breathe, Miss Church. Continue your focus." He stepped in briefly and adjusted her right elbow out a few inches. "Now you are in Tierce, parry number three. Do not move. Tell me again why you are standing this way."

"I'm at entering distance from which to launch an attack, Sir." Kate grit her teeth and tried to put her mind above her pain as she'd done so many times before.

"So the blade and your hilt face outside. What does this do?" he questioned.

"It protects the outside line of my body, Sir." She was audibly starting to pant. Kate was wearing similar fencing uniform garments. Sweat trickled down her back from her collar and the loose tendrils of hair that escaped from her former neatly pinned bun. She was forbidden to rub it away.

"Good. Extension!" He barked loudly enough that it echoed the walls of the gymnasium. It was a large room with extensive round topped windows on the southern side. They required extra metal framework that was painted a deep grey and stood out from the surrounding maroon brick. Various exercise equipment and targets lined the other walls. The afternoon sun poured in only a few feet away from the teacher and student, casting a warm golden light onto the pale wooden floor.

Kate extended her arm. Pain formed a buzzing trail along its inside.

"Directly at my face, Miss Church. As straight a line as possible. Remember, you are to be a threat to me." His eyes bored into hers. "Now back."

Kate drew her elbow in while her legs quivered.

"Extend." This time he was much quieter. Out went Kate's arm.

He walked around her, taking in every inch of her being. He'd been told that she was special. They were right. He'd never had a female student like her. Most did not make it through the first fifteen minutes of the beginner's class. She had made it through hours of fencing preparatory work. Perspiration soaked through the back of her jacket. Her face was flushed.

It reminded him of the last woman he had been with a few weeks prior. A lovely and sweet but deadly being that he'd bedded, and then slashed her throat as ordered. The redness of her face as she climaxed was glorious. His knife, hidden underneath his pillow, was horrific. Her eyes had closed long enough for him to procure his weapon. After his duty was finished, he pulled from her body, covered her face with a pillow and wrapped her in the sheet where she'd experienced life's greatest ecstasy for the last time. She would miss an Engagement that would've taken her to Chicago with Lord Wilson.

Within ten minutes he was fully dressed and returning home. The Member that he'd assassinated was already dumped in the river by the porter of the hotel, where he'd agreed to meet her and exchange information.

"And back." Master Richards commanded. He couldn't ignore that Kate had a lovely ripe bottom that hugged her pantaloons and despite her sweat, the scent of lavender lingered.

Kate retracted her arm yet again. Her shoulder blades felt like hot pokers had torn through them. Her chest heaved with deep breaths.

"Relax. Very good, Miss Church." He again stood before her.

"Ahhhh, ugh." Kate almost collapsed to the floor and dropped her sabre with a clatter. She bent forward with her hands on her knees, sweat dripping in small plops on the floor.

"Oh Miss Church, that is not a way to treat your weapon. Pick it up," he ordered coolly.

"Yes Sir." Her words came wearily. She stooped down for the sword, her hand so tired she could barely grasp it.

"Now again, posture. But this time only feet. Remember, right foot, step." He tortured her. It was time to truly start testing her stamina.

Kate purposely stepped forward without complaint.

"Extend."

Her arm again aimed at the face of her target.

"Lunge."

She pressed into a deeper bend of the right leg and straightened the left. He said nothing for almost thirty seconds. Kate thought that surely she would vomit. Her breath now came in heavy spurts. She licked her parched lips but did not complain.

"Back."

Kate returned to her crouched position and prayed for a moment to relax. It did not come.

"Now again, step. Then extend and lunge at the same time." He tried not to grin. She had gumption, desire. He wondered if this extended to her performance in the bedroom.

Kate stepped, but her knees buckled and faltered. She fell on her side with a dull thump. Her sabre slid across the floor landing precisely at Master Richards's feet. She tried to sit up, but the room was spinning.

"Oh dear, Miss Church. Come on now." He tilted his head coyly with a click of his tongue. She looked like a wounded bird with her arms flayed about like broken wings.

"Yes Sir." She turned onto her hands and knees. Her mind reeled back to Iris, when Drasco and his men had intended to drag her to her death. Chin's voice came to her for the first time in weeks. *You are strong.* Kate inhaled and pushed off the floor with such force she almost fell backwards. Her Master extended his hand but she ignored it and stood tall on her own. She tilted her chin in silence, her nostrils flaring. The defiant fire in her eyes almost branded him.

Master Richards turned away quickly and picked up her weapon. He liked her passion, but her sudden resolve was unexpected. He grinned and handed the sabre to Kate. "Well done Miss Church. Well done. That should be enough for today. Please, come sit for a moment."

"Thank you Sir." She exhaled with such tenacity that he felt her hot breath graze his cheek.

Kate crossed the room and put up her sword in an almost robotic fashion. She then followed her master to a corner of the room with a small plain wooden desk and two chairs. He pulled one out for her and Kate sat upright with polite perfection. She patted her face with a towelette. He poured a glass of water and set it in front of her before pouring one for himself. They drank in silence for a moment. This had become the pattern after every lesson.

Master Richards marveled at her ability to fight and then to suddenly become so lady-like that he'd forgotten that she'd killed before. That rare off and on switch of emotions worried him. He'd only been at the Society a few weeks, but had known so many skilled women over his lifetime. However, none had measured up to their reputations, unlike Kate Church. He poured a second glass for her and spoke a few standard words of wisdom.

"Well done Miss Church. You are taking to the basics quite well. Soon we will start true fencing, sparring. I will teach you how to read your opponent, even through a mask. Body language is of the utmost importance. So I will see your tomorrow, the same time. Please recover well." His manner was professional and quick. He stood and offered his hand to her. This time Kate took it and rose with such grace that Master Richards pursed his lips to ignore her disheveled beauty.

"Thank you Sir." They bowed and left the gymnasium to an outer stairwell. They climbed the steps together, again in silence.

Kate used every ounce of strength left to hide her pain as they went up two flights. At the top were two doors: a general office to the right for instructors and a dressing room on the left for students.

"Good day, Miss Church."

"Good day, Master Richards."

With untimely precision they entered their respective rooms. Kate shut the door behind her and slid to the floor. Her clothes clung to her in a sticky mess. Her body was like that of a limp doll. It would be a few moments before she would be ready to undress.

In the neighboring room, Master Richards jotted a quick note on Kate's progress to Lord Wilson. Nothing too gushy or dramatic, just a simple, "Your Member is much improved." He disrobed and hurriedly stepped into a misting chamber, for today something was different. Once clean, he donned a silken robe and a monocle with a pointed cone of brass. The opening at the end was about a sixteenth of an inch. On the side of the eye piece was a small notched cog.

Master Richards had come to like Miss Church. Perhaps more than he should. He found that a lovely painting in the general office he shared with several other trainers was on the adjoining wall to the trainee's room. This wall was only plaster over wood frame and about four inches thick. Over the course of a few days, he'd managed to slowly carve out a hole from behind the painting. It was a couple inches wide on the instructor's side and tapered to only a pinhead through the room of the trainees.

Today he would test his handy work. He removed the painting and set it aside on the desk. With his body flush against the wall, he turned the gear on the monocle. Its cone extended and focused. Within a few seconds he could see directly into the adjoining room.

He watched Kate undress and clean. The way she enjoyed her misting enthralled him; her eyes closed and their lashes dripped with moisture. The water and soap ran smoothly along her skin. The ending blast of warm air hardened her nipples and blew her hair into wavy golden threads.

He resisted the urge to pleasure himself and checked her body for details. The rumored tattoo was there, but nothing else. When she began to dress, he retracted his scope, stuffed the hole with a bit of cloth and returned the painting to its proper place. He too dressed and prepared to leave. He shared this room with many others. The hole must never be discovered as this was not a Society approved endeavor.

"Now, see here. You left yourself vulnerable. Remember, center control and King's safety. If you need more time to think, do it." Lord Wilson politely suggested a chess move to Kate. "Try pawn at E4." He wanted to go lightly on his new Member. She'd barely had two weeks of rest and then had delved right into all sorts of activities.

The time off had been good for her. She'd become rosy-cheeked and robust in the right places.

Kate placed the pawn at E4 as requested and looked up. She was still uncertain of what she was doing and the frustration showed on her face with a firm line of her lips.

Lord Wilson moved his pawn further in to H3 with no emotion.

Kate remembered to protect her King and slid it to G1 and set a pawn to G4. She tried to think of the board as a battle with the pieces, like soldiers, moving out in order of their rank.

"Much better. However-" Wilson then moved to H3, later to G2 and took her King. "Checkmate."

Kate looked defeated as she sat back in her chair. Strax was present and he whined a bit. Wilson had taken quite an unexpected liking to the canine. He was grateful he saved it, not just because the dog made Kate happy, but it also drew her to Wilson Manor like a magnet. "It will take more time, Miss Kate. Be patient. Think strategically, because if you blunder you will most certainly lose."

"Of course." Kate still seemed a bit overwhelmed and certainly distracted. She leaned over to pet her furry companion. Lord Wilson watched their interaction with a raised brow in curiosity. Yes, it was certainly one of the best rescues he'd made.

"Why don't we take a break? It'll be tea time shortly." Lord Wilson wanted to check on her progress. Her attendant had reported that she'd had a few nightmares, but otherwise appeared to be getting enough rest. Her various instructors were pleased with her studies so far.

"Yes Sir, that would be lovely." Her eager smile was radiant. She loved the petite sandwiches and snacks at 4 p.m. The time Kate was spending at the Manor was glorious. She felt welcomed, enjoying some of her meals there, having some time to spend with Strax and Lord Wilson. He was strong, but kind. Their interactions had been professional and polite for the most part. But every once in a while, he was a tad more gracious. He seemed genuinely curious of how her classes were going. For the first time in a long while, Kate felt safe, and especially so with Lord Wilson.

Kate had met Dr. Harrington, the young professor who lived and worked in the cellar. She'd already begun to share some of his workspace in her endeavor to develop new weaponry that took her fancy. Her umbrella rifle had been perfected and was now standard issue for ladies and those gentlemen who tended to work in inclement weather.

"May I inquire about your studies, then?" Lord Wilson questioned as they temporarily abandoned their game. He moved the chess board to his desk as he continued the conversation. "What did you learn today?"

"Madame Prix and I talked about different signals this morning, fan language and the like."

"And did she give you a fan?" Lord Wilson raised his brows knowingly.

"Yes, but not one like hers, if that's what you mean. Although I can use it as a prototype." Kate's eyes lit up.

"Good, so she gave you some ideas then?" Her Senior was grateful for the enthusiasm. Kate hadn't been excited about etiquette. She had some manners, but she needed a higher caliber of stature for future Engagements.

"Oh yes." Kate's fingers continued to run through Strax's fur. Their conversation was interrupted by the buzz of their timepieces on the table. Leeds brought in their beverages and afternoon repast without a word. They sat silently as he set their plates from an ornate tray, poured their tea and handed a bone to Kate for Strax. The canine sat up and begged until Kate offered his treat. Strax moved to a cushion to enjoy his snack. Leeds left as quietly as he'd come and Lord Wilson began again.

"And how are you getting on with your physical education?" This was information he was most excited to hear. Kate was strong and almost completely recovered. He couldn't imagine what she'd be able to do once properly fit. He added sugar and cream to his tea while hoping for a positive answer from his charge.

"Today Master Richards showed me tierce form. He explained the stance and we practiced for a while." Kate stirred her tea with a sly smile and then sipped. Kate had taken well to exercise, although Lord Wilson noticed her flinch when she poured more tea.

"Excellent. And your recovery afterwards?"

"Well, a bit sore in the arms I must say," Kate admitted. "But I've been to the salon for massage and Dr. Finch said I have only one treatment left." Her face was angelic. Lord Wilson's heart warmed to see her so happy.

"May I?" He turned to her and offered his hand. Kate flushed. Dr. Finch hadn't said anything about Lord Wilson inspecting her back. But he was her Senior after all; she didn't see a reason to refuse.

"Well, of course." Kate stuttered and stood. He led her across the room to the section which held his laboratory equipment. Lord Wilson peered about the grounds. They were nearly empty as it was tea time, a very common time for Discussions. "Come behind this panel. And know that I will not hurt you Miss Kate. Do not be embarrassed."

Kate faced out the window as Lord Wilson slowly undid the lacing on the back side of her dress and opened it wide. With a gentle tug, he'd undone her corset and pulled up her under-dress. Kate shuddered.

"Are you alright Miss Kate, no pain?" Suddenly, he could barely stand next to her without wanting to touch her. His curiosity became more than just about her scars.

"Oh no, just a bit of a chill." She tried to stifle a nervous giggle.

"Just a moment, I promise." Her scent intoxicated him as he looked over her skin. It was almost healed; just the faintest of pinks where the deepest lash points had been. "Turn to the left just a bit." And then he did touch her; ever so slightly at the small of her back, to guide her rotation. It electrified him.

She flinched at the unexpected caress.

"Oh so sorry, just a quick turn to the right. No pain?" She'd been through enough hurt to last a lifetime. He was enthralled that Kate was healing.

"Oh no Sir." Kate warmed. His hand was strong against her back. She closed her eyes and grasped the edge of the panel. She wanted him to undress her fully, to take liberties with her. Her knees started to quake.

He felt her again as he turned Kate back to facing outside again. Her skin was so soft beneath his fingertips. Just a hint of the side of her right breast peeked out. He licked his lips and swallowed hard. Lord Wilson felt the urge to reach from behind and cup her chest. He could see her reflection in the window. Kate's eyes were closed. She looked heavenly in the afternoon sunlight. He could take her right there. Push her against the glass and feel the part of her that was all woman. *Stop it*, his mind fought back with all its reasoning and muster. He cleared his throat. "Very, very good progress Miss Kate. Dr. Finch is correct. One more treatment should be sufficient." He quickly redressed her from the back to avoid further temptation. He only struggled with a last ornate button closure at the collar.

"Oh, I can reach that." Kate spoke with a jittery lilt, opened her eyes and tried to come back to reality. His breath had tickled her from her neck to almost her bottom. She'd wanted so much to collapse back against him, for his hands to guide her and touch her intimately. She clutched the front of her dress with her right hand as if she could rip it to shreds. *No, no, no*, Kate chided herself. She shouldn't feel that way. There were repercussions. She stiffened, reached over her head and fastened the button as Lord Wilson backed away. As Kate turned, Strax barked. He'd been very properly trained since coming to the Manor, so something must be afoot.

Lord Wilson was already examining his pocket watch that had buzzed over the head of the canine. Kate was grateful he didn't see her flushed face. "Well Miss Kate, let us finish tea, and then I have business to attend to." Kate continued to hide her face, crouched down and pretended to comfort Strax.

"Oh that would be lovely, Sir." She inhaled and after a few moments finally seated herself back at the table. Her heart had finally stopped pounding.

Lord Wilson set his timepiece down. *Thank God for it*, his mind tumbled. He'd been seconds away from doing things that would cost them both dearly. He poured a fresh cup of tea. "More tea, Miss Kate?"

"Yes Sir. Please." Kate sat straight as a board. So stiffly that Lord Wilson wondered if he'd just imagined the chemistry that had just happened between them.

That is, until he offered her a chocolate. "A sweet?"

"Yes Sir." She pulled a piece from a small dessert tray that Lord Wilson extended to her. Kate dared to look at him directly as she tilted her chin and let the chocolate slide against her lips, her fingers lingered. She chewed slowly and deliberately smoothed her lips. "I would like another, Sir." She whispered. He hadn't yet set the tray down.

"Of course." He looked down at the tray briefly. When his eyes came back up, her mouth was still a bit open.

"Thank you, Sir." This time she popped the candy daintily into her mouth and washed it down with a sip of tea. "That was exquisite." Kate's eyes were aglow and she had just a hint of a clever smile. She wanted him to know that she had desire in her heart, however subtle.

Lord Wilson took a piece for himself and swallowed. "Yes, they are. Indeed they are." His pocket watch buzzed yet again and the spell was broken. "Well Miss Kate, I have things to attend to. Enjoy your studies and I will see you tomorrow."

This should not happen again, Lord Wilson warned himself.

"I look forward to it, Sir," Kate teased. She felt confident and worldly.

"As do I." He ushered her down the spiral case and into the garden, trying to ignore her good natured banter. "Good evening Miss Kate." Kate had turned to go, but he stepped forward and pulled her back.

"Miss Kate, the King's Gambit is a risky opening move. I just want you to remember that when we next play." Lord Wilson tried to veil a reprimand for her flirtations.

"Oh I will Sir. I most certainly will. Good night Lord Wilson." Kate walked briskly away to the Main Hall. *Risky moves indeed*, she smiled.

7 A FIXTURE LAPSES

On a late November evening, Nathan Halton walked down a dirty alley in Boston. A chilly wind blew old newspapers around him in frantic circles. Mr. Halton was a short, stubby man, much like the cigar he chewed on. He wore a ragged cap and tattered coat that flapped against ruddy brick walls as he skittered along. After several minutes of trolling the backstreets of the most downtrodden area of the city, he stopped at a beat-up doorway. Only a fading gas lamp to the right of the door let him know he had reached the correct location for his meeting.

Mr. Halton rapped twice and gazed at the alley. He'd done this dozens of times, but he was getting nervous. Despite the chill outside, he was almost sweating with anxiety. He couldn't wait to get a drink.

The door groaned open and only a black gloved hand came through the opening. A plain envelope was passed to Mr. Halton. The moment he snatched it, the door shut, and he could hear a rusty bolt seal it with a clang. After he'd safely tucked it in his coat pocket, he dashed away with his information, as light flurries of snow began to dance from the sky.

Once he was back on the street, Mr. Halton paused briefly to double check that his payment was there. A sum of one hundred dollars cash made his heart pace. He continued on, ignoring the pleas of the beggars and miscreants on the curb.

He hustled to a basement establishment, swung open the door and hopped to his favorite seat. The other patrons continued to play cards, drink, and muddle over each other's old tales. The bar tender said nothing as he poured Mr. Halton's drink. The scruffy man liked a good bit of liquid courage to propel him on his mission. His tasks were never easy, as Mr. Halton always delivered bad news. He was a Fixture of the Society, permanently placed among the lowest of humans as a grave digger.

Working in a cemetery didn't pay much. So when a scout from the Society saw a man down on his luck, Mr. Halton was observed, his background checked, and when cleared, promptly recruited to be an angel of death of sorts.

When a Member was fully ensconced into the Society, any relations, even if they were distant or claimed no responsibility for the person, were notified of the "death", falsified of course by the Society. In that way, those in mourning would not come looking for the dearly departed. Those recently expired would have had some monstrous end, like an explosion or fire, that would leave no remains to claim. Usually a small sum of cash was paid by their employer. In very few cases, of those families most attached to a loved one, a notification of a grave marker in a distant city was given.

It made perfect sense that cemetery and undertaking personnel delivered such news. Mr. Halton had been such a worker for the Society for about twenty years. He was already in his late thirties when initially approached and didn't have any family. He immediately received lighter duties at the burial grounds where he worked. All his living expenses were fully paid; food, shelter, and the like. His life with the Society even included the affections of a new lady of the evening, a Miss Meredith Pratt.

Miss Meredith Pratt was a long tenured Fixture of the Society. Unbeknownst to the Fixtures she served, she was a Senior Member. Miss Pratt had grown up in whore and boarding houses up and down the east coast, wherever her mother and two aunties could find work. They never stayed in one city very long. Miss Pratt's father was most likely a wealthy gentleman who had used her mother, during a single roll in the hay, for his practical sexual purposes. Despite doses of hideous, fowl tasting, sickening potions and several attempts at serious falls, her mother could not rid herself of the pregnancy and Miss Pratt came into the world unwanted. But despite her lack of education, Miss Pratt's mother realized that her child could be used in various schemes to increase their financial situation. Once young Meredith could speak, she was taught to use her urchin charms to beg and steal. Over and over, she played the orphan, managing to avoid the local clergy who tried endlessly to give her a good home. If anyone got too close to the Pratt ladies, they moved on. At least until a couple of brothers took a shine to Miss Pratt's aunties.

The enterprising young men seemed to have plenty of cash. After a few visits to the flop house where the Pratts were staying, the gentlemen realized it would be much more economical to take the younger two Pratt sisters with them. Meredith was ten years old when her aunties left her mother.

It had been a very cold night and the eldest Pratt sister had only had one visitor. Little Miss Pratt sat quietly in the cold hallway as her mother serviced the man. As he left, he felt sorry for Meredith and knelt down next to the trembling child.

"Can you keep a secret?" He whispered. The man had a strange accent that sounded oddly pleasant to the young girl. He placed a gold coin in her worn mitten while speaking directly into her ear. "Don't ever give this to anyone. Keep it to yourself, and if you ever need help, come to the address engraved on the back. You promise me this, eh?" He touched her chin and tilted her tiny face to look at his. Out of the corner of her eye, a shiny pocket watch gleamed in the dull light of the hall.

"Yes Sir," Meredith squeaked.

"You promise?" he asked again.

"Yes Sir."

"Good girl." The man stood and left abruptly. As he exited out the front door, Meredith's aunties and their new gentlemen friends came in. The ladies were clearly inebriated, stumbling about the hall until they reached the one bedroom apartment the Pratt ladies shared. Their giggles echoed off the walls and made Meredith grin. They had been happy as of late, but Miss Pratt's mother never smiled with them.

This was again true when Mrs. Pratt opened the door to her two younger sisters, her face grim and her eyes hollow pools. "Where have you been?" she hissed. "Did they give you money? Or just pay for a show?" Meredith's mother eyed the gentlemen with a nasty glare.

"Oh for God's sake. What's wrong, you jealous?" one of her aunties slurred.

"You know she is. She's an old whore and made us just like her. But we ain't doing this anymore. These gents are going to make proper ladies out of us." The other sister clung to her date as if she was on a sinking ship and he was the only post to hold on to.

"Get your things ladies, and we'll be on our way." One of the gentlemen brushed a gloved hand over his top hat. The other checked his time piece. Meredith noticed that his pocket watch looked very much like the one from the gentleman who'd given her the coin and just left.

"You can't leave," the eldest Pratt sister griped loudly.

"Watch us. We're going." The two younger Pratt women pushed their way into the room. The collection of their items only took a few minutes. Meredith looked up at her mother. She had never seemed so worried before. Her hair was just starting to turn ashen, her skin taking on a yellow pallor. Suddenly her aunties burst forth with two small sacks.

"We're only taking what's ours. Just our things." The middle Pratt sister stuck out her chin.

"And Meredith. She doesn't need to be a whore, like her mother." The youngest sister reached down to grab the youngest Pratt, only to be slapped by her oldest sister. She fell on her side and one of the gentlemen helped her up. The two men gave each other knowing looks as they helped the ladies with their things.

"You can't have her, she's mine." For the first time, Meredith saw her mother cry. Tears rushed down her face. She rang her hands over her old dress in frustration.

"You keep her then!" The middle Pratt sister's voice boomed as they turned and left. The gentlemen said nothing. "Stubborn hag!"

"I will," the eldest Pratt sister mumbled while she grabbed Meredith's collar, and dragged her into the room. She slammed the door shut with a grunt.

Outside her aunties were gone for good, never to be seen again. The gentleman that had visited the eldest Pratt sister just moments before, was sitting outside in a small carriage. One of the aunt's dates tipped his hat his way and the two couples disappeared into the night. The lone gentleman was disappointed to see that the little girl had not left with them. That man had hoped to ensure the safety of little Meredith and had done what he could. Any woman that would whore out her sisters would certainly do that to her child.

And that is precisely why a young Director Roth recruited the younger Pratt sisters to the Society and not Meredith's mother.

Miss Pratt's mother cried all night and was so immersed in her sobs that she didn't notice that Meredith turned her shiny new coin over and over in her hand as she would become prone to do in times of trouble.

When Meredith came of age and it was obvious that men took a liking to her, her mother didn't hesitate to notice. Mrs. Pratt was now suffering from the effects of various diseases. Only the most wanton and desperate wanted her services. Meredith, on the other hand, was lovely. She was lithe with gentle features, shiny brown hair, and hazel eyes that hid her lack of nourishment.

She was still stealing or would beg. But now men's eyes would rake over Meredith and wanted to give her more than money. "It's time to put you to work," her mother squawked one bitterly frozen morning. Her voice was now raspy and she struggled to breathe. Mrs. Pratt had taken to drinking heavily to quell the coughs and her misery. They ate once a day, usually bread or whatever Meredith could pinch. On this cold January day, they had a leg of goose and a half loaf of bread. Mrs. Pratt looked up from their measly meal.

"Yep, today, you bring a man home. Or two or three. And you do like I did. Let them touch you. Whatever they like. And make them pay first before you bring them back here."

"Momma-" Meredith started to protest.

"Now, Meredith, go!" Her mother used almost every last ounce of her energy to bang her fist on their rickety kitchen table.

Meredith stumbled out into the snow and tried to hold back the tears that burned her eyes. She went to the corner where men leered at her many times before. She turned the coin over in her pocket to try and stop her anxiety. By late afternoon, the streets filled with people going home. A decently dressed man approached and asked if she needed company. She could only nod in the direction of her terrible living quarters. He tried to make small talk as their footsteps crunched in the newly fallen snow. When they approached her dilapidated building, the man stopped and spoke lowly. "Not here." He looked around then grabbed her hand. "This way." He led her a few blocks away, not far from the open market.

He guided her into alley trimmed with ash pits, trash and a single black cat that meowed in protest then strolled away. He pressed her body against the cold brick while he lifted the hem of her dress. His tongue darted wildly in her mouth. As a light snow fell around them, Meredith gave her virginity to a man who was desperate, his wife pregnant and ready to give birth. He was not unkind to her, but the pain shot between her legs like a sword. He finished with a satisfied grunt and handed her five dollars. "That's a good girl, eh? Sorry Miss, I'm in a bit of a hurry. The missus could give birth any minute and I got mouths to feed." He yanked up his trousers and dashed out without another word.

Meredith tugged at her clothing and tried to arrange it without furthering the searing pain. She shuddered and tucked the money into her collar. In her haste to leave the slovenly room at the boarding house, she hadn't even brought a pocketbook. *So this is what it feels like.* Her mind fogged over. *I don't think I want to do this again.*

Her heart was heavy and her insides rattled with hunger as she stumbled through the increasing snowfall. When she passed the market, the stalls were closing for the day. She crossed the street to wait until the last shop owner closed up. Within seconds of his leave, Meredith and several others came out of the shadows to salvage spoiled goods. Even with five dollars in her dress, Meredith dared not spend it and raise her mother's ire.

With the piercing cry of a policeman's whistle, the forsaken crew hurried away, the contrast of their dark tattered clothing against the snow making them seem like crows scattering in the wind from above. Once Meredith was safely three blocks away, she bit into a molded bit of bread and an end of cheese. Both were bitter, but she didn't care. She devoured them and then started on two sausages that were still warm, but burnt to a crisp. The slimy grease ran down her fingers and she licked them clean. There was a third sausage and another end of cheese that she so desperately wanted to eat, but Meredith generously saved it for her mother. Finally sated, she sat in the darkness just on the inside of the overhang of a deserted building. Then it hit her. Uncontrollable heaving sobs crashed over her. She buried her head between her knees. *Would it always be like this*? She wondered how long she could do these terrible deeds. Her crotch still throbbed in pain and she grew angry at her mother. A vile pit of nastiness formed inside her for a moment, but it ended as a well-to-do couple walked by her.

"You alright Miss?" the husband inquired.

"She looks quite upset." Meredith overheard the woman whisper to her spouse.

"I-I am fine. I am so sorry to trouble you. I got a bit lost, you see." Meredith bit her lip. Another lie, another story, all because of her mother. She faked a smile and looked at the couple. They were fashionably attired and had a carriage waiting for them. She could easily sit next to the wife and steal the contents of her bag. She could have them drop her off just a bit further up the road in a safer neighborhood, in front of a house that wouldn't be hers.

"Oh dear, would you like a ride?" The man offered her his hand and helped her up.

"You poor thing," the woman said in a light pitch.

"Oh no, no. I couldn't. I'm not far at all really." Meredith straightened and tried to stand tall.

"It's not safe at night Miss, surely you know. A lot of thieves live not far from here." The man had tender eyes and a pleasant smile. Suddenly, Miss Pratt felt an epiphany warm over her. *I will no longer steal. I will earn my way,* she resolved.

"No thank you. But it's a kind gesture." Meredith grinned almost ear to ear. Something changed in her that day.

"Are you certain Miss?" the man inquired one last time.

"Oh yes, I am." Meredith was completely certain. She hurried home and bounced into the room.

Mrs. Pratt was drunk on what little sherry she'd managed to procure from a neighbor in return for letting him suckle on her old withering tits.

"Well, about time you're home. It's dark you know." Her mother could barely lift her head.

"I know. But I made five dollars and I have some food," Meredith offered brightly. She set down the sausage and cheese and handed her mother the money.

With a nasty scowl and flick of her arm, Mrs. Pratt knocked the food off the table. "You dumb bitch. You only made five dollars? And can't you smell that food is rotten?" Her mother got up and wobbled towards the bedroom. "Tomorrow, you go out and make three times as much, you hear? And don't come back until you do." She slammed the bedroom door so hard it made Meredith's teeth rattle.

Any hope that Meredith had found was gone in that instant. Her sobs went unheard as her mother passed out on the bed. She turned the coin over and over again in her pocket as she fell asleep on the floor of the kitchen. At daybreak, she left the room to use the common bath and gingerly wiped at her swollen lady parts. Spots of dried blood dotted her old knickers.

She returned to the room with her mother still asleep. Meredith was broken that day. She thought herself locked into a future of pleasing men and her obstinate mother.

Her mother's harsh words bounced in her head for the next couple of months. "You're a lousy whore." Meredith continued to fake pleasantries on the street corner. Most men would not come home with her. Instead they took her to the back lots of abandoned buildings, carriage houses, and on one occasion an empty church rectory. *Surely I am going to hell*, Meredith thought. She'd grit her teeth as men fucked her. Pretended to smile when they collapsed on her with release. But Meredith did not steal again. She earned her money, more than enough to pay for food and the alcohol that kept her mother quiet. More than once, a carriage with a well to do madam stopped by her corner. Meredith was far prettier than most of the ladies working the streets. However, she would decline offers. She continued to polish the coin in her gloves to help ease her fears. She couldn't abandon mama. No one wanted her mother any more, not even Meredith. But Mrs. Pratt was her mother, and she had guilted her into submission.

Meredith hated her mother as the winter dragged on. If sober, she griped about everything. If drunk, she snored or coughed incessantly. Meredith made it a point to regularly visit a gentleman that served wine to upscale families. In return for her temporary affections, the savory liquid he supplied allowed Meredith peace from her mother's inebriated rants. On more than one occasion she stayed the night in his wine cellar.

After one such evening, the restauranteur liked Meredith enough that he allowed her to sleep in one of the vacant servant rooms. The warmth was heavenly. The room clean and the sheets crisp. Meredith slept well into the next morning. When she awoke, he told her he could no longer supply her with wine as the master of the home suspected someone of stealing. Meredith would not be able to return. The older man stroked her cheek and gave her twenty dollars. "I am so sorry, I wish you well."

Meredith was again devastated. Her feet felt heavy on the wet brick as she walked home. She trudged along not wanting to spend the money on liquor but also not desiring to hear her mother's horrid speech. She paused at the steps of the very church where a young minister had taken to her in the rectory. She uttered a simple prayer. *Lord, free me of my mother, please.* With that plea, she resolved to buy food instead and face her mother's wrath.

But her prayers were answered that day. When she returned to the boarding house room, it was eerily quiet and chilly. The stove hadn't been lit yet that morning. Meredith felt the iron furnace and it was as cold as the weather outside. "Mother?" her cry echoed.

No snoring, no hacking, she mused. "Momma?"

The bedroom door was open just a crack. Meredith inhaled and slowly pushed it open. The room was dark with the old curtains drawn, but even she could see that her mother was dead; her body motionless in the filthy room. Meredith drew back the curtains and sat next to the old woman for a moment. A pang of guilt stabbed at her heart as a single ray of sunlight illuminated her mother's face. Her eyes were blank holes and a small stream of phlegm mixed with blood dried on the dirty bed. Despite her deadly wish and anger for her mother, Meredith closed her eyelids and kissed her forehead. She packed what little things she had left and vacated the boarding house for good. None of her neighbors heard or saw her leave that day. They were all enslaved to their own dramas of poverty and sin. As she started towards her usual corner, Meredith wondered what she would do. It was just her now, she was on her own. She rubbed the coin that had been her talisman for over seven years now.

As if in a dream, she pulled it out slowly. The well-polished gold shone in the winter sun. She remembered the man with the kind face. There was an address, 1224 Park engraved along the edge and a number on the other side, in the center, sixty-eight. She hailed a carriage and took a ride to a place that was her future.

The door to a nondescript brownstone opened slowly. A butler peered out. "And what would your business be Miss?"

Meredith took a deep breath. "A kind gentleman gave me this and asked me to come here." She handed the man the coin with trembling hands.

The butler took it, squinted briefly and smiled. "Do come in." He opened the door wide. As he waved Meredith in, he inquired. "Your name Miss?"

"Meredith Pratt." She tried to sound formal but she instantly felt like she didn't belong. The foyer had well-polished floors and thick carpets which looked better than the old dress she was wearing. A couple months ago, Meredith had rescued it from a wealthy woman's trash outside her home where Meredith had just slept with her husband.

"Yes, Miss Pratt. This may take a moment. Please, come this way." He led her to a sitting room lined with plush chairs, slick tables, and beautiful pieces of art. "Please have a seat. Would you like something to eat and drink?"

Meredith was taken aback at the stranger's generosity. "Why, yes, I would."

"Very good Miss." The butler slipped out quietly as Meredith studied her surroundings. She sat in the parlor, amazed at the refined furnishings. Her hand ran over the velvet arm of her chair. It was so incredibly soft beneath her fingertips. Meredith reached in her pocket for her coin, but once she remembered she'd given it to her greeter, she began to twiddle her thumbs instead. She'd checked and rechecked her hair before she left, trying to look like a proper lady instead of a whore that had turned tricks the night before.

The clicking steps of two other gentlemen distracted her thoughts. A taller, finely clothed man and another servant entered the parlor. The tall man addressed her. "Hello Miss Pratt, I'm Mr. Mason. I have some refreshments for you. Please eat and drink as much as you like." He waved his hand to a manservant who brought in a silver tray with tea, an assortment of petite sandwiches, and sweets. He poured a cup of the soothing liquid. "Cream and sugar Miss?" Her face flushed in embarrassment as her stomach growled in anticipation. The wafts of delicious food teased her nostrils.

"Yes please," Meredith stuttered.

"Enjoy Miss." He too left so quietly that Meredith swore she could hear her own heart beating in the silence.

Mr. Mason smiled. "I'll be back in a moment Miss Pratt. Enjoy your snack." He left with a nod and a quick turn.

She lifted the cup of fragrant tea to her lips. The sweet warm liquid delighted her tongue and she drank the cup in one long swish. As she finished swallowing, she reached for one of the sandwiches, a tender morsel of beef with gravy. The greasy dressing ran down her fingers and she suckled them in between bites. She filled her tea twice more, and ate all the sandwiches before delving into the sweets. There were petite fours with delicate iced flowers, chocolates, truffles and peppermints. As Meredith plowed through her dinner, the butler had passed her coin on to a secretary.

He in turned hurriedly wired the number to a discreet location of the Society. At that remote locale, a receiving Member pulled a volume from a large library, its content numbers embossed on the spine. The receiver was able to locate Meredith's number in his log and was able to confirm it to the secretary in Boston. He smiled as he relayed the information to Mr. Mason, for he knew a once desolate child had made it to adulthood and into the Society. "Send word to Director Roth in St. Louis," he ordered.

If a child, once given a coin, came to the Society as an adult, the original recruiter, if still alive and in good standing, would have first refusal of the new Member. Meredith would not be denied.

Mr. Mason returned to the parlor as Meredith had taken one last bite of a caramel. "Did you enjoy your meal Miss Pratt?"

"Why yes, thank you." Meredith tried unsuccessfully to stifle a burp. Mr. Mason pretended not to notice her lack of manners and continued.

"Miss Pratt, a long time ago a man gave you this coin, correct?"

"Yes Sir." Meredith began to shudder as she remembered the night her aunties left her mother.

"Well Miss Pratt, this gentleman, let us call him Mr. R., has many resources. He would like to make you a very kind offer of employment. But first we'd like for you to stay at another home close by. One where you'll be catered to and be able to rest at no cost whatsoever to you. Then after you've had time to think about it, we'll most likely send you on to meet your benefactor. Would you be interested in such a possibility?"

Meredith was overwhelmed; the rich foods, the pleasant service, the ornate home. She wondered if this man wanted a mistress. She stood and was so jittery that she almost knocked over the empty tray. "I'm so sorry. I'm not quite so sure. I-I don't feel as if I should be here." Her words echoed in the parlor.

"Oh dear, please sit back down. You are in no danger here. And there is no need to feel unworthy. Mr. R. selected you for a purpose. And certainly you've not got many good prospects at the moment?" Mr. Mason looked over her worn dress with a raised brow.

"Well, yes. I mean, you're right."

"Of course I am." Mr. Mason laughed heartedly. "Please sit. Do you have other belongings? Family we need to contact?"

Suddenly Meredith remembered her mother and the tears poured out in droves. "I am so sorry."

"Oh Miss, have I upset you? Please tell me what's wrong." Mr. Mason coaxed.

"My mother is passed, just today. I have nowhere to go."

"I see." Mr. Mason put a finger to his chin. "Well, Miss Pratt, about this rare offer. Mr. R's business will supply everything you will ever want. Food, shelter, a very good life. We'll even take care of your mother's funeral expenses. But you must leave today. Do you think you'd be ready to do just that?"

Meredith rediscovered the new courage she'd found the day she turned her first trick. She swallowed the lump in her throat. It was now or never. "Yes, I am."

"Alright then, if you'd follow me please." Mr. Mason led her to a small room just around the corner from the parlor. It had a mini wash room, a shelf of several large tomes and a few plush chairs not unlike the parlor. "Someone will be here to assist you in just a moment. Please relax and enjoy some of the books."

Meredith looked troubled, her brow furrowed. "But Sir, I don't quite know how to read."

Mr. Mason smiled. "Oh not to worry Miss Pratt. We'll teach you absolutely everything you'll need to know."

Within the half hour a lady's maid had helped Meredith into the finest clothing she'd ever worn. Her hair was styled into a tidy bun topped with a large bonnet. A carriage arrived and took her to a safe house owned by the Society. That eve, over a splendid feast, she had a long conversation with a fine lady about what was to be expected of her. Later, Meredith had one of the most peaceful slumbers she would ever experience. Ironically, across town, a young Mr. Halton tossed fresh dirt onto the newly buried Mrs. Pratt.

St. Louis, November 1895

Mr. Roth didn't like the news he read. A Fixture in Boston was lapsing. One who had a most important job, to bury the dead and all their secrets. Mr. Halton had been getting drunk more often and a few unkind words had spilled out. "One should not cause such a distraction." He mumbled to himself then smiled.

The upside to this debacle would mean a visit with someone he cared very much about, a Miss Pratt. Word was sent to her location and by the next morning, she stood in his doorway much like she had almost twenty years before.

Meredith was still lovely. But she was no longer the shy, abused adolescent he'd received. The Society had been very good to her. Once educated and her confidence boosted, she proved to be smart as a whip and a force to be reckoned with. Her experience with the unsavory side of life gave her a unique approach to men and their weaknesses. Meredith worked her way through small assignments, from a regular Member to a Senior Member with assassination skills.

Currently she was the Madam for the entertainment house on the St. Louis Society grounds. Occasionally she would visit and stand in for a Fixture Madam at other similar houses on different Society grounds if necessary, until a new one was promoted or recruited. And in extreme cases, she would be sent out to "clean" particularly difficult messy situations that involved ladies of the evening.

It was she that made sure that each visiting Member and their chosen companions were not going to cause any issues for the Society. Meredith had one other job which she quite enjoyed. When Mr. Roth needed company, he choose Miss Meredith for the evening.

On those nights, Meredith would dine on sumptuous meals with Mr. Roth in his private quarters in the Main Hall. Afterwards, long eves of tender intimacy would commence. Their agreement as lovers was not known by most in the Society. It had been one of its best held secrets for over fifteen years.

Today Meredith wore a lovely deep wine-colored dress that brought out the hazel green in her eyes. "May I join you?" She grinned, shut the door behind her, and promptly sat on the edge of Mr. Roth's sturdy desk.

"Please do, Miss Meredith." He returned her warm smile. And so the Discussion began between two of the highest Members of the hierarchy of the St. Louis Society.

"I gather that this is not a cordial visit." Meredith tilted her head in the way that told Mr. Roth she meant business.

"Unfortunately no. We have a Fixture that's gone awry. One that we can't afford not to handle, in Boston."

"Boston?"

"Yes. A cemetery worker."

Meredith frowned. She knew that like the Angel of Death, all that they delivered was bad news. "Hmm. I see."

"We don't want the Boston office to get involved in his Termination. He can't be tipped off. I'll need you to go as soon as possible. I fear exposure for any new recruits."

"I see. Consider it done. I trust I'll leave tonight then?" Her voice upturned and a different kind of smirk crossed her face.

"That would be correct." Mr. Roth stood from his desk and leaned forward, placing a gentle hand under Meredith's chin.

"So we have this afternoon Thomas?" she whispered.

"Yes, Meredith. Yes." His lips grazed hers as he pulled her into a passionate embrace. The two lovers enjoyed themselves on Mr. Roth's desk as a cold November rain poured outside.

St. Louis, MO

About a week before Miss Pratt was summoned, Kate swallowed hard and gazed out the window of Wilson Manor. *How can I do this*? She must do it. After a few more moments of consternation, she put her hand to paper and wrote exactly as Lord Wilson ordered her. How different this day was from just a week before, when they had flirted over chess?

He sat at one of the plush chairs sipping tea, observing her task, while she penned a letter from his desk. Lord Wilson didn't like to see her so upset. But this was one of the most important doors to close on her past. She had been a distraction as of late. He'd tried to be a bit cold towards Kate. She was just too tempting at the moment.

Kate folded the paper and tucked it into an envelope with a heavy sigh. She wiped a few tears from her eyes as she handed it to her Senior.

"Finished then?"

"Yes Sir."

He rose, and in a gesture of affection pulled her close to him and let her cry into his shoulder. "Now there, remember, a last cry."

After a few moments, Kate found her emotional strength and pulled away.

"Better now?"

"Yes Sir."

"Alright then, let's have a bit of tea, shall we?"

The two enjoyed a standard tea without any further interruption. The Discussion had already taken place. The letter she had written was the last form of contact Kate would have with her sister, Abby Tomley. She had penned that she was happy, all was well, and maybe, she would visit sometime in the spring. The last part of the letter about a possible trip to Boston was a complete and utter lie.

Boston

Mr. Halton enjoyed his fifth drink and droned on. His bartender would not stop him; he knew Mr. Halton was flush with cash. He always came to drink when he'd been paid. It had been happening for over ten years now, just about the same time Mr. Halton decided to hide his drinking from the Society.

The endless times he'd interrupted families with destitute news got to him. He was continually depressed. No amount of money or whores could fill the hole he'd felt, although his new lady Miss Meredith seemed to help. The Society had provided her for less than a week and he'd already visited her twice. She was affectionate and sweet. She asked a lot of questions which made him feel special.

However, he was so ruined by alcohol, he didn't even realize those visits ended without copulation. Mr. Halton usually babbled semiconsciously until he fell asleep. Meredith listened to every innocuous word.

As the bartender poured a sixth drink, Mr. Halton's odd moments were noticed by a tall, dark-haired gentleman, who worked for a group much opposed to the Society. Cecil Ellis was the oldest Ellis son. He purposefully overheard every guttural moan from the drunken Fixture. Not a single detail was lost. When Mr. Halton downed his last drink and stumbled into the darkness, Mr. Ellis was not far behind. And as he'd come to watch Mr. Halton over the last few weeks, Cecil recognized a familiar pattern. Only tonight, change would come to the sad life of Mr. Halton.

Mr. Halton fell into his carriage in the throes of inebriation. After a half-hour nap, the cold finally awoke him to duty. He bade his Driver to take him to the address that was on the card he'd been given with his pay. In the chilly stillness of early eve, the Driver pulled up to the fine home of Ferris and Abby Tomley. Mr. Halton stumbled out and rang the bell.

An older black butler opened the door.

"Sir," Mr. Halton slurred. "I have some news for the gentleman of the house. May I come in?"

Silas, the Tomley's kind servant stepped back at the insidious smell of the portly, drunken man before him. "Wait just a moment." He shut the door and summoned the master of the house, Mr. Ferris Tomley.

Mr. Tomley peeked out the window. "Did he say what he wanted?" A small pit knotted in his belly. His sister-in-law, Kate Church, had tangled with some dangerous folk, but all should be decent by now. Abby had just received a letter that her work was going well.

"No Sir." Silas looked worried.

Mr. Halton knocked hard on the door and yelled through it. "If you please, I have an urgent message regarding a family member, Miss Katherine Church." He then belched loudly.

In the shadows only a stone's throw away, Cecil Ellis inhaled sharply. He had only hoped to cull general knowledge of the Society in order to infiltrate its walls with information from the grave digger. Rumors abounded that Kate Church's family was relocated in Boston. So when a drunken cemetery worker, oddly flush with cash for a man of his profession, started to let things slip at a certain watering hole, it was fairly easy for Cecil to convince a bartender to just listen in a bit then pay off for the intel. And now Cecil was more than pleased to hear the name of his father's killer without even having to eavesdrop through the Tomley's windows. He could scarcely believe his luck as he pulled out a very special spyglass and began an intense observation.

Ferris Tomley flung open the door at the sound of his sister-in-law's name. "Please come in. And be a little quieter if you would please." Silas ushered the drunken man inside, as Ferris checked outside. The streets were empty. He shut the door, ran to the parlor and grabbed Abby from her cross stitching. "Come quick, we have word about Kate." Abby was so startled she dropped her crafting and hurried behind her husband to the foyer.

"Well Sir, go on, now that I have the lady of the house present." Ferris frowned. This man was clearly not sober and it set him on edge.

"I have a note here, from Acme Shaft Company in St. Louis. I'm sorry to inform you that Miss Church perished in an explosion yesterday. Small fire, but unfortunately she was killed." He swallowed another burp before continuing. "They've already buried her remains. I am so sorry. You'll be receiving a stipend of $10,000 for your loss from her employer. Here is the information you'll need." Mr. Halton handed them the small slip of paper with bank information that could not be traced to the Society. Suddenly he was well aware that this had been his worst performance ever of his usual task. He broke out in a profuse sweat. "I'm so incredibly sorry." He made another poor attempt at apologizing.

Abby fell to the floor in tears. "Oh God, no." Ferris struggled to hold her and Martha stepped in to help.

"Oh child, oh no." The ladies held each other as the gentlemen spoke just a moment more. Ferris felt the knot in his stomach grow tighter as Silas showed the ruffian out. *Something had happened to Kate*, he was certain. *But who was really behind it?*

Meredith Pratt bit her tongue as Mr. Halton stumbled outside and made his way down the block. She too had followed the slovenly Society Member and knew that his time to be Terminated had come. Just as she prepared to step forward to dispose of him before he reached his carriage, another figure emerged and ran across the yard to the back door of the Tomley home. She grabbed her pistol, but was too late. Within seconds, there were several bright flashes behind the curtains of the home of Ferris and Abby Tomley. Meredith gasped and stepped back.

Inside, Cecil Ellis had effectively assassinated Ferris and Abby Tomley and their two servants, Silas and Martha. From his vantage point with his clever gadget, he had seen where the family had been standing. Cecil correctly assumed how to quickly kill them all by coming in the back door, running swiftly through the kitchen and down the hall to the foyer.

The men were so engrossed in scanning the paperwork for details, that they were much too late to halt the interloper. Abby and Martha's last sight on earth was the muzzle of a silent weapon exploding in their faces. Just as quick as he'd arrived, Cecil turned and ran back outside. He swiftly kept on running into the alley behind. It had taken less than 12 seconds to complete his revenge.

Mr. Halton was too far away and drunk to notice anything had happened. He fell into a deep slumber as his carriage pulled out. He wanted to rest before visiting Miss Pratt.

Maybe a roll with her would make me feel better, he pondered as the alcohol finally took complete hold of his senses. His driver grimaced as he slapped the reigns and wondered why his passenger was still alive.

Miss Pratt decided to give chase. Any information at this point could be helpful. She tore after the assassin, knowing he could turn at any corner, and that she could be in grave danger. She was light on her feet and ran almost without a sound. She stopped at the first cross way of the alleys behind the Tomley home. She paused and heard the rapid steps of her adversary going further away to the left. She changed direction and intended to cut him off.

Cecil was smiling as he changed his pace to a brisk walk. *Mother would be so pleased,* he mused. He purposefully turned a corner and looked over his shoulder at nothing. His pistol was still warm in his holster and he treasured the feeling. He continued to walk with a wicked grin just as a gorgeous lady of the eve approached.

"My, what a lovely smile. Are you looking to share that happiness?" Meredith Pratt asked saucily of her new found prey. She looked directly at Cecil, taking in every detail, his clothing, hair, and eyes.

"Oh no Miss, I must be on my way, although you are quite intriguing." Cecil deftly dodged her and continued on, not looking back. The only woman that would be pleased tonight was his mother, with the news of the death of Kate Church's family. He'd been extraordinarily lucky to have found Mr. Halton through a well-paid bartender. He did not have time for any female entertaining.

But he should have paid a bit more attention. His well-trained ear of an assassin recognized the click of a gun barrel. He broke into a crooked run just as Meredith fired a shot into his back. Despite the burn in his shoulder blade he turned another corner and picked up his pace. He made a break for the nearest main street and hailed the first driver he could see.

With a flash of cash, Cecil was hurried away by his happy driver. Meredith cursed as she watched from an alley way. She'd wounded him, and would never forget his face. She ran back to the Tomley home. The street was still empty. The surrounding residences were filled with clueless neighbors beginning to settle in for the eve. Like Cecil she entered from the back. The smell of gunpowder tickled her nose. Mentally she prepared herself for the task at hand.

As she assumed, the assassin was well trained. All four of the Tomley's had been shot square in the forehead. She was lucky he hadn't shot her in alley when she approached. But playing the whore had worked. She had something to give Mr. Roth besides the paperwork she collected from Mr. Tomley's cold hand. She avoided the spilled blood while turning out the lights and dousing the flames of the fireplaces.

Meredith then caught a coach to a safe house not far away. Of all ironies, it was the very house she had stepped into when she was barely a woman forced into prostitution by her mother. Telegrams were sent, plans were set into motion.

In the very early hours of the next morning, two men delivered firewood to the Tomley residence. Their bodies were taken out in large crates topped with freshly cut wood. Any curious neighbors were told that there was a death in the family and that they had moved. They were cremated and their remains buried next to Henry Church in St. Louis.

Meredith would personally return these remains as requested by Mr. Roth after she attended to other business. After her brief stop at the safe house to secure these plans, Meredith prepared herself for a task she'd completed dozens of times with incredible efficiency.

She arrived at her small temporary apartment to find Mr. Halton passed out on the stoop. Meredith was not pleased, as she needed him inside. "Now, now Mr. Halton?" She shook him until he awoke. It was less than two hours since he'd delivered his last message. "Come inside, it's cold."

"Ah yes, my angel." He sputtered awake and clamored into the plain brick building.

"I gather you wanted to see me," Meredith cooed.

"Ah yes, busy evening you might say." Mr. Halton stumbled behind his new mistress as they passed the desk clerk. He was still quite intoxicated and didn't notice that Meredith had passed the gentleman, a certain Mr. Mason, a small note with a quick flick of the wrist.

"Oh my," she whispered. "Must I take good care of you then? A different room perhaps?" She stopped abruptly at a door halfway down the hall.

"Whatever you say." He chuckled as she turned the knob.

"You first." She smiled warmly, but her heart was cold as ice as she opened the door to a drafty darkness.

"Well then." He stumbled forward.

"If you please." Meredith batted her eyes coquettishly.

"But there's no light in here-"

Meredith shot him flat in the back of the head, watched him fall down onto an empty mattress with a small thud, popped her pistol into her bag, shut the door and locked it behind her. She walked back to Mr. Mason, handed him the key without a word and went upstairs to her room. *This had gone horribly wrong,* she worried before falling into a fitful sleep.

Mr. Mason sent a regrettable telegram to Director Roth before he too went to bed for the eve.

At Director Roth's insistence, Kate Church wasn't told of what had transpired in Boston.

Lord Wilson sat across from his longtime friend in the Director's office. His eyes narrowed at the terrible news. "So, all four of them, gone." Lord Wilson leaned forward for a freshly lit cigar from his Director.

"I'm afraid so. Mr. Halton was already marked for Termination. It was just a shame he hadn't been taken out before delivering word."

"And the assassin was wounded?" Lord Wilson tried to take some comfort that the aggressor was injured.

"Yes, in the shoulder. Miss Meredith took quite the risk. But she did see his face and we have scouts on the watch now." Mr. Roth leaned back. "She should be back tomorrow. Arrangements have been made. I'm so sorry Christopher."

"I am as well. This is horrifying. Did he mess anything else up before?"

"Not as far as we can tell. But the bartender had been paid by someone. We think the assassin. He's not on anyone's regular payroll, so we're going to leave him alone. I don't think he's good enough to recruit or pursue out of retaliation."

"A pity," Lord Wilson mumbled.

"Again, I am sorry. Miss Church made some enemies, we know that. It's unfortunate that her family got caught in the cross-fire. But she will never know."

"You have my word." Lord Wilson stood and shook hands. He left Mr. Roth's office and sent word for Miss Kate's afternoon classes to be cancelled.

After lunch, Kate received an Invitation to see Lord Wilson after 1 p.m. at Wilson Manor for lunch and the remains of the day. The last visit ended with unpleasantness. Her last letter to her sister Abby shook her to the core. The realization that she'd never ever write her again made her stomach churn. She smiled as she touched the familiar parchment. It had been a few days since she'd been invited to stay so long.

Her same happy face arrived at Wilson Manor shortly thereafter.

Lord Wilson winced and inhaled deeply as he watched her approach the grounds. Her face was alight despite the late autumn chill. Leeds met her at the library doorway.

"Good Afternoon Miss Church. May I take your coat?"

"And you as well Leeds, thank you." Kate's manners had continued to improve. She was rosy cheeked and elegant in a pale lavender gown with a wide banded sash around her middle and full sleeves.

Lord Wilson managed a satisfied grin. "Welcome Miss Kate." His heart pinged for a moment. She was lovely. "Please come to your usual seat." He pulled out her chair.

Kate sat with a refined posture. She was eager to be at Wilson Manor again. She had missed it of late, buried in study, practicing hard. He'd seemed distracted, perhaps even angry over the last few days since she'd had to write the letter. So she'd done everything to appease him. Going to classes, focusing on small tasks she was given. Doing everything to the T. Even her last class with Miss Prix was flawless.

Lord Wilson sat across from his charge. Inside his heart was breaking. Kate had been so well as of late. Not a single outburst or misstep. But her past mistakes inevitably caused the death of her family. He would not chide her for this, for she would not be told of the deaths. He even had considered hypnotizing her, but no one could ever completely forget something so tragic. There was no current way to erase someone's memory.

"Sir, you seem preoccupied." Kate took off her gloves while trying a gentle audible pry.

Lord Wilson shook off his doubts. "I have some wonderful plans for this afternoon, Miss Kate. Something I think you're rather going to enjoy. But first let us have lunch. And I'd like to hear of your progress in your studies. I've received very good reports from everyone."

"Yes, I've learned a lot. I feel like I'm finally getting a grasp on fencing."

Their food arrived from Leeds and they finished their conversation over roasted pheasant, grilled squash and corn.

"Splendid. And your manners continue to improve." Lord Wilson smiled. She needed the etiquette, but he didn't want that fiery passion in her to go away. There could be fighting in the future and she needed to be able to protect herself. "And don't forget to keep practicing other weaponry, your whip especially."

"Thank you Sir."

"And speaking of your whip, I have a well-earned surprise for you. Are you finished?" A clever grin marked his face.

"Yes Sir." She had no idea why he was suddenly so giddy.

"Come." He led her inside the Manor where Mrs. Leeds waited at the bottom of the stairs. "She will assist you up top." Lord Wilson looked above.

"Oh, thank you Sir." Kate hadn't been upstairs before.

Lord Wilson waited until the ladies had turned the corner before collecting Leeds and going up behind them.

"In here Miss Church." Mrs. Leeds unlocked a door not far from the top of the stairs. She waved her hand over a copper box and a series of ornate lamps on the walls illuminated the room. It was a splendid lady's quarters, even rivaling her room in the main hall. Thick golden curtains were closed over the windows. A marbled fireplace with cherubs carved into its mantle sat in the center of the room. A small book shelf was between it and one of the windows. A table for two was in front of the illustrious fireplace. Two large wardrobes lined a wall near another door. There was a vanity and a small desk with the standard basket and tubing that dropped down from the ceiling. Next to the vanity was a privacy panel and chair draped with a lovely gown, boots and other riding accoutrements. Kate's mouth fell open.

"Oh my…"

"Let me help you my dear." Mrs. Leeds assisted in dressing Kate. When finished, they gazed in a long mirror. "Lovely. Lord Wilson will be pleased."

"Am I going riding?" Kate asked incredulously.

"Oh, that is for him to tell you Miss." She beamed as if the buttons on her dress would burst underneath her apron. "Let us go downstairs shall we?"

Lord Wilson and Leeds waited at the bottom. Kate wore a grey riding coat trimmed with a black velvet collar, cuffs and pockets. A dainty lace pocket square peeked out. A ruffled blouse collar eased through the top. Lord Wilson was mesmerized yet again.

"Well then, you look properly attired." He smiled and took Kate's hand. "Come this way." He led her outside to another small building about one hundred yards away. It was well hidden by a group of trees. Once they passed the small grove, the smell of horses was unmistakable. They came around the side to a waiting groomsman that opened the door to a petite barn.

"We're going riding?" Kate sounded like a happy child.

"Yes. Come see." He led her inside. There were three stalls, the first empty. The second held a black stallion. "This is Midnight." Lord Wilson stroked his face. "And this, I believe is yours…"

Kate was stunned yet again. Sonny stood in the last stall. "How did you..?" She had to touch her old friend to believe that he was really there.

"Never mind Miss Kate. Are you prepared to ride?"

"Yes!" she squealed. The groomsman led the horses out and then helped Kate mount Sonny. Once seated, Lord Wilson led the way to a thickly forested patch. The air was chilly and steam rose from the nostrils of their rides.

But the hearts of Kate and her Senior were warm. A gentle breeze made the highest branches of the nearly empty trees sway in the bright light of the afternoon sun. Squirrels darted about the dead foliage looking for last treasures to bury before hibernating.

They came to the ridge of a small creek and stopped by a cluster of aromatic pines. Birds chirped in the crisp air as if prepping for one last meal of worms before the ground hardened for the frozen winter.

The stream gurgled a few feet below. The shallow waters so clear, that the rocky bottom could easily be seen.

"What do you think Miss Kate?"

"Splendid. Magnificent." In the crisp, cool autumn sunset Kate's face was full of the sun's last glow of the day. She radiated a golden hue and her eyes sparkled. She closed her eyes and inhaled. A brief sadness came upon her. She remembered Blaze, her favorite horse before Sonny and riding on the Parker's property. How Michael Parker had made her feel. She opened her eyes and felt as if she'd just been dreaming.

Lord Wilson watched her with a protective eye. He didn't want old memories to take over. "Fantastic then. Please take it all in Miss Kate." He waited a few more moments. A few deer emerged from the opposite tree line and came forward to drink. Kate watched in awe as they slowly drank then made their way downstream.

Lord Wilson savored this moment and reminded himself to be patient. "Well Miss Kate, we must go," he whispered.

"All right then."

They rode back to the Manor on the same path with the sky overhead turning to golds and purples as the sun set. Lord Wilson took great care in helping her dismount even though he knew very well she could do it herself. He let his hand rest on the small of her back even after she'd reached the ground safely. He still held her as he spoke. "Did you enjoy that Miss Kate?"

"Yes!" she gushed.

"Good. Please remember how precious these days are." He paused and looked at the sun dropping below the horizon. "I want you to be happy here." He bit his tongue to stop what he really wanted to say. How important she was to him. How he'd grown to love her. That he could hardly wait to have her always at the Manor.

"I am. I really am. Thank you."

"Oh, you'll thank me later, I'm sure once we start the more dangerous Engagements," he teased.

"Do tell," she bantered back.

"Not yet. They come to us as we're needed. But for now, a game of chess?" He pulled back from the spell he'd been under for the last few hours.

"Yes."

"Come then." He took her hand and led her back to the Manor. He had completely forgotten about her family's death until they were inside the library. "Mrs. Leeds will help you change and we'll have tea time and chess then."

"Yes Sir."

As he waited for Kate to return, Lord Wilson sat at his desk and peered out into the growing darkness. He had a new secret to keep and he despised it. It was one he did not cherish; unlike how he felt about the woman he'd wisely recruited.

Boston

Miles away, a new cemetery worker was promoted to replace Mr. Halton. His first task was to bury the lapsed and now dead Fixture.

8 THE CRUISE

Kate's day started simply. She rose before 7 a.m. as an Invitation whooshed into her basket before breakfast. Her attendant threw open the curtains to reveal a dark grey autumn morning and then turned her attention to her mistress. A cool breeze rattled the window pane.

Her attendant shook her awake. "Miss Church, you've received word."

Kate stumbled out of bed, grabbed and then threw on the robe handed to her. She plucked the usual card with its embossed seal from her desk. With a deft slash of the opener, Kate sped through the details, her eyes darting over the fine parchment. There was a Discussion at 10 a.m. in the garden with Lord Wilson. An early Invitation was unusual, so Kate hurried to dress. Her previous Discussions had almost always been at tea time at Wilson Manor. She remembered those first Engagements fondly, smiling as she and her attendant laced up her boots.

Although she was still in training, Kate participated in a couple of Discussions and Engagements in her first few weeks at the Society. But like the first challenges she had experienced in Iris, these had been relatively easy tasks.

She was sent to observe a bank transaction between a Member and a Fixture that worked in a financial institution in the city. Kate pretended to draw money from a fake account as more than one hundred thousand dollars safely changed hands only feet from her location. The clerk smiled at her. "Mrs. Wren, that is thirty dollars for you. We are so pleased that we can serve you. Would there be anything else?" Kate dropped one of the bills just long enough to get a side glance at her targets. The gentlemen had gone their separate ways, the exchange completed. The clerk peered over the gated counter.

"Oh how clumsy of me. Here it is." Kate smiled at her contact from below and placed the cash inside her bag. "Thank you so much." She stood, walked away without a sound, and went virtually unnoticed. Kate's plain grey dress faded into the various stone buildings that surrounded her. Carriages and people filled the streets with dust and the clatter of hooves on the cobblestones. After a block and a half, she spotted her driver. She touched her grey feathered black fascinator to signal. The plume was almost as soft as her black velvet gloves. She played a bit with the simple wedding band as she waited for her ride and a brief pang tugged at her insides. *Could she ever be married?* Being called Mrs. was, well, kind of nice. The thought wisped through her mind like a tendril of smoke. The driver pulled aside in a black short covered carriage with a single horse. Kate pinched her hand to bring herself back to reality.

"Good afternoon, Mrs. Wren." He nodded and assisted Kate to the carriage.

"Good day, Sir." Once inside Kate relaxed and her mind wandered again. There were no notes to make; she was to see Lord Wilson in person. The thirty minute drive had given her a moment to ponder. *Would every day be like this? Or every other day? Doing minimal tasks, reporting, and then back to studying and hopefully spending some time at Wilson Manor?*

Lord Wilson crossed her mind. Since the day he'd checked on her scars, he'd rebuffed even the mildest flirtation from Kate with a somewhat blank stare. Even the day they went riding he remained distant. He was still incredibly kind; helping her with her chess game, and recommending books. But now there were tea times without him and Kate took walks with just Strax. Had she mistaken his helpfulness for affection?

She remembered Dr. Finch's warning. "He is not your lover." As her first few weeks of the Society passed, Kate had almost wanted it to be so. But it simply wasn't allowed. Dr. Finch and Madame Prix had both encouraged her to learn as much as possible. To be strong, but ladylike, because it wouldn't be long before she could be paired with someone. "A year will pass quickly, Miss Church." Dr. Finch reminded her with a gentle tone on one of her follow up visits.

But would it be Lord Wilson? Or someone else? A tingle crept up Kate's spine. *Was Master Richards a possibility?* He was attractive, strong and lithe. He made fencing look like ballet; his smooth sword play effortless, yet deadly. Occasionally, Kate swore there was a twinkle in his eyes, the bright blues shining as she challenged him during their sparring.

Kate's musings were interrupted as they pulled into the Society grounds. Her pocket watch pulsed with perfect timing. Her driver dismounted, assisted her with a quick "Good Day", and was off to the carriage house.

Kate walked up the marble steps of the Main Hall, her heels clicking along with the other Members comings and goings. She waltzed straight through the foyer, passed the fountain and out the French doors to the promenade.

Several Members were seated outside enjoying one of the last lovely early afternoons of fall. A gentleman had pulled off his top hat and was adjusting a large arm bracer. Its metal pieces reflected in the sunlight. Two other male Members played cards. One had a monocle that glowed a deep green. The other adjusted a series of coils that seemed to be bracelets around a leather cuff as he drew a card. A couple sat at one of the far tables deep in conversation. The gentleman wore a cook's clothes, but the lady adjusted her fascinator that was falling out of her bright pink hair. Kate had grown accustomed to the costumes of her neighbors and didn't bat an eye. Each Member had gifts and talents. It wasn't up to her to question them.

Kate strode into the Garden with a happy gait. "May I join you Sir?" She greeted Lord Wilson.

"Of course, please." He stood as Kate sat and then joined her on their bench. And so the Discussion began. "I trust all went well on your first Engagement from here?"

"Yes, the exchange happened as planned. No noise or distractions." Kate reported to her Senior.

"Well done then Miss Kate." Lord Wilson nodded with approval. His timepiece buzzed but not hers. "I must be off. Business to be had Miss Church." His voice lacked emotion.

"Tea time today, then?" Kate piped up.

"Not today Miss Kate. My business will keep me busy into the evening. I think it'd be good of you to relax tonight. Perhaps read one of the books you've borrowed?" His face was so even tempered that his wrinkles were barely visible.

Kate shouldn't have invited herself over. Still, a part of her felt dejected. "Oh, of course, Sir," she said feigning a weak smile.

They stood simultaneously. "Good afternoon Miss Church."

"Good Afternoon Sir." Kate nodded politely, although her heart was in flux. They walked in opposite directions.

Kate felt listless and decided to stay on the promenade for a couple of hours until teatime. She would join the others in the Main Hall for the afternoon snack instead of Lord Wilson. *Maybe it was time to make some acquaintances?*

Her body was relaxed, almost reclining in her seat, but her mind still tumbled. Her eyes wandered over the flowers, but she looked right through them. Her fingers pressed over the chain of her pocket watch, making mini linked impressions in her velvet gloves.

Kate had been told that on days she'd have Engagements, she would not have classes or training. "A weak person cannot complete strong work" the ethic went. But now she was bored and didn't feel like resting. In fact, Kate felt the opposite. When her timepiece buzzed, Kate walked inside with her fellow Members almost begrudgingly. Tea was not what she was thirsty for. She would drink it though, acknowledge the others with slight movements, go upstairs alone, and unsuccessfully try to study before having a good cry at bedtime.

Kate's time alone did not go unnoticed. From the training wing of the Society, Master Richards observed Miss Church's melancholia. He stood at full attention, his hands clasped at the small of his back. As Kate left her table, Master Julian Richards turned away from the window of his room, heavily decorated with trophies, swords, shields and armament. For a moment, he wondered if he could add Miss Church to his collection. This was not to be, as Master Richards was not the fencing instructor's true family name and his alliances belonged to another. He released his hands from behind his back and let the forefinger of his left hand slide along the blade of one of his prized rapiers with a sigh. The splice immediately leaked a dark crimson. He pulled it to his lips and suckled. *If only this was Miss Church's lips.*

Lord Wilson returned to the Manor with entangled emotions. It had been a little over a month since she'd arrived, but Miss Kate had completely upstaged his usual thoughts. And on top of keeping his passion in check, he now held the secret that her family had perished.

He had trained many other Members, both male and female and sent them on to duty. Although attracted to some of the ladies, he'd never quite found the one he was searching for until Miss Kate. As a younger man, his heart had been broken and he'd thought it unrepairable. Now close to fifty, he was tired of being alone. He hadn't exactly chosen this life, but it had been good for him. The finest foods, clothes, and furnishings, all at his fingertips. He practiced and studied his botany unsupervised. He had complete control over the serum. At last, after some initial word from scouts in the field, a talented woman had been found. One that could be his charge, and perhaps even his equal. Now she was here.

Miss Kate had awakened a long dead desire in him. He couldn't act on it now; he'd have to be patient. In the meantime, Kate was prepared to do more for the Society. *Balance in all things*, he chided himself. Lord Wilson tried to hide his feelings as he came home.

"Good day Sir." Leeds took his hat and coat. "All well this afternoon then?"

"Yes, very well, thank you." Wilson hurried to his desk, jotted down several notes on a card and handed it to Leeds. "Please deliver this to the post today."

"Of course Sir. Should Mrs. Leeds prepare for Miss Church at teatime today?" Leeds could tell his master seemed distracted.

"Hmm, not today. I'm going to finish some things here then blow off some steam. I'll be having tea elsewhere today," Lord

Wilson muttered. Leeds turned away from his charge, unhappy at the code he'd just been given.

Leeds was concerned for Lord Wilson. He'd been so happy with Miss Church at the Manor. It was much more than an instructor/tutor relationship, certainly more than a fondness. In the times she came to learn chess, the arts, and sciences, he noticed that Lord Wilson was at his happiest. His master had always been impeccably groomed, but since Miss Church's arrival, he wore his suits with a flourish, putting one of his special greenhouse flowers in the lapel. He requested more polish on his shoes and had not a hair out of place on his head.

He heard his Master tidy up his desk and call for him. Leeds brought his hat and coat. "Will you be back for dinner, Sir?"

"Most likely not. Do not wait up for me. I will handle my evening tasks later." Lord Wilson hurried out as the sun lowered on the horizon. He'd left in such haste that Leeds couldn't get a 'good evening' in. The servant shuffled away, knowing that he should not judge and most certainly could not do anything to change his Senior's mind.

Within the hour, Lord Wilson had enjoyed a burlesque show and satisfied his needs with Miss Candice at the gentlemen's club. She had not seen Lord Wilson for almost eight months. And it had been almost two years before that. He dined with her in her private quarters and enjoyed her pleasures again for dessert. Miss Candice never complained as he called her Kate during their moments of ecstasy. He left late in the eve, still as conflicted and unsure as before. Patience had never been his strong point, but decisiveness usually was.

He'd already sent over Kate's next Invitation. Lord Wilson cursed himself for bowing to his masculinity and not waiting for Miss Kate. He should've been more careful in deflecting her affections.

"One should not be so soft." He mumbled that eve as he fell into slumber.

The next day, after her morning class with Madame Prix, Kate was pleased to find an Invitation for a Discussion that afternoon at 4 p.m.

Somehow, she mused, *I've made him angry or displeased.* She assured herself that she would be on her best behavior. After all, the first Engagement had gone well.

There would not be tea, just Discussion. Again she met Lord Wilson in the Garden. Kate was on time and waited for her Senior.

"May I join you?" Lord Wilson's British lilt came crisply.

"Of course." Kate returned the standard agreement with a pleasant tone. And so the Discussion began and plans were set in motion for the next day's Engagement. There was to be no dinner or visit at the Manor that evening. Kate did not ask and Lord Wilson did not offer. And as it happened the night before, they separated, both equally frustrated at their situation.

Kate had a larger role in a money drop in Lafayette Park the following day. She handed her contact a small case, full of money, in exchange for a lunch pail that contained the frozen heart of a person that had betrayed the Society. How and why the treason happened was of no concern to the new Member.

At precisely 4 p.m., with the buzz of her timepiece, Kate delivered the organ to her Senior in the Garden. Lord Wilson waited for her.

"May I join you?" Kate gave a wry smile. She'd been only slightly apprised of what was in the container.

"Of course, please do." Lord Wilson stood and accepted the heart of the traitor. And so the Discussion began. He gingerly set the pail down and turned to his charge. "Any complications?"

"None whatsoever Sir." Kate sat tall. "May I make a comment however?"

Lord Wilson raised his eyebrows. Questions on Engagements were not usually taken. "Go on, but proceed with caution, Miss Kate."

"May I ask why we would retrieve such an item? Experimentation perhaps?" Kate inquired with a tinge of curiosity.

"As in all Discussions, confidentiality is key. I will answer this question, however, as it pertains to other things we must discuss." There was a hint of sadness in Lord Wilson's eyes. He lowered his voice. "Know, Miss Kate, that we are always being watched, always heard. And there are sometimes those that should not be doing so. That is why we are here in the Garden. It's one of the most sacred of places here. Do you understand?"

"Yes, of course." Kate was immediately reminded of the seriousness of her decision. She should not have been so flippant.

"Remember the penalties for breaking our tenants are severe." He stiffened and motioned to the pail. "This is an example of such punishment. This is the heart of a woman, one who not only betrayed the Society, but her Senior Member, who was her husband as well. He is high ranked and well respected. He is a proud Senior Member in another city. My understanding is that the heart will most likely be taxidermied and displayed as a trophy." Lord Wilson continued as his brow furrowed with concern. "Do not be so soft, Miss Kate. I will not be unkind to you, but know that it pains me to correct you." He leaned in closer to his beloved Member. "Miss Kate,

I should not ever want for this to be you." He brushed the back of his hand along her cheek. "You do understand?"

Kate paled. "Yes, of course Sir."

He removed his hand. "You have come so far in such a short time. Let us not waste your efforts." He gave a mild smile. "Now, I must take this piece and usher it onto its owner. Tonight, please rest, because bigger things are to come. I promise you. Good afternoon, Miss Kate."

Kate shuddered as she stood with her Senior. She had forgotten how cold he could be. "Good afternoon, Sir."

The two parted with many things understood but none of them said aloud.

Kate shook her head in an attempt to forget those previous Discussions, and focus on her current one. She hadn't been to the Manor for almost a week. There had been a mild reprimand, yet praise for her last efforts. Unlike her Engagement in Chicago, these minor trips outside the Society walls had gone off without a hitch. But they had also opened the door to feelings that would have to wait to be acted on. She brushed off the memories and drove herself to complete attention.

Lord Wilson was waiting in the Garden. Kate strode in, her nose upturned, her gait confident. A cool fall breeze blew at her royal blue dress coat and teased the ribbons on its matching hat. The colors matched the tint of her eyes. As she approached the bench, the morning sun broke through the clouds casting a golden glow on Kate. Lord Wilson swallowed.

"May I join you, Sir?" Kate gave the standard inquiry.

"Of course." Her Senior Member tried desperately not to grin. She looked lovely, as if a seraph had arrived to take him to heaven. *If only she could,* thought Lord Wilson. He waited and then sat with her. Her manners had escalated in the time she'd been away from the Manor. Kate floated into her seat. Mrs. Prix was to be appraised of her good work. And so the Discussion began.

"We've come upon a desperate situation, Miss Kate. As you know, you've secured two of three keys that are intrical to a machine that is of utmost importance to the Society. Some time ago, these keys were stolen. Taken by those who are far less kind than us, with dubious intentions. We've received word that a Mr. Percy won this last key in a poker match just a week ago. He is usually not so lucky. He has fondness for drink and ladies of the evening. He's made several withdrawals from his bank accounts in the last week in order to pay for his temptations. His resources are completely depleted. Mr. Percy booked a gambling trip on the Ester, a riverboat which will be sailing here tomorrow. He has boarded upriver, most likely hoping to recoup his losses. We have reason to believe he has no idea of the value of the key he's holding as he has not tried to sell the jeweled top or offer it in any game so far. We think he's now desperate enough to add it to the pot in a high stakes game tomorrow night."

Kate smiled inside, warmth rushed through her veins. The idea of gambling again intrigued her. "Tomorrow?" she inquired.

"Yes. We leave before dawn. We must be very careful on this Engagement. There is a strong possibility that other players may recognize you, including Mr. Whitney." Kate had to stifle a giggle at the thought of the flirtatious man from her past. "Having a disguise or alias would be moot. We also have word that Mr. Whitney is trying to procure that key in exchange for a large sum from a mercenary who is unable to complete the task himself. I would gather that he has been hired by those that intend to hinder us." Lord Wilson paused. He was asking his Member to take an incredible risk, exposing herself outside of the Society's walls. "Are you prepared for this Miss Kate?"

"Yes." Kate spoke confidently. Her eyes even, her stature strong.

"Very well then. No classes, training, or tea time today. Please take time for leisure." Lord Wilson's voice was filled with intensity. "I will see you tomorrow Miss Kate, bright and early."

"Good day, Sir." Kate stood with him. Her skin tingled with anticipation.

The Next Day, Hannibal, MO

"You must play your absolute best." Lord Wilson was stern, his lips pursed. "Mr. Whitney will know you're good. He's competing for that key. You'll have to force Mr. Percy to give it up. He will be wearing a red velvet vest and green-tinted spectacles. Win at all costs. Flirt but don't act salaciously. Win gracefully. Pout in a lady-like fashion when you lose."

"Of course." Kate primped in the mirror in a room of the quaint country inn that had been arranged for their preparation. They had left the Society grounds before dawn. Lord Wilson stepped outside on their balcony to take stock of the surroundings while Kate dressed into more appropriate evening wear. The sun was setting over the last of the fall foliage. The grand steamboat, the *Ester,* was slowly making her way to Hannibal on her route. A curious group had gathered on the dock to watch her approach. Still others sat on the porches of local establishments enjoying various food and beverage selections. Coaches came and went, stirring up dust devils in their wake.

When Kate had finished, she peered through the door, and then stepped out slowly. Lord Wilson returned to a vision of loveliness in a light blue corseted dress with a plunging neckline. It had off the shoulder caplets which revealed a lovely pearl choker that rested over her collarbone. She wore long black gloves and a fascinator with matching light blue feathers in her flowing hair.

"Can you tie me up a bit?" Kate smiled. "I couldn't quite reach the last lacing." She'd become used to having someone else dress her. But then she paused, forgetting about her flirtation warnings.

"Become a bit spoiled, have we now?" Lord Wilson chided and ignored his own cautious thoughts. "Turn around then." He pulled the lacing and retied it, resisting the urge to run his hands along her bare shoulders. "All better?"

"Yes, much better." She tried to ignore his attention and finished adjusting her hairpiece.

"Alright then. Off you go. Godspeed Miss Kate." Lord Wilson bolstered his Member. "Will meet you at the rendezvous point." His hand gently grazed her shoulder. He was sure she could handle the mission, but a part of Lord Wilson's heart ached. He didn't have a good feeling about the coming eve.

"That was some hand. How about another drink?" Mr. Whitney purred. The poker game started at 7:30 p.m., a half hour after the Ester left the dock. It was now almost 9 p.m.

"Don't mind if I do." Kate almost crowed in return. It had been a very good evening for the lady from the Society. Mr. Whitney waved at the bartender and a smooth concoction was sent over in short order. As the barmaid handed him the drink, he slipped in a small tablet that dissipated instantly. Kate took the glass from Mr. Whitney and began to sip while the dealer shuffled the deck.

Some of the players were running out of money, including Mr. Percy. Only a few chips stood in front of him. His tell was a gentle tugging of his ruddy beard. Kate was surprised he still had any facial hair left after his losses. She was winning handsomely. She was certain that Mr. Percy would have to give up the key soon.

Kate took another drink. The warm sweet liquid made her lightheaded. She began to relax while a sense of giddiness enveloped her. Focus on the game at hand was lost and womanly sensual desires rose to the surface of her emotions.

Mr. Whitney could see that his poison was taking hold. Kate swayed a bit in her seat. He hurried the current round along as best he could while not being obvious. He put his hand on Miss Church's thigh under the table. She giggled in return as the other players wondered what was amiss.

Kate's vision became cloudy. *Did I really just twitter aloud? What has gotten into me?*

She had won most of the games and the third key was in the current pot. Mr. Percy had finally offered it up. Perhaps he still didn't know its real value.

I could win. Oh, but Mr. Whitney's hand felt delicious on her thigh. She wanted it to go further up to places where it really mattered. Her mind hazed over with unclear thoughts.

"Miss Church, it's your draw," the dealer intoned sternly.

"Oh yes, it is." She laughed, falling deeper under the spell of the tainted absinthe Mr. Whitney had given her. She blinked and drew a Jack of Spades. "I'll check," she mumbled.

Mr. Whitney exhaled; he had a horrible hand. He tapped his foot in anticipation as the others folded, one by one. That is except for Mr. Percy. "I'll raise you one hundred." The table looked to Kate in unison.

Her eyes stared at her hand; she was going a bit numb except for her lady parts.

Mr. Whitney barked, "I'm sure the lady would like to match that." He squeezed Kate's thigh and she jumped. Surely she had the better hand, Mr. Whitney reasoned.

"Oh yes, one hundred," she sloppily pushed her chips forward with a satisfied chirp.

"Mr. Percy, your hand?" the dealer inquired.

"I'll check." Mr. Percy was not amused. The woman was suddenly acting strangely. She'd been quiet as a mouse before. *Was she throwing him off his game? Trying a different tactic?* He couldn't afford to lose.

"Miss Church?" The dealer smiled at the odd turn of events.

"I'll check too." Kate laughed with an enormous belch. She covered her mouth politely, shocked that she'd let the gas emerge. "So terribly sorry, excuse me." Giggles ensued again.

"Mr. Percy, show your hand." The dealer was now thoroughly entertained. The biggest pot of the night was at stake and the most likely winner was clearly no longer sober. Mr. Percy flipped his cards. "Two pair, Aces and Queens," the dealer bellowed. The other gamblers whooped and chortled. "Miss Church? Your hand please."

Kate's arms were heavy as she flipped her hand. "Oh how pretty," she whispered, not realizing she'd just presented the best hand in poker.

"Miss Church wins. Royal Flush, Spades, Ten through Ace. Your winnings Miss Church." The dealer was pleasantly stunned as he pushed the large pile of chips, cash, the key and a few other assorted trinkets to her. Whistles and sighs filled the room. "Another game, lady and gentleman?"

"Oh-" Miss Church started but Mr. Whitney stopped her, practically pulling her from the chair.

"I think Miss Church has had enough for this evening." Mr. Whitney wore a devilish grin and slid the cache into her bag as Kate wavered. The other gentlemen laughed.

"Oh yes, enough. I'm….out," Kate stuttered.

"Good night gentleman." Mr. Whitney tipped his hat to the losing group. He pulled Kate by the waist and led her out. "Let's go to your cabin Kate," he whispered saucily in her ear as he pulled her along, helping her hold the bag full of riches.

"Oh….yes." She laughed, her nether regions aching, her mind let loose of all humility. "Ooops. I have…I have to-" Kate stopped.

"What?" Mr. Whitney hissed.

"I have to…tinkle," Kate slurred.

And I have to do something else, she thought, her subconscious valiantly tried to come forward. *Something to do with a key.*

"Now?" he grumbled. She nodded and whimpered. "Alright then, but outside!" If she went to the Ladies' parlor he surmised, he could lose her and the money. They went out to the deck. It was chilly and their breaths sent small fogs into the air.

"Be a gentleman and hold up my dress," she wailed while leaning on the rail.

"Shh! I will not do such a thing," he replied sternly. She could drown, *but why should I care?* Mr. Whitney thought. He had the money, although the possibility of fucking her brainless body made him stir with excitement. But he suddenly realized he didn't have her bag. In the rush to get her out, the purse still dangled from her arm. He stared at her as she dropped it beside her with a clunk.

"Well don't watch then," Kate replied with a huff and hiked up her dress. As Mr. Whitney turned round, the cool air provided a moment of clarity to Kate. *Key is in the bag. Key goes in shoe.* She drowsily pulled the key out. "Oh so pretty," she mumbled aloud, almost dropping the valuable piece.

"Hurry up will you!" Mr. Whitney cried impatiently and fought the urge to peek over his shoulder. He had yet to hear the splatter of her bodily fluid as he faced away from her.

Shoe, Kate thought drowsily. She turned her heel out and plopped the key into its secret compartment.

Now to urinate, her bladder aching. However, it would not come until she squelched her embarrassment by singing. Kate had one hand on the rail while simultaneously holding up her dress as she squatted much like an impregnated duck. The other hand pulled her bloomers aside as she warbled a bit of La Traviata.

"Get on with it, stop this foolishness!" Mr. Whitney grit through his teeth. Just then the familiar sound of relief broke Kate's obliteration of Verdi's opera. He sighed as Kate finished.

Woozy, she bent for her bag and almost fell over, the purse nearly sliding off the deck. Mr. Whitney heard the commotion. He turned and pulled her up. "Enough of this silliness." He rebuked her sternly.

"Please don't be mean." Kate pleaded like a child.

"Oh no dear, I've been impatient." He pretended to be sweet; he needed that money and the key. "Let's go then. Where to Miss Church?" He grimaced and picked her up.

"Cabin 23," she whispered merrily, her eyes blinking more slowly. *Thank God* he thought, just down the hall. He carried her quickly, setting her down briefly to unlatch the door. He lifted her, they stumbled inside, and he propped her against the nightstand.

"Here now, take another sip." Mr. Whitney pulled a flask from his waistcoat.

"Oh lovely." Kate laughed and downed a full shot. Mr. Whitney grinned wickedly, knowing it would only be a few more moments before she'd be under. "Oh, I'll have another if you don't mind." She tippled back another drink, and then tossed the flask back to her naughty companion. "Alright then," she boldly proclaimed, "Throw me on the bed and have your way with me." Kate had a teasing look in her eye for a brief moment before the room began to spin. Seconds later her eyes closed as she collapsed into the arms of Mr. Whitney.

"What a shame." He smiled, picked up her limp body and laid her on top of the bed. He so wanted to stay and have her at last, but there was no time. They should be docking soon and he couldn't risk waking her without escaping with the money. He sat beside her for a moment, brushing her soft golden locks from her face. "Good bye Miss Church." He kissed her gently on the lips, quickly grabbed her bag, and stole quietly from the room.

"Goggles down." Lord Wilson gave an audio command and night vision goggles mechanically drew from his bowler to over his eyes. He had taken the river path by horseback for the last quarter mile, riding silently in the dark with Strax and Sonny for Miss Kate. He was to meet her at the next port, but the Ester had run aground and panic had ensued.

Lord Wilson's special spectacles allowed him to see that the boat's guests were quickly evacuating, even in the darkness, but so far Miss Church was not out. Strax whimpered as Lord Wilson dismounted; he sensed his master's distress. The huge steamer had clearly taken on enough water to sink it. He waited for ten agonizing minutes as the large groups of passengers turned to just a trickle. Miss Church was not among them. He stooped to Strax, "Alright boy, go get her!" he urged. The pit-bull took off through the edge of the woods and into the river.

His pocket watch began to pulse rapidly with a red light, then more slowly. Finally it stopped and the color faded out. Lord Wilson made a decision, one he technically was not qualified to make. He pulled out a different timepiece and hurriedly wound the hands backwards exactly fifteen minutes. He felt sick to his stomach, as dizziness overcame him. He leaned against a nearby tree and closed his eyes for a moment. Then he opened them and inhaled.

Kate was groggy. Her body didn't want to wake up but a persistent and unpleasant sound was making her head ache. It sounded a bit like barking. *Who had a dog?* Her hazy mind drifted, but the sound only grew louder. She could not ignore it. As her eyes opened, Kate felt afloat and indeed she was. Her bed was sifting about the room in three feet of water that teased the edge of her dress. With great effort she sat up to see Strax swimming and barking. "Oh good boy," she cooed woozily. He stopped, satisfied that his mistress had finally awoken.

She heard the yells of passengers and crew as the massive boat shifted uneasily. She looked round to see that her bag was gone. So was Mr. Whitney. *Oh what happened to Mr. Whitney?* She remembered he had taken her to the cabin but then what? It didn't matter now, the water was rising quickly. She would drown if she stayed.

Kate slid into the invading cold river water. It jilted her awake in a most horrible fashion. A large bureau had bounced into the cabin door after Strax had come in. The hefty piece of furniture knocked the door haphazardly off its hinge, partially blocking the doorway. Kate swam to it but couldn't get a decent grip on the latch. The influx of water kept pushing her back. Fortunately she'd packed her pistol and whip to her thigh. She reached under her floating skirt to procure her trusted tool.

The first time she cracked the whip, she hit the outer door frame, missing the handle. But on the second try she'd braced herself on the bedpost and the whip curled tightly around the door latch. Kate pulled herself to the doorway and was able to force it open just enough for her and Strax to swim through.

Water poured into the hallway as trunks, baggage, and furniture tumbled about. Kate knew they were close to the exit to the deck. But still, in the short distance to the exit, she sustained massive bruises as the floating pieces hit her violently. Strax had locked his jaw onto her laces as Kate pulled them both out onto the deck. Only the top of the rail was above water. Kate hobbled over it, taking her faithful canine with her.

Fortunately her side of the Ester faced the closer shoreline. With a few strokes in the river she felt the sand under her feet and was able to get aground. The crew were helping a few people just a bit up the shoreline. It was dark; Kate wouldn't be seen. She sat for a moment on the sandbar as Strax licked her face. "Good boy, good boy!" she whispered.

"Yes indeed he is." Kate was startled that Lord Wilson had found them. "Shhh…come now. Into the woods." He helped Kate up; they strode into the dark foliage and paused at the horses once they were out of sight. "Miss Kate, what the devil happened?"

"I was drugged by Mr. Whitney. Then the ship ran aground, I think. But I have the key." Kate spoke wearily. She turned the heel of her shoe and plucked the key from its hiding place.

"Well done Miss Kate." Lord Wilson encouraged. "And to our fellow Strax. I was almost ready to come after you, but I was certain he could find you much more quickly. Are you alright?" He pulled a blanket from her horse.

"I got out just in time. I'm a little battered and cold." She was indeed shivering; Lord Wilson could feel her tremble as he wrapped her. "Let's get you back and into some dry clothes." Deep inside he was elated she hadn't drowned. He was literally at the water's edge when she popped out the exit. Now he had to keep her from freezing.

They mounted and rode down to the landing where the Ester was supposed to have docked. Word had just reached those waiting to board of the steamer's unfortunate wreck. In the bustle of confused workers and guests, Lord Wilson, Kate, and Strax were barely noticed as they hitched their horses to a waiting open shipping wagon. He lifted Kate and Strax in the back. Kate was briefly reminded of the night they first met in Iris. How a star-filled sky had mesmerized her and led her to a destiny she couldn't have ever imagined.

They rode off until they were out of earshot, then Lord Wilson finally spoke. "There's some fresh clothes and more blankets in that trunk. We can stop if we must, but you need to get out of those wet clothes. I promise I'll be a gentleman."

"Keep going." Kate sighed. "I'll dress under the blanket." There were only men's clothes in the trunk, but that would suit her just as well. She struggled out of the soaked dress and despite the bumpy river road, was properly attired within a few minutes.

"I'm finished," she said quietly, as the fresh clothes warmed her.

Lord Wilson had to bury the desire to glance at Kate. He cleared his throat. "Very well then. There's a canteen with water and some bread in that trunk also. Why don't you rest then? I'll wake you. We should be at the grounds in about an hour." Lord Wilson cooed to his lovely charge, grateful that not only had she completed her mission, but she was alive. He was starting to regret sending her off into these situations.

"Thank you, rest I will then." Kate pulled fresh blankets over her and Strax and soon fell into a well-earned slumber. In a short while, Lord Wilson was on the main road to Lafayette Square and was able to pick up speed to carry them home in record time.

Back at the Ester, Mr. Whitney's body was caught in the roots of some fallen trees a few feet under water. But he hadn't drowned. A bullet hole dotted his forehead. Kate's purse was now in the hands of another.

Boston

Mrs. Ellis wrapped a velvet shawl around her shoulders. The November cold of Boston did not agree with her even though her London heritage made her more than familiar with wet, chilly weather. Neither did being newly widowed, and receiving word that the third most important key was now in the hands of the Society, bode well with her. The telegram had been veiled in code, but the message was clear. The American they'd chosen to aid them in securing the key had failed. The third Ellis son had dispatched of Mr.

Whitney and would remain in St. Louis until further orders would come.

Her face bore a nasty snarl as she rolled some tobacco into the telegram and smoked it. She puffed with disdain as she crumpled Mr. Ellis's fake death certificate, marked as Mr. Reed, and pitched it into the fire. The words on the document weren't real, but Mr. Ellis's demise at the hands of Miss Church was. The blaze roared briefly at its feeding. The remaining ember of her unplanned cigarette came to her leather gloved fingertips. She pinched it out with a small hiss.

Mrs. Ellis tried to comfort herself that her second son was now deeply embedded in the Society and her first born was soon to join him. But first Cecil, the eldest Ellis son, was recovering from a successful mission about ten miles outside of Boston proper. He'd exacted the revenge his mother so wanted. Ferris and Abby Tomley and their two servants were dead.

"An eye for an eye." Mrs. Ellis cackled and stoked the fire. The reflection of the flames flicked over her good eye and in the ruby red ring that had recently been refilled with an astute poison.

The next morning Lord Wilson arose to news from Dr. Finch that Miss Kate was recovering well from her unexpected swim. He was dressed even before Leeds came to wake him, even though he'd only slept a couple of hours. "Leeds, please summon Dr. Harrington to a short breakfast Discussion."

"Yes Sir." Leeds hurried down to rouse an important Member of Wilson Manor. But Dr. Harrington was also already awake in the cellar of the Wilson estate. He was going over a series of machines, tinkering and adjusting. This particular set of instruments was regularly hidden from view. Even the Leeds and Kate, did not know of their existence.

Within the half hour, the two gentlemen of Wilson Manor were enjoying a light breakfast.

"So it worked?" The young Dr. Harrington grinned under his thin mustache.

"Yes, splendidly so. The extra timepiece turned back perfectly." Lord Wilson returned his Member's enthusiasm. "No word of any disasters? Changes?"

"None, Sir. Not one anywhere in the world. Although I'm still waiting to hear from a smattering of other offices when they awake."

"Well done, Sir. Well done." Lord Wilson slapped the shoulder of his assistant with gusto. "Did you feel it?"

"Only a moment where I thought for sure I'd made a notation on an experiment. But I definitely remember the equipment coming to life." Dr. Harrington paused and his voice turned a bit somber. "And Miss Church?"

"Recovering. I will see her later today." Lord Wilson took a pleasing stab at a thick sausage on his plate. "No one but Director Roth will hear of this."

"Of course, Sir. Excellent news, Sir."

"It is. You Sir, are a life saver." Lord Wilson finished his breakfast and shook the hand of his protégé. "I cannot be more grateful." Truer words couldn't have been spoken, because Kate Church had died the night before.

All had seemed lost in the darkness for the Ester, but someone had signaled the captain in time to avoid the heaviest part of the sandbar.

That help came from Lord Wilson, who had just the right equipment to take a subtle action that caused a far larger reaction.

The steamboat had run aground, but took on about five feet less than it had fifteen minutes before, when the water had been high enough to drown Miss Church before Strax could reach her. No one on the ship would remember the wrinkle in time.

The Ester had miraculously been saved, the damage much less than expected and was towed from the sand. However, time travel or not, fate caught up with the beloved steamer later that winter, when she hit a snag from which she would not recover.

Thanks to the brilliant mind of Dr. Harrington, Kate would live on. She rose late the next day feeling unusually blessed, as if she had been given a second chance. Indeed she had.

9 A NIGHT AT THE OPERA

On a cold grey December mid-morning, as Kate mulled over a study of rapier weaponry, the familiar sound of an Invitation sliding into her desk basket drew her eyes away from her studies. Just as common to her, was the red "W" imprint in the wax seal on the envelope. Kate leapt from her desk to read it:

'Dear Miss Kate:

Engagement this evening at 5:30pm. Dress like an elegant lady, we will masquerade as the espoused Lord and Lady Carrington. Rest today; it will be a long evening at the Opera and then of Investigation and Observation. Costume to arrive at 3:30 p.m.

Sincerely,

W."

Kate's heart was warmed and was instantly curious. It had been almost a month since the near disaster on the Ester. After several days of ordered rest, Lord Wilson let the Engagements fly. Kate had two to three simple tasks a week. Each Discussed and implemented in between her studies.

She would only visit the interior of the Manor once a week, usually on Sunday for dinner and chess. "I would like for you to be more independent Miss Kate," Lord Wilson urged.

Secretly, after almost losing her forever, he could not bear to have Kate in such close approximation for long periods of time. He feared not being able to love her in public would drive him mad. So for now, meeting socially once a week with her felt proper. He would cherish those dinners for the remainder of the days, but managed to compartmentalize his feelings otherwise.

The rest of the day would drag in anticipation for Kate. She had a simple lunch in the Main Parlor; some turkey with a sweet grainy bread spread with butter and grape jam, and tea with milk and two teaspoons of sugar. The room was filled with Members and conversation, but she did not hear a word. She was imagining what an opera would be like with Lord Wilson, her "husband", Lord Carrington, for the eve.

These types of Engagements were not usually performed by non-married Members of the Society, but the shortage of female recruits and active Members made it necessary at this time. Senior Member males were well educated on proper behavior with their Senior or Active female counterparts. Any relations or distractions could jeopardize a critical Engagement and result in serious losses of life or information, especially during an Observation. A Member needed to be especially watchful at such times.

Kate returned to her room and napped restlessly until Miss Beatrice knocked at 3:30 p.m. "Miss Church, I have your costume ready." She entered the room and placed the tissue wrapped garments and two boxes on the bed. She gently opened a blue velvet coat with a matching bustled skirt and waist sash. The larger of the two boxes held freshly polished black boots. The smaller, when opened, revealed thick dark woolen tights, black bloomers, several large strands of pearls with matching teardrop earrings, silken opera length gloves, a soft black velvet hat with an oversized blue plume and a velveteen bag with a slight bulge. Another knock at the door and a second attendant brought in a large mink coat. Kate was stunned at the rich clothing. "Accouterments meant for a fine lady, let us dress, Miss Church."

For the next ninety minutes the attendant styled Kate appropriately, giving her a generous pompadour with ringlets at the sides of her cheeks. The outfit fit well and brushed softly against her skin. The pearls draped neatly over her breasts. Kate felt different: wealthy, strong, and powerful.

"Now Miss Church, I am told there are items you must review in your bag. I will leave now to allow you that opportunity. Be safe Miss." The attendant shut the door quietly behind her.

Kate peeked into the lovely small purse. The bag contained an ornate and heavy set of opera glasses, a note, and a brilliant emerald ring. The note was strict and simple, "We will have Discussion and information on the glasses during the carriage ride. Wear the ring over your glove on your wedded ring finger. Act like an elegant lady and be alert for Observation. The weather is quite cold." Kate wrapped herself in the mink and walked quietly to the Main Hall entrance. She did not want to draw any unwarranted attention.

A second mention of Observation and unpleasant weather in the purse note made Kate uneasy. It was likely that they would follow a fellow Member; one capable of deceit and insubordination. She would soon learn that the Member was Miss Fahey.

Madeline Fahey was a rising Member at the Society. She was brilliant from the start; the youngest from a large well-to-do family but slightly rebellious. Madeline had refused her betrothal much to her family's distaste, and chose to attend university instead. She had a penchant for literature, especially historical military actions and conquests. Mr. Roth had heard of her knowledge of strategy, cartography, and gift of languages. He recruited her at the tender age of twenty-three. More importantly, she was a stunning creature and could easily disarm any man interested in her beauty. Miss Fahey was bewitching and used her feminine wiles to her every advantage when allowed and it was deemed necessary.

Madeline was now barely thirty, lean and tall, 5'10" with long black locks, magenta lips and violet eyes that sparkled from pale skin. Even among the few women in the Society she stood apart. Her original Senior Member had wanted to marry her after only a few Engagements, and was denied. He, totally smitten and dejected, shot himself early one morning outside the far reaches of the Garden.

Mr. Roth determined that she was sharp and clever enough to report to him directly. He appointed her to a Specialist position working in the Library, developing plans for securing documents and codes. And if necessary, she would work her charms in order to procure information during Engagements. Supposedly she had such an Engagement at the same opera performance Miss Church and Lord Wilson would be attending.

Precisely at 5:00 p.m., Madeline met with her Driver and headed for the Opera. He was a bit surprised at the sudden addition to the Schedule, but knew that she must have an urgent Engagement for him to be called so quickly.

At precisely 5:30 p.m. Lord Wilson's Driver first assisted Miss Church into his carriage then Lord Wilson himself. "Good evening Lord and Lady Carrington," he greeted and spread a grey woolen blanket over their laps.

"And to you as well," replied Lord Wilson kindly. They looked quite the handsome couple as the dapple grey steed led the carriage into the cold December evening. "Lady Carrington, you are quite beautiful." He looked over her and kissed the shimmery emerald. She blushed and he continued, "I am pleased you could join me."

"And I am as well," she responded politely with warmth in her voice. He was handsome in topcoat and tails. Her heart pattered. And so the Discussion began.

"As you know, we are Observing this evening, watching for the slightest hint of espionage, deceit, or impropriety on the part of another Member. This Member is Miss Fahey."

Kate drew a quiet breath. Miss Fahey was popular among the male Members and her reputation was of a stellar researcher and strategist, yet cagey on Engagements. Rumors abounded that she would use her body as much as her brain, and was just on the verge of breaking the Society rule, *'Do not draw attention to oneself.'*

He started again. "She has many secrets of the Society at her access and has made an Engagement unapproved by her Senior Member. We have a contact with the Opera that has provided us information. She has made a reservation for two for this evening. This contact will recognize us by our names and your ring. He will seat us in the balcony where we can Observe. We believe that she may also have made reservations at the Bixby Hotel. The reservations were made under Lord and Lady Roth, a serious challenge to our Director's reputation and safety. We have similar arrangements in order to follow and detect what we can. We are only to Observe and not act." This was serious business indeed.

He continued the Discussion, "The opera glasses in your bag are twenty times the normal sight strength. You can turn the handle to the right to tighten focus. It will magnify with each click and turn. We each have a pair and our contact will direct our vision to where she is seated. We must be watchful at all times and play our roles carefully; we must not be discovered. Do you understand Lady Carrington?" She smiled at his role playing.

"Yes indeed Lord Carrington," she replied, just as the carriage pulled in front of the Opera House. Miss Fahey had arrived only ten minutes before and had already taken her seat. The Driver crisply pulled the blanket away and assisted the covert Members. Kate and Lord Wilson exited the carriage and walked regally up the stairs, watching the crowd and slipping discreetly into the entrance where ushers opened doors and greeted the incoming audience. The room was loud with cheery voices and the sounds of warm beverages being served.

"Lady Carrington, smooth your hair with your ring finger and turn right," Lord Wilson whispered. Kate lifted her gloved hand and the emerald sparkled enough to catch the attention of the contact, a tall bald usher waiting on the stairs to the balcony.

Just as a host was preparing to ask for tickets and their names for announcements, their contact gently tapped him on the shoulder. He waved them over to the marble stairs on the right side of the Opera House. They passed several other guests down a long corridor of red balcony curtains, the very last of which was theirs. He parted the long tapestries with a wink, "Welcome Lord and Lady Carrington," took their coats, and seated them.

Kate was stunned at the beauty of the House; the red velvet seats, rich wood trim, and gold scrolls lining the walls and well-polished marble floors. Gas lamps glowed like small rising moons above each seat section. The usher gave information in a hushed tone. "See, center aisle, our side, ten rows from the front. She arrived about fifteen minutes ago. She is alone, but there is an empty seat next to her. Part the curtain should you need anything."

And there Madeline Fahey was indeed, in a black dress with lace and satin trimmings. Kate and Lord Wilson pulled out their glasses.

"Do you see anything on her person?" he asked.

"Yes, she has a large black bag that she has placed on the empty seat," Kate replied. "And a smaller one wrapped on her wrist."

"I see it too. Oh look. She's getting up." Miss Fahey arose, stepped into the aisle and left the larger bag behind. "Follow," Lord Wilson simply ordered and remained seated.

"I'm off." Kate stood gracefully, parted the curtain and nodded at the usher. He would also stay; there was a good chance that Madeline was headed for the ladies parlor. Kate walked down the corridor with a pleasant face and was down the stairs to the main hall within a minute. It was just in time to see Madeline go through the opened door of the parlor. Kate waited briefly, she mustn't be seen.

Madeline was keenly aware of competition at the Society and although Kate was lesser ranked, she was older, wiser, and seen as a more appropriate female for both Engagements and possible companionship with a male Member. Madeline was not popular with the other females; she sometimes spoke harshly to others and seemed to create unnecessary drama with false bravado usually reserved for the male Members. It was this sort of behavior that received some covert attention from those higher up in the Society's ranks.

Kate had had only polite conversations with Madeline in the Library and the Ladies Salon at the Society. She remembered their first meeting, in particular because she was so brash. Just a short while after Kate had arrived, she was still recovering from the shooting in Chicago and had gone to the salon for a massage. The scars had just started to fade from her back and ribcage. She was wrapped in a fluffy towel in the steam area, warming her muscles before treatment when Madeline strode in completely naked holding only her towel. Kate politely nodded and turned her head. "Oh you are the new one aren't you? Hello, I'm Miss Fahey," Madeline introduced herself and extended her hand. *How odd*, Kate thought as she tried not to look, but shook her hand. As she lifted her hand,

Kate dropped her towel in error. *Oh this is not going well at all,* she thought, *pull it together.*

"I am Miss Church." Kate returned pleasantries as she bent and gathered her towel.

"What kind of hell have you been through?" Madeline burst incredulously upon seeing her scars.

"Oh, I had a life before here. But that was then and this is now." Kate replied in the standard phrase that was uttered when other Members were too curious about the past.

"Haven't we all?" Madeline twittered in a slightly wicked fashion. "So you are hardly new here?"

"I like to say experienced, somewhat the wiser with time." Kate knew her verbal baiting tactics and would not be lead into divulging.

"You are so coy-" but before Madeline could finish, the attendant arrived to take her to the massage room. The attendant glared at Madeline's outright nudity. Madeline beamed back naughtily. The attendant ignored her and as they exited, Madeline cheerily burst out, "Pleasure meeting you!" It echoed down the hall. Kate and the attendant looked at each other briefly and rolled their eyes. *She is over the top and of high risk,* Kate observed. And she was more than right.

Kate walked into the Ladies Parlor focusing on the task at hand and quietly scanned the lounge. She just caught the backside of Madeline heading into the water closets. As soon as she heard one close, Kate walked in and chose the stall next to hers. Kate heard nothing but urination and the possible snap of a pocket watch. Perhaps she was biding time? The familiar flush and unlocking of the door let her know that Madeline had nothing on her person. But something must be in that bag in the Opera seats. Kate waited a few more moments and returned to the balcony. The contact opened the curtains for his special guest.

"Anything?" Lord Wilson whispered.

"Nothing. Maybe a check of the time, she must be waiting for someone?"

"Yes and there he is." He nodded towards the aisle. A tall, well-groomed man was ushered to the open seat next to Madeline. He was formally dressed in tops and tails. Kate and Wilson adjusted their glasses. The man kissed Madeline's hand as she lifted the bag towards him. She deftly showed him the edges of what appeared to be papers of some sort. "Did you see anything?"

"Yes, papers. Specifically I think architectural drawings. I could just barely see the edge and think I saw a roof and steeple. Possible an interior floor plan," Kate replied confidently. Wilson was amazed at how quickly Kate took to things. He'd seen a bit of building, but she had managed to see some details. Madeline had moved the bag to the floor as her guest sat.

"Well done." Just then the lights dimmed and the opera began. "Keep watching." Lord Wilson whispered. There was very little action during the opera itself. Wilson stole a few secretive looks at Kate. She looked lovely in the glow of the stage. He wondered if she'd been to an opera before. She was so focused and intent on her task; he liked her dedication and tenacity. These were the reasons he had brought her to the Society in the first place. But a small pang of romantic interest stirred deep in his soul.

Miss Fahey and her companion were quite still until almost the very end. Her hand slid off her lap and onto her companion's leg. Madeline then leaned in ever so slightly and whispered to him.

"Did you see that?" Kate noted.

"Yes." Lord Wilson replied. The lights came up and Madeline quickly got up with her companion. He grabbed the oversized bag from under her seat.

"Quick!" Lord Wilson jumped up and parted the curtain. Their usher had their coats readied and they hurried down to beat the crowds to the carriages. They were at the top of the stairs just in time to see them heading out the entrance. Wilson and Kate swiftly made their way down and outside. Their driver was further back and they walked to him instead of waiting; they did not want to follow too closely. A light snow had covered the ground and sparkled white in the gas lamps. They were soon on their way to the Bixby, with Madeline none the wiser that she was being followed.

The Bixby was just a few blocks away. Wilson and Kate waited around the corner until Madeline and her companion were in the hotel lobby and their driver had pulled away to the stables. They then went to the Grace Inn, a less extravagant hotel, across the street from the Bixby.

The Grace had the feel of a hunting lodge, with mounted heads of various animal prizes on the walls of the foyer and into the small main hall which was empty. Wilson only nodded to the desk clerk. He replied "You can sign in here Lord Carrington," but instead of offering the hotel log he simply slid it back in the counter drawer.

"Kate wait here at the door, be watchful." Lord Wilson ordered as walked back out. He crossed the street with an observant eye and strode into the Bixby. He addressed the desk clerk in a disarming fashion, "Hello, perhaps you can help me. I sat with our neighbors at the opera, a Mr. and Mrs. Roth, and they left behind their glasses. Would it be possible for you to please take this to their room?"

"Oh so sorry Sir, the Roths have checked into their room and did not wish to be disturbed," the clerk explained. "But may I put the glasses in a safe place behind the counter?"

"Absolutely," Lord Wilson replied as the clerk took a small worthless pair of glasses and slid them into a mailbox for room 410. And with a quick "Thank you sir," the Society Member was out the door, but he didn't cross the street.

Instead, Lord Wilson went around the corner and knocked over several large buckets of rubbish then stood behind the edge of the neighboring building. He made quite the commotion. Of course the clerk came out and went into the alley. He cursed aloud at the apparent mess a bum had made. Meanwhile Lord Wilson had slid back into the Bixby and had taken the glasses back from the room 410 mailbox. The night clerk had successfully been distracted and wouldn't remember to tell the Roths that they had forgotten their glasses.

Lord Wilson strode into the Grace, entered, and nodded to the clerk "410". The clerk handed them a room key, "It's 511 Sir. I'll have some tea and scones brought up in a moment. I'll be at the desk should you need anything."

Lord Wilson and Kate went up to the room taking a petite lift made of intricate iron. Wilson spoke quietly as they went. "We should have a direct line of sight into their room. We may be lucky enough to see what they are planning if they leave the curtains open." Lord Wilson opened the gate and they went straight to the room without a sound. He adjusted a lamp and surveyed the room quickly. It was very simple, a single bed, a nightstand, two chairs with a low table at the window and a minute washstand and mirror over a basic fireplace already in use. He opened the curtains. It was a bit chilly and as Wilson stoked the fire, there was a knock, two short raps followed by three longer ones.

Lord Wilson motioned to Kate and she answered; their clerk had their tea and snacks. They would need them for the long evening to come, it was already 11 p.m. The clerk instructed with caution, "The water closet is down the hall and to the left."

"Thank you," Kate replied. She put their tray on the low table and closed the door as Lord Wilson adjusted the chairs at the window. He took their coats and hung them on the backside of the door, then pulled their glasses out of her bag. They sat and so a small Discussion began.

"This may be long Kate, but please do what you need to in order to stay awake. We can have more tea if necessary. We'll use our opera glasses to Observe. Their room at the Bixby should be easily viewed from here. We must try to determine what they have. If it becomes tedious, we can take turns. Will you please pour the tea?"

"Of course," Kate replied and offered Lord Wilson a cup, then poured one for herself. Suddenly activity drew their attention to the Bixby. Curtains were opened and there in a fully gas-lit room stood Miss Fahey and her companion. She was turning to a nightstand and opening her oversized bag. The companion had tied aside one of the curtains. Wilson and Kate could clearly see into the room through their glasses. They had already removed their coats and appeared to be ready to conduct business.

Madeline sat on the bed and pulled out the same paperwork that was observed at the Opera. She unfurled the large pages on the bed. Again they could see it was architectural drawings, but of what? Her companion took them from her and put them back into the bag. He then handed her a brown leather satchel from which she counted several large stacks of money. When finished, Madeline set her cash aside.

"This is horrifying," Lord Wilson commented with a snarl. "This might be it, be prepared to follow. We need to try and find out who this person is." But he was wrong, as Lord Wilson stood, the situation across the way changed. They would not be leaving so soon. The companion had pulled Madeline off the bed and into a deep embrace, kissing her passionately. She clutched his back then pulled away suddenly to remove his suspenders and crisp white shirt. The buttons nearly burst off with her enthusiasm.

Lord Wilson was quite stunned at the turn of events. "This is not good at all." He sat back down in his chair.

Madeline and her companion were quickly and passionately undressing each other, not caring that they could be seen so easily through the open window. Kate looked at the street below for a brief moment; it was abandoned and the neighborhood was asleep, oblivious to the action at the Bixby. But Kate and Lord Wilson were well aware, both becoming uncomfortably so. The companion, only in his trousers, had pulled off Madeline's dress to reveal lacy black undergarments. He unlaced her corset and her pert breasts popped over the top side as it fell to the floor. He threw her onto the bed and tore her garter and stockings off. Her black hair had come undone and contrasted sharply with the white sheets on the bed. She, now completely naked, looked at him knowingly, through her violet eyes. He dropped his trousers to reveal a thick muscular body and a rapidly hardening groin. He pulled her ankles to his shoulders and not so much made love to her as thrust at her like a captain harpooning a sea serpent. He was rough and Madeline was grasping onto the sheets and one of the bed posts as he took her. This was unexpected. "Miss Kate, please, look away," Lord Wilson muttered in disgust. "There is no need for you to see this."

"Yes Sir." Kate was completely stunned at the turn of events at the Bixby. She got up from her chair at the window and sat at the edge of the bed facing the fireplace, watching the flames lick along the logs. *What would happen? What an act of treason.* She sat bone straight and nibbled nervously on a scone. Across the room Lord Wilson shifted uneasily in his chair. The tension in the room mounted.

"Miss Kate, why don't you try to rest for a while? I can wake you if necessary." Lord Wilson looked at her somberly, trying to gauge her reaction to the atrocity. She blushed.

"I will—I need to use the facilities." Kate responded softly and left the room for the water closet. As she walked down the hall, her head spun, not quite believing what she had seen.

Meanwhile Lord Wilson watched as the companion had flipped Madeline on all fours taking her from behind. He started smacking her bottom violently, leaving red welts and she bit onto the sheets so as not to scream. Lord Wilson was somewhat repelled, but could not stop watching the repulsive act. The companion pulled Madeline's hair, thrust harder and then suddenly climaxed on her backside. He pulled her back over, rudely collapsed on top of her and crudely wiped his brow and groin with the sheet they lay on. Wilson was grateful that Miss Kate was not present. He poured another cup of tea and attempted to eat a scone.

After a soft knock at the door, Kate reentered the room. It was now almost 1 a.m. Wilson nodded towards the bed. Kate sat completely on the other side of the bed for a moment, pulled a pillow towards her, and exhausted at the long day, fell asleep fully dressed on top of the sheets.

At the Bixby, Madeline and her companion washed briefly and climbed into bed with each other after turning off the lights. And so Lord Wilson sat until he heard Miss Kate's breathing steady as she fell into slumber. Lord Wilson stood, walked across the room, pulled a blanket from the end of the bed and gently covered her like a child. Her face was angelic in the firelight. He wondered for a moment how it would be with her. If he could marry her and be her lover, it would be different, he was sure. He would give her pleasure, but would love and respect her.

Kate had been so headstrong, so independent yet physically and emotionally wounded when he had recruited her. Yet she had become a compliant and eager student. She had revealed only one lover to him. Would he be able to satisfy her, to get her to love him? He had hoped that she would be his permanent companion at the Society, but there were never any guarantees. Lord Wilson shook his head at his foolishness, tossed another log on the fire and sat back at the window until 4 a.m. He then gently shook Kate awake. She would need to learn to stay alert and be observant, unfortunately. "Miss Kate?" he touched her shoulder.

"Yes." She sat up quickly and rubbed her eyes.

"Your turn to watch, they're sleeping, so just let me know when they awake," he instructed her. Lord Wilson stepped out for a moment, going down the stairs to inform the desk clerk and their driver of the change in plans. They would most likely remain the rest of the night but leave early. Kate wiped a bit of water on her face, tidied her hair, and clothing then sat at the window. She had known men like Madeline's companion in Texas. They were truly wicked, but what shocked her more is how much Madeline seemed to enjoy the pain. She did not understand it, but reminded herself that humans were animals, and it was not her job to judge. She kept watch on the now quiet hotel.

Lord Wilson returned, they grimaced at each other silently and he rested on the bed. He wondered how disturbed Miss Kate was. Surely she knew evil like this existed, but had she ever seen anything like that before? He did not look forward to having that Discussion. He drifted into a brief sleep and awoke to Kate's gently tapping on his shoulder, it was 5:30 a.m.

"Lord Wilson, there appears to be some movement across the street," Kate briskly informed. Wilson jumped up quickly as Kate handed him his glasses. They stood at the window looking at the Bixby. Miss Fahey and her companion were washing and dressing. It had started snowing again.

"Quickly Miss Kate." Lord Wilson rushed, grabbing their coats. He wiped his face while she carried the bags. They stole out of the Grace, with quick discreet looks at the desk clerk. He in turn signaled their Driver.

"Good Morning Lord and Lady Carrington." Their Driver greeted pleasantly considering the hour. He again wrapped a blanket on their laps and offered them hot tea. Kate eagerly took a cup and Wilson proceeded to give him instructions.

"Miss Fahey and her companion will exit. If leaving together, it will hopefully be an easy follow. If they separate, we need to follow the man." They waited around the corner of the Grace, the Driver acting as lookout. He signaled and jumped up to his seat. He almost had slipped in the fresh snow which was now falling harder than before.

"Two carriages Sir, and the companion has a large black bag." He informed them and they started their pursuit. Miss Fahey's carriage was already leaving in the direction of the Society Grounds. The companion's was just pulling away from the Bixby in the opposite direction. Their Driver started very slowly after, but tried to pick up pace. The snow was now falling heavily, the streets were slippery, and it was becoming very difficult for anyone to see in the early morning darkness of winter. Even with lights on the carriages, it was dangerous to be traveling in the onslaught of blizzard conditions. "Sir, I'm losing him." The Driver shouted as they turned a corner and the carriage slid sideways a few feet. The horse whinnied and snorted and Kate fell into Lord Wilson's lap. White-out conditions had taken over, snow was blowing into the carriage and even Lord Wilson was having trouble seeing the Driver. He wrapped the blanket tightly around Kate and kept her on his lap.

"Alright then, go back to the Grounds, let's try to avoid Ms. Fahey." Lord Wilson yelled as the winds howled. "What a mess." he looked disappointedly at Kate. "Are you cold?" he said kindly, their faces close in the freeze.

"I am alright." Her cheeks were pink and her eyes sparkled despite the lack of sleep. His hands were deep in the fur of her coat, embracing her. *What a trooper*, he thought; almost no sleep, forced to watch an obscene act, and now trying not to freeze to death. She did not complain, not a bit.

The Driver turned the carriage and headed back to the Grounds. The snow continued to fall heavily. Lord Wilson instructed Kate quietly and sternly breaking the small romantic spell between them. "When we arrive, we'll come in the side door and the Driver will head for the stables. Go straight to your room, avoid other Members if at all possible. I'll have an attendant bring your breakfast. Then rest for the day. We'll have a brief Discussion in the Garden at 4:30 p.m. No one must know of this. Understood?"

"Yes of course," Kate replied, realizing the seriousness of what had happened overnight. The snow lightened with the dawn as they pulled onto the Grounds and into the stables at 7 a.m. The Driver quickly assisted them from the carriage and helped them inside. Lord Wilson whispered to the attending stable porter who immediately took their coats and hats.

"Lady Carrington it has been my pleasure." Lord Wilson acted out one last scene of the espionage.

"And mine as well Lord Carrington," replied Kate sweetly.

He pulled her close and whispered, "Hurry Miss Kate, be careful and confidential. Not a word, it looks to be quite cold today.

Rest well, good day." His eyes embraced her with sincerity, he kissed her gloved hand and turned towards the offices.

Kate scurried to her room. Only a few moments passed before her attendant knocked and quietly entered with some hot tea, biscuits and eggs. Miss Beatrice helped Miss Church undress and Kate ate without word, as she was suddenly so very hungry. The attendant turned down the bed, turned up the heat, took her dishes, nodded to Miss Church, and left. Kate tucked into bed and fell into a deep slumber. The attendant would return with snacks and fresh clothes at 3:30 p.m. and Kate's pocket watch would pulse at 4:25 p.m. reminding her of her Discussion with Lord Wilson. As she prepared for her latest Discussion, part of her wondered if last night had really been just a chaotic dream.

10 THE GARDEN IS FED

Madeline Fahey counted her money under a blanket in her carriage as her Driver wondered what kind of mission she'd been on that had kept her overnight. He had no idea of the trouble she had started. The snowstorm delayed them on their return from the Bixby and Miss Fahey did not take her Driver's concern of the weather too kindly.

"What do you mean we have to stop?" She demanded in a vile rant.

"The snow is too thick, Miss. We'd be stuck anyway." The Driver panted over the driving snow. The winds pelted his face like sheets of cold metal.

"If we must then," Madeline acquiesced.

Just a few minutes later, when visibility had been completely lost, they were forced to stop at a roadside inn. It was not in the best area of town. A few bums were passed out in the wispy corners of the new fallen snow. Madeline held her bag in a viselike grip. She had earned this money. No one was going to take it from her.

As her Driver made arrangements at the inn, Madeline recalled the evening before. She held her breath for a moment and grimaced. The man who fucked her was only supposed to take the plans for the Society grounds. She hadn't agreed to sleep with him. But she did what she believed was necessary, anything to get away from the restrictive Society.

An unknown contact inside the Society had sent her a note just two weeks before. When it dropped into her basket, Madeline expected an Invitation from Director Roth. Later contacts were made through discreet notes in the Library.

"Oh Director Roth. What a fool you are," Madeline murmured. She believed she had him whipped. Once she finished training, she'd made sure she reported to him directly because the Senior she'd been assigned to, Larimore Stills, was an incredible sap.

Madeline won over the weak-minded and bookish Mr. Stills with her charms, but she planned to be rid of him as soon as possible. She tempted him from the first day under his tutelage. "Darling Larimore, why must we play these silly games?" She cooed at him during their first Discussion.

"Miss Madeline! You know you are not to call me by my first name. And how ever did you find out about it?" He tried to sound angry, but his heart couldn't bear to be cruel to her.

"Oh does it really matter? This foolishness about pecking order only makes people feel unworthy." Madeline managed to sound both dejected and haughty at the same time. Her eyes were soft but her nose upturned.

"Miss Madeline, you are most worthy. You know you were chosen to be here. But you must call me Mr. Stills, at least for now. Would you please?"

"Well, when we're alone like this, does it not feel childish to you?" Madeline reached over their Garden bench and touched his hand. "It's impersonal." She fluttered her eyes as she whispered.

"Hmm." Mr. Stills had risen to a Senior Member based on his vast knowledge of accounting, not experience. He was unmatched for the feminine wiles of Madeline Fahey. "Alright. But only when we're alone. We pass outside these walls, it's Mr. Stills to you."

"Oh thank you, Larimore. I knew you'd see that this is not kind. What a dear you are." And so their Discussion never really began. Rather, it floundered terribly.

They only had one Engagement. Madeline was supposed to drop off a bag of cash to a proprietor of a small café as she and Mr. Stills enjoyed a cup of tea. They arrived without incident to their rendezvous.

"May I take your coat?" Their host offered.

"Oh yes, delightfully so," Madeline twittered loudly. "I just love this small café."

Mr. Stills was so aghast at her chatter that he almost forgot to give his own coat to their host. Once seated, he finally started to speak. Mr. Stills cleared his throat. "Miss Madeline-"

"What a lovely day to be out. Isn't this exciting?" She interrupted him with an ooze of charm.

"Miss Madeline. Stop," he tried to hiss under his breath.

"Oh so sorry. Don't mean to be a bother." Madeline pretended to mope as the server brought their tea. This was supposed to be her signal to make her money drop. But she didn't move. Instead she stirred her drink listlessly.

After a few moments Mr. Stills began to panic. He nudged her knee under the table.

"Oww, damn, now why on earth would you do such a thing?" She cursed lightly.

"Miss Madeline, remember your task." He frowned.

"Humph, if you insist." She finally rose and took two steps away before remembering she needed her handbag. Mr. Stills tried to ignore her forgetfulness and attempted to focus on sipping his tea. She slid to the counter of the café and approached the cashier. She looked over her shoulder and winked at Mr. Stills. He in turn, spilled tea on his new suit.

"Sir, can you tell me if you have a powder room at your fine establishment? Oh and I think I'd like one of these candies. I'm certain you wouldn't mind if I tried one." Madeline cooed as she placed a peppermint in between her velvety lips. "Um, delicious I must say."

The cashier was alarmed. His contact was to ask for the ladies facilities and then hand him a small paper bag without a word. He gulped and said nothing, for he wasn't supposed to speak.

"So silly of me, I should pay for that." Madeline lacked subtlety as she dug in to her purse and finally popped the small bag of money onto the counter. "Thank you so much for your hospitality." She crowed and finally headed for the restroom.

Mr. Stills was frozen in his seat. He'd overheard ever single bit of the extensive and unnecessary chatter. He was worried for their safety now. Almost anyone there could've seen the exchange. He clutched his cup so tightly that the tea inside began to shake in the wake of his straining hand. He dare not look in the direction of the cashier.

Meanwhile the cashier had never moved so fast to hide something from the counter top. He began to vigorously wipe down the bar as if his life depended on it. He purposefully looked down to avoid any possible eye contact with anyone in the café.

Five minutes passed. Then ten. Finally Madeline returned to the table. Mr. Stills had worried that Madeline had bolted. When she sat, Madeline acted as if nothing was wrong and went straight to drinking her tea with a forced grin.

Mr. Stills exhaled. "Finish and we leave." His voice was as dry as kindling wood.

"Alright then," Madeline purred. After a few seconds of silence, she complained, "I've had better than this sludge they're serving here."

"Now Miss Madeline, now." Mr. Stills spoke through clenched teeth. "Not another word." He stood and their host brought their coats. They walked outside in silence. Their ride approached and assisted them in. As they started off, Madeline dared to speak, but he cut her off. "Not a word Miss Madeline. Hush."

About halfway back to the Society grounds, Madeline knew exactly what she was doing. She feigned a good cry. It started as a silent tear. Then some sniffles. Finally she wracked with sobs.

"Good God, what is it?" Mr. Stills stammered.

"You know I only want to please you. I-I haven't been given much opportunity to be with a man like you before." Madeline soaked her handkerchief. "You know I want to help, Larimore."

"Miss Madeline, please stop." He pulled his own cloth and handed it to her. "You did, well, alright. We just need to be more careful next time. You never know who'll be watching."

"Well you didn't say thank you. How was I to know I did well?" Madeline continued to let the tears fall.

"Miss Madeline, you know we are to Discuss things later. Calm down now, please. And remember you have to call me Mr. Stills. Alright?" His voice came out sweeter than even he expected.

"Well alright then." Madeline faked a smile.

"Now there's my girl. Trust me, things will get easier. We'll have a Discussion tonight. I can move it to the Main Hall instead of the Garden. Would that help?" He caved to her.

"Oh yes Mr. Stills, yes Sir."

"That's better then. I know you'll get the hang of this." Mr. Stills tried to ignore the pinch in his side. Perhaps all the stress had gotten to him.

Later that eve they met in the Main Hall just inside the parlor.

"This is more appropriate don't you think?" Madeline's violet eyes sparkled at her Senior and teased him further.

"This will be the only time we can do this here. And we'll make it quick. You did a fine job today Miss Madeline, but there's much more room for improvement." Mr. Stills tried to encourage his charge.

"Well then, so I can at least pass muster." She turned her head away but teased with a wicked side glance back. "I really can do much better I assure you."

"Oh, of course you can Miss. Really. You know, if you make good progress-" Mr. Still's voice quieted, "We can be together, always."

"Really?" Madeline continued to play the ingénue.

"Well sure. And you'd get to live with me, upstairs. On the third floor." He then let his secrets loose, including his room number, a major infraction on her Senior's part. He finished with a quick, "Now we mustn't tell anyone. You understand don't you?"

"Of course, Mr. Stills." She responded to him properly, letting him believe that he'd gotten through to her. Instead the wheels of a dastardly plan churned in her mind.

"Very well then. I will see you tomorrow. Good night Miss Madeline." He rose and assisted her from the table.

"Good night Mr. Stills." Madeline strolled away, confident that she had Mr. Stills wrapped around her finger.

That night Madeline allowed her attendant to help her prepare for bed. The moment her assistant left, Madeline pulled out her most revealing negligee and covered herself with a coat. Most of the Main Hall was asleep. She had worked out the code for the lift for the third floor after Mr. Stills revealed it had something to do with the birth of their nation. 1776 was indeed the correct sequence to take Madeline to the regulated and secretive third floor. In short order she found the men's wing and Mr. Still's room. Madeline held her breath and knocked as quietly as possible. Much to her delight he answered the door almost immediately.

"I am not in need-oh Madeline." He was shocked at her presence. "You shouldn't be here, but come in." He pulled her arm. "Please tell me you are not in trouble." He gushed once they were inside with the door closed behind them.

"I don't think we should wait." Madeline let her coat fall aside.

Mr. Stills was weak. He was under his charge's spell and she used her power to completely disarm him. He made love to her gently, especially since she hadn't been with a man before. He took to her slowly with kindness.

When his face was buried in her breast, Mr. Stills did not see Madeline's eyes rolling in exasperation. Mr. Stills was far from her first lover. In fact he was closer to her fifteenth, even despite her young age. Every moment with him had been a lie.

Madeline hated men like him. She liked a firm hand, even enjoying spankings as a child. So she misbehaved at every opportunity. And once into adulthood, she thoroughly enjoyed being incredibly naughty.

Afterwards, Madeline left Mr. Stills, certain that she had her claws embedded into his very soul. Now she would use him to move up to more powerful, stronger men. She had enough information to use Mr. Stills to rise up in the Society without him. *It would take a little work,* she assured herself as she tucked into bed much later than her attendant believed.

But things progressed much more quickly than even Madeline could have expected. For the next morning, Larimore Stills strode in Director Roth's office full of pride and argument. Instead of winning Madeline's hand, Mr. Stills received a strict rebuke and immediate suspension. He was quarantined to his room for thirty days. Madeline Fahey would be assigned to another Senior after a few days of intense study alone.

One day and one night alone in his room crushed Mr. Stills. He did not eat or sleep. He could not live without Madeline; she had convinced him of that. So before dawn, on the second day of his suspension, Mr. Larimore Stills pulled his pistol from his desk, strolled out of the Main Hall, and about 100 yards outside the furthest edge of the Garden, shot himself in the head.

Later that day, Madeline was summoned to the Director's office. She wasn't told that Mr. Stills hadn't expired, only that he had moved due to insubordination.

Madeline managed to hide her happiness. She could now aim directly for the top.

After a short Discussion, Madeline convinced Director Roth that she should report to him directly. "He put me in danger, can't you see? Why should I be placed with someone of a much lesser caliber? Goodness, I wonder what horrifying plans he would have had for me." Madeline winced, pretending to be scared.

"Agreed, Miss Madeline. You have excellent skills that are of great use here. I would be happy to be your Senior and apologize for this unwanted attention from Mr. Stills. Please know that he has been dealt with. Any further direction and education will be professional," Mr. Roth assured her.

Director Roth was true to his word. He was kind, yet direct. Madeline flirted with him mercilessly at first. But when he deflected all her attempts at attention, she took a different tack and appealed to his intelligence. He was made of sterner stuff than Mr. Stills. He didn't fall for her over the top feminine graces. She quickly became one of his favorites, brimming with information and detailed ideas that could be implemented by others. But after a year, no offer of marriage came from the Director.

When Madeline tried to broach the subject, she was met with almost no emotion from her Senior. That day burned a hole in Madeline. She would never forget being called to his office for Discussion. The Invitation was polite, referring to her first year tenure at the Society. *Surely he will want me,* Madeline smiled as she strode to his quarters. *How could he refuse?*

"May I join you Director Roth?" She entered the room after a polite knock.

He stood and waved his hand to the chair in front of his desk. "Please do."

With early disappointment, Madeline noted he didn't want to be seated next to her on the sofa near the window. Little did Madeline know that the spot was already reserved for a woman she hadn't or wouldn't ever know anything about. Meredith Pratt understood her place in the Society, and had never had to push for it.

And so the Discussion began. "Miss Madeline, as you know,

you have been at the Society for over a year. After a rough start, I have been impressed by your studies and work. I am proud to announce that not only are you considered a full Member, but a Specialist. I'm going to assign you to the Library for strategic, top secret research. You will be promoted to private quarters on the third floor." Director Roth grinned. "Congratulations."

Madeline was speechless. And incredibly angry. But only the clenching of her bag could've betrayed her true emotion. "Oh thank you, Sir."

"You deserved it, Miss Madeline. I am proud to call you my Member."

"So I will still report to you then?" Madeline tried to hide her worry. She didn't want to be assigned to someone lesser. Not when she had managed to get to the top so quickly.

"Of course. But, you are strong enough to work without supervision. I will occasionally Discuss or Engage with you as needed. Again, congratulations on your new rank." Mr. Roth leaned back in his chair.

"Thank you Sir. Thank you so very much." Madeline rose and he stood, as if only it was a formality and not because she was a lady that deserved his respect. They shook hands and Madeline left.

Once the door closed, one of Mr. Roth's secretive shelves pulled aside to reveal Meredith Pratt. "May I join you?" Her face stern with her lips in a firm line.

"Of course." Mr. Roth began his second Discussion in only ten minutes. "And your opinion?"

"She's dangerous. Be glad she's on our side, at least for now." Meredith spoke with candor and a directness that Director Roth had always favored. "You were wise not to pair her with anyone else. See how she does on her own for a while. The loss of Mr. Stills was odd. I mean, they were probably mismatched from the start, at least in carnal knowledge, but I think she put him to madness."

"Likely so. Thank you for you unbiased analysis. Although sometimes I worry about what you just might think of me," he cajoled.

"Oh you know." Meredith's voice lowered. "I think you are just lovely."

"I think I'd like for you to join me on the sofa for a while." The Director took off his jacket as Miss Pratt locked his office door.

Madeline stalked down the hall enraged. *How could he not want me? Why?* The thoughts burned through her mind as she went outside instead of into the hall for lunch with the others. She sat on the promenade for a while. Her face had paled and her lip upturned in a snarl of disdain. Though chilly outside, she hadn't bothered to put on a coat. "Someone will want me. I will make them notice me."

The next few years tumbled onto each other, full of research, some Engagements, but mostly boredom. There were times when Madeline thought she'd met her match, but for some reason, the Director never paired her with another male. So she took every opportunity to meet everyone, especially all the Society males, even in the most casual and unacceptable of ways.

Finally, one male gave Madeline the attention she craved. He sent her an Invitation she could not refuse. She did not meet him in person. Instead, this unknown Member sent her information through the Society delivery service. Other instructions came through letters stuffed into books at the Library. The last one was delivered in a book about the history of fencing. Ironically, the same book, devoid of the inflammatory letter, was picked up the next day by Kate

Church for study.

The letter gave a detailed Engagement with the opportunity to leave the Society for good; further details to come later. She would procure certain documents in exchange for a phenomenal sum. Somehow this mystery Member was able to discern that she had access to such plans. It was this espionage that landed Madeline Fahey into her current situation.

Her Driver was able to secure some hot tea from the Inn's staff and Miss Fahey insisted on staying in the carriage to drink it. "We should leave as soon as possible," she huffed.

The sky finally lightened, as did the snow, and she bullied her Driver to hurry back. "Come on now. We must go," Madeline hollered from the carriage.

Madeline didn't think she'd be caught. She reasoned that only a little time was needed to gather her things and leave. She clutched her bag filled with cash and dreamed of the coming days. Her companion of last evening would have more treason money if she could supply a few more items to him later, including her pocket watch. He also promised her more episodes of unbridled passion. Madeline smirked as she remembered his raw desire from the night before.

Men are fools, she mused. Miss Fahey had traded in blueprints of certain secret Society buildings to her companion for more than enough money for her escape from the Society. She thought no one was the wiser to her theft and that her Senior Member, the Director, was under her spell. She couldn't have been more wrong.

When they pulled into the Society grounds it was 7:15 a.m., the snow had stopped and the sky was clearing as the sun was rising. Madeline walked briskly into the Main Hall as if nothing had happened and went directly to her room. There were some Members about, but none had noticed her. As she opened the door to her room, she saw the familiar card of an Invitation sitting in its basket. *It must've arrived late last evening,* she pondered. Her heart sunk and her gut wrenched as she opened it. It read simply "Discussion, 8 a.m. in the Garden". *Damn it,* Madeline thought, she would most likely have an Engagement that day. *I could do a double shift of spying, then leave,* she planned.

Miss Fahey would have to do just that. It was now too late for her to exit unnoticed and Director Roth was most certainly awake and preparing for their Discussion. On this point she was correct.

Lord Wilson had already parted from Miss Church and knocked on the door to the Director's office. Only a few moments before, Director Roth's attendant opened the door for Lord Wilson and then showed himself out so that the two Seniors could have a most important Discussion in private. It was obvious that the Director had not slept as horrid dark lines inhabited his under eyes. He poured some tea and listened to Lord Wilson's brief details of the events of the previous night.

"I'm sorry to have delivered such poor news." Lord Wilson finished his verbal report and rose to leave.

"It is done then." The sun was shining, but he continued in a sad tone, "It will be a cold, dark day." They shook hands and Lord Wilson left for the Manor.

The attendant returned and reported to the Director that Miss Fahey had not yet come in. Director Roth handed the attendant an Invitation and he left immediately to deliver it.

With a heavy heart, the head of the St. Louis Society unlocked a drawer at his ornate oak desk and pulled out a simple box containing a plain but effective pistol. He loaded it and carefully tucked it into his waistcoat, finished his tea and headed for the Garden.

Madeline quickly packed a few things with the dirty money and hid everything in a large case in her closet. She changed clothes, fixed her hair, and egotistically fantasized about how she would live outside the Society. She strode quietly from the room to the lift. Promptly at 7:55 a.m., as she left towards the Garden, her pocket watch began to pulse and she lifted her parasol to block the rising glare of the winter sun.

The Garden was muffled with almost six inches of snow but the paths had already been cleared. As Miss Fahey turned towards her bench, she saw Director Roth waiting, his dark coat standing out against the sun brightened white drifts. "Would you care to join me?" he said politely as she approached.

"I'd be delighted." She faked a smile and sat on the cleared bench. And so the Discussion began. She thought she was ready for whatever task he had for her.

Again she was wrong. Madeline Fahey put her parasol down beside her and looked up. The last thing she would feel was the cold metal of Director Roth's pistol on her forehead. He shot and Terminated her at point blank range. The red splatter of her blood colored the snow behind the bench. With a firm hand on her shoulder, he quickly pushed her body down on the bench, wiped the pistol with a crimson cloth, snatched her pocket watch, and walked away without a word. Two Gardeners immediately popped out from around the corner, efficiently placed her body, parasol, and the ruined snow in a large wheelbarrow, covered it with a blanket, and rolled it away. Visitors to the Garden that day would have no idea what had transpired earlier.

The ivy along the inside wall of the Grounds would grow greener that spring, fed from the body of Madeline Fahey. An interesting irony that she would be buried at the very wall she had planned to climb to begin her new life outside the Society.

11 AN AFTERNOON UNEXPECTED

An exhausted Lord Wilson entered the Manor. It had been a long night and knowing that Madeline Fahey was already Terminated, dampened his mood further. *What a terrible blow.* Telling his Director the night's events was a regrettable duty. And having observed Madeline Fahey's outrageous sexual behavior with Miss Kate present made him both restless and embarrassed. It was 8:15 a.m. and Leeds had a light breakfast of tea, biscuits and jam waiting for him.

Lord Wilson picked at it, was tired and wanted to sleep, but his mind was filled with erotic images of what he had seen. The pale, sensual beauty of Miss Fahey interspersed with the raw, heated desire of her companion twisted in his mind. He was conflicted between arousal and disgust as he nibbled.

He dreaded the Discussion regarding morals and behavior that he would have with Miss Kate later in the day. He wanted to be sure that she never fell into the same trap that Miss Fahey had. There was a fine line between doing the job that the Society expected and letting oneself fall to the depths of despair. The organization needed all kinds of people; what Members did behind closed doors was usually their business. Miss Fahey had put herself on display and now plans of some sort had been stolen. *Not too hard, not too soft,* the most challenging Society tenant to balance, was broken by a now departed Member.

As Lord Wilson set down his fork and wiped his lips, he swore that he would do his best to keep Miss Kate on that fine line. They would both need some time to rest before their next

Engagements. Lord Wilson would soon be recruiting in the field and couldn't be distracted while doing so.

He trudged upstairs to the master bedroom, opened the curtains and the window next to his bed with a slow drag of his arm. The air was filled with the scent of winter snow and fireplaces burning on the grounds. He undressed, letting his clothes fall sloppily to the floor, wiped his face wearily, and climbed into bed naked. As he fell into a fitful sleep, a sharp knock awoke him.

The door opened with a rush of cool air that slapped Lord Wilson to attention. There Kate stood in a soft black velvet coat, trimmed with thick elegant lace. She was bathed in the rising sunlight of the bedroom window. She looked radiant despite their lack of sleep the night before. Her eyes sparkled and her cheeks were a rosy pink.

He was startled and sat up thinking that Leeds had forgotten something. "Miss Kate, what's wrong?" he stuttered and worried what kind of emergency had taken over the Society for her to have come to his door.

"Nothing. I mean, well, I could not sleep. My mind would not rest. I could not stop thinking about you. I had to come see you." Her words burst forth breathlessly as Kate approached the bed. Her blue eyes deepened with passion. "I need you. I can't contain what I feel any longer." Kate dropped the coat to reveal a mere wisp of a white cotton shift that stopped at her knees. The neck laces were undone revealing a tender collar bone and the top of her chest. Her nipples poked curiously through the garment, excited by the subtle breeze in the room. "I want you to take me now, please," she cooed.

He could only nod, his mind spent and completely lost of all proper thought. Lord Wilson lifted the covers, sat at the edge of the bed and helped her remove her lingerie. He pulled her onto his lap and felt the warm soft skin of her buttocks and thighs against his groin as she giggled. Her delightful body tinged his skin with fire.

"Kate, you are, so, lovely," he murmured, cupping her face then kissing her fully. "I love you." Her hair was undone and her soft blond locks fell onto his body tickling his chest. His hands grazed over her full breasts and rosy nipples. They travelled down and ran over the silkiness between her legs. Her mouth was warm and his tongue slid easily from her lips, down her neck, and to her bare chest. Her hands ran through his hair and down his back. He had wanted this terribly from the day he'd found her. It was wrong; they could both be Terminated, but he didn't care. His heart pounded through to his head and his groin throbbed. It stiffened against her backside and pleasant moans emitted from her lips.

Lord Wilson lifted Kate onto the bed and entered the sweet tenderness of her body. She cried out in ecstasy and trembled as she accepted him fully. The outside world was gone; there was nothing but their love. This was what he had wanted to give her all along—his mind, body and soul. He would give up everything to be hers. He would surrender all.

Just as his passion grew, he thought he heard another knock at the bedroom door. *Had she shut it behind her?* He couldn't remember. Again there another series of knocks, confusion and words that didn't sound like Kate's melodic voice.

"Lord Wilson, Sir? Are you awake?" And suddenly he was indeed awake, passionately clutching his pillow. *Drat, an exquisite sensual dream. Why couldn't this be real?* Again a heavy knock. "Sir? You have an appointment today?" Leeds was insistent.

"Yes, yes, just a moment!" Lord Wilson shouted through the door. He grabbed a nightshirt and noticed the sun was now setting and the room was chilly. His pocket watch was pulsing on the nightstand. It was 4:35 p.m. and Discussion with Miss Kate was supposed to be after tea time, at 4:30 p.m. sharp. He was late. "Damn it." He jumped up quickly, pulling on some trousers that Leeds had thoughtfully put out the night before, and opened the door.

"Prepare my coat please." He snapped at Leeds as he rushed to the washroom. Once inside, Lord Wilson closed his eyes at the wash stand and for a brief moment the dream came back. He relieved himself quietly, his breathing hard, his body tensed at a final release, then relaxed. He wiped his face and quickly combed his hair and beard. Looking in the mirror for a brief moment, he saw a man whose face was flush with excitement. One that looked youthful and happy. Lord Wilson chuckled to himself, *how silly.*

Then more seriously, *how could I allow my subconscious to think about her in such a fashion? It's becoming hard to hide my feelings.*

He dashed through the Manor while throwing on clothes and his coat. Strax barked after Lord Wilson until Leeds was able to hold him. Embarrassed and behind schedule, he ran from the Manor, across the Grounds, and to the Garden, almost slipping several times on the snowy paths.

It was 4:40 p.m. and Kate was pacing at the bench, her mind filled with awful thoughts. Her pocket watch pulsed in her gloved hand in her pocket. She checked the time again; it was getting dark. *Had Miss Fahey's departure caused an unknown rift in the Society? Had Lord Wilson not acted properly and been Terminated? Should I go see Director Roth?*

Kate did not want to be assigned to another Senior Member. Lord Wilson could be strict, but was often kind and even fatherly at times. She was drawn to him, but consistently denied her feelings. *There's a definite connection, I'm certain. But where are we headed? What would I do without him?* Her mind was completely muddled. At last, her worries were interrupted by hurried footsteps on the path.

Lord Wilson knew he was late and thus breaking a rule, although a much smaller infraction. He turned a corner and there

Kate paced at their bench. She wore a long black velvet coat that covered her body, and he grinned remembering the more than pleasant dream. As he approached, he noticed her curvaceous dark silhouette contrasting against the white snow. She turned and smiled gratefully, upon hearing him arrive.

"Miss Kate, would you care to join me? I regret my tardiness." He spoke with haste and waved a gloved hand towards their bench.

"I would be delighted," she quivered, relieved that he was there at last. And so the Discussion began.

"As you know, we are often asked to carry out difficult Engagements. Some are easy, some unpleasant and some very, very dangerous. A Member's good behavior in completing their work is key to our missions. When a Member chooses unwisely, they put the whole Society at risk and for the greater good, they must be Terminated so that they do not infect our community." Lord Wilson was dour and direct. "Obviously Miss Fahey not only engaged in espionage for which the Society faces a serious threat, but she behaved in a manner that was not ladylike. Others could have seen her tawdry acts and caused disruption or called attention to our mission. I know that this was discussed in your initial training, but I must reiterate the seriousness of this situation. Do you understand this Miss Kate?"

"I do." She acknowledged him with a succinct nod. The sun had set and more than the air was chilly in the Garden.

"Good." He continued in such a way that rattled Kate and made her more anxious than before. His voice was deeper, stronger. "I want you to understand that you were chosen because of your high moral values and discernment as well as your skills and intelligence. You have not killed without provocation or awareness of its consequences. When you went back to Texas before coming here,

I was questioned by higher authorities as to whether I had made a good selection. I understood that you had unfinished business, but that brashness almost made you non-eligible for Membership. I was able to persuade otherwise, as you know, but I will remind you, once again, that rules here are strictly enforced and I would not want a good Member to be Terminated. We all have regrettable pasts that offer us wisdom, but we must use that knowledge only for the greater good moving forward. Miss Kate, should you ever be Terminated, it will be I that will perform that task. I hope that you will never put me in that position. Do you understand?" he questioned once more. Despite the cold weather beads of sweat formed under Lord Wilson's bowler.

"Yes Sir." Kate's heart began to pound, while suddenly very, very conscious of the higher authorities that existed in the Society. A pang of regret flooded her as she remembered her previous flirtations.

Now Lord Wilson spoke more personally, "Miss Kate, I know that you have had relations with men." He coughed uncomfortably and paused.

She interrupted quietly, almost in a whisper, "One."

Lord Wilson remembered her confession in Iris and revelations under hypnosis. But he hadn't pried about other dalliances. She had always acted as if she'd had a wealth of intimate experiences, but apparently her wisdom and carnal knowledge were two different things. She looked calm, innocent, and slightly embarrassed, much younger than her age.

He stammered slightly and refocused. "Miss Kate, I will not judge your morals or previous experience. Please know that not all men lack that courtesy and respect of what you witnessed last eve. Male Members should be gentlemen and ladies should be gentlewomen. The Society does have those Members which act on the underbelly of the outside world. I am sorry that you had to witness such a seedy and bawdy act. You will not be asked to perform such duties as they are ground for Termination, do you understand?" He drove his point one last time.

"Yes, Sir." Kate replied, sensing his discomfort and realizing she may have said too much in the past.

Lord Wilson tried to quell her embarrassment, "You have become quite a lady, Miss Kate, and we have high expectations. So far you have met all of them and I hope that you will continue to do so. Thank you for your service, I am grateful to be your Senior. Additionally, thank you for your concern about my well-being." He touched her with a genteel hand. "I could see that you were upset when I was late today."

"I was." Kate confessed. "And thank you as well." She finally relaxed with a weary smile. But the relief was temporary.

"I want you to know that you won't see Miss Fahey on the Grounds anymore. You do understand what I mean by that?" Again, the conversation became thick with tension.

Kate gulped. "She has been Terminated." Her voice was veiled in softness.

"Correct. Nothing is to be said and no one will say anything further." Again Lord Wilson stopped fearing that he'd gone a bit too far. "It has been my pleasure to have you here. Please continue as you are. I am certain we will have another Engagement soon." He stood, held her hand and led her off the bench. "It looks to be a lovely evening." Indeed it was, despite the chill. The stars had come out and a full moon was rising over the grounds. "Good evening Miss Kate."

"Good Evening, Sir." She replied with a firm handshake and they parted ways, each of them sensing that something had changed.

He wondered more of her past; she'd had so many scars. Kate was kind, yet strong and violently committed when necessary. He prayed that she could hang on through her training. The Society needed her. "I need her." He muttered under his frosty breath on his way back to the Manor. "Don't be too soft Kate."

Kate walked with purpose to her room. She was mindful that he cared for her, but just couldn't express it at this time.

A strong force of nature developed warm hearts betwixt them. A bond had been strengthened. The fascination phase of their relationship had ended.

A strange new reality had arrived. They would have to work together to survive, but Kate had to learn to succeed on her own.

I must be patient, I must wait, and above all, I must succeed, Kate mused.

For the first time since Kate had arrived at the Society, Lord Wilson paused, watched her walk away from the Garden, and secretly hoped that the dream he'd had that day would someday become reality.

12 CONSUMPTION

A gray day without rain is boring. Kate stood at the window at the beginning of what appeared to be a most dreadful and dull day. Her assistant cleared away her breakfast tray as Kate traced every wrinkle of her hands. Strax whined uneasily at her feet.

"Will that be all Miss?" Kate's helper let her gaze linger on her charge. Her mistress had been upset of late. Despite sumptuous meals, her excellent tutelage, and a short break from Engagements, Miss Church hadn't been eating much. From her pink and swollen eyes, her assistant had gathered that she hadn't slept well either. But Kate's help had no idea of the secretive traumas she'd experienced over the last few weeks.

"Yes, I'm finished." Kate's voice was barely above hearing level. Miss Beatrice left quietly, leaving Kate to her thoughts, none of which were happy.

As she moved to her vanity, Kate remembered what her mother used to say, "when it rained the angels were crying". *Why weren't they crying today?* Clearly Kate had been upset and she powdered her face in a vain attempt to cover her reddened complexion. Kate smoothed over the black dress with a little train she hadn't worn in quite a while. The Widow had returned for a newly departed friend. The memorial service for Jilly Browne would be today.

After the Termination of Madeline Fahey, Kate's life at the Society slowed down. There was more intense study, but also more time for independent work. The only visits to the Manor were for tea on Sundays. The first tea after Miss Fahey's demise was tense.

"Miss Kate, as I mentioned before, things will change very soon. There won't be time for chess, tea, and the like. You'll be here less during the coming weeks, but thereafter you'll be attending more Engagements, some on your own, and more work in the field. I want to prepare you for the intensity. I'll need you at your best." Lord Wilson set down his cup with polite precision.

Kate finished nibbling on a thin oatmeal cookie. It melted in her mouth with smooth sweetness. She quickly lost the taste for it with her Senior's words. She tried to read him without flirtation. "Immediately?"

"Yes, starting tomorrow." Lord Wilson refilled their cups. "Remember we spoke of this last week?"

"Um, yes, Sir." A wrinkle danced across Kate's forehead. The sun had set and the Manor's library took on a dark air. "More study?"

"Yes, but you can still have scheduled rides. And Strax will come home with you to the Main Hall tonight for a while." He set the pot down. "Milk and sugar as usual, Miss Kate?" He played his role well. Kate needed to be independent for just a while, to make further connections within Society. Not necessarily friends, but Members on which she could rely, even for small comforts.

"Sugar only please, Sir." She still could not read his emotions. Kate was trying to hide her anxiety from showing, but thoughts of being away from Lord Wilson made her stomach churn. Creature comforts like milk in her tea would not curb her stress.

Her pallor was obvious to her Senior. He raised a brow at the lack of milk. "I want you to know you are not being punished. My stature here requires many duties, including keeping up with new equipment and training others." His attempt at assurances backfired.

Immediately Kate wondered if a new female Member would be joining them. She looked down on her plate with a withering grimace. "So…" She swallowed and failed at concealing her concern. "New Members coming aboard then?"

"Of coursc." Lord Wilson laughed solidly. "There are always new Members. Members grow old and retire or pass away. Fresh recruits bring new life blood and ideas to the organization. All are made the same offer you were, Miss Kate." He leaned in and whispered. "You know I cannot tell you much more. But please don't look so forlorn."

Kate blushed at her jealously. "Of course."

They ate in silence for a few moments. Kate let her eyes wander. Flurries danced along the outside of the library. Their once perfect snowflakes melted slow deaths against the warmth of the Manor's windows.

Lord Wilson inhaled. Kate looked lost while staring at the grounds. He changed tactics. "You are happy here, Miss Kate?" His voice dripped with sweetness.

"Oh yes, of course, Sir." She snapped back to attention.

"Good. If you are ever unsatisfied, I want you to tell me. Don't let your feelings go awry. Miss Fahey's situation was tragic." He touched her hand in a way that had become so pleasing to her in the short time they'd known each other. "You were selected for a reason. Many reasons, in fact. Some which may not be clear to you now, but please be patient. Good things are to come, you do know this?"

"Yes of course." She finally let her fears fade. His charm and the tea soothed her.

"Very good then. You'll get notification when you are next needed. Use this time to relax, learn, and make stronger connections." He paused. "If something should happen to me, Miss Kate, know that I would want you to stay and be happy here." Lord Wilson cleared his throat after the honest admission had escaped his lips.

Kate again blushed at his concern. "Yes, thank you Sir."

"Good. Tomorrow expect something different on your schedule." Lord Wilson winked and stood. "May I help you with your coat?" He didn't wait for Leeds. Lord Wilson desired to give her just a touch more personal attention.

"Yes, thank you." Kate smiled as his hands lingered on her shoulders after she was properly attired for the weather. She whispered "Good night Sir," as she turned to face him.

"Good night Miss Kate, enjoy your day tomorrow." Lord Wilson opened the door and resisted the wildest urge to kiss her.

As Kate walked home to the Main Hall, she had not the foggiest idea of what her Senior was alluding to.

Mr. Antonio Vincent stood behind his three female students and corrected them in a silky Italian accent. "Lift your chest, hold your abdomen in tightly."

The ladies, including Kate, stood with imaginary dance partners. Each had arms extended for their lead.

"Ladies, when you waltz, it must be smooth. You must be light of the feet. No man will want to resist you." The instructions rolled off his tongue. "Now turn right; turn left. With grace and ease. And again."

Kate hadn't danced for so long; she'd forgot how much she'd enjoyed it as a child. Mr. Vincent nodded his approval in her direction.

"Miss Church, Miss Browne, well done. Oh, stop, Miss Cutter." Mr. Vincent rushed over to the last woman in their line. "See now. Chin higher. Look at your companion with kindness. Desire. He is to be your suitor, even if for one song. You must dance as one." Kate and the other lady in line, Miss Jilly Browne, tried to stifle their giggles.

"Now, now ladies, again. One, two, three. One, two, three. We do this over and over because tomorrow you will have partners and you will not want to damage their feet, ahh?" Mr. Vincent made a small joke and the ladies twittered.

After an hour, their lesson was over. Mr. Vincent gazed proudly at his pupils. "Remember tomorrow, we practice with some of the gentlemen. Thank you ladies and good day." He strolled to his office outside the dance studio. His steps brushed on the polished wooden floors.

The ladies headed for their dressing room with broad smiles and tender hearts. Their instructor was by far the kindest and most flamboyant man any of them had met so far at the Society. They spoke of him as they dressed. It was a rare time for them to be without supervision or attendants.

"Did you hear the way he rolled his tongue? Such a lavish accent." Miss Cutter swooned in a thick countrified tone. With her awkward poise and stumbles on the dance floor, Kate wondered how well she was doing with Madame Prix. Miss Cutter had a plain face with wide brown eyes, ruddy, almost unruly red hair, and tanned skin despite the weather. She was tall and of stocky build. Kate was almost certain she'd been recruited from a farm.

"And gallantry. So polite and well mannered." Miss Browne agreed. To Kate, Miss Browne was a harder read. She had shiny light-brown hair, hazel eyes and creamy skin which was prone to freckles. She was petite in stature, and moved with a grace that gave her a pixie-like air. She could easily pass for an adolescent, perhaps even younger, Kate mused.

"Yes, he is quite the gentleman. Very dapper." Kate chatted freely with her companions. They didn't have to address each other formally here. "However, I think he might be a dandy."

"A what?" Miss Cutter looked up from tying her shoe laces.

"A gentlemen that likes other gentlemen," Miss Browne piped up. "I think you might be right on that."

Miss Cutter blanched. "Oh my."

"But remember, ladies, discretion is key." Kate, being the eldest of the three, gently reminded her classmates of Society rules, even though it was she that brought up the subject. Kate didn't want Miss Cutter, the most obviously naïve, to set her sights on a Senior that wouldn't ever be available.

"True," Miss Browne replied. "I'm looking forward to finding out who our partners will be tomorrow." Each of the women had been there less than a year and had reached a level of education where they would be trained with others. This would be the first time that gentlemen Members who were not instructors, would be joining them. An excitement filled the room as their banter rose like chattering sparrows.

Kate wondered if Lord Wilson would join them, but her mind immediately filled with self-doubt. She remembered the previous day's conversation. She was certain he'd have left the grounds already. Kate had forgotten what it was like to be alone.

"So Miss Church, would you like to join us?" Miss Browne broke into Kate's muddled thoughts.

"I'm sorry, for…" Kate stuttered.

"Lunch? In the Main Hall. I don't think it would be too much trouble against the rules?"

"Yes, yes I would." Kate pushed herself back into reality.

The ladies were leaving the dance hall when Miss Cutter's attendant met them at the door. "Miss Cutter, I've been sent to collect you. You have an unscheduled Discussion immediately with your Senior." The help was practically bursting with joy, so Kate surmised it must be good news.

"Thank you ladies, I must go." Miss Cutter blushed while she was led away.

"Good luck," Kate urged after them.

"Yes, good luck," Miss Browne chimed in and turned to Kate. "Well, are you still up for a bit of company?"

"Yes, yes I am." Kate reminded herself that she needed to be seen, to make contacts. "Let's go."

They made their way through the vast Main Hall to the dining room, passing dozens of people. There was an odd buzz of activity. Kate almost said something when Miss Browne interrupted. "My, there's a lot of Members about today."

"Yes, I was going to say the same." Kate was almost dizzy at the scores of people rushing to and fro, carrying all kinds of gadgets and wearing odd bits of clothing.

The dining room was packed with a noontime crowd, most of which were male. The host greeted them warmly as he checked off a reservation list. “Hello Ladies, we are a bit full today, but if there are just two, I’d be delighted to seat you.”

“Yes, just us,” Kate responded with a light tone. She was still astounded at the crowd. They followed the host to a small table for two at one of the windows. It was blindingly white outside. Kate realized why so many were indoors. It was the weather.

“Look.” Kate gestured to the window as she and Miss Browne were seated.

“Oh.” Miss Browne was just as surprised.

“Ahh yes, ladies. A sudden snowstorm. Started only a bit ago, but there’s already several inches on the ground. From what I understand, it will be a genuine blizzard. Many changes in plans and activities. But not to worry, we have plenty to eat today.” He set down menus as a server brought tea and water. “I’ll return for your orders in a bit.”

An odd feeling came over Kate as they peered out the window. At first she thought it might be anxiety over where Lord Wilson was at the moment, but it was something different. She and Miss Browne both turned away from the window at the same time. Kate opened her mouth, but again Miss Browne spoke first.

“Do you see it?” Miss Browne looked down and pretended to scan her menu, but her eyes flicked to the inside of the room.

“Yes.” Kate whispered and swallowed hard. There was a sudden stillness in the dining hall.

Almost every man in the room was watching the pair. Whether discreetly over a newspaper, a hot cup of tea, or side glances with other gentlemen, the focus of the room was Kate and Miss Browne.

"Oh my goodness," Miss Browne twittered. "No rings?"

"Not any that I can see." Kate responded after taking secretive glances at the left hands of the men around them. "Miss Browne, is your Senior here?" she asked, her voice taught with concern.

"Um, no. I mean he's here, but preoccupied today. And yours Miss Church?"

"On an Engagement."

"Oh."

"This is odd."

"Yes, it is." Kate sipped. "Keep pretending not to notice."

Just as the two began to feel like a circus sideshow, a waiter dropped a tray of dirty dishes. The clash of falling china seemed to break the spell. The room slowly returned to life, although more than several men continued to peek at them.

"They act as though they've never seen a woman." Kate giggled.

"Have you not noticed it before though, Miss Church? The stolen glances?"

"Um, well, somewhat. But I've been so deep in study."

"Oh, so that's why I never see you on the first floor." Miss Browne made kind conversation.

"Well, I live on the third floor." Kate replied.

"Oh." Miss Browne looked a bit shocked. "I thought you were new, just a few months in, like myself."

"Yes, but, I'm somewhat elevated. You know I can't say much more."

"Of course not. But that's an honor. You do look wiser than the others I've met." Miss Browne paused. "It's strange to have a conversation like this. Almost a real one, do you know what I mean?"

"Yes. In fact this is the first time I've had lunch with another lady here. I mean to actually sit with someone other than my Senior. Usually I've sat by myself or had lunch at the Manor."

"Me too." Miss Browne raised a brow. "Wait, did you say Manor? Like one of the homes outside?"

"Yes." Kate grinned. "Please know that I am not in any way bragging."

"Oh how exciting, Miss Church." Miss Browne squealed. "What's it like? Is he handsome? Older? Most of those men are. And of highbrow stature. A Manor! Is it gorgeous? Oh my." The words tumbled out until their server returned. Miss Browne cleared her throat.

They ordered their meals with ladylike manners. When he was finally out of earshot, Kate spoke. "You know I can't say much, but it's a good life. It really is." Kate found herself beaming. "And you?"

"It is good. I didn't come from much to start with, really. I can't complain now, that was then, this is now, you know. But they let me bring my cat." Miss Browne's voice was so gentle, Kate wondered how she'd come here.

"I have my dog." Kate laughed.

"Oh that's lovely." Miss Browne almost snorted, then coughed. "Oh excuse me." She sipped some tea.

"Are you alright?"

"Um yes, it's just a tickle I've got." She sipped again then whispered. "I know you can't say much, but what are your Engagements like? I mean, do you go out?"

"Yes. They've been, well varied, and sometimes a bit dangerous." Kate had to hold back. She'd only met Miss Browne today. But she had such a sweet inquisitive nature. "And you?"

"Well, you notice I'm quite petite. Childish looking, don't you think?" Miss Browne tilted her head in a knowing fashion.

"They put you in, well, um—" Kate couldn't believe her ears.

"Schools, yes. Sometimes churches. You see, remember they don't involve children. But I can pass for an older girl fairly easily." Miss Browne smirked. "Although I'm tired of continually meeting new classmates, except for you of course."

Their food arrived before either could divulge any serious secrets. They ate in silence as men came and went by their table, taking the long way around to the exit or pretending to visit other gentlemen. One started to pause at their seats when Miss Browne's face lit up. Their interloper soon disappeared at the presence of someone very well known to Miss Browne.

"Hello Mr. Scott," Miss Browne greeted her Senior. He was a tall, handsome young man with sandy blonde hair and light blue eyes. Kate estimated that she was older than he by more than a few years.

"Good day, Miss Jilly. May I join you ladies?" He warbled pleasantly in a southern drawl.

"Of course Sir. This is Miss Church." Mr. Scott not so much looked over Kate, but seemed to be stunned at her presence.

"Oh yes. How lovely to meet you." He shook Kate's hand firmly. He motioned to a server who quickly offered a third chair to their small table. "My usual please." He ordered with such finesse that it put Kate off guard momentarily.

"Likewise Sir." Kate gave her most pleasant grin to Miss Browne's Senior Member. Again the movement in the room seemed to have slowed. Kate turned to see several men give each other exasperated looks and tried not to laugh at their disappointment.

"So Miss Church, will your Senior be joining us as well today? Lord Wilson, I believe?" His questioning was almost stern in nature. So much so that Kate wondered if they shouldn't have had lunch together at all. *But Lord Wilson did say I was supposed to make connections, did he not?*

"Lord Wilson?" Miss Browne smiled in surprise.

"Why yes, that's right." Kate tried to relax. This was not a secret. He'd addressed her as Miss Kate many times in front of others. She was his Member.

"Miss Church, that's outstanding. He has a brilliant reputation." Miss Browne was still amazed, her mouth open.

"Yes, he does. He was my Senior as well, before I started reporting to Director Roth." Mr. Scott was precise in words. "And it is outstanding. You are indeed something special, Miss Church."

Their pleasant conversation was broken by a coughing fit from Miss Browne. Mr. Scott patted her back gently as she sipped on tea. He motioned for the waiter. "Fresh water and more tea please. With honey." He looked gingerly at his charge. Then Kate saw it, the unmistakable look of love on his face as he eased her through the spell.

Miss Browne's face had reddened, but was now coming back to its freckled pink creaminess. Mr. Scott was encouraging in the way he refilled her tea and poured in copious amounts of honey. Then helped her drink it, urging her to sip slowly. He leaned towards her with such devotion that it was obvious that she was selected by and for him. With Lord Wilson and now Director Roth's direction, he was definitely of a higher caliber, even at a young age. He'd been allotted a female Member. "Well now, that's better," Mr. Scott cooed.

Kate inhaled sharply at the revelation. Her head clouded. She wondered if the attraction between her and Lord Wilson was this obvious. She had been told they could be paired off, but it could take a year. Madeline Fahey had been paired with Director Roth, but there was no appearance of romance there. At least not that she knew of. Other female attendants, Dr. Finch, Madame Prix-all had rings. *Was there a chance I'll be given to someone? Could I refuse if I wanted?* The thoughts played in her mind as Miss Browne came around to feeling better and her focus shifted back to the table as her new friend giggled.

"Oh how silly of me to have choked." She laughed with a merry grin.

"Well then, I think we should be off. Who knows what this weather will bring, eh?" Mr. Scott helped Miss Browne from her chair and the host came to assist Kate.

"Indeed," Kate mused aloud. There was definitely something in the air and it was much more than the flurry of snow outside.

Kate returned to her room to find that her fencing lesson had been cancelled for the day. A part of her wanted that physical release and pined a bit. She had hoped it would distract her from thinking about Lord Wilson that afternoon.

Warmth surged through Kate's body like a dip in a pleasant bath, with the water slowly enveloping every inch of her skin. The source of the rush surprised her, for Kate was in the arms of Master Richards as they twirled in the dance hall. She no longer regretted missing her fencing class the day before as her fencing instructor had agreed to volunteer at her dance lesson.

"Lovely, lovely, ladies and gentlemen." Mr. Vincent encouraged the pairs of students waltzing in perfect synchronicity. "Such grace and carriage." The instructor was grinning ear to ear. The music slowed and Mr. Vincent flipped a switch on the wall which stopped it completely. "Well done. Let us take a few moments to rest."

Kate finally caught her breath and looked directly into the eyes of her dance partner. Master Richards's eyes gleamed and a tender smile engaged her. He was still holding her even after the music had stopped.

"Miss Church, would like some water?" Miss Browne asked as she poured glasses for herself and Mr. Scott. Her Senior was there for reasons now obvious to Kate. They were meant for each other, melting into one another across the polished wooden floors. Kate shook herself to attention.

"Why yes, thank you." Kate turned to see a concerned look on Mr. Scott's face. She was still in the arms of Master Richards. She slid away while trying not to blush.

"I think we could all use one." Master Richards lingered behind her. Kate felt the tickle of his breath on the back of her neck which set new waves of excitement through her body. She closed her eyes briefly, almost fainting at the pleasure that raced in her veins. When she opened them, she was looking into the horrified eyes of Mr. Scott.

Miss Browne was immune to this strange visual display. Her throat was burning, her chest suddenly filled with heavy pain and beads of sweat formed on her brow. She was racing through a second glass of water when the coughing began. Huge gasps that seared her upper respiratory system.

Every eye in the room was now on her and Kate's moment of surreal ecstasy was immediately forgotten. "Miss Jilly!" Mr. Scott pulled her to his side, massaged her back, and gave her a cloth for her mouth.

"Oh no." Kate hurried forward and began to fan her. Master Richards dipped his handkerchief into some of the cold water and dabbed at her forehead. Even Mr. Vincent came running from the back of his office. After about a minute, the coughing ceased. Miss Browne had pulled the cloth away to sip some water, when the group gave a collective gasp. Blood and phlegm covered it.

"I think we should stop for today. We need to get you to the infirmary." Mr. Scott dabbed at her lips with a fresh handkerchief. It too was covered in bits of gooey vermillion.

Miss Browne tried to turn her head away. "No, I'm fine, really. I just had a spell."

"You've been having a lot of them lately," Mr. Scott chided. "You're leaving for the infirmary. That's an order." Her Senior took control. Kate watched Miss Browne whiten.

"Why don't we clean you up a bit before you go?" Kate offered, hoping to defuse the tension between them.

"Yes, that would be wise," Mr. Scott agreed.

"So we shall carry on tomorrow?" Master Richards tried to sound cheerful.

"Yes, whoever is able can come tomorrow." Mr. Vincent assured.

"Alright then, let's see if we can get you on your feet." Mr. Scott assisted Miss Browne until they reached the ladies dressing room.

"I'll help from here," Kate assured. "We'll be out shortly, gentlemen." Once inside the changing room Miss Browne collapsed onto a couch with a thud.

"Ohh, how embarrassing," she moaned.

"It's not your fault you're not well. Let me help." Kate tidied up Miss Browne's hair as they spoke in confidence.

"I know, but…"

"I'm sure Mr. Scott understands," Kate filled in the blanks for her new friend.

"So you see it?" Miss Browne's eyes widened with happiness.

"Yes. I do. You're a good pair." Kate tended to Jilly's face, patting it dry, and then added a bit of powder.

The conversation paused as Jilly straightened her blouse and Kate made herself tidy. The silence was broken with a tentative question. "Miss Church, I'm hesitant to ask, but do you feel the same for your Senior, Lord Wilson? I mean, why isn't he here today?"

Kate was stunned, but tried not to make it obvious. "You know I cannot say. But you also know that we're only a handful of women here." Her voice lowered to a whisper. "My Senior is on a long Engagement. I don't quite know for how much longer."

"How do you deal with him being away for so long? I mean, do you make visits to the Hysteria Room?"

"I'm sorry, the what room?" A shadow fell over Kate's face.

"Oh, you haven't needed it then," Miss Browne twittered. "You must have supreme self-control."

A puzzled wrinkle formed between Kate's eyes.

"I can't tell you, but you'll know, I'm sure." Miss Browne stifled a giggle. "Please, I can't say any more."

"Alright then." Kate was still perplexed. She hadn't heard of such a place in the Society.

"But you have so much attention, you probably don't need it. I mean, Master Richards seems to, well, I mean, you know." Miss Browne stumbled over her words. "The way you dance together is magical."

"Oh." Kate tried to stop a smile, then her conscience came to the surface. "Miss Browne, you know you can't say anything. I'm not promised to anyone yet. I've only been here a few months. And you know, we shouldn't have this conversation." Kate raised her chin in defiance.

"I know. It's just good to have someone to talk to."

"Yes, but we mustn't. We should get going. I'm sure the gentlemen are worried."

"Discretion then, Miss Church?"

"Yes, discretion, thank you. Well said."

The two ladies gave each other sympathetic hugs before stepping out into the dance hall. And then Miss Browne had another fit of hideous coughs.

"Let's hurry, good day everyone." Her Senior carried Jilly out. The others watched them go. Kate's skin crawled with a sense of foreboding.

As Mr. Scott helped Miss Browne stumble to the infirmary, she coughed almost incessantly. During this particular attack, Miss Pratt passed them in the hall and had just removed her gloves. She discreetly tried to hide a yawn as she did not sleep well the night before. She opened her mouth just as Miss Brown had a terrible spell and molecules of infection attached themselves to the lips and nose of Miss Pratt.

Kate reread the note in her basket:

Dear Miss Kate:

I have been apprised of the consumption that has invaded our Grounds. You are to report to Dr. Finch immediately for serum treatments. You and you alone will receive this medication. No one is to know of this. As always discretion is key.

I understand several of your fellow Members have taken ill, including Miss Jilly Browne. Miss Kate, I know that you have the best means at heart, but under no circumstances are you to provide her with serum. Please understand that I am acting for what is best for your well-being. We will discuss this upon my return. Rest when necessary. I will need you at your best. Destroy this letter upon reading.

Take care,

W."

Kate crumbled the fine parchment and flung the letter into her fireplace where it was engulfed by the crackling brilliant flames. "Fuck no," she cursed and sat at her table. Strax got up from his bed and barked. "Oh no, not you sweetie." She reached down to pet her faithful companion, then sat at the window while her breakfast grew cold.

Kate's fingers played along her neckline as she realized how long it had been since she'd used foul language. Iris was long gone. She looked through the window at the continuing snowfall as bitterness rose. Anger welled into slow tears that trickled down. How could she not help Jilly? She'd been so sick for days now.

It wasn't fair. He's not here anyhow. The disturbance rotted her mind, left her listless and without hunger.

A knock from her attendant brought her to the present. Kate dabbed her eyes and smoothed over her hair. "Please come in."

"Miss Church, you have an appointment with Dr. Finch in fifteen. Sorry that this was not scheduled, but you must be there."

"Of course, thank you," Kate replied in a stoic fashion, her lips in a rumpled line.

"Very well Miss, may I take your tray?" Kate didn't want it, but remembered Lord Wilson's warning. He did care for her. She needed to be at her best.

"No, let me finish. I'll be done in a bit." She faked a smile and dug into her breakfast.

Fifteen minutes later, Kate sat in the parlor outside of Dr. Finch's office. Someone was coughing terrible fits inside. Kate trembled in her chair. She recalled people becoming ill in both Iris and St. Louis. Sometimes it was something simple. Other times, people died horrible deaths. Kate had a sinking feeling that this time was going to be more of the latter.

An attendant suddenly came through Dr. Finch's door. She wore a light kerchief over her face. "Dr. Finch would like for you to come back in an hour if you could?"

"I will." Kate stood and left for the library as the pit in her stomach grew.

Over the next few weeks Kate visited Dr. Finch daily for small doses of serum. "You get a teaspoon a day for at least the next two weeks. This should prevent you from falling ill. You won't have to worry about coming in contact with others. You can even visit Miss Browne at the Sanatorium."

Kate tried to hide her anger in not being able to help Jilly. The serum helped though. The careful administration of healing spoonfuls made her feel almost giddy afterwards.

But later Kate's emotions would crash. She'd ride Sonny out to the Sanatorium. She remembered seeing it the first time on a ride with Lord Wilson. He'd pointed out the group of three small buildings. One was a pleasant Victorian mansion. This home was for healthy retirees, those Members who were still able to care for themselves. The second was a Germanic brick home of three stories which served as a last haven for those who were deathly ill.

The last structure was made of a very plain brick. It too acted as a hospice at times, for this place housed those believed to have serious contagious diseases for which there was no treatment or cure, even with the advanced medical knowledge of the Society. Some got well. Some lingered for long periods of time. Others died. This building was where Jilly Browne and suddenly scores of other Members were being housed.

Some days Miss Browne seemed well, with perhaps a few light coughs during their conversations. Other times she was so ill that Kate would only stay a few moments. On one of these poorer days for Miss Browne, Kate came home to another note from Lord Wilson.

"Dear Miss Kate:

I must send you on an urgent small Engagement. It will be within the Society's walls. At precisely 8 a.m. tomorrow, while most others are at breakfast, you will go directly to Director Roth's office. His attendant will be aware of your arrival and you will have access to his office. If you are questioned, you have an appointment with Director Roth.

The attendant will leave you in the office to take the following action. You will go behind his desk and look at it. On the right is a small statue of a soldier. You will attempt to lift it. When you do, a small compartment will open from the right side of the desk. Inside will be a list titled "Alias". It will be short, so I want you to memorize the names on the list as quickly as possible. You cannot write them down in his office.

You will return the list to its hiding place by lifting the statue again and immediately part from Mr. Roth's office. Again, it is imperative that you do not write the names down there.

Instead you will write them down from my desk at the Manor. You know of where my stationery is and Leeds will be prepared for your coming. Write down only the list of names. You will fold the letter as I do, and use my envelope and seal. Leeds will be prepared to take it from you as soon as you are finished.

Afterwards you are to continue on as usual.

I hope that you are doing well in your studies and that you are in good health. Should you not feel well, please see Dr. Finch immediately. I understand that many others have fallen ill with consumption. Again, discretion is key. We have much work ahead of us. Please be prepared.

As usual, destroy this letter upon reading. Thank you for your services.

W."

This was unusual, Kate worried. But it was Lord Wilson's handwriting. If something was wrong, surely she'd be stopped. This list was important enough not to be taken back in physical form across the grounds.

Kate didn't sleep well that night. She noticed less traffic in the halls. Classes with Madame Prix, Master Richards, and Mr. Vincent were cancelled intermittently. She hadn't been to the Manor other than in passing on her way to the stables to ride Sonny. The Society was in peril, she was sure of it.

When the sun rose Kate was already dressed, much to her attendant's surprise. She had walked Strax before dawn. Her pocket watch buzzed just as she approached the Director's office at 8 a.m. His attendant opened the door, allowed her inside and left, just as Lord Wilson's letter had described. She crossed the room in silence and stood behind the desk. The small soldier statue was easily found. With a light grasp and lift, a small side tray popped open as promised. The list was there, just four short names:

Bunting

Fox

Gotham

Parsons

They were simple enough and in alphabetical order. Kate read and reread the list. She closed her eyes and visualized the words on the page. In her mind they looked oddly familiar. Her eyes popped open as she realized why; they were all subjects of nursery rhymes. Kate smiled as she placed the list back into its compartment and again lifted the soldier. The tray snapped back into place.

As Kate hurried, her coat sleeve caught on a small wooden box on the corner of the desk. Although not physically attached to the desk, it held just as many secrets as the list that Kate had just procured.

It fell to the floor and its lid came off. Out tumbled a small picture and a coin. "No. Oh no." Kate looked around feverishly to see if anything had opened or closed. After being certain nothing was out of place, she quickly picked up the items. She could not control her curiosity. The picture was of a lovely woman that looked vaguely familiar. On the back side were two handwritten initials "M.P." The gold coin had been rubbed quite a bit over time, but Kate could still see an address on the edge and a number "68".

Kate tried desperately to erase them from her mind, but they stuck with her as the list had. She tucked the trinkets back into the box and placed it back onto Mr. Roth's desk. She opened the door to the approaching attendant. There was only silence as he closed the office door and she departed.

Kate acted as if nothing was wrong. But everything was. People were dying. Jilly was sick. She'd been asked to procure some confidential information from and for the most powerful man in the Society. Lord Wilson was away. And Master Richards, well, he made her feel special. Desired.

Kate tried to shake off these obtrusive thoughts as she walked over the white laden paths of the Grounds to the Manor. It had continued to snow off and on for days now.

The Manor looked like a beautiful crystalized castle while encased in the frozen precipitation. Kate smiled as she climbed the cold stairwell to the library. Again her timepiece buzzed as Leeds opened the door.

"Good day Miss Church."

"Good day."

Kate made a beeline for the desk, wrote the list, and sealed it as directed. She handed it to Leeds with a polite nod. Within two minutes, this portion of her task was completed. She turned to leave when Leeds stopped her.

"Miss Church, Lord Wilson has sent something for you. Please sit at the table and I will bring it momentarily."

"Alright then." Kate tried not to worry. She was supposed to return to the Main Hall. *Why a sudden change of plans?*

Leeds returned with a grin. "You are to open it here. And I am to bring you breakfast, which shall come in a few minutes. In the meantime, I leave you to your package." He set the brown paper and twine wrapped box on the table. Leeds was beaming when he left without a sound as usual.

Kate tore open the package with a flourish. Lord Wilson's familiar parchment card was set atop a black velvet box. It read:

"Know that you are in my thoughts and that I cannot say much more. You will take the gift with you. Unfortunately you must feed the card to the fireplace once you open the box.

With much care,

-W."

Kate's heart flopped in her chest as the room seemed to spin around her. Was she dreaming?

She lifted the lid wondering what could possibly be inside after what had been written in the card. An ornate heart shaped music box glimmered in the pure white reflection of the snow falling outside. The musical piece was a deep burgundy shade with gold trim and elegant flowers painted on its lid. She lifted it and turned the crank. "Serenade" by Schubert began to fill the room. As she looked closer, there was an inscription on the inside:

"These violent delights have violent ends.

And in their triumph die, like fire and powder,

Which as they kiss, consume."

"Romeo and Juliet, Shakespeare," Kate whispered to herself. Was this real? She closed her eyes for a moment and opened them to be certain. She offed a glove and pinched the backside of her hand until a bruise had begun. "Oh God, oh my."

She stood and flicked the card into the fireplace. The flames brightened with what seemed to be happiness at being fed such elegant paper. Kate gripped the edge of the mantel to steady herself.

Is this all in my mind? He feels this. I feel it. Inside her heart was full as if it would burst. Her head blissfully satiated. Suddenly her face was hot, her whole body afire.

She turned to watch the snow fall outside as if it might cool her senses. Her fingertips grazed the glass as she remembered how it felt when he had checked her scars. How delicious he smelled. The way his hands sent a charge through her. Kate closed her eyes as rapturous tears rolled down her cheeks. She sank to her knees as the sweet music was all she heard. The rush of memories overcame her. How fine the wool of his suit felt under her fingertips. How he'd pushed her to the edge of madness. The way his eyes saw all the way to her center and held her soul captive.

Kate sobbed in earnest, while crouching on the floor. Her cry shook her to the core. *I love him. How can I keep this hidden?*

"Miss Church? Are you alright?" Leeds brought her breakfast in and set it down immediately upon viewing her crumpled stature.

Kate snapped back to the present. "Yes, yes. Can I please have a moment to collect myself?"

"Of course Miss. Your meal is on the table. You can call for me when you're finished." Leeds extended his hand and helped her up.

"Thank you." Kate wiped her tears with the back of her glove as Lord Wilson's assistant left. She sat at the table. Suddenly she was ravenous, her face almost buried in the plate. Kate ate as if it were her last meal, licking her lips, feeding a deep set hunger.

When finished, Kate sat back in her chair and let her eyes close again. For the first time in weeks, she felt satisfied. Her hands rested in her lap and her head fell forward as she began to nap. Mrs. Leeds tapped her shoulder. "Miss Church, you can rest on the settee if you like?"

"Yes, yes. That would be wonderful." Kate's eyes were still heavy as she crossed the room. Mrs. Leeds covered her with a quilt and Kate was soon fast asleep. She napped throughout the morning, all of her worries suddenly forgotten. This was well, because some of the worst was yet to come.

Jilly Browne's condition worsened, as did so many of the others. Unlike the day that Miss Browne and Kate ate in the dining hall, the Society grounds seemed vacant. Only the most pertinent Engagements were in operation. At least half the Members were in quarantine. About a tenth had been sent to the Sanatorium, some never to return. Christmas and other holidays were coming. Some effort was made by staff to make the Grounds look jolly, but an underlying specter of sickness and death haunted the Society.

Kate made daily visits to Miss Browne without issue. The serum was protecting her. It made her complexion radiant and Kate was vibrant in every physical aspect of her being. It was as if every detail of her life was sharper than knives crafted by the hardest steel.

She took walks with Strax and long rides with Sonny, even in the snowy cold weather, when no classes were to be had.

The day after Kate received the music box, she awoke feeling good physically. Her emotions were another matter. A suspicion boiled deep in her gut. Something was very wrong. She couldn't quite put her finger on it, but she tried to prepare herself mentally for whatever might come. She rode out to the Sanatorium fully armed.

When Kate arrived, she learned that Miss Browne had been moved to the hospice wing. The attending nurse urged her not to go. "Miss Church, are you not in quarantine like the others? We are still admitting new patients and cases on a daily basis."

"I will be fine. I assure you. I have visited Miss Browne for a while now and I have no symptoms of consumption." Kate was tart in her response. She had to see Jilly today. It could be her last.

"All right then. But know that we cannot be responsible for any illness you might contract and word will be given to your Senior." The attendant was equally as sharp, her eyes almost piercing Kate over the top of her surgical mask. All the staff had taken to wearing copper and brass contraptions that continually misted the wearer with medicines and nutrients. "You can go unassisted, the hall to the left. Miss Browne is in the room on the right, at the very end." The terrible irony of Miss Browne's placement in the hospice made Kate's heart fill with sorrow. *This is literally her end.*

Kate walked slowly down the hall, noting the names on the charts on the closed doors. She heard a loud beep and rustling about from medical staff in the one of the rooms with an open door. It was hastily shut by a doctor leaving the room. Kate couldn't help but notice he carried away a red pocket watch that was rapidly fading to black.

Kate inhaled and carried on, trying to pretend all was well. As she neared Miss Browne's quarters, she passed a room with a door left slightly ajar. Kate fought the urge to spy, but caved when she saw a patient she recognized inside. Kate glanced up and down the hall. No one else was about, and so she peered in. Inside two ladies were resting, obviously heavily sedated to the point where they could not cough. They were both attached to odd bits of equipment, none of which were helping them live. They simply let them continue to exist for a while longer. One of the women, despite her sickly appearance, was so familiar that Kate did a double take. She was the woman that was in the photo on Director Roth's desk.

Kate didn't debate. She stole into the room to get a closer look. She checked over the woman's chart at the end of the bed, scanning over the most pertinent details:

Meredith Pratt, female, aged 38.

Senior Member, Thomas Roth. Attempting urgent notification due to Engagement.

Extreme rapid onset of consumption.

Treatment-all means available.

Prognosis-fatal.

Kate nearly dropped the chart. She took a quick last look at Miss Pratt. The Director's paramour had been admitted only a few hours prior and was gravely ill. Kate paused. Lord Wilson's instructions explicitly forbid her to use the serum. She pursed her lips and turned out of the room with her heart in flux.

Kate went to Miss Browne's room while trying to hide her tears. This could be the last time she would see her. *I need to be cheery, positive. Definitely kind,* she groomed herself. Kate opened the door to a touching scene.

Mr. Scott was sitting in a chair and holding Miss Browne's hand. His eyes were filled with tears as his other hand wiped her forehead with a moist cloth. Even though her eyes blinked intermittently, Kate could see the love in them.

"Hello Miss Browne." Kate attempted to sound happy, but when Jilly's watery eyes glanced in her direction a lump formed in her throat.

"I think it would be alright if you called her Jilly now." Mr. Scott looked devastated, his face had grown pale and his clothes crumpled. He stood with a weariness that looked more appropriate on a man much older. He pulled another chair over for Kate. "Please, sit. She's not supposed to talk much, but would you like a few moments alone?" He looked at the both of them. Jilly nodded. "I'll be back in a moment dear." He kissed her forehead with such tenderness that Kate swore her heart would break. Mr. Scott left the room while shutting the door behind him.

Kate sat and started to speak. "Jilly-" Miss Browne tried to motion with her weakened arms towards her mask. "Pull down?" Kate questioned and she nodded.

Jilly inhaled with a horrid raspy breath. Kate could smell the putrid infection from her lungs. With great effort, Jilly motioned for Kate to lean in. Kate moved quickly to the bed while sensing Jilly's time on earth was winding down.

"Oh Kate," Jilly whispered. "Such a good soul." Her body struggled with each word. "I will be gone soon. I want to tell you something." Kate's face was now almost directly against hers. "Don't wait, don't care for the rules. You must tell Lord Wilson. You know." Jilly's eyes fluttered, Kate panicked and tried to put the mask back on but Jilly gripped her hand with what little strength she had left. "Tell him you love him. I know you do. I see it in your face when you speak of him. Promise me?" Jilly's eyes had a glimmer that belied her illness.

"Yes, yes I will." Bitter tears streamed over Kate's cheeks. She could not believe she was making a promise to another dying friend.

"Time is short, yes?" Jilly managed to smile.

"Yes." Kate replied.

"Don't let Mr. Scott be bitter?" The sound of her lungs filled with death's call made her sound more desperate.

"Of course I will. I promise. I know you love him." Kate squeezed her hand tightly.

"Alright then." Jilly paused. "You need to go. But, again, love, don't wait. Yes?"

"Yes." Kate smiled through her cry. "I'll get Mr. Scott then?"

Jilly nodded and Kate returned her medical device. She rose and like Mr. Scott, gave a sweet peck to her forehead. "I love you, Jilly. We are friends forever now."

Miss Browne smiled and slipped into slumber, comforted that she had passed on her dying wisdom. Kate stepped out to Mr. Scott checking his pocket watch in the hall. It had just started to pulse a light pink. "I am so sorry, I cannot find the words." Kate tried to comfort.

"Just do as she asked, Miss Church. Don't wait." He urged and ducked back into the room.

"Ah, well done Miss Church, but you seem a bit distracted today." Master Richards grinned at his student as he offed his mask. They had sparred for almost a half hour. Kate hadn't had a lesson in a few days, but when she had been told she could resume classes, she didn't hesitate. "Let's have some refreshments. Are things alright then?" he pried.

Kate tried to hide her melancholy feelings from Master Richards. "It is just difficult with so many, well, of the illness that abounds right now." Kate commented her voice dry with weariness.

"Yes, hideous, isn't it? We are both lucky to be well." Master Richards's eyes locked on her. He was happy to see that she had survived the disease that had plagued the Society.

It was one that he had helped implement. During his first week after he was recruited by a Senior Member, another fencing instructor that was a Fixture in the field, he'd smuggled in several vials of fluid that seemed to be cologne. He did not hesitate to put droplets of the contaminated mixture into everything he could. Water that students drank. The fountain inside the Main Hall. Eventually finding the main plumbing system from plans obtained from his superiors and filling it with whole bottles of infectious poison. However, despite his orders, he did not intend to harm Miss Church. In fact, he wanted the opposite.

"Yes, we are." Kate turned away to set down her weapon. As she stood, Master Richards had come up swiftly behind her.

The warmth of his body against her backside stunned her. "Kate, I am so glad you are alive. You have no idea of what you mean to me." The heat of his breath burned against the tender skin of her neck. She shuddered as his hands grasped her shoulders then ran down her arms. He caught her off balance and twirled her around to face him. "You know that I love you."

Before Kate could respond, his lips were against her own, his hands gripping her upper back and then her waist. His tongue dipped deeply into her mouth, quashing any words Kate tried to emit.

Her body responded against her will at first. He felt so good against her, the temptations of his flesh overwhelmed Kate and she kissed him back. His fingers slipped to her backside for a squeeze, then returned to her upper body and finally to her head, pulling her hair loose. Ironically it cooled Kate's head for a moment, just enough to bring her back to proper thought.

Her arms had fallen loosely to her sides, dangling like a doll's. Strength awoke in her and her hands flew to his chest to push him away. "No." she mumbled, turning her face away from him.

"No?" He laughed. "That kiss was no?" He still held her hair and teased it.

Kate opened her eyes fully while stepping back. "Yes. I mean, no. We need to stop."

"Oh come now, Kate, how silly. We are adults aren't we? Why do we need to follow antiquated rules?" He chided and tried to reach for her chin.

She responded with a nasty slap to his face that echoed through the room and made his lip bleed and cheek redden. "No. You know this is not proper." Kate stood stiffly. "We could be Terminated."

He replied with a deep-throated chuckle. "Oh really. Do you fear that? Dying for the greater good?"

A queer feeling overcame her, much like when Drasco had tried to kill her in Iris. She was in the presence of darkness. But unlike Drasco, Master Richards had been an evil temptation that was masquerading as kindness. "I made a promise." Kate spoke with defiance. Promises, to Riley, to Lord Wilson, to Jilly. "I keep my promises."

"Oh so you say. Wait until they start taking from you. Your friends, your family. I mean, you gave up everything to come here, did you not?" He removed his gloves and dabbed his bloodied lip with one of them in a fine manner. "Kate, the things you do not know about your beloved Society." His eyes became steely dark pools as he ranted and stalked around her like a lion in prey. "And Lord Wilson, your Senior. Quite the character. A puppet master really. You do know you are just a pawn for him, don't you?" Master Richards seethed.

"That was then, and this is now." Kate tilted her nose up in retort. She tried desperately to keep him engaged in conversation while planning to escape. The weapons were now out of reach. Their passionate kiss had moved them about ten feet away from the table and arms storage.

"He has you, doesn't he? There are things he could give you? But he won't quite put himself out there where love is concerned, will he?" Her instructor was now her foe, embattling her with words that he spat out to induce the deepest of harm.

"You're wrong." Kate immediately thought of the music box. Lord Wilson had given her hope. He was coming back, she would have to be patient. But how long could she wait? Her mind faltered. But she'd just promised Jilly she wouldn't. "I won't wait." Her admission slipped out and surprised her.

"Can't you see? You shouldn't have to." He rolled his eyes. "I can take you now to where you can have all of this and more. Why are you in such denial? Did you not just kiss me like a lover?" His voice took a passionate tone. "Come with me Kate, please?"

"No." She crossed her arms, her voice flat. "You can leave without me." *You are strong now.* Her old mantra echoed.

Master Richard's wicked laugh bounced through the room. "Oh Kate, how nice of you to let me leave. But can't you see it's me who's letting you live? Did you think that you survived all of this just because of luck?"

Kate couldn't believe her ears. "You started the consumption?"

"Oh darling, and so much more. You have no idea. The Society will be destroyed and you with it." He stepped towards her with a nasty growl and pulled on one of her hands. "But, I can keep you. This is your last chance." His voice turned back to that of tenderness and he again leaned to her. "Say you'll be mine?"

"Never." Kate kicked his knee and dragged her boot down the front of his shin. Master Richards fell forward and grabbed her hair as she turned to run. He yanked her tresses so hard, the force pulled her back onto him as they fell to the floor.

He rolled and pushed her face down with one hand. His body had broken her fall, but her cheek ached from the crash against the floor. She tried to reach up to free her hair but his other hand grabbed both of hers to fully pin her down. "So you like it from behind." He hissed and salaciously licked her ear.

Kate squirmed beneath him. "No. Please, stop."

"Oh, I like hearing you beg. It can be like this all the time if you like it rough." He panted wildly while his fist tightened around her wrists. "You know this excites me. Having you underneath me. You are such the tease, Miss Church." His other hand released her hair and slid aside her hip. He moved back ever so slightly to allow his hand to explore her crotch through her training trousers.

"No." Kate whimpered. She desperately tried to push him off, but it only furthered his hardening groin against her buttocks.

"Kate, I don't have to hurt you. I can be tender. It's up to you. All you have to do is say yes." He removed his hand from her crotch and ran it along her side. He gripped her hip again, but this time released his body away enough to flip Kate onto her back. He was on all fours, preparing to press himself directly against her. Her panicked face looked into his as she tried to free her hands from his vise-like grip. His voice became unexpectedly soft. "Don't make me do this. Believe me, I am a gentleman. I will take such good care of you. I love you. Will you let me?"

Kate saw her chance and feigned relaxation. "I-I" She purposefully stuttered. "Won't!" She kneed him in the groin and he fell awkwardly on his side. Kate rolled and scrambled to her feet. The door was too far way for her to run out. She instead stumbled towards the armor cabinet.

Master Richards, overcome by both the desire to catch her and to kill her, made a quick recovery. Kate could hear him slipping on the floor behind her just as she was gripping her sabre. By the time she turned to face him, he too was grabbing his weapon. Kate gulped. He was already trained and six inches taller. The odds were not good on a physical scale. She would have to continue to beat him with mental tactics.

They faced each other, tips up. "Oh Kate. You are quite the minx aren't you? Full of fight, passion. Tell me, are you the same in the bedroom?" He charged forward and the fight began.

"Wouldn't you like to know?" Kate smirked. Their blades crisscrossed in a ballet of metal, then both stepped back to pause.

"Yes, I would. You know, I'm a much younger man than that old fart Lord Wilson. I can't imagine he knows how to satisfy you."

He attacked again, this time with a back-hand from the left that cut a few inches from Kate's hair. She stepped back in parry, just in time to see the locks fall. "Oh, I think I want to keep those. I like how you smell Kate. I could keep those strands in a little box, you know?" They measured each other, walking in a slow circle. "Or," he sneered, "I could be in that sweet little box of yours."

Kate attacked in anger and without focus. He easily met her challenge, forcing her to step back several times as the clashing of their swords echoed in the gymnasium. He pushed forward, just barely slashed her left arm and drove her back to the break table. Kate fell against it, but manage to roll off the side. As she crashed to the floor on her bottom, the pain shot through her spine with enough fire that she dropped her weapon. A thin line of blood seeped through her jacket.

He stood over her. "Kate, darling, we do not have to fight like this, hmm? Surely you know I have experience, talent. You cannot win against me, why bother?" He stuck the tip in her face and flicked her cheek. A fine point of vermillion immediately came to the surface of her skin.

"You'll have to kill me. I won't quit." Kate warned as her chest heaved. She tried to push herself up, but now the brutal pain burned through her legs and arms as well. Just as she thought she couldn't take it anymore, the agony stopped. Her skin tingled and ceased bleeding. Kate then realized the serum was still in her system. It was healing her wounds as they were happening.

"I could cut you to pieces if you like. But you're a tough one, I'd like to see you fight for your life then." He lifted her weapon with his sabre and dropped it into her lap. "Come on now, get up. Remember, this is how you want it." He turned away from her and walked a few steps. "I'm waiting."

This is my chance. Kate feigned weakness coming off the floor and pretended to drag herself forward in a crouched position.

Master Richards looked over his shoulder, then turned to face her. He flung his arms wide open. "I'm still waiting." He laughed with eyebrows raised in jest.

"You'll have to wait forever." Kate gazed through the hair that had fallen over her face. She pounced and made a single quick stab at the direct center of his chest.

Kate punctured his heart and pulled her weapon back so quickly that it sounded like a wine cork popping from its bottle. The narrow dot left behind soon exploded into a broad crimson patch on the fencing jacket of Master Richards.

He slumped forward onto his knees, his sabre clanging to the floor. His mouth fell open and his eyes widened in shock. "Nooo. Oh Kate, how I loved you." His words gushed out in a crippling moan as he collapsed on his side. Master Richard's eyes fluttered as his chest gurgled blood onto the floor. With two last slow heaves, he expired.

Mr. Scott charged into the room. "Miss Church, please-" he paused at the horrific scene before him. "Oh my God. What happened?"

"He tried to kill me. He's a spy." Kate was soaked in sweat and panted aloud.

Mr. Scott rushed to her side. "Please hurry, oh God, Miss Church. Miss Jilly has died."

"What?" Kate almost fell where she stood.

"I'll handle this, get changed." Mr. Scott ran for an attendant while Kate pushed upstairs to the student's room. It felt odd for her to be entering on her side without her trainer on the other. She trembled in the aftermath of the subterfuge. He'd said the same things that Lord Wilson had months ago. Similar promises. But Master Richards had confessed his love, even in death. And Jilly had passed. Kate's head fell into her hands as she wept.

You are strong now, again rattled in her head. Kate gathered herself and stood. *I did what I had to do.*

By the time Kate had dressed, two men from the Garden had been called in to clean up a very messy situation in the gymnasium. And so Master Richards, the alias for Julian Ellis, the second Ellis son, had died, consumed by his love for a woman whom his mother despised.

A few hours later, Director Roth and Lord Wilson were on a train bound for St. Louis from Boston. They had spent several days on covert missions. First they had tried to secure intelligence on the assassination of Kate's family. With a bit of effort, they were able to bribe a certain bartender for information. This was the same man who had served Nathan Halton his last drinks. Combined with the description of the man Meredith Pratt was able to provide, the two gentlemen were able to divulge some details from a porter at the hotel where the assassin stayed.

This led to a doctor who took cash payments from desperate individuals. For more cash, the physician then had a name for the man he'd treated for a bullet wound to the shoulder, a Mr. Frank Parsons. After several wires and connections, it was discovered that Mr. Parsons was staying in St. Louis. Parsons was on the well-protected alias list. A list that was updated only when a certain group was active against the Society. Its only copy was held by the Director. This did not bode well for Director Roth and Lord Wilson who realized they must return home immediately.

Their second task was much more frustrating. Finding the man that Madeline Fahey had sold her soul to had been a lost cause. They had hoped to find a connection to Mr. Parsons. Miss Fahey's personal effects didn't leave any clues. Whatever plans she had sold were long gone and the trail cold. Both high ranking Society men were worried.

"Miss Kate said it looked like a steeple. Perhaps they are planning on infiltrating one of our churches? Or robbing the banks?" Lord Wilson offered a theory.

"Possibly. With this latest development we must be on guard. Who knows what they are after?" Director Roth frowned over their paperwork.

Their train made a brief stop in Cleveland. The customary knock brought them both to attention. Their porter rushed in and shut the door behind him. "You'll want to read this." He shoved a telegram at the Director.

"By God!" he exclaimed. "Your Miss Church is quite extraordinary. She just killed our mole, it was Master Richards."

"Richards!" Lord Wilson bellowed. "Bastard. And I thought he was only after Miss Kate's heart."

"Yes, seems she finished him off during a fencing duel. My Mr. Scott, despite his sorrow, managed to go through his office afterwards. It appears that Richards started the consumption threat, and was spying on students through a hole in his office. That's not all. His last piece of mail was halted. A short letter addressed to a Mr. Parsons. Actually just two words, consumption completed."

"Good God man. There's our link." Lord Wilson sat on the edge of his chair. "They're after Kate, whomever they are."

"Christopher, I think at this point we do know who they are." Director Roth was concerned. An old grudge was coming back to haunt them both. "Miss Church has only stirred up old adversaries. I believe it's the same ones who want the keys."

Lord Wilson agreed. "I think it's high time we sent them a message."

"Yes, indeed." The Director paused and wrote down implicit instructions for the porter. "Have this done immediately. Today. We want them to know just what they're dealing with."

"Yes Sir." The porter left the room as the two Seniors lit cigars. For a moment it was quiet. It had been quite the journey for the two men trying to safeguard all around them.

Finally the Director spoke. "It's a shame about Jilly Browne."

"Yes, yes it is."

"And you denied Mrs. Finch use of the serum?"

"Yes, and Miss Kate acting as a dispensary as well."

"It must be hard determining who shall live and who shall die, eh?" Director Roth seemed not at all pleased.

"Remember Thomas, we can't give it to everyone. We have to think of the consequences. Should everyone have it? Then all ailments are cured, hmm? But what then if it's overused? It loses its power, the ability to heal? The natural human immunity then relies too much on outside cures?" Lord Wilson argued. "Then we have no other recourse. We can't just find other plants or hope there's one like it. We have to conserve. I know not of any other plant like it in the world."

"But you didn't hesitate to use it on Miss Church? And other subversive tools as well, for another beating away from death's door?" The Director alluded to the time travel device that Dr. Harrington had developed.

"You know, as well as I, that she is my last chance. I will not find anyone else like her." Lord Wilson sat back in his plush seat. "Besides, would you not do the same for Miss Pratt?"

"Point taken." The Director doused his cigar. Neither gentleman realized how relevant their conversation was at that very moment. Miss Pratt was on the verge of dying. And because of the delicacy of their mission, Director Roth had no idea he was losing his love.

Kate climbed through the window with her heart beating so hard that she swore it would pop through her chest. Most of the lights were out in the Sanatorium. The halls were still except for a couple of the patients that had managed to survive the consumption and were still coughing in recovery.

Kate remembered exactly which room was Miss Pratt's from her visits to Jilly. She had scaled the flowered trellis of the hospice outside, and despite its frozen nature, climbed quickly to the room.

Only hours before she had debriefed with Mr. Scott. Kate had been given the evening away from work after a visit with Dr. Finch. She'd bathed, eaten a quiet dinner in her room and carefully hidden a small bottle of serum she had stolen from the doctor's office. After witnessing so much death earlier in the day, and knowing that Meredith Pratt and Director Roth were attached, she did not want anyone else to suffer. Kate rode Sonny to the Sanatorium as soon as most of the Main Hall had quieted for the evening.

Miss Pratt had the room to herself; apparently her roommate had died. The neighboring bed remained bare. Kate was relieved that the door to the room was only opened a crack.

Meredith lay dying on the bed, tucked tightly in. She was heavily sedated in order to quell her cough. But she was still wheezing through some contraption that she was attached to. It blew warm air into her nostrils but didn't seem to be helping much, if at all. Her skin was a sickening grey green. Kate hoped she wasn't too late. The consumption had crashed through Miss Pratt like a train off the rails. Jilly had probably been sick a few weeks. Others had almost healed. Meredith was deteriorating in less than forty-eight hours.

Kate approached the bed slowly, every ounce of her being ready to dart out at a moment's notice. She dared not get caught. She covered her mouth with a handkerchief and then rubbed her fingers over the bottle of the serum in her left pocket.

She touched Miss Pratt's shoulder. Her eyes fluttered. "Meredith, not a word. It's Kate Church, Lord Wilson's Member. I have something for you that should help. If you can hear me, blink once," Kate commanded.

Meredith blinked.

"Alright then. I'm going to put this sticky liquid to your lips. If you can't swallow, just try to lick it, okay? If you understand, blink," Kate encouraged. Meredith blinked again.

Kate pulled the cork off the small bottle and tugged on Meredith's lower lip. She poured in a few drops. Meredith licked her dry, cracked mouth.

"Again, alright?" Kate whispered. Meredith blinked a third time. Kate put more drops on her lips and waited. After a minute, Meredith closed her eyes and the wheezing stopped. Kate drew in her breath, fearing she had died.

But Meredith's mouth fell open and Kate could suddenly hear air reaching her lungs. Kate poured more liquid onto her tongue. "Go on, drink."

Meredith's lips became pink and color returned to her face. Her eyes opened fully as she took a deep inhale. "Don't say anything." Kate cajoled as Meredith was fully conscious. "A last sip."

Meredith nodded this time and was able to swallow another teaspoon on her own. "Mmm."

"Better?" Kate smiled and untucked her from the bed.

"Yes, yes." Meredith cried and tears rolled down her face.

"Shh. I'm going to pour some water for you. Try and drink it." Kate helped her sit up, held the glass and Meredith swallowed it whole with gusto. She was so vibrant and alert that Kate was frightened that she'd given her too much. "How do you feel?"

"Hungry." Meredith giggled. "Oh my Kate. I'm fine. I feel well."

"Good." Kate sat on the bed, removed her kerchief and held her hand. "I know we all have secrets Meredith. I'm going to have to ask you to keep another. I can't tell you about what I've given you, only that it works miracles. Understand that we cannot speak of this any further."

"Of course not," Meredith promised.

"I must go. Rest well." Kate brushed her forehead with a gentle kiss and tears fell down her cheeks.

"I'm fine, Kate, really." Meredith grinned.

"I know, I know. But Jilly Browne died today. I didn't want to lose anyone else." Kate stood.

"I'm so sorry Kate." Meredith began to cry too as she realized that her stature in the Society probably saved her life.

"Thank you, but don't be. I'm glad it worked." Kate paused as footsteps echoed in the hall. She winked and stole back out the window.

It was just in time. A nurse came in and immediately noticed Meredith's improved condition. "Oh my, Miss Pratt, it's a miracle."

Miracle indeed, Kate smiled as she hurried down the lattice work and back to the Main Hall.

Mrs. Ellis could not believe her ears. "Yes. Julian, mother." The youngest Ellis son informed his mother of his brother's passing. They were staying at a small hotel in St. Louis proper during what had been a couple of weeks of heavy snowfall.

"And how?" She hissed, sitting taller in her chair. Her voice was as cold as the frost on the window pane.

"A duel of sorts. We don't know exactly how he was discovered, but Miss Church stabbed him during a fencing exercise." Atticus Ellis knelt down in front of his mother and held her hand. "I am so sorry."

"Is that is all that is left?" She nodded towards an end table. On top of the beautiful piece of furniture was an even more elegant silver fencing cup trophy that Julian Ellis had won years ago. He'd displayed it in his Society office with pride, even while masquerading as Master Richards. It had been left with their hotel lobby attendant only an hour before. Although his name was not engraved on the outside, his ashes had clearly been deposited on the inside. It was a not so subtle warning to the Ellis family.

"Bloody fool," Mrs. Ellis cursed. "That bitch has stolen two of mine. How dare she? She must die." She cackled, jumped up from her chair in a rage, and slapped her hands on her desk. They landed over detailed plans of the Society Grounds just a few miles away. "They all should die." Her chest heaved in anger. "We need to pack immediately. They know we're here. We move forward with Cecil's plan to get the keys back. Get Mr. Gotham into position as well."

"That was as splendid a sendoff as a place like ours could give." Miss Pratt followed behind Kate as they left the small chapel on the Society grounds a day after Miss Browne's passing.

"Yes, it was. The flowers were lovely, very fragrant, and sweet." Kate muttered, still saddened by Jilly's death and missing Lord Wilson terribly.

The skies remained grey over the grounds as other Members passed them and headed back. Mr. Scott paused briefly. "Words cannot..." He fumbled over his speech.

"There are no words for times like these, Mr. Scott." Miss Pratt reached out and held his hands tightly. "Director Roth and Lord Wilson deeply regret that they cannot be here today. They should return very soon and will be in contact with you then."

"I am so incredibly sorry for your loss." Kate encouraged with a hand on the gentleman's shoulder.

"Thank you ladies, I must be off." He pulled away with his head down against the cold.

Meredith paused until Mr. Scott was out of earshot. "Kate, that could've been me too. I can never be grateful enough, and I can't express it anymore." Meredith whispered as the December winds blew stiffly around them. "But we shall be friends, shan't we?"

"Yes. Absolutely." Kate wiped her tears.

"Tea then?"

"Yes. Tea would be lovely."

As the two ladies left the chapel, the snow began to fall again. *Frozen angel tears,* Kate mused, her heart aching for all she had lost.

13 A FEW WORDS ABOUT LORD WILSON

Lord Wilson relaxed in his lounger while sipping hot chamomile tea and pondering his future with Kate. He'd brashly sent her a gift while away. Mr. Scott had alerted him and Director Roth that Master Richards had become far too close to Kate. Lord Wilson, feeling not only her endangerment, but an ominous cloud of jealousy, sent the music box to her as a sign of hope. The bold move had more than served its purpose.

"Sir, will Miss Church be coming over this evening?" Leeds interrupted his conflicted thoughts.

"No, but she will tomorrow, for lunch and the remains of the day. There will be much to discuss." Lord Wilson would have to know absolutely everything about Master Richards. He'd nearly killed Kate, which made his insides pinch painfully. He didn't think he could bear to lose anyone else.

Did I make a mistake in bringing her to the Society? Director Roth had not been pleased with her initial behavior, but Lord Wilson had convinced him that it was just one slip in judgement, that she was worth the risk, and that he was to be personally responsible for her. Lord Wilson hoped that she would calm; he did not want to kill her spirited nature but did not want that same drive to get Kate assassinated. It was that balance that made a good Member.

Oddly enough, Lord Wilson himself had those same character traits. To tame them had been quite a challenge.

London, England, 1869

"That boy needs to settle down." The elder Lord Wilson chided as he watched his eldest son Christopher ride recklessly through their fields.

"Oh dear! He's always been such a spirited boy. Smart, but not overtly bookish like Daniel." Lady Wilson twittered as she finished a book of poetry. "In fact, he reminds me more of you every day."

"Bah." Lord Wilson turned from the window. "Please tell me I was never so silly in courting you."

"Hmm. Perhaps. But don't forget, he's had other interests. Like plants." Lady Wilson grinned at her eldest son's variety of activities.

"Maybe. But now, only uses his study of botany, to acquire the rarest of roses for all the young ladies." Lord Wilson smirked.

Outside, a young Christopher Wilson demonstrated his talents as an excellent horseman. He pushed his steed over the highest fences, much to the chagrin of his friends and several available ladies watching. The power of the race excited him, setting his blue eyes afire.

"Come on now Christopher! You can't charm all the ladies." Fenton Crisp called out with a hint of disdain. Mr. Crisp was almost on par with the young Wilson. He was a handsome lad, with dark locks and mysterious eyes. Mr. Crisp was clever, sometimes boastful, but could back up his grandiose statements with a vast scientific knowledge. His only folly was a penchant for strong liquors, for which he'd earned the nick name Crispy.

"Well, just maybe I can." The younger Wilson winked at a lovely woman, who'd just moved into his family's territory, as he dismounted. He hadn't talked to her yet, but Crispy had at least gathered her name, Helena. "Well Crispy, I say, I think you owe me twenty quid. I cleared every fence with nary a nick on this fine horse of mine."

"Oh, didn't I see the top slat of the fifth mark quiver a bit?"

"Humph, but it did not falter. Twenty, sir. But maybe, I'll buy you a round with that at the club." Christopher snickered as he handed his groomsman his crop.

"Can't say fairer than that." Crispy closed in on his friend as he forked over the money and whispered. "And perhaps no fairer than the new lady about town. A blue blood at that."

A crew of young folk gathered around the dashing Lord to be. The young women gossiped about his bachelor status. The men quipped about their latest escapades. But this new girl, Helena, caught Christopher's eye. "Lovely," he commented to Crispy. *Pretty*, he thought, but he was in no way ready to settle down. In fact maybe a bit of entertainment at the club was just what he needed that evening. Those plans were soon dashed.

His father's valet, Mr. Spencer, rushed out to the small group from the Hall, and handed Christopher a note. "Young Wilson, Sir. You've received a calling card from a neighbor. Your mother has asked that you return this request post haste."

Christopher looked at the invitation and almost bolted from the group. His head whipped about in an odd fashion. "I must go, some business to attend to, I'm afraid. I'm sure Crispy will keep you entertained." An old friend of his, Professor Thaddeus Barker, had returned after five years. Christopher dashed towards home much to the disappointment of the onlookers.

"I did not want to comment in front of your present company Sir, but your mother mentioned that Professor Barker is very unwell. His manservant apparently remarked that he has come home to die."

"Thank you, Spencer. Pull my things, I will dress immediately." Christopher broke into a trot up the hill to Wilson Hall, a home that had belonged to his family for at least a hundred years, built on land his ancestors had owned for centuries.

June 1857

"Now see here young man, seems you've obtained quite the scrape." A kind older man examined Christopher's freshly cut knee. "But, I think with a bit of magic, perhaps I can help."

"Oh that would be very good Sir. I'm ever so sorry my pup got into your garden." The boy was sincere in his apology. A winsome look crossed his pink cheeks.

As if on cue, the lad's beagle sat up with a friendly yap. The sound echoed through the small greenhouse of Professor Barker. "Ah, and I think that's an apology from her. What's the hound's name?"

"Lolly Belle. My father believes that she already has the makings of a great hunter."

"By jove, I think he's right too. She got that squirrel that's been eating my best berries." He tore a plump leaf from a small potted plant that stood apart from all the others on his pruning table. "Now this will sting for a bit." He pressed the foliage against Christopher's knee and a thick purple gel stung the young man's skin.

"Ouch."

"Hmm, just another moment." The Professor smiled as he wiped away the excess with a soft cloth. "There now, see? All better."

Christopher peered down in amazement. "It's gone."

"Yes indeed." The studied gentleman chuckled. "But as we promised before, tell your mother that the tear in your trousers was from young Lolly Belle taking a friendly jump at you. Understood?"

"Yes Sir." The curious child looked around the storage house filled with all kinds of odd greenery. "Do all of these plants have magic?"

"Ah well, on my many travels, I have discovered several of them do have particularly wonderful qualities. Would you like to learn more?"

"Yes sir, very much so." Lolly Belle howled in approval.

"I would enjoy having a new pupil. I'm fairly certain your father would approve."

Their friendly conversation was interrupted by a rap on the door. "Do come in," Professor Barker called out.

"Hello Professor." A very tall, sturdy young man with a bit of a northern lilt entered the greenhouse. He wore spotless military garb and had the posture of a well-to-do soldier.

"Well if it isn't Lieutenant Roth. Lieutenant, please meet young Christopher Wilson. He of Lord Wilson, the benefactor of my research and this lovely facility."

"Hello young man," the soldier bellowed. He had a deep voice despite his age of only twenty years. He turned to the Professor. "I wanted to tell you that I've been assigned to the Indian rebellion. I leave tomorrow."

"Ah, India. What a splendid place. Of course I prefer the African continent, but I believe that you shall find much adventure there." The Professor mused over his past travels. The boy turned away from the conversation of the two men, his curiosity peaked by the rare things that surrounded him.

Still, the older man lowered his voice. "I don't suppose that this will be a long skirmish, so when you return, I think that we will have much to talk about. I know that we have not been acquainted very long, but I believe I know of an employer that would be more than excited to have a man in their stable that's reached an officers rank at such a young age. Your military prowess will impress them much more than I can express. In addition, if you should hear of any rare, say, botanical finds on your trip, I would much appreciate a sample." The Professor was very keen on collecting what he could.

"Of course Sir, I'd be delighted." The soldier had been very pleased with this relationship as it had come with monetary benefits and a bit of prestige. Professor Barker was held in high esteem in educational circles, but had managed to maintain a low profile. Not everyone got to know the man behind the greenery as much as the young soldier had.

"God speed Lieutenant."

"Thank you Professor." The soldier left with a tip of his cap almost as quickly as he had entered.

"Don't be too soft," the Professor whispered.

Lieutenant Roth would indeed return a year later, not with samples, but to take up the offer of his new found mentor.

Professor Barker turned to his new student and grinned. The boy and his dog were absolutely rapturous in the tropical environment, moving from plant to plant while examining every inch of the place. And so began Lord Christopher Wilson's education which was well beyond anything his tutors could teach.

That day in the greenhouse was the first of hundreds. Young Christopher would finish his other studies as quickly as possible so he could hurry over to the greenhouse to learn more of the unique specimens within. The Professor also taught him of the wild beasts that roamed the far reaches of the planet and of the exotic environments they lived in. "They say the sun never sets on the British Empire. I will tell you, this is true young man. But we must respect and protect all that we have. And furthermore, all that we discover. That would include the serum. You must never tell anyone of what you see in here. Understood?"

"Yes Sir." The young Wilson replied earnestly, his eyes wide in amazement.

The Professor would often leave on trips, extending his finesse and knowledge around the globe. He was a supreme gatherer as well, ever mindful of the delicate balances of nature.

He instilled this pride to his pupil and eventually entrusted him to care for the greenhouse while he was gone despite having three manservants at his beck and call. Christopher also took great care in illustrating, documenting, and noting the characteristics of all specimens, work he delighted in.

The elder Lord Wilson was quite pleased with this relationship. The Professor visited Wilson Hall frequently as the Lord was his benefactor, although ironically, his Lordship did not know of some of the secrets he son was learning.

1862

Shortly after Christopher turned seventeen, he was summoned to the Professor's cottage for an urgent private meeting. The eldest Wilson son hadn't been to Professor Barker's greenhouse on a regular basis since he'd started formal education. Christopher grew into a tall, gregarious fellow while attending some of the best schools in England. His thirst for knowledge was almost insatiable. His father was grooming him to take over his estate and Wilson Hall.

Upon Christopher's arrival to the greenhouse, there was much scurrying about the grounds. "Welcome back young Wilson!" The Professor greeted him warmly. "My, what a strapping lad you have become."

"Thank you Sir. It's good to see you too."

"My dear young man, I believe that I have taught you everything that I know. I have asked you here because I need to make quite the extended adventure, this time to some of the deepest jungles of Africa. Your father tells me that you'll be learning much of his work soon, so I wanted to discuss a few things. Please sit down." The conversation took a serious tone as they sat down for tea. Christopher did not know it yet, but he was starting his very first Discussion. "I'll be travelling to quite a remote location. I've been there before, when I was a much younger man. Not much older than you are now. But I need to return fairly quickly, an urgent matter has come. I intend on coming back, however, should I not, you will inherit all of this."

"I'm sorry Sir, what?" Christopher sat taller in his chair. None of this was expected.

"Yes, I have been a tenant of you father's for quite some time. And this is his property. The greenery is mine. I have spoken to

Lord Wilson and he agrees; he would be delighted if you would keep this." The Professor ached to tell him more, but could not.

"I don't know what to say, Sir."

"Just promise me that you will take care of it. You'll guard the serum with your life. Not even your father yet knows of its existence. Should matters change, let's say the greenhouse is to be sold, or damage occurs from some unexpected source, I have someone for you to contact." The Professor stood and pulled out one of his oldest botany manuscripts. "On the inside of the first page, see here." He pointed directly to a name and address duly noted on the page. "You will contact this gentleman. You can entrust any of this to him. Do you understand?" Mr. Roth's information was written in small script on the page.

"Yes Sir." The young man was still stunned at the turn of events.

"Very well then, young Christopher. Continue on as you have. Your father will be proud."

"Thank you Sir."

"Thank you Christopher. Be on your way young man." The Professor gave his pupil a sturdy handshake before the young Wilson departed. Once the door shut behind him, there was a rustle of plants and an old friend emerged from a darkened corner of the structure. The professor smiled. "What do you think Mr. Roth?"

"I think that he will be an excellent benefactor like his father. And he has my information for emergencies." The former lieutenant stepped fully into the light of a lamp. Mr. Roth had retired from the military a wealthy young man and now worked for a very sincere organization. "I'm sorry I won't be here as often. It seems I will continue to travel as well."

"Of course not. You have work to tend to in the Americas. It's growing and so should we. Extending our reach there will not be a challenge." The Professor took a long look over the various foliage. "Africa is an entirely different matter."

"Indeed. Godspeed Sir." The young Member shook hands with the Fixture.

"You as well Mr. Roth." The two men parted for their respective missions.

1869

Helena Wickford smiled over her shoulder at the attractive lord to be. Her bare shoulders intrigued Christopher Wilson. He wondered if her breasts would be that same creamy pink.

"I am certain that she is interested. Look at that, now she's fluttering her fan." Fenton Crisp whispered to Christopher. They stood in the ballroom of Wilson Hall. Available ladies had been invited to meet the man would who inherit it and so much more.

Only a week before, Professor Barker had died after returning from his long trip to Africa. Christopher had been given a chance to say goodbye to his favorite mentor. And as promised, Christopher inherited all of his property, including the prized plants. The young Wilson didn't quite understand the complexity of owning such an interest. He would find out soon enough.

At that very moment, his attention was focused on the young woman who'd caught his eye about a month ago during his riding bet with his friend Crispy. "Hmm, I'm sure they are all interested, some perhaps in just my fortune. That is for certain. But the Wickford girl, is she smart enough to play coy?" Christopher remarked with a smile.

"I'd say." Crispy chortled. "And you should play back. Look at that raven-haired beauty by the piano." The two took a long look at another young woman across the room. Christopher knew that parties like this were necessary for his future, but a part of him had no desire to be confined just yet.

"So many hens. Almost too much for the cock." Christopher mumbled.

"These women are all here for you." Daniel Wilson laughed at his brother's reticence as he joined the two gentlemen.

"She's lovely. However, she was jilted a week before her nuptials. Rumor has it, her former fiancé found her cold. And he is the last of his name. There has to be a child to carry it on. I don't think she expected to have any relations with him whatsoever." Crispy's eyes raked over their target.

"Cold? She looks absolutely frozen," Daniel chimed in. He was only four years younger than his brother Christopher. He was jealous that his brother would inherit the family title and he relished Christopher's discomfort with the ladies vying for his attention.

But it wasn't for the lack for wanting to bed each of them. Christopher liked being the young man about town. During his last year away at school, he'd lost his virginity to a much older woman who ran the kitchen for the lads. Chicken soup would never be the same again.

"Pity. A waste of beauty." Christopher's eyes wandered back to Helena. He engaged her smile. Before Crispy could say another word, the young Lord to be was already asking her to dance.

"Did you have a good evening then? I quite like the young Wickford woman. Her family has just inherited some property adjoining ours."

The elder Lord Wilson poured a drink for him and his son in the drawing room after the party. "And she's quite pretty I'd say. Although no woman would look better to me than your mother."

"Yes. She seems intelligent as well." Christopher took a glass from his father as he reclined casually on a settee. He was attracted to Helena, but didn't feel the need to settle down yet.

"A very good quality in a young lady; important to have a woman of stature and not just some coquettish girl." Lord Wilson sipped at his brandy. "We'll invite her parents over for tea and formal introduction." He paused at his son's lackluster reaction. "My son, your future is here. You are educated. Right now I'm healthy and so is your brother. But still you need to prepare to take over the reins here."

"Father, I know. I just-" The younger Wilson started in mild protest.

"There can be no delay. Come here," Lord Wilson interrupted and walked over to his desk. Christopher stood and approached as asked.

The elder Wilson proffered a key from his waistcoat, unlocked a drawer and pulled out a thick leather-bound ledger. He placed it on his desk with a thud. "My son, what I'm about to show you is of the utmost confidence. It's a record of payments, donations really."

"To whom?" Christopher was startled. He father had shared everything about his business once he'd returned home from school. He was already taking well to managing the Wilson's extravagant grounds.

"I'm not certain really. Payments are automatically deducted from an account on a monthly basis. There is a trust I've set up that will continue to do so, in perpetuity. I started this process years ago at the request of Professor Barker. I want you to understand that you will never have access to this money and it is for the greater good. However, the estate is yours. And of course your brother Daniel will receive enough for a comfortable life after my death. I'm telling you this now because you must be ready. I want you to be prepared for change. I am responsible for our grounds and the village below it. You must be of noble means to retain our family's good name. I'm counting on you Christopher. The time to step forward is now. You understand?"

The younger Wilson had never seen his father so serious and it made his heart pace uneasily. "Yes, father."

"Very good. We'll look forward to meeting Miss Wickford's family then. Hopefully she will be a good match. I only want the best for you." Lord Wilson touched his son's shoulder with a fine pat. But he needn't worry. Christopher was soon smitten beyond his imagination.

"A June wedding would be splendid." Lady Wickford agreed with her hostess and soon to be mother of the groom, Lady Wilson. "Warm, but not too unbearably hot. Good weather in which to travel."

Christopher Wilson tried to feign interest in the upcoming nuptials. It wasn't that he wasn't ready for marriage, he loved Helena. But the copious amount of planning bored him to tears. He wished it was already his wedding night, although he'd probably gone a bit too far with Helena already. She tempted him so.

It was a few months after he'd first laid eyes on her at the party at the Hall. The expansive home would also host the wedding, as the ladies and help determined over a luncheon. After food was served and the meal finished, the men were grateful to take a stroll outdoors. Christopher winked at his soon to be lady of the house as they left.

The initial meeting with the families was more than pleasant. For an only child, Helena was not spoiled. She was genuinely kind and whip smart. She had a lilting laugh at the silliest of jokes. But most of all, she was a trifle naughty when they were able to steal bits of time alone. Today would be no different. After the men returned, dessert was served and the two stole a moment in the drawing room.

"Kiss me," Helena demanded with a captivating giggle that shook the loose golden curls that framed her pale face.

"Shhh." Christopher tried to quiet her, but he was giddy with desire himself. He had been with other women, painted ladies from the club for the most part. But Helena was different. She had a natural poise that made his heart ache. "I'll kiss you."

His lips brushed slowly against her while his hands ran over her shoulders and then caressed her back. He couldn't wait until he could touch inside her clothes, to let his fingers wander the softness of her skin. For the first time in the younger Wilson's life, he was truly in love. She returned the kiss with a gentle pull on his tongue. His whole body burned as he forgot every other previous dalliance. Helena would be his and there would be no others.

Unfortunately for the Lord to be, this bliss would be undone.

Christopher Wilson struggled to open his pasty shut eyes. They and his right calf seared in pain. A warm, sticky wetness covered his face. As he pawed slowly and then blinked, Christopher could finally see that his hands and his clothing were splattered with blood. For a moment he completely forgot where he was. He'd fallen on his side facing some of the wet spring greenery on his family's estate.

Although his arms were sore, much like the rest of his body, he was able to push himself up to a sitting position. He adjusted his vision again only to be horrified at the sight of his leg. His calf muscle had been ripped from his body with the remaining flesh and bone completely exposed. He inhaled sharply while grasping at his cravat. Although he moved quickly to tie off the wound, it felt like an eternity. His ears roared with a dull pang and his head felt afire. Finally his eyes cleared enough for him to examine the world gone wrong around him.

The day had started well enough. Helena had come to picnic with the Wilsons just a few months before their nuptials. Spring seemed to arrive early with splendid clear blue skies, so the carriage was left open.

Helena wore a lovely blue and gold dress that brought out the pink in her skin and green in her eyes. A stunning bonnet protected her brilliant strands. As a gentle wind blew, all he could think about was how he would have her for eternity soon. His parents were holding hands while the sun shone down on them. He remembered thinking that he wanted that happiness for his own marriage when suddenly there were sharp bangs and then darkness as he was thrown violently from the carriage.

He saw only the fields and the road that ran beside their creek. He couldn't walk, so he began to crawl to the road at a snail's pace. When he reached the well-worn wheel path, he could see tracks of the carriage that veered off the cliff to the water below. He again tried to stand, but fell forward at the edge. He howled at the sight of the over turned carriage, his own voice rattling his eardrums in a terrifying buzz. The horse had broken free and sipped leisurely at the water, unaware that the persons he guided through the fields only moments earlier had perished.

The bullet ridden bodies of Helena Wickford, and Lord and Lady Wilson were strewn about the rocky bottom of the stream. As young Christopher tried to fully comprehend what had happened, he slipped into unconsciousness.

"Sir. Sir, Christopher. Christopher Wilson?" A doctor prodded at his new patient.

"Hmm, yes. That would be me. I think." Christopher's eyes fluttered open.

"You've had a terrible accident, Sir. You're in a hospital. Can you see, Sir?" A tall dark-haired man gazed at Christopher's face.

"Yes. I can." The room slowly came into focus. It was small and plain, with various carts and shelves aligned to the walls. He didn't recognize any of it. "Can you hear me alright?"

"Yes," Christopher muttered.

"I'm going to look into your eyes. You've been out quite some time with an incredible blow to the head. A couple of days, really." The doctor peered at the young Lord for a moment. "I'm going to let you rest for a bit, then we'll run more tests. If everything is well, you'll probably be able to leave in a few days."

Suddenly visions of the accident flashed through his mind. "My family?"

"I'm sorry Sir. Your parents and fiancé have perished. However, you brother Daniel is here." The doctor lowered his voice. "I'm so sorry for your loss. But I must tell you, there is so much more to learn about the accident and your condition. You mustn't say anything to your brother until you're up to speed young man. Is that understood?"

Christopher had not a clue what his doctor was insinuating, but he had neither the strength nor mental capacity to deal with it. "Yes," he mumbled furtively.

"Good, now please listen carefully. The accident you were in was made to look like a robbery. All items of high value were taken off their persons. But I assure you, it was not. Your parents supported a cause that is unknown to most. It is a secret society, funded through many like your family. Those that are opposed to this notion intended to assassinate them in order to cut off these funds even though your father had no other direct link to this organization. Once your engagement was announced, I'm certain that they wanted to stop the transfer of monies from your father's generation to yours. Lord Wilson did speak of this to you recently, did he not?"

"Yes."

"Good. What they did not know, is your death wouldn't have stopped this trust, as you were already informed. Now, for the most important part. You will be a benefactor like your father to this group called the Society, but you will be offered a more active role in this process. Those that wished to harm you and your family? They still think that you're dead. The Society has been sent to help you recover and determine what role you will play. I am sorry that you have unwillingly been put into danger, but your life has been spared, and choices must be made. You will have a short time to make them. Do you understand this?" At that very moment, the young Wilson was set on a course to his destiny.

"Yes."

"For the next part, I'm going to lift your blanket. You may be horrified. Do you remember what happened?"

"Yes, I took a blow to the head. And my, my leg." He stuttered. Christopher expected his appendage to be gone.

"We saved it, through very generous modern means known only to the Society. Take a look." The physician pulled up the cover with a whoosh. "Let me help you up."

Christopher could not believe his eyes, his calf looked normal. Swollen, yet the flesh appeared to have returned. "What the devil?"

"Not sorcery, machinery. See here." The doctor pressed a tiny latch and the calf opened. The muscle was gone, completely replaced by a small steam machine that pumped life through his leg. "You will be shown how to maintain it. Parts can be replaced and it should last a lifetime. Without this, you would have bled out, even with your makeshift tourniquet. Our Members found you just in time. Your head is another matter. A bullet grazed your temple and you soundly hit the ground. We stitched up the gash, but you're going to have concussion symptoms for a while. That is why we'd like to contain you here, for your recovery."

"Where's here?"

"You are at the village doctor. But we've given him a bit of a holiday to have his exam room and upstairs quarters just for you. We'd like to keep you in hiding for at least a few days. Word of your family's death could not be hidden. Would you like to remain dead?"

"What?" A shock waved over the young man.

"This is your choice. We can say you survived the accident, but not your injuries. We'll announce your death. Your brother Daniel will take over the estate. He's much too young, so we'll have advisors to work with his barristers."

"And the other option?"

"We'll say you're in a coma. Not too loudly of course. You'll be transferred back to the Hall in a few days. Only Daniel and our group will know of this scheme. Your family's staff will be given time off to grieve. They will eventually be replaced with other knowledgeable folk and given employment elsewhere, unless there is someone currently there who could be trusted?"

"Spencer. He was my father's manservant. He was to stay on even after his death."

"So you would like to remain alive to the public for now? But in a state of coma? Just know that once the air is cleared, you could remain a target for those that wanted you dead."

A fire rose within the young Wilson. "I want to live, because those bastards will die for what they've done."

It was just after dark when the new Lord Wilson left the Hall for the cottage that once housed the Professor. Spencer had been entrusted with the care of the plants until Christopher recovered. He stumbled into the greenhouse and found the plant that contained the fresh serum. He pulled two of the plump leaves, squirted one into his mouth, and then rubbed the second against the gash on his temple. Then he sat in the Professor's old study chair and relaxed.

Soon the headache and dizziness was gone. The deep cut warmed with a sting and then cooled. He felt over the skin. It was smooth without a trace of damaged tissue. He pulled more of the plant leaves into a bottle and corked it shut. He also plucked a few of the roses. They reminded him of the Professor.

"Thank God for the Professor." Christopher grimaced. He felt the best he had in days. *I will be well, and there will be revenge.* He promised himself as he returned to the Hall. Lord Wilson had made a deal with this new Society. He would be a Member. He was convinced that his family's blood had not been shed in vain. The warm spring wind pulled at his coat as he strode to the countryside home. There would be hell to pay and he now had means to collect.

He passed the family burial yard on the way back to Wilson Hall with the wet grasses cooling his feet. He paused over his parents graves as the moonlit shadows of tree limbs danced over the stones. What honorable people they'd been, giving back when they had no reason to do so. This generosity had saved his life.

Helena had been buried there too. Her family wanted her at rest where they knew she'd been most happy. *It had been with me,* Lord Wilson thought. The Wickfords chose to move back to their country estate. Lady Wickford could not stand being so close to where her daughter had died. They would start anew. And by some odd miracle, a year later, the Wickfords produced a male heir for their family and Helena was eventually forgotten.

But not by Christopher. He knelt next to her headstone, and for the first time since the ambush, he cried bitterly in the dark, his tears stinging his skin as they fell on the roses he'd leave behind for her.

Daniel Wilson was still adjusting to his new way of life at the Hall. He'd only just turned eighteen, his parents were dead and his brother severely wounded after a violent robbery. The staff had been completely changed. He had no idea of how to exist with this new reality. The only comfort was that Christopher starting to heal – at least physically.

Lord Wilson's emotional state was a different matter. He was more focused, having taken control of the estate. He had no patience for silliness. Gone were the flippant quips and flirtations with the ladies. Even visits from Crispy didn't lighten his mood. He'd taken to long rides around the grounds, much more study, many physical pursuits, and spent extended hours in Professor Barker's old cottage.

Daniel was never informed that his brother was training to be one of the most deadly spies on the planet. The young Lord Christopher Wilson was becoming a man to be reckoned with.

1874

Lord Wilson lit his cigar and let the tobacco ease through his lungs. He sat in the ornate London offices of his new Senior Member, Mr. Roth. The rooms were built inside an impressive stone castle. The surrounding buildings were just as fortuitous. It was one of the oldest Society compounds in the world.

"I just wanted to congratulate you Lord Wilson. Your work in our community has been quite stellar. Not only have you recruited one of our best scientists, your friend Mr. Crisp, but you've managed to dispense of those who murdered your family. I am impressed that you've continued the endeavors of Professor Barker as well. I cannot be more pleased to inform you that you are now elevated to a Senior Member yourself. Of course, since I am traveling to the Americas on a regular basis, there will be more responsibilities. And you'll be able to select a female under your tutelage for eventual permanent assignment. I think you already have someone in mind?"

Lord Wilson smiled. "Yes, I believe she's perfect."

"Very good. Miss Quentin will be notified of her new Senior. Again, congratulations." Mr. Roth smiled. He had watched Christopher since he was a boy. Professor Barker had kept on eye on him so that the Society would have both the Wilson money and his botanical secrets protected. He never imagined that Christopher would become a Member himself. His family's death at the hands of the Mass was unexpected. Revenge wasn't always the best driving force for the greater good. However, in this case, it gave the Society a perfect gentleman and now perhaps a lady to join him. And the death of the three assassins that killed the Wilson family sent a clear message to the Mass that their interference would not be tolerated by the Society.

Mr. Roth took one last drag on his cigar. Lord Wilson deserved a good woman. Helena, his deceased fiancé had been collateral damage. Plenty of women, in and outside of the Society found him attractive. There had seemed to be no other for him. That is until he worked with Elizabeth Quentin for a while.

Fenton Crisp sat in the dining room of the Society compound just outside of London. He'd finished several experiments with fantastic results that morning. He couldn't wait to share them in a Discussion with Mr. Roth later that day. He'd waited five years to be promoted to Senior. Although he'd had his share of all the wine, women, and song the Society would give him, he was ripe for promotion. And just perhaps, a permanent female partner. He didn't want one of those former prostitutes or waifish girls. Crispy wanted a woman he'd seen on a regular basis for quite some time. In fact, someone he'd known for as long as he and Lord Wilson had entered the Society. Unfortunately it was the same woman that Lord Wilson had ever so slowly fallen in love with.

Lord Wilson and Miss Quentin entered the room to join him for lunch. Crispy's heart leapt at the sight of her. She looked radiant in a burgundy gown accented with brown and gold tassels. Her light brown hair was pulled up neatly under a mini bowler. Her hazel eyes seemed to sparkle with flecks of gold. Miss Quentin was as beautiful as the first day he'd met her in the library. He remembered how he'd come to do some research with Lord Wilson on the history of certain armaments when he saw her working the stacks.

"Hello, Miss. Could you guide us to anything on armor?" Crispy grinned at the lovely young woman holding a small pile of books. Lord Wilson seemed uninterested. Instead he gazed at the rafters of the castle.

"They must be centuries old," Christopher mused aloud.

"Her?" Mr. Crisp was horrified.

"Oh no, the support beams."

"I should apologize for my friend. He's enchanted by the architecture, Miss?" Crispy caught the attention of one of the few females at the London Society.

"Miss Quentin. Librarian at your service." Elizabeth returned a grin. She liked the attention, it never bored her.

"Let me help you with those." Crispy reached out, but tripped on the thick floor covering and instead fell into Miss Quentin, who started to topple.

Lord Wilson's attention turned to the thuds of books pounding the floor. He slid over just in time to catch Miss Quentin in his arms. That brief moment started her fascination with Christopher. Crispy landed on the floor in a sprawled mess as his face reddened in embarrassment.

"Sorry chap." Lord Wilson set Miss Quentin onto a chair and offered his longtime friend a hand.

"How silly of me," Crispy moaned.

"Oh the pains of education," Lord Wilson quipped.

In the coming months, Christopher seemed to be immune to any flirtations from Miss Quentin. Mr. Crisp noticed every nuance, each gentle movement of the librarian, so far as to receive one gentle reprimand from Mr. Roth to focus on his studies.

But as time moved on, Lord Wilson's wounded heart slowly healed from the loss of Helena. The female entertainment provided by the Society bored him. He desired a real partner. A woman of distinction. He wanted Miss Elizabeth Quentin to be that lady.

Miss Quentin was of noble birth, but her father had lost everything to a rather treacherous drinking and gambling addiction. Her mother died from a fall down the stairs in their lavish home after a most serious argument. Stories abounded that Elizabeth's father had pushed her.

Elizabeth's brother didn't appear to like women very much but agreed to a shell of a marriage. His fiancé's family soon got word of his homosexual leanings and broke the engagement.

The elder Quentin, in severe desperation, attempted to sell her and the estate off to whatever man of even halfway decent intentions approached. But Elizabeth insisted she would not marry for trade. She was educated and independent from birth. She ignored her older brother's warnings that such bold qualities would only leave her a spinster.

After a third rejection of a poor marriage proposal to his daughter and a night of precarious carousing, the head of the Quentin household put the cold butt of a revolver to his temple and ended his miserable life. Word of his demise spread quickly among their region. After a shameful funeral, a certain Mr. Roth offered Elizabeth a chance he'd offered to dozens of prospective Members. Initially she declined, but a week after her father was buried, her brother left to India with another man, and the estate was put up for auction. Mr. Roth again made an appearance, this time at the home Elizabeth would be forced to leave. This time Elizabeth accepted Mr. Roth's offer.

She thrived at the Society. Her knowledge and curiosity were rewarded. She was surrounded by men that appreciated and respected her. Eventually Lord Wilson recognized this radiant being that the others were vying for.

That day in the library where Mr. Crisp fell, was one of the happiest in her life, for suddenly Elizabeth knew exactly what she wanted. Unfortunately, so did Mr. Crisp.

Although almost as strapping as his friend Lord Wilson, Crispy wasn't nearly quite as genteel. He loved his books and treated his women in the same way. Something to be opened, devoured, and then closed at the end of the day. He had the reputation for frequenting the local Society watering hole and then imbibing with the women.

Elizabeth noticed this, and despite his flirtations, had no desire to be with someone who might even have the slightest propensity to overindulge in spirits like her father once did.

As Lord Wilson's stature grew, he was chosen to tutor several select students in the botanical sciences. It was no mistake that he was gently prodded by Mr. Roth to take on Miss Quentin as one of those chosen few. Over hours of books and studies, and the pruning of rare roses, the fate of the two nobles in the Society was sealed, as Mr. Crisp was soon to find out. His mind cleared of the old memory as Lord Wilson and Elizabeth approached his table.

"Good day all," He greeted his companions. "It is lovely out, isn't it?"

"Yes, it is. Fantastic really." Lord Wilson pulled out a chair for Miss Quentin.

"A perfect day." Elizabeth radiated the beauty of a woman newly engaged to the man she loved.

Crispy was blind to the stunning ring she wore and the way Lord Wilson tended to her. “Perhaps we should eat outside?”

“Well, first we have such good news to share.” Lord Wilson touched Elizabeth’s hand as he sat beside her. “Miss Quentin and I will be wed this summer.”

“I’m sorry?” Mr. Crisp stuttered. Surely he hadn’t heard correctly.

“Yes, it’s true. I guess I’ve finally come to my senses,” Lord Wilson laughed heartily. “Miss Quentin was able to persuade me,” He teased.

“Ah, I will hear none of that. We all know how the Society works,” she gently reprimanded. An undeniable electricity sparked between them.

Across from the happy pair, Mr. Crisp was falling apart inside. His appetite was lost. His brain buzzed in anger. Finally he was able to gather enough fortitude to speak, but his voice lacked enthusiasm. “Congratulations. That is wonderful.”

“It will be exciting, and Crispy, we’d be honored if you would stand for us?” Lord Wilson asked.

“Of course.” Fenton Crisp could barely get the words out. He wanted to vomit even though his stomach lacked food. Bile backed into his throat.

“We would so appreciate it, thank you so very much Mr. Crisp.” Elizabeth tilted her head in a most polite fashion.

Mr. Crisp sputtered. “You’re most welcome.” *Bitch!* His mind screamed. “But I seemed to have forgotten, I’ve a Discussion this afternoon to prepare for. I’m sorry to leave, but please, enjoy your lunch.” Before they could respond, he stumbled from the table, completely devastated in the wake of their happiness.

"We have them." Lord Wilson peered through a special spy glass designed by Mr. Crisp, one more powerful than anyone had seen on the planet. "We'll enter the building from the west side. From there we'll be like shadows." He, Miss Quentin, Mr. Crisp, and Miss Avery had scoped out a warehouse near the Thames for an intense Engagement.

Miss Avery was new to the Society, but much older than her companions that eve. Her whole family had been military veterans. There were rumors that some were traitors to the monarchy, but those doubts were ignored because of her complex set of skills. No one expected an elegant woman in her late forties to poison and murder. Miss Avery was an assassin assigned on this mission to kill members of the Mass who'd stolen and smuggled complex equipment from the Society Castle. The others would come in from various positions to retrieve the materials once she'd dispensed of their enemies.

The Mass had long been a threat for the Society and its Members, but since the Revolutions in France and America, the most disillusioned people had increased in their ranks. They somehow managed to have structure without rules. Although they claimed to live a dystopian existence and crave anarchy, they regularly backed certain disruptive pillars of society, from priests to politicians. Many an argument could be made that the Society operated in the same fashion. To those Members who harped on that position, they were tersely reminded that the Society existed for "the greater good" and anyone who disagreed could let a door hit them in the arse on the way out if a bullet to the head didn't reach them first.

"I'm getting into position." Miss Avery jumped up from their covert rooftop location. A vivid streak of grey accented her raven black hair. Her dark eyes seemed to melt into her skull that was perched on top of her rail thin body. Her clipped accent only sharpened her demeanor.

She strapped on the largest gun Lord Wilson had ever seen. The barrel alone was almost four feet long. It had an extra cartridge that held over sixty rounds of immense horrific bullets. For a reed thin woman, she possessed incredible strength. Miss Avery lifted her weapon like it was an empty hat box. She ran down the fire escape with her black evening cape flowing behind her as if she were a wayward crow.

"Mr. Crisp, when she reaches the door, you are to follow. It should be about thirty seconds." Lord Wilson ordered as he checked his timepiece.

"Spot on, Sir." Mr. Crisp had not received his expected promotion. Instead he was now under his friend's command. The only redeeming quality of this relationship was that he would occasionally see Elizabeth. His heart had never healed in the months since their engagement. He harbored a dangerous bitterness that unknowingly threatened those around him. His pocket watch buzzed at the appropriate moment. "I'm off." He too left the roof across from the warehouse, but left via an interior stairwell where Miss Quentin stood watch.

"Godspeed!" She whispered as he rushed past.

He wouldn't reply and tried to ignore her kindness. His jealousy burned deeply inside him as he took each step down the four-story building. He hoped that she and Lord Wilson would marry soon and perhaps he could go back to Mr. Roth's direction. Mr. Crisp could not take the emotional pain much longer.

Another thirty seconds passed before Lord Wilson stood. "Miss Quentin, we're off." They too exited down the inside stairs. They hurried across the street to an iron spiral staircase that led to a cage and pulley system next to a large group of skylight windows. Lord Wilson and his charge stood just off to the side of the opening behind some roofing supplies and spied on the four men guarding the stolen goods. From their vantage point they could also see Miss Avery was ready to enter shooting. Mr. Crisp would be around the corner as back up. All of their pocket watches were set to buzz in precisely one more minute.

Suddenly there was a loud click in the alley behind Miss Avery and Mr. Crisp. The Mass spies ran through to the East side of the building in the opposite direction. Miss Avery cursed to herself "I thought there was only one way in." She began to shoot early but her targets had seemed to disappear. And indeed they had, to an underground bunker attached to the sewer tunnels below the building.

Miss Quentin stood directly in front of the windows to get a better view of the plan gone wrong while Lord Wilson looked into the street for the source of the odd sound. Unfortunately, the strange noise was a remote device to set off a bomb.

Just as Miss Avery fired off the first shots at her targets and Mr. Crisp followed behind, the blast unfurled its deadly destruction upon the building. Miss Avery and Mr. Crisp were tossed to the ground like dolls. Lord Wilson was slightly protected by the entrance to the interior lift, but Miss Quentin took the full force of the blast with screaming shards of glass running through her body which fell to the cobblestones three stories below. Her head made a sickening crush against the street as blood and brain matter splattered around her broken body.

"Noooooo!" Lord Wilson screamed as the blast jarred every inch of him. He held on to a support beam of the pulleys as his legs shot out behind him. Heat seared his skin and charred the hair on this head.

Meanwhile inside the warehouse, Mr. Crisp had been knocked down flat on his back. His mind went black as he hit the floor. He'd been burned, but not mortally so. He would have permanent scars on his hands and face, but he would live. Some of the storage crates had blocked the worst of the flames for him.

It was not quite the same for Miss Avery. She missed the flames, but a shard of metal flew through her gun scope and took her right eye with it. She writhed on the ground screaming in agony as bits of blood leaked through her fingers. Her desperate cries awakened Mr. Crisp.

He sat up and shook at the sight of his damaged hands. He stood slowly, like a poorly made tower ready to crumble with the slightest vibration. Parts of the warehouse were engulfed in flames. In this hell, he saw visions that would forever haunt him. Miss Avery rolled side to side clutching her face. He looked for his cohorts up at the skylight which was now a gaping hole of twisted metal and fractured glass. Crispy turned to go out, as every inch of him ached with a brutality he'd never experienced before.

Lord Wilson had clutched on for dear life and dropped to the planks that bordered the lift. He blinked and checked himself at the top of the stairwell. Did he really see Elizabeth blown away? He grabbed some serum for a quick swallow. He exhaled and lay back down for a moment while it took hold. He heard the terrifying moans of his crew. Finally his heart stopped racing and he stood. They had been ambushed.

Lord Wilson took the steps slowly to the street below, trembled in fear, and began to cry as he neared Elizabeth's body. He knelt at her head and pushed her bloodied hair from her face. Her eyes were frozen open. The glass peppered her body with deep gashes. Her fluids seeped into the wool of his trousers. "No, no, no." His insides collapsed, his heart crushed.

"You killed her." The weakened voice of Mr. Crisp was behind him. "You did this. She wouldn't be here if it weren't for you. Nor I. You fucking bastard. You killed her."

Lord Wilson turned to his friend. He was blackened with thick smoke. Bits of his clothing had burned completely off. "I can help. Please let me."

"No, no. You've been quite the help. You, with the stick up your arse nobility. The 'for the greater good' bullshit world you brought me to. You're a God-damned prick." Mr. Crisp fell against the wall of the burning warehouse as Lord Wilson stood. The sounds of a horse approaching echoed in the alley along with the flames that licked at the frame of the building. It was going up like a box of matches.

"Crispy, no. We were tricked. This was not meant to happen." Lord Wilson stepped forward as their driver arrived.

"You took Elizabeth from me. You already had Helena and you fucking killed her too! Wasn't once enough for your ego?" Mr. Crisp stood again as he cried. "I can't follow you any more Christopher. I don't want to die like this. I want to die on my own terms." With that he rushed into the burning warehouse.

The fire was generating enough heat that Lord Wilson dared not follow. He could not save his friend or Miss Avery.

"Lord Wilson, my God." Their driver had just arrived and started to pull him away. "Good God man, get into the carriage." Christopher stood for a moment at the horrific scene. "We must go now Sir, it's going to collapse."

"I can't leave her." He moaned even though it was far too late to help Elizabeth.

"Sir, I will force you. Now." The driver was a burly man and yanked impatiently at his Senior. Lord Wilson finally relented. He fell into the carriage as the driver bolted to his reigns. They were only a block away when the whole structure caved. Onlookers and firemen had started to come forward as others, like Lord Wilson and his driver, ran away.

Why do I survive? Why do all those around me seem to die? Lord Wilson closed his eyes as the carriage shook to and fro. *I will avenge again, I swear it.* He clutched his pocket watch just as the red face went completely black. Everyone connected to him was deceased.

About a mile away, another carriage hurried through the streets of London. It carried a very special cargo for the Mass. And she was livid. "You were supposed to let me shoot them and then leave." Miss Avery hissed as a medic attended to her empty eye socket. Her recruiter, a Mr. Ellis, felt badly for his new found spy. He liked her. She was wickedly sharp and an incredible lover.

"I am sorry my love. Our bomber acted in haste, but we succeeded did we not?"

"Are you sure? I thought I heard voices outside. And how is it a success if I lost a fucking eye!" She spat.

"Oh, my dear. But you can still see me with one eye. And we'll get you the loveliest patch that money can buy. Perhaps even some vision in the future?" Mr. Ellis soothed.

The medic gave her a sip of a special medication as she suffered.

"Hmm perhaps." She moaned as the heroin took hold of her pain and she drifted off.

This promise and more would be kept. Miss Avery would wed Mr. Ellis. And despite her advanced age she would bear him three sons that would be just as evil as them both.

1877

More than three years had passed since the ambush that killed Elizabeth and Lord Wilson's closest friend, Mr. Crisp. After the blast Lord Wilson retreated to the Society a broken man. He requested and received permission to work strictly as an educator within the Society's grounds for the safety of both him and his pupils. He moved from Wilson Hall to distance himself from his brother Daniel, who still believed that his older brother worked somehow in the House of Lords. His days were spent teaching. Long evenings were filled with night terrors of all he'd lost.

Only one thing sustained Lord Wilson. A Dr. Arav from the East Indies was visiting London and had been referred to Lord Wilson via Mr. Roth. After several visits to the infirmary and Dr. Arav, Lord Wilson was captivated by the doctor's mind control. This new found fascination with hypnotism sustained Lord Wilson. His interest in the study of the mind returned a semblance of order and control to his life.

Meanwhile, his brother Daniel married a lovely young woman, Beatrix. Although not from noble means, her family had made millions in international trading. She was the youngest of five. Her parents were delighted to have finally married off their last child. So much so, that they chose to spend the rest of their lives traveling.

His family's money continued to fund operations for the Society. He never questioned where or how it was dispensed. This was another secret Lord Wilson regrettably kept from his brother. For on the third anniversary of the warehouse explosion, Wilson Hall was leveled by a mysterious fire. Daniel, his new bride, and the staff perished. As he buried the last of his remaining family, he remembered the promise he'd made at his parent's and Helena's graves.

There would be revenge.

The very next day he approached the Director for a return to field work. He was granted his request with an enthusiastic yes. He was immediately assigned to Engagements with Mr. Roth.

"Good God man, it's marvelous to have you back. It's been quite boring without you." Mr. Roth greeted his new partner. He had worried for Lord Wilson long after Elizabeth's death. His face lacked color. He'd seemingly lost his bravado and taste for adventure.

The ambush hadn't been his fault, but the weight of it burdened the talented Member with a reputation for acting with too much haste. After some careful research, Miss Avery's true intentions and infiltration were discovered, but the damage had been done. Further on, intel discovered that Mr. Crisp had survived the fire with a little quick thinking from Miss Avery and had joined the opposing forces.

Although Lord Wilson's sabbatical had been self-imposed, it would've have been forced without hesitation anyway. Mr. Roth feared that the young Christopher he'd watched over would not find his way back. The Lord's atonement period and new found inquisition methods put him back into the good graces of the Director. Mr. Roth hoped that Lord Wilson could still find happiness with a gentle woman, as he had with his new bride Annabelle.

"Thank you kindly, Mr. Roth." Lord Wilson smiled at his longtime friend.

"I am pleased to tell you that we are to start recruiting efforts immediately."

"You mean, now that you are happily married, I must be too?" Lord Wilson laughed.

"We need to look for all kinds of Members." Mr. Roth's tone changed. "I was concerned for you Christopher. I don't want you to rush back in if you don't feel you're ready."

"Thank you for your concern, but I am more than ready." Lord Wilson lifted his chin and set off at a brisk pace towards their ride for a new Engagement.

As Lord Wilson strode towards their carriage, Mr. Roth whispered to himself "Don't be too hard." He didn't want his friend to die like so many others had.

"All you have to do is sit on the bench and pretend to adjust your shoes. Pull the package from under your skirt and leave it under the bench. Then you'll circle the park once. Take your time before coming back to the carriage. Quite simple, yes?" And so the first Discussion began for Pippy Wills. She was his first female recruit after several months of intense Engagements.

Lord Wilson was driven by passionate revenge. More than several Mass spies met their ends at his hands. He was cunning and ruthless. Mr. Roth had to remind him that they had plenty of assassins at their disposal. Out of respect, he returned part of his focus to recruitment which led him to this Engagement with Miss Wills.

"Yes Sir." Lord Wilson's new Member nodded her head eagerly as if it were to bobble off her neck at any moment. Her Senior appreciated her enthusiasm. She was very young, all of eighteen, from a poor family, and had retained more than a touch of her cockney accent.

"Very well then. We'll wait a few moments, and then the driver will help you exit from the carriage. I'll be watching, but remember you must act as if you are alone."

"Yes Sir."

Lord Wilson looked over his charge. She was eager and ready. His pocket watch buzzed. "Go now." He opened the door and the waiting driver assisted her out.

Lord Wilson watched as she did precisely as planned. Pippy crossed the street without a care in the world. About thirty feet into the park, she sat at the appropriate bench and left the package as directed. She pretended to adjust her hat as well. *Nice touch,* Lord Wilson thought. She then strolled away. One minute later their contact pretended to lose a newspaper at the same bench. The drop had been a success. Pippy enjoyed the park for bit, taking one full round as ordered, before returning to the carriage.

"Well done Miss Wills, well done. Driver?" Lord Wilson tapped the door. Pippy's first Engagement had been a success.

This little act of espionage was noticed by one Mr. Fenton Crisp, who inhaled the cold winter air with a rattle in his permanently heat singed lungs.

1879

"Why don't you love me?" Miss Wills cried and collapsed in a chair inside Lord Wilson's office. "Has all this been for nothing?"

"Miss Wills-" Lord Wilson tried to calm his Member.

"Don't 'Miss Wills' me with that Society rubbish. It's because I'm plain isn't it? All that noble blood can't possibly boil for a simple girl like me." Pippy stood abruptly and started pacing in front of his desk almost stomping her feet in frustration.

"Miss Wills, stop now. Quit acting like a spoiled child." Lord Wilson sat forward in his chair like a cat ready to pounce. He was trying his best to control the conversation. One that they should not be having.

"Or is it you don't like females? Haven't you noticed I've become a lady? I mean, you do seem to spend quite a lot of time with Mr. Roth. Rumors abound you know." She squinted at him and glibly turned to look out the window.

"That is quite enough!" Lord Wilson shouted as he stood behind his desk. "Act like a lady. Sit down. Now!" It had been almost two years since Miss Wills had come to the Society. She'd finally reached a level of possible attachment. It took her longer than most, not for lack of trying, but for lack of education. Today's Discussion was unexpected. Pippy had been notified only a half hour before by the Director that she was now assigned to another Society Member-a good, younger man that would be a much better match for her. Upon this notice of replacement, she immediately flew into Lord Wilson's office without Invitation.

Miss Wills sat visibly shaken at the outburst from her Senior. "Here, take this." He handed her a kerchief. "For heaven's sake, calm down." *Don't be too hard,* Lord Wilson reminded himself. He paused, poured a glass of water and handed it to her. "Are you composed now?"

"Yes, Sir." The words came timidly in direct contrast to only seconds before.

"Good. Miss Wills, when you came to the Society, you were offered many things. Although I admire your gumption, I was not to be one of those given to you. If I led you to believe otherwise, I am sorry." *Cushion the blow,* he reminded himself. "While I do think that you are lovely, it is in your best interests to get along with your new Senior. And although I consult with Mr. Roth frequently, I assure you, that when I take someone to my bed, it is of the female persuasion. And Mr. Roth is happily espoused. Please know that none of this is any of your business whatsoever. However, I am choosing to be kind as I believe you have misunderstood our arrangement. I am your Senior. I've educated you to the best of my ability." Lord Wilson sat back in his chair. "It is time for you to move to someone who is better suited for you."

"Apparently you've never had your heart broken, have you Sir? Is that why you're such a cold bastard?" Her words came out in a slow bitter trickle.

Lord Wilson held back the pain that clogged his throat. "I have been hurt in ways you can never imagine, Miss Wills. This is the last conversation we shall have in this office. Again, I am sorry that you feel wronged. Know that many changes are being made here due to those who wish to harm us. Any chink in the armor is a weakness they look to expose. If you continue to have issues, I suggest you see the Director immediately. Am I clear?"

"Yes, Sir." She meekly acquiesced to him.

"I want you to look outside at the snowfall for a moment. See every unique flake. Every sparkle." Lord Wilson cooed. "Do you see them?"

Pippy's eyes fluttered despite her best attempts to stay focused. "Yes, very, um, pretty."

"So you'll take my suggestions?" Lord Wilson spoke more softly as she slipped under his mild hypnotism.

"Of course Sir." Her face went blank and her limbs drooped over the chair.

"Good, you'll awake when I count to three, and you'll be completely satisfied at today's outcome, correct?"

"Yes Sir."

"Very well." Lord Wilson smiled. He hated doing this, but he didn't want Pippy's last memories of him to be unfortunate. "One, two, three."

Her eyes popped open, and she looked round the room in confusion.

"Very good, you may leave now." Lord Wilson returned his focus to paperwork on his desk and tried to slow the rapid beat of his heart. He liked Pippy. He didn't love her. He hoped she would grow to love the man she'd be given to.

Miss Wills stood to leave, and then turned suddenly. "I wanted you to know that I'm sorry Sir. I-I didn't mean to, um, cause trouble."

"You're forgiven." Lord Wilson looked up briefly while fighting the urge to give her a fatherly hug. "Good luck Miss Wills."

"Thank you Sir. And to you as well." Miss Wills stepped out in a far more quiet fashion than when she'd come in.

Lord Wilson again sat back in his chair and gazed outside at the snowfall. He remembered Helena and Elizabeth. *Am I to die alone? What is a life without passion?* He didn't have the heart to take on another female operative. But he wouldn't have to as he was soon to find out.

"I'm sorry, did I hear you correctly?" Lord Wilson raised a curious brow at Mr. Roth.

"Yes, St. Louis, the direct center of the country. A booming city, ripe for us. The grounds are immense. Five times the size of what we have here. Their Director passed away recently, an elderly chap, not quite up to snuff on modern advances. The wild west has yet to be tamed and it has given the world a whole new breed of characters. The Society wants fresh blood. Explorers. Those with a sense of adventure."

"Loony bin bastards?" Lord Wilson joked and puffed on a cigar.

"More recruits as soon as possible. I've been awarded the Directorship and I'd like for you to be my second in command. You'll have your own mansion on the grounds, your own staff. The choice is yours, Sir." Mr. Roth grinned.

"Greenhouse?" Lord Wilson bantered. It was good to see Mr. Roth so happy. His wife, Annabelle, had died mysteriously on a non-covert trip outside the Society's walls, a poisoning at a tea party. Her demise was never explained, but it was widely assumed that The Mass was still at hand. In the few months since her passing, Mr. Roth buried himself in Society work. It was Lord Wilson's turn to comfort his grieving friend.

"Of course, we'll have a most advanced greenhouse built to your liking." Mr. Roth's voice slowed. "And it's a chance to start over. For both of us." He examined the end of his cigar and inhaled deeply.

"Indeed. Cheers, to starting over." They hoisted their drinks and toasted their new endeavor.

A few months later, the two Members were safely relocated in their new home. Solid Members were quickly recruited. Director Roth became a leader to be admired. Lord Wilson was pleased that his plants had survived the move from London. A few samples were left behind in case of tragedy, but his most precious specimens thrived in his new greenhouse. Only one short note from the London Society Director spoiled their homecoming.

Pippy Wills had been killed on Engagement much like the one that ended the life of Elizabeth. The two men had no doubt that The Mass was still hard at work at eroding their good deeds. It was time to leave personal regrets behind. Revenge would come another day. The pair would create a better Society elsewhere.

1895

Lord Wilson examined the dossier with a more stringent eye. The day before, Director Roth had given him the file of a Miss Katherine Church, who liked to be referred to as "Kate", according to the detailed documents. He'd flicked through the pages with haste as Director Roth offered some insight on the possible recruit.

"She is precisely where we need to be. Sister Theresa has procured one of the keys. But Iris is falling apart. We need to try and extract her. Mr. Drasco is already working for The Mass.

"There's not a gentleman who could do this?" Lord Wilson questioned.

Mr. Roth laughed. "Miss Church is a bit of a maverick against these rabble rousers apparently. She also has family here in St. Louis, but she's been gone a long time. Can't say further than that, you'll need to investigate as soon as possible. Besides, we need more ladies."

"That we do." Lord Wilson smiled. So many young men had joined. They could only get so many prostitutes to stay. "I'll be off in two days."

"Godspeed my friend." Mr. Roth boomed as Lord Wilson exited. His longtime Member needed a lady himself, much more than he realized. Outside only the most close of acquaintances at the Society, Lord Wilson had become a cold man. Revered for his knowledge, admired for his skills, but slightly pitied by those who knew him best. Wilson Manor had never had a lady of the house since he'd moved in.

"More tea, Sir?" Leeds brought in a fresh tray.

"Yes. Are my things packed for tomorrow?"

"Yes Sir."

"And the items from the rail office were procured?"

"Yes. Although, they are quite damaged." Leeds handed his Senior two sheets of dog-eared papers. After a quick glance, Lord Wilson noted that it contained what he wanted, the former St. Louis address of Miss Church.

"Well done. Thank you Leeds." He took a last look at the documents' details. His prospective Member was a bit older, thirty-six. Never married. *I wonder why?* He pondered. "More than proficient with guns, adept horsemanship. Prefers men's clothing." Lord Wilson continued reading to himself and chuckled. "Appears to be kind to others, including foreigners." *She has a heart. Not too hard, not to soft.* He would soon find out if this was true. He needed a good female, perhaps even one for himself. Rumors abounded of The Mass resurgence in London. They too were seeking fresh blood and had stolen three keys that were of the utmost importance to the Society. To have one back in the hands of a Society Member had been a small miracle.

He closed the file with a quick flick and tossed it into his briefcase. Miss Church seemed well on paper. He hoped he could bring her in to work for the greater good. Lord Wilson would soon learn that he'd chosen wisely.

14 TEMPTATION

The day after Lord Wilson's return was supposed to be one of debriefing with Kate. The plans had been set for them to dine together and have a lengthy Discussion. Upon the day he arrived home, after much thinking, Lord Wilson prepared to make careful allusions to their future. He had brought Kate so far and without the Traveler, would've lost her for good. *Thank God for her resilience,* he thought as he prepared for a breakfast with Director Roth. He didn't think he could live through another death of someone he loved.

Lord Wilson's heart took a tumble when an urgent message from the Director arrived. There would be much more than a meal today. Within the hour, a serious Discussion was at hand in Mr. Roth's office.

"Sorry for the change of plans old chap. But we just found out that the Ellis clan has moved. This was certainly expected after our gift to them." Director Roth measured his friend's reaction. He was relieved to see enthusiasm and color in his face at the mention of the old enemies.

"Quite." Lord Wilson tried not to gloat over the way Master Richards was given back to his family.

"We have word that a Mrs. Bunting and her two sons have come to an inn just on the other side of Lafayette Park. This, of course, is a little too close for comfort on our part. We need Observation on the park and the house. You'll have a new driver, because, as you know, unfortunately, your previous one died in the epidemic." His words took a nasty turn.

Like Lord Wilson, the Director couldn't wait to see Miss Pratt after her stupendous, yet suspicious recovery from the consumption. But he didn't resist the small opportunity to dig at his old friend.

"Yes, tragic. But Dr. Finch has assured me that no new cases have been reported and all patients are now on the mend." Lord Wilson dug into his eggs with the eagerness of a man hungry for something much more than food.

"Change of heart then?" The Director raised a brow. He was secretly angered at the control Lord Wilson maintained over the serum.

"Yes." Lord Wilson sipped his tea and continued. "It seems to have benefitted Miss Pratt as well."

"Hmm and rather quickly I should say, even before the others." He hinted at Kate's involvement in Meredith's recovery, a poorly kept secret amongst all involved. "I am grateful."

"It was too late for Jilly." Lord Wilson's words were tinged with regret. "Mr. Scott is still devastated. If I had known it was a disease planted from an adversary, I would have acted differently. But that was then and this is now." Lord Wilson looked out at the sun beaming onto the Grounds blanketed in thick white snow. A pang of guilt shadowed him. He hadn't intended on being so blasé on the wave of sickness that ravaged the Society.

"Yes indeed. We've cut our losses before. Yesterday was no different. Mr. Scott will be rewarded with someone of his choosing when he is ready. Today begins anew. And we have a good chance of disposing of an old enemy." Director Roth tried to avoid sounding callous. Both men had suffered similar devastating casualties. It was part of the Society environment. "Cigar?"

"Yes." Lord Wilson leaned in for a light.

Little did they know of how close their past was to catching up to them.

Kate read the Discussion cancellation with disgust. She stomped her foot and pitched it into the fireplace. Her reunion with Lord Wilson was put off for yet another day.

"Miss Church, is there something else I can do?" Miss Beatrice felt the tension from her Member.

"No, but thank you." Kate grimaced. "I will have lunch here today. Maybe study in the library. I'll probably go for a ride later." Her heart dropped and felt heavy in her chest. She missed Lord Wilson to the point of silliness. She cursed herself for being so brooding and emotional.

So much had happened since he'd been gone. It felt like a lifetime since he'd left. Her fingers ached for the smoothness of the chess pieces. She craved the smell of the leather bound books in the library. Kate remembered how just a few days before, she had discovered his love for her, while listening to the light chimes of the music box. "You can go." She uttered flatly to her assistant.

The moment her help closed the door, Kate opened her desk and pulled out the box. Strax whined at her feet. After a gentle pat on his head, she sat on the floor next to him and wound the key. As the pleasant music filled the room, quiet tears rolled down her face. Her canine looked up with a sad expression. "I know, you miss him too. We'll see him tomorrow." She stroked his soft fur and tried to bury a worry that wouldn't quite go away. Yes, she would take a ride that afternoon. The cool air would hopefully clear her head.

"There you are Sir, a blanket and hot tea in the decanter." Lord Wilson's Driver threw a blanket over his new Senior.

"Carry on then." Lord Wilson tried to focus on the task at hand. He could be sitting in the cold for hours waiting for any of the Ellis family to part from their temporary home. They may not leave at all since low clouds had blown in, covering up any chance of sunshine in the late afternoon. "So much for a break in the weather." He muttered under his breath. He was bundled up in woolen clothes, a fur coat, and two blankets. His driver's face was covered with a low cap and a huge woolen muffler that left only his eyes exposed.

But what truly kept Lord Wilson warm were thoughts of Kate. He was disappointed at not being able to see her, but this Engagement couldn't wait. Those who'd wanted to destroy the Society were close enough to warrant an immediate stake out. The Mass still haunted him.

Lord Wilson looked at his pocket watch as the sleigh carriage started off. They departed for the park where they would find a covert spot from which to observe the inn. He shuddered as a brisk wind blew in darker clouds.

The timing of this gale couldn't have been more important. As the carriage eased its way outside of the grounds, Kate had indeed taken Sonny for a ride. She cantered out the back of the Main Hall before riding along the main entry ways' hedges. Kate's curiosity led her to the Society's entrance. She was eager to see how deep the snow was on the bordering neighborhood street.

Just as this gusty winter wind picked up, Kate passed Lord Wilson's carriage leaving. The coach had all the windows drawn to keep out the cold. The driver's thick scarf blew aside and he almost lost his hat. More than a chill passed through Kate, because the driver looked oddly familiar.

She stopped Sonny and tried to jog her memory. There was something sinister lurking, but she couldn't quite place him. Going on gut instinct, Kate halted her ride and went to the Society stables just as the skies opened with a thick snowstorm.

Two groomsmen popped out as she approached. "Miss, you can pause for a bit, but riding horses aren't stabled here. There's a storm blowing in, you'll want to get back immediately." A Senior Member warned her.

"I'm sorry; I'm here on urgent business from Lord Wilson." Her heart pounded with worry.

The two men exchanged nervous glances and the Senior spoke again. "Well Miss, he just left."

"Yes, I know. But he has a new driver. Is there any way I could know his name?" Kate questioned.

"Miss, that's confidential."

"That Driver may also be under my direction as I am Lord Wilson's Member." Kate frowned down upon the men. "I would suppose you can't tell me how long he's been here either?"

"No Miss, of course not."

"But if Lord Wilson was in danger and you were to be responsible for his death, then would you let me know that Driver's name?" Kate was exasperated. "Please, I need to know."

Again, the groomsmen looked concerned. After a deep exhale, the Senior relented. "Well it seems to be an old German name, Athom, or something of the like."

"Is it written down? Do you keep a log?"

"Of course Miss."

Kate dismounted before he even gave permission to view it. "Hurry!"

They bolted inside the stable office and the Senior horsemen pulled a fine thick leather bound book from the shelf. "See, here."

Kate's eyes scanned to the name, *Athgom.* "This here? Athgom?"

"Yes, Miss."

Kate closed her eyes. The alias list popped into her head. *Athgom looked like Gotham. The letters are mixed,* she panicked. "Notify Director Roth that Lord Wilson is in danger. Now! Don't hesitate." Kate hollered as she ran to her trusty companion, her feet trudging through the thickening snow. She had to catch up to his carriage.

Kate mounted and slapped the reigns. "C'mon Sonny." Her faithful steed charged through the snow leaving a mist of flurries behind. She hoped she'd be able to follow the sleigh's trail before the snow filled it. As her steed went into full gallop, she tried in vain to remember where she had seen him before.

It wasn't here in the Society. It was on an Engagement. But which one? Her mind was a blur with the white of the snow.

Kate could just barely make out the carriage rudder tracks. It appeared that they were leading to Lafayette Park. Trees emerged from the white out as she passed some of the lovely, stately homes that surrounded the park. As she entered near the Police Station, she could finally see the shadow of the carriage plowing through. Its pace had picked up considerably and jostled its inhabitant.

Inside Lord Wilson gripped the door handle which had frozen shut. He had been shouting at the driver to no avail. "Slow down! Are you mad? You'll kill us both!"

Kate gained speed and was almost aside the wayward vehicle.

The cold blasted her face and stung through her gloves. They were moving at a breakneck pace towards the north end of the park. As Kate closed in, the driver lost his muffler and saw his pursuer. Suddenly, she got a good look at him. It was the man that Madeline Fahey had sold the mysterious plans to.

He made a sharp turn in front of Kate, cutting her off. Sonny reared up, but Kate clung on, gripping the reigns with whitened knuckles.

Inside the carriage, Lord Wilson fell away from the door and crashed into the other side of the seat. "Shit!" He cried out as the pain jarred his shoulder. Only the padding of the blankets cushioned his slam into the hard wooden construction. His head pounded with ferocity and anger that yet another mole had managed to infiltrate the Society. He gripped on to the seat with every inch of strength as the sleigh did a complete turnaround and headed for the frozen-over lake.

Kate soothed Sonny and again took off after them. A flurry of Canadian geese scrambled and honked as the chase approached the edge of the frozen pond. But the ice was not as thick as Mr. Gotham had hoped. When the carriage bounced onto the lake, the blades sliced into it. It fractured immediately and the sleigh toppled sideways into the cold water below. The driver was tossed from up top and crashed head first onto the blue glazed waters. Lord Wilson cracked his head with a dull thud on the ceiling and fell unconscious.

Kate had paused at the edge and watched in horror as the sleigh crashed. She jumped from Sonny and tentatively stepped out onto the ice that hadn't broken, while knowing that the slightest move could pull her under. As she approached the scene, Kate cracked her whip and caught one of the blade supports. She pulled herself to the edge of the water as the sleigh bobbed perilously.

"Lord Wilson! Wilson!" Kate screamed over the howling

wind as she pounded on the door, her hands feeling as if they would fracture. She steadied herself against the carriage while she freed her whip. Kate eased along the edge of the ice with gritted teeth as she unburdened the work horse. The animal was able to find some footing in the shallow water and made it to shore. Kate was able to peer between a coverlet and the frame of a window to see that Lord Wilson's body was submerged and locked just under the water line. Her heart fell. *You are strong. You must do this. He will die if you don't.* She encouraged herself.

Kate clamored up the faltered vehicle, praying she could get to Lord Wilson. The door was still stuck, so Kate busted through the window with the handle of her whip and a loud pop. Glass flew into the wind that blistered her bare face.

A few feet away, a stunned Mr. Gotham came to his senses. He shook his head and pushed himself up slowly onto the slippery ice. Upon seeing Kate, he reached into his coat to pull out his revolver, but fell as it went off. The bullet ricocheted off one of the blades with a bang as he attempted to stand again.

Kate, alerted by the ping of the bullet, again used her trusty weapon. With a quick flick, she struck out and sent the whip around Mr. Gotham's neck. It coiled around him like a deadly python. His hands grasped at the leather while Kate pulled as hard as she could, the muscles in her arms strained to control him. She dug her heels into the step board and yanked while Mr. Gotham slid face forward on the ice. He sputtered violently but could not speak as she slowly choked the life out of him. His face reddened until at last, his eyes closed, his body went limp and he expired.

Kate reclaimed her whip with a lyrical snap and leaned into the carriage, while gripping the edge of the broken window. Lord Wilson was completely soaked in the chilled water, his head dangerously halfway between the water and air. Bubbles gurgled around his mouth as Kate jumped fully in and pulled his upper body out. The water shocked her into deep breaths as she held onto him with every ounce of strength left. Blood poured from a gash in his forehead and trickled vermillion streams onto her coat.

"Wilson!" She pushed him onto his back as he coughed up water. She patted his wound with her frozen gloves. His eyes opened slowly as he finally could breathe. Kate had never been so happy to see the blue of his eyes.

"Kate?" He muttered. His eyelids fluttered like dying moth's wings.

"Yes, yes. You've been in an accident. We have to get you out of here." Kate herself was weakening. The cold was freezing every bodily fluid.

"Oh, Miss Kate." He moaned and grabbed his thigh.

"Your leg?" Kate covered his hand.

"Yes, we need, we need to get dry as soon as possible. I will explain later. But here..." He pulled a familiar small bottle from inside his coat. "Serum, quick sip."

Kate partook of the magical drink and quickly handed it back. Her Senior needed it more than she.

He took two long draws. "Alright, let's go."

It seemed to take an eternity for the two to climb out of the upturned carriage, onto the fragile ice and back to shore. The blizzard howled a frenzy of frozen death around them. Sonny and the sleigh horse waited impatiently as the pair finally made it onto the snow.

"We need to find shelter now, or we'll freeze to death. The serum will only help for so long." He looked furtively through the snow with squinted eyes.

"The police station? We passed it on the way in?" Kate offered.

"Too far." He gasped. "There. The boat house." He pointed to a shadow of a building.

The two stumbled while trying to lead the horses around the edge of the lake. They too were suffering the effects of the storm. Their shelter may have only been thirty feet away, but the whipping winds slowed them to a snail's pace. Drifts had started to form against the door of the large shed as night fell. Lord Wilson picked up logs of firewood stacked up next to the door and busted the lock. The door creaked open to almost total darkness. "Inside quickly!" He yelled. "Bring the horses."

The animals protested, but Kate managed to pull them in as Lord Wilson frantically tried his lighter. He tossed it aside in frustration while Kate pushed the door closed behind them. The winds whistled through cracks in the building.

"No light?" Kate moaned.

"No." Lord Wilson grumbled.

"Wait, my pistol." Kate pulled out her gun that stuck to her wet skin. "Where's the fireplace?"

Lord Wilson stooped to the floor, almost begging his eyes to adjust to the lack of light. He felt cold metal along one of the walls. "Most likely here."

"Guide my hand." Kate urged.

"You're not going to shoot are you?" He asked incredulously.

"No." Kate followed his hand until they could feel the metal plated hearth.

She knelt down to feel some ash left behind. “Reach for coal, sticks, anything that might light.” She opened the small globe of her gun and dribbled some of the good ole potent cactus fuel from Texas on to the floor of the fireplace.

“I’ve found dry firewood,” Lord Wilson said.

“Excellent! Do you have any flint?”

“No.”

“But a pocket knife?” Kate asked.

“Of course.” In the darkness, Lord Wilson grinned at his resourceful charge.

“Here, hand it to me.” She reached up and felt over his crotch by accident. “Oh, so sorry.” Kate was grateful he couldn’t see her blush.

Lord Wilson stifled a guffaw. “It’s here.” He came to the floor next to her.

“Alright, put the wood in the fireplace, then lean back. I’ll strike the liquid on three.” Kate ordered. “One, two, three.” She flicked the knife tip on the metal and it sparked a small flame from the gun’s supernatural fuel. Kate pushed forward some of the lighter wood and started a proper fire. The horses whinnied at the bright flash that filled the room.

“More wood?” Lord Wilson admired his Member. Her face was aglow with the firelight, the shadows of the flames dancing across her rosy cheeks.

“Yes please.” Kate smiled in satisfaction as he handed her a few dry bits of timber. In the new found light, Kate was able to procure a kettle on the floor next to the fireplace and placed it near the flames to warm.

Lord Wilson stood slowly as his leg burned. His artificial calf ached and caused him to drag it across the floor with a dull scrape. He brought the horses to the tallest part of the room, opposite the hearth. After he tied them up, he rustled about some cabinets, looking for supplies.

Kate watched her Senior. Her heart felt woozy to see him in pain. "Are you alright?"

"Yes, but I'll be better if we can find blankets, towels, anything. We need to get out of these wet clothes. We must be dry to stay warm."

"Oh." Kate blushed again. "Well, let me get a bit of snow to melt for the kettle. We can at least have hot water." She opened the door and grabbed a few quick handfuls to wipe out the kettle. She made haste with a few more to melt over the fire. Lord Wilson stopped his search briefly and watched with awe as his insides warmed.

"Miss Kate, you never cease to amaze me." He smiled as he turned over one of the small stored boats and pulled it towards the fire as it creaked over the floorboards. He took off his coat with enthusiasm and placed it over the skip. "I'll need your coat, scarf, and hat. All your outer wear." He commanded in a polite tone.

"Of course." Kate started to undress and handed him her things. He set them over the turned boat as well. He upended a second one with a loud crack on the floor.

"We need to get the horses dry as well." He motioned to their rides and offered a hand to Kate to help her from the floor. Electricity jumped between them, but they both made efforts to ignore it; work must be done. They removed the saddles and blankets in a hurry. Lord Wilson draped them over the second boat and began to search again while limping.

"I should do that, you're hurt. You had quite the tumble, Sir." She tried to joke through chattering teeth. Although the small room was starting to warm, Kate's clothes had frozen on her skin.

"I've got it." Lord Wilson finally opened a small cabinet with a single woolen blanket inside. It too was cold, but dry. "Here, take off the rest of your things and put this on."

Kate hesitated as her mouth fell open. Despite the temperature in the room, she became unduly hot.

"Do it or you'll freeze. This is no time for modesty. I will look away as you undress. Then you will do the same for me." He flipped a tarp off a set of oars on the floor and then set it in front of the fireplace. "Our clothes will need to dry. I'll set them over some of these paddles."

Kate tried to disrobe quickly with her back turned to Lord Wilson. Her clothes clung to her with a soppy, chilly wetness. She had to peel them off ever so slowly. Her dress wasn't so bad, but her underthings almost seemed to take her skin with them. Bits of drafty frozen air gave her goosebumps and hardened her nipples. Once naked, Kate wrapped the wool blanket over her, trying to cover as much as possible. She positioned herself directly in front of the fireplace.

Lord Wilson was almost true to his word. While shuffling through the boathouse's pantry for supplies, he'd found some toiletries including a small shaving mirror which was already perfectly placed for discreet peeking. He couldn't resist stealing glances at Kate. She was every bit as lovely as he'd imagined. Her skin glistened in the firelight as he found a few tin dishes, dried fruit, cheese, and nuts.

"I'm finished." Kate stuttered.

"Alright then, here, put these close to the fire so we'll have a little warm food." He handed her a small stack of supplies. "And if you'd be a gentlewoman and close your eyes." His face was so close to hers, Kate almost melted as she complied.

He abruptly turned back to the cupboard, and offed his boots and soaked suit. His underclothes were molded to him. He was especially careful in removing the cloth from his mechanical calf. The gears had frozen and it needed some attention. He'd found a bit of lard with the stored items and hoped it would work to get his leg up and running. He peered over his shoulder. Kate was absolutely still.

She's so obedient, so trustworthy. He so desperately wanted to reveal himself to her without a stitch on, but fought the urge. Instead, he sat down next to her and pulled the tarp over himself. "Okay, you can open now."

He was taken aback by her beauty. She'd let down her hair and the wet tendrils dripped over her blanket covered shoulders. "You'll want to shake these out a bit to dry." He gently tugged at one of the damp locks. He smiled at her as she took a corner of the blanket, dabbed at his forehead and removed traces of blood from the carriage accident. "Ah, I'd forgotten about that. The cut is gone isn't it?"

"Yes, that serum is, well, fantastic." Kate grinned and finally started to heat up under the blanket. There was an awkward moment of silence between them as the fire crackled with life.

"I meant to tell you how sorry I was about Jilly Browne. But I hadn't known that the disease had infiltrated the Society by disastrous means. You managed well despite being at the hands of a vicious assassin. I want to apologize and commend you for your actions." He paused and tried to gauge her reaction. "There are so many things that I want to tell you Kate. But I must wait. You do know why?"

"Yes." Kate pouted. For a moment she was genuinely angry

at all of the Society rules.

"But there is one thing I can show you now, because there really isn't a way of avoiding it." He lifted the tarp up from his partially artificial leg. "You must know that what you see, as always, is between us." He tenderly pulled the latch and opened the compartment to his mechanical calf.

"Oh." Kate was stunned. Bits of metal flickered in the firelight. "What happened? Is that the only part of you like that?"

"Yes, yes." He warmed some of the lard on a plate and then drizzled its melted oil onto the frozen parts. "That is why the serum didn't help my limp. I had an injury a long time ago, from quite the accident. I can't say much more than that, but a fine Society physician put my leg back together." Suddenly the gears started to turn and a look of relief washed over Lord Wilson. "Ahh, that is so much better."

He put the remaining melted fat out in front of him. "So, we have something to dip our fruit and nuts in. And as you see I found some coffee beans we can roast. Would you mind putting some of them into the pot?"

"Of course." Kate dropped the beans into a shallow pan and soon their aroma filled the boathouse.

Is this what it's like? Her mind questioned. *To be domesticated? Would all their future moments be like this?*

"Let me feed the horses." He stood and gave the beasts some of their cache. "It's still very cold over here, but I think they'll be fine."

Kate stole a glance over her shoulder at her Senior. He'd draped the tarp around his waist and held it closed with one hand while the other tended to the animals. He was decently fit, with strong shoulders and a lean middle. The muscles of his arms and back rippled with every move. With the boat cover dragging behind him on the floor, Lord Wilson looked the part of a Greek god, as if he'd been modelled from clay. Deep inside, Kate felt that old stirring of desire and suddenly wanted to act on it. Just as that thought crossed her mind, he spoke again.

"But for us, I think some coffee and getting closer to the fire should help." He looked in Kate's direction just as she turned away and started to crush the roasted beans. Her head and arms were the only bare part of her, but it aroused him, knowing that underneath the blanket was the sweetness he'd longed for. He came up from behind her to stoke the fire. "We should have enough firewood to make it through the night. Go ahead and eat." He resisted the urge to touch her hair again. It was still damp, and the air still wasn't warm enough for his liking.

"Thank you." Kate delved into their stash of food as Lord Wilson shared with her. They sipped on the tart coffee as the night grew even colder.

The orange radiance of the fire tinged her skin with a pleasant tickle. The reflection of the flames danced in her eyes. After about five minutes of silent snacking, Lord Wilson could barely contain himself. The way she brought the bits of fruit to her lips reminded him of how she'd tempted him with the chocolates. But now Kate was only doing what was natural and helping them survive. He resisted his impulse and cleared his throat. "Well, we should save some for breakfast."

"Yes, yes we should." Kate put the food aside, wondering what would happen. The temptation was raging through her and she shuddered. She was chilly but her heart was afire.

The boat house was still cold with some drafts wafting behind them. They wouldn't freeze, but Lord Wilson knew that they needed more heat. "Kate, we need to be warmer than we are. I can see you shuddering. So we will lie in front of the fireplace, you in front, and me behind. I will tell you now, that I will remain a gentleman. You will do as I ask?"

Kate was stunned. "Yes, of course."

"Very well then." He patted the floor in front of him. "Here, try and rest."

Kate lay down while still wrapped in the blanket. He spooned against her, with only the wool between them. He wrapped himself around her and whispered. "Good night Kate."

"Good night." Kate finally was warm enough to realize two things: Lord Wilson had stopped calling her Miss and that she was exhausted. She soon fell asleep tightly bundled in his arms, the back of her head against his chest.

Lord Wilson cherished this moment. Her slow breaths warming his hands under her chin. Her plump buttocks cushioned into his lap. After she'd fallen into slumber, he ran his fingers through her hair with a light touch. The strands were almost dry. Content that she was safe, he finally was able to rest.

Kate's slumber didn't last but an hour. Although Lord Wilson was asleep, his teeth were chattering next to her ear. *Oh, this will not do, not at all*, she laughed to herself. He had given her the comfortable covering. *His backside must be frozen away from the fire. That tarp is anything but pleasant.*

Kate mulled over the consequences of sharing the blanket. They had some serum left, but they were trying to save it for the ride back should the weather improve. They needed to conserve the firewood. Who knows how long they'd need to stay if the storm didn't break? She tentatively pulled her hands out to feel his. They were almost warm from the fire. She discreetly tried not to disturb him as she felt up and around the back side of his head. It was cold.

Lord Wilson didn't stir, but this was no way to sleep. She caved. *Hell with this. What happens, happens.*

Kate opened the blanket and turned to face him. He awoke with her body stirring against his.

"Hmmm." His eyes opened as she tucked the blanket round both of them. "Oh." He mumbled in surprise.

"It's too cold for you. Your teeth are chattering." Kate whispered.

"No, no. Turn back around." He tried to turn her hip but she was already pressed against him.

"Nope. I won't." She buried her head under the cover and onto his chest.

The teasing softness of her skin fully awoke him. "Kate. No." He again tried to push her away, but she clung to him, her hands holding the blanket around him.

"It's not fair for you to be cold." She persisted.

"No, Kate. You need to let go." He groaned in exasperation. He pulled his hands to his sides and she still was too close. She shook her head under the blanket. "What if I ordered you, Miss Kate?" His voice was stern.

She finally popped her head up. "I will do as you ask, as always. But I won't rest if you can't." Kate pleaded.

He rolled onto his back as she finally let go. His eyes gazed into the fire for quite a while. Finally he sat up and pulled the blanket up to her neck. "Kate, I know that you probably can't have children. But I have no means of, well, protection. Besides that, I am a man of my word." He touched her hair. "You are everything I have ever wanted. I value every ounce of your being. You do understand how hard it is for me to resist you?"

Kate smiled ruefully. "Yes. I'm sorry."

"Then again, you're correct; my coldness will not help you stay comfortable. If I allow you next to me, I take full responsibility for my actions, but you must as well. Understood?" He tried to ignore the ache in his groin, the desire to be with her fully.

Lord Wilson had a sadness in his eyes that shocked Kate. They wouldn't die out here, but they could be Terminated later.

"Yes, I won't tempt you. I promise." Kate's smile disappeared as she gave him her earnest word.

"Come then, sit in my lap. Open the blanket. I will not judge." Wilson put the tarp aside momentarily as Kate slowly pulled the wool down. Kate tried not to look at his crotch as she slid onto his thighs. He was truly a man. He looked into her eyes and pulled the blanket around them both, then put the tarp on top. "Rest your head like before." He whispered. "Shall we try this again now?"

"Yes." She mumbled with pangs of guilt running through her.

"Good night Miss Kate."

"Good night, Sir."

With a few neighs of the horses, the two were at last warm enough to slumber in the bitterly cold night.

15 A RETURN

"No relations then? Really Lord Wilson, I'm impressed with your fortitude." Director Roth poured a second cup of tea for his once frozen friend.

"You have no idea." Lord Wilson smirked.

"I almost want to apologize for our archaic rules." The Director hid his bemusement with a wipe of his lips from his napkin. "It's a shame that you can't both receive some sort of credit for the ability to save each other's lives."

"Hmm, yes. A pity." Lord Wilson shared his Director's opinion.

"My biggest concern is the infiltration of our grounds. This is the second Ellis mole to penetrate the Society in only a few weeks. The subterfuge of Madeline Fahey has released a cluster of violence upon our Members. We need to get a hold of this situation immediately. I'll keep you posted on the results from our clean up team. Such a shame we couldn't retain the body of Mr. Gotham. I suppose our delivery of our faux Master Richards prompted the Mass to react quickly. The ashes more than confirmed his aborted mission. At least we know that they received our message."

"Indeed." Lord Wilson dug into another sausage. He was famished from the night before in ways one could barely imagine.

Much earlier that morning Lord Wilson had dressed and prepped the horses so Kate could continue to sleep. *So much loss and tragedy, yet her heart is still open to love*, he pondered. She deserved the extra rest. He could at least give her that. Last night he barely resisted giving her everything.

Kate awoke just as he was ready to take the horses out. There was just a hint of natural light in the room and she squinted around in awe.

"Good Morning, Miss Kate. Your clothes should be dry. Why don't you dress while I ready things outside?" He was fully prepared for the frigid weather. "The sky is clear, but it's still quite cold. We can eat a bit and head out before the full dawn. I don't want too much of a scene. We need to hurry back to get this mess covered up." He stepped out before Kate could reply.

Kate shook herself awake, clamored off the floor and threw on her things. *Did last night really happen?* She'd warmed the remaining coffee and food just as Lord Wilson returned.

"Hmm, wonderful smell." Lord Wilson swooped in beside her at the hearth and popped a warm almond in his mouth.

"It is, isn't it." Kate grinned and handed him a cup that was as warm as her heart in that moment.

"Here, sip a bit." He handed her the bottle of serum with just a few drops left.

"Yes Sir." She took a drink and passed it back as it heated her tongue. He scooped up a few bits of fruit and downed his coffee.

"Eat quickly now." He hand fed her the rest of the dried fruit dipped in the lard.

Kate's insides tingled but she wasn't sure if it was from the serum and hot food or how Lord Wilson was being so kind to her.

He pressed a last walnut against her lips. A bit of the fat dribbled on her chin. He wiped it with his fingertips and then licked them. "How barbarically sinful to eat this way." He chuckled. Before Kate could respond his finger was at her mouth again; his face so close she could feel his breath. "Oh you have a bit, just right there." But instead of wiping it clean again, he kissed her fully on the mouth for a brief moment. "There that's better. Come along now." He took her hand while he rose up and pulled her with him.

"Oh, thank you." Kate was still stunned by the kiss. It had been so quick but incredibly sweet.

"Coat?" He whisked her heavy cover off one of the boats, gave it a brisk shake and helped put it on. He paused with his strong hands on her upper arms and tickled her ear. "Not a word of last night to anyone, Miss Kate. Agreed?"

"Yes Sir."

"Alright then, outside. I'll douse the flames here." He poured the remaining water onto the fire. "Watch out for the manure."

Kate stepped out into a bitter cold that slapped her awake. *Did that all really happen?*

Sonny grunted a good morning as she prepared to mount him. Day was breaking as the remaining clouds of the night before blew off to the East. She looked out to the lake. Lord Wilson's carriage was still upended and stuck into the thin ice. But she didn't see Gotham's body. Suddenly she was distracted by a rapidly approaching crew. Their horses kicked up a dust of snow across Lafayette Park. A familiar face led the pack.

"Miss Church, are you alright?" Mr. Scott pulled his muffler aside to speak clearly.

Lord Wilson stepped out at their arrival and bellowed before Kate could even open her mouth. "She's fine. And so am I." There were ten men and two sleighs filled with plenty of supplies.

Kate was suddenly grateful that she wouldn't have to ride Sonny back in the cold. She swore her bones were still frozen solid.

"Very good then, Sir. The storm blew in before we could set out last night. Appears you had quite an evening." He nodded towards the carriage.

"Yes, and a bit of a mess inside," Lord Wilson replied. The Security men dismounted and set to work cleaning up all traces of the Society Members' night in the boathouse.

"Well then, Sir. A warm ride for you and Miss Church. Director Roth will be pleased at your return. Good day Sir."

Before Kate could even speak one of the gentlemen carried her to the sleigh and tucked her in. Lord Wilson was next to her in seconds. Sonny and the carriage horse were given blankets and riders. Soon they were whisked back to the Society.

"Mother, they're leaving." Atticus Ellis peered through a spyglass from the inn window. He was almost relieved at their departure. The youngest Ellis son was tired of holding watch at the chilly window.

"Hmmm. And they were there all night then." Mrs. Ellis was still in her nightclothes, but her attire didn't dampen her acidic mood.

"Yes." Atticus set the glass down with a gentle thud. He hated delivering bad news to his mother. She'd lost so much.

"And Mr. Gotham?" She reclined on a settee near the fire while sipping hot tea.

"Expired. We managed to retrieve his body without incident."

"Hmm. Pity. But Cecil is safely embedded now?"

"Yes, since Boston. He's been active a few days now. He's sure to get more pertinent Engagements by being the right blend of gentleman and killer." Atticus hoped his eldest brother could do what others, including his other brother Julian, had not.

"Splendid. So, not all was lost." Mrs. Ellis looked at her youngest with a fondness. She didn't want to expend another one of her children. But Cecil would exact a severe revenge on her enemies. Mrs. Ellis just didn't realize how soon he would have the opportunity to do so.

It had been a horribly long twenty-four hours. After his briefing with the Director, Lord Wilson hurried back to the Manor.

"So happy to see that you are well, Sir." Leeds was genuinely pleased that his Senior had returned safe and sound. "And Miss Church?"

"She is well. Resting for a while. She will be here for tea and dinner, if you would please make arrangements with Mrs. Leeds."

"Excellent, Sir."

Lord Wilson turned to his desk. For a moment he thought of the last evening's adventure and his body ached with want of her. He enjoyed surprising Kate with the stolen kiss. *That's the second time,* he pondered. Again, he wondered how long he could continue to hold out for official word from those who held the highest powers in the Society.

Kate gazed in the mirrored wall in her bath. Despite the ravages of near death, cold and whatever disasters that were thrown her, she was a survivor. *You are strong.* "Yes I am." She smiled at her reflection. Ming and Chin's words were still a mystical mantra for her. She flipped the control button and her reflection disappeared as she eased into the warm waters for a quick soak.

Kate was grateful that the serum had saved her once again. Her thoughts travelled to Lord Wilson as she stepped from the tub. It had felt so wonderful to have rested against him. She looked forward to a morning nap, then maybe she could revisit him in her dreams.

She was certain if she hadn't been exhausted, she wouldn't have been able to resist. Like Lord Wilson, she wondered how long she could wait. Kate had just finished dressing as the familiar whoosh of an invitation landed in her basket. She opened it without hesitation.

Dear Miss Kate:

So much has happened in such a short time that we need to discuss today. Please arrive at 3:00 p.m. at the Manor for a long Discussion, tea, some time to relax and initial planning. You may bring Strax. We have much work ahead of us.

Sincerely,

W.

Kate held the invitation close to her heart as she fell into a blissful morning slumber.

Mr. Cecil Cole strode through the Main Hall of the Society with a devilish air. Not a bit of information around him missed his gaze. He memorized every face, every gadget, and every piece of décor he passed. Information in the right hands was deadly. And the hands of Mr. Cole were deadly indeed.

He'd only been in the Society for a short while, but he'd made certain his reputation preceded him. He'd been in the military, was an excellent marksman until after several wars and conflicts, fell on hard times and resorted to crime. He made good money as a gun for hire. At least that was what his faux dossier led his Society recruiter to believe.

His cover was so well received that he'd already been sent out on Engagements as an assassin; a role he had trained for in his true life as the eldest son of Mrs. Ellis.

He returned to his room after a kill Engagement. This one had been easy; a butcher that was a Fixture had been skimming off his profits for quite some time. That kind of trickery could be punished by lesser means. But when that same butcher had an affair with a Senior Member's wife, his life was expendable.

The Fixture didn't see it coming. He'd only known that his mistress had disappeared. He figured she'd returned to her husband and that he was already forgotten. Only her heart made it back to her husband. It was in the pail that Miss Church had delivered to Lord Wilson only a few weeks earlier.

The butcher's demise was much less dramatic. On that fateful night, he closed his shop for the evening and set out from the back door. Immediately after he'd locked the door, he came face to face with Mr. Cole. Within seconds the butcher was dead, his pockets emptied, and all of his money drained from his store to make it look like a robbery.

For his valuable precision, Mr. Cole made it very clear to his Senior that he would not be patient like the others. He would be rewarded quickly and handsomely. Because of his proven prowess and chosen profession, he was given more access than most. Like Kate, he was given a higher entry status: a room on the third floor, all the entertainment he could handle and as much killing as he could muster. Mr. Cole was very adept at making death seem like something else entirely: staging fatal accidents, accomplishing quick clean hits, and the occasional disappearance.

He could not, however, change the appearance of his shoulder. He took some tonic to the scar. The wound from Miss Pratt still stung in the mornings. It reminded him that he needed to watch out for her, if only for a little while longer, in order to accomplish his mission undiscovered.

"You've upped your game Miss Kate." Lord Wilson leaned back in his chair with a smile.

"I think I have," Kate felt the smoothness of Lord Wilson's queen under her fingertips. "Check mate."

The two enjoyed tea and chess as Strax lay asleep at Kate's feet. Both were of like minds, wishing that it could be this way always.

"Do you tire of the games, Miss Kate?" Lord Wilson asked as he put the chess board away.

"Depends upon the game and how it ends," Kate bantered and then dared to ask the same. "Do you?"

He turned around to face her cleverness. "Depends on the players. As we spoke of earlier, the people who tried to assassinate you and me, well, they are old enemies. Same players, but it's a new game. They want three keys. And they are the Ellis family, and part of a much larger organization that is similar to the Society." He poured a fresh cup of tea for both of them while preparing to explain. And so a new Discussion began.

"The Ellis family has ties to mine and Director Roth's joining of the Society. What I'm about to tell you stays here as always, Miss Kate," Lord Wilson warned.

"Of course, Sir." Kate stopped nibbling on an oatmeal cookie and sat up straight in rapt attention.

"Our separation from the Ellis clan was not pleasant. The Director and I chose to work for the greater good here at the Society. They obviously went another route, even to another country to work for a group called The Mass. The three keys that you have helped us procure, belong in that country, the home of my birth, England. They help run a massive machine in the underbelly of London, but only if you have all three. We don't know exactly how the machine works or what it does, but the keys were stolen for nefarious purposes, of that we are sure. We are certain that the Ellis family took those keys to implement a much larger plan.

The holder of the keys controls the machine. As we speak, two of the keys are being returned now. One is being held back and we are to deliver it in person. This we'll speak of later.

Obviously you thwarted Mr. Drasco and eliminated Mr. Reed, who by the way was Mr. Ellis, the head of the family. He was the father of Master Richards, also known as the Ellis's middle son, Julian. These good deeds, unfortunately, brought you to The Mass' attention. However, you then won the last key on the Ester." Lord Wilson's face broke into a smile. "Which reminds me of something I must show you. Please come." He stood and offered her his hand. She felt blissfully safe in his arms as helped her with her coat. They went outside and their steps echoed down the spiral staircase, Kate going first and Lord Wilson following behind.

He paused briefly outside of the lab. "I know that you have worked on some special projects here. There is one very important piece of equipment I must share with you. Very few know of its existence and I must have your word."

"Of course, Sir."

"Very well, then." He opened the door and a whisk of warm air and Dr. Harrington greeted them.

"Oh, hello Lord Wilson and Miss Church," the young technician greeted in a cheery tone.

"Hello Dr. Harrington. I've brought Miss Church to show her what we had discussed earlier."

"Ah, yes. Please do come." The Member waved his hand to a corner Kate had looked over before, but not really seen. It had always appeared as an old piece of equipment blanketed by tarp. With a quick flick of his wrist, the cover was removed and a shiny copper and brass framework glistened in the low lights of the workshop. It was in the shape of a trapezoidal box of about five feet high and six feet wide at the base. The front was completely closed off by a blue-colored glass. On the inside of this window was a panel with a row of numbers, various gauges, knobs and switches. A round, shallow impression was bordered by a large red switch. The back side was bordered with a simple narrow burgundy velvet covered bench. Behind the seat was a box lined with pumps and gears. A small chimney puffed poofs of steam after its inventor flipped the red switch.

"Oh." Kate piped up in astonishment.

"This is what we call the Traveler." Dr. Harrington presented in fine fashion. "It is a machine that travels through time."

"What? How is that possible?" Kate questioned.

"Through quite a bit of science really. And something that we use every day," Dr. Harrington continued. "First, it has a powerful energy source of its own. When I first assembled it, the fuel needed to run it really wasn't available. It burnt through a pile of wood in seconds, and coal in mere minutes. I had to scrap the first furnace. Then we tried potent explosives, none of which worked and some of which shaved a few moments from my life when I wasn't certain I could transfer the energy. But thanks to you, Miss Kate." He waved his hand over a cap on the side. "We can fill it with only a glass of the fantastic green liquid from the cacti you discovered in Iris. It generates more than enough power to work for fifteen minutes. Just enough window, we hope, to accomplish our most urgent needs. And it has worked, for at least that time period."

"But how does it work?"

"Well, back to our everyday use. The higher level Society Members all have pocket watches. All of these time keepers are linked to a secret Society resource. A pulse, if you will, that controls all of our time and our bodily links to it. When I've coded the watches to the machine through a magnetized divot, it reads the pulse of the watch holder, and pushes them through time."

Kate looked puzzled with a wrinkled brow and turned to Lord Wilson.

Lord Wilson smiled at her befuddlement. "There is much more science and physics behind this than he can explain, but listen, Miss Kate."

"Right now, it can work remotely through only two existing demo model timepieces, mine and Lord Wilson's. However, Director Roth and now you, Miss Church, will have access to the Machine via your timepiece. All you need to know is how to work it. Please come, step inside and sit." Dr. Harrington took her hand.

Kate sat on the bench, her face illuminated by the equipment. "Alright then, show me."

"I am going to program your watch first. Your timepiece please?"

Kate offered her pocket watch to Dr. Harrington.

"Now then, I'm going to set it in the round hole there. It's magnetized and will stick instantly." He only had to set the watch in front of the panel and it was sucked into the hole. "Now I'm going to press this green button." Once he depressed the key, her pocket watch gave off a familiar buzz and the machine gave a small hiss. It buzzed twice more; Dr. Harrington removed it, and handed it back to Kate.

"So now you can use the machine. In order to move through time, you must pick an exact date and time. Note that we move time for everyone, not just the person with the timepiece. This is why the Traveler must remain secret. We have not tried to move Members to other locations. We assume that they will be in the spot they were during the original time period. So you will set the date here." He pointed to the row of numbers. "I move this daily, to the current date, so that should something drastic happen, Lord Wilson or I could at least buy ourselves fifteen minutes to hopefully change the outcome of whatever hell has happened upon us. Then you set your watch back fifteen minutes from the time you want to move, then place it in the hole it was just in. Lastly you'll press the red switch. Time movement will be instantaneous. You may feel some temporary nausea or dizziness, but all should be well."

"So how far have you tried to go back?" Kate was incredulous.

"Well, only fifteen minutes, really. This piece is still in the prototype stage. There is a strong want for people to change time.

The results on a change in history could be disastrous. We have yet to move further back with dates, but the ripple effect could be crippling. We must proceed with extreme caution."

"So it has worked before?" Kate was impressed.

"Um, yes." Dr. Harrington blushed.

"I think that should be a good enough explanation then for, um, the technical part. A moment, Dr. Harrington?"

"Yes Sir." The young Member left the lab and stepped outside with a "Good Evening". Lord Wilson paused until the door closed with a quiet thud.

"So it really works? Did you try it?" Kate asked.

"Yes, a few weeks ago."

"And did I know this?"

Lord Wilson looked somber. "Please sit down, Miss Kate." He pulled up two of the laboratory chairs for them. As she sat, he took her hand. "Yes, yes you did. Do you remember anything strange about the night on the Ester?"

"Um no. I mean I was drugged and I was pretty woozy."

"Miss Kate, I don't mean to startle you, but there's a reason I'm allowing you to know the secrets of the Traveler. We know it works because of you. That night when the Ester ran aground the first time, you died."

The first time? The words shot through her head. Kate was suddenly sick to her stomach. "You mean, I died on the boat?" Kate's voice cracked through her lips.

"Yes, you drowned before I could send Strax after you."

"You, you did this, for me?" Kate's voice quivered. Tears ran down her face as she shuddered. "Oh, oh my God."

"Yes. I set time back and was able to get a warning to the Ester about the sand bar. They were able to alter course enough to control the damage," Lord Wilson stuttered. "I could not lose you Kate." He paused and pulled her close.

Kate buried her face into his chest feeling the steady beat of his heart against her temple. *How could I ever have doubted?* "Thank you."

"Please, remember all this and keep it to yourself." He pulled up her chin and wiped her face. "I'm giving you access to the Traveler in case something drastic should happen. As we spoke earlier, there are serious forces that intend to do us harm. Obviously, they are not finished and won't be until we are eliminated. The weather is going to continue to be cold. We need to be ready for any changes. We need to stop them."

Kate was exhausted. The previous weeks' adventures had tapped out almost all of her reserve. She clung to him wordlessly.

As if reading her mind he spoke quietly, "This has been an incredibly rough period, Kate. I'd like to take you to the greenhouse for some warmth." He looked at her with tender eyes and led her outside to the radiant building.

They stood for a moment on the walkway that trimmed the greenhouse. Their figures appeared as shadows before the glowing glass. Again, there was no Miss before her name, she wondered. He held her hand as a lonely crescent moon rose. "I am grateful for what you did for me, that you took initiative and saved my life. It is a debt I cannot ever repay, really." His voice was melodic and warm. "Are you happy here Kate?" His eyes were sincere.

"Yes. Yes very much." Kate looked at him earnestly.

"I-I want to tell you." He stopped and touched her face. Kate flushed as her heart ached. "I have loved you from the first moment I saw you. I had so hoped you would come here and want to be with me. I know it is a tremendous rule I am breaking, but I must know, do you feel the same?"

Kate's mouth fell open. She could barely think. Was he judging her? Should she resist him? But the words poured from her lips before she could stop them. "Yes, yes I do."

Wilson breathed a sigh of relief. "May I kiss you?" he whispered.

"Yes, I want you to." If this was a test, she was failing miserably. Her voice so thin it barely peeped out. Lord Wilson removed his top hat and pulled Kate closer with his other hand, putting it in the small of her back. She closed her eyes as he leaned in for a delicate kiss. Kate became light headed as the featherlike brush of his mouth excited her. She puckered and returned his pleasant affection. The kiss became more sensual. He drew her directly against him, intoxicated by her scent, her soft lips. He could resist no longer. Their mouths opened in their passionate embrace.

He pulled away and Kate opened her eyes slowly. "Oh Kate, I must tell you that this is wrong. But if you will wait until August next year, you can stay here at Wilson Manor if you would have me." The words tumbled from him like fallen cards.

Kate looked at him oddly, her soul held in suspense. "What?"

He explained. "Once you have been here for a year, you're considered properly trained. I know that you have heard of this formality, and it is true. The Society wants a full year for you to become seasoned, then the Society would choose a new Senior for you unless I objected." He paused and looked a bit distressed. "Or you could be my permanent partner. We could be married." His face begged for her to speak.

"What about now? What will happen?" Kate was frightened; she so loved Lord Wilson.

"Nothing will change for now. We will attend Engagements and follow all rules. You can visit the Manor as always. But we must be extremely discreet. You must not say a word to anyone, not even Dr. Finch. I promise you this. There are no others, Kate. I will not touch you again until I am allowed. Will you wait for me, for all this time as Member and Senior until we can be together?" He held her so tightly as if she would break if he let go.

"Yes." Kate smiled. She liked the strength of his hands on her. It reminded her of when she first met him in the desert and he lifted her into the wagon.

"Very well then. I want to show you something." He led her inside the structure to a corner she hadn't explored. He helped her off with her heavy woolen coat, laying it over an exquisite iron bench. He removed his outerwear and placed it next to hers with a gentle rustle.

The area held a rare array of roses she'd never seen before. Their brilliant hues filled her heart. "This is what you are to me, Kate. Beautiful, rare. And sometimes a little dangerous." He smiled as his finger grazed a thorn of one of the plush blooms.

"Well, thank you." She blushed. It was suddenly very warm in the greenhouse.

"Kate, you have never asked for additional rewards. You've performed admirably without subflurious compensation. Today, I am authorized by Director Roth to give you whatever payment you desire. A large sum of money, some private time away from study.

Anything you ask is yours." His voice lowered as he waited for her reply.

"Anything?" Her eyes widened with surprise.

"Yes." He wondered what he could possibly offer that she didn't already have, other than freedom outside the Society's walls.

Kate's mouth opened but the words would not come.

Suddenly, the misters of the greenhouse came on, the light sprays soaking them both. Kate began to laugh in light cheery echoes. "Must we always be wet?" Her eyes danced. Wilson joined in her mirth.

"So Miss Kate, what is it you want?" The water seeped down his face as he grinned. He pulled out a kerchief and wiped the moisture from her cheeks and forehead.

"I think out of these wet clothes first." A softness entered her eyes as she cajoled. "Then I want you. I want you, Christopher. Now. I'm not waiting anymore. Fuck the rules." She stepped forward and kissed him.

As Kate spoke his Christian name for the first time, it sent a shockwave through his body. His hunger would be satisfied; he would not be patient.

This time, neither resisted the other. Lord Wilson pulled away briefly to place his coat on the hardened wet brick of the greenhouse. He quickly offed his dampened suit coat, vest, and shirt for some added cushioning. He let his suspenders fall to his sides as he returned to her, bare-chested.

He unbuttoned her dress coat and helped her peel it off. The water had seeped through her pale blouse and the pink of her nipples showed through. He released the lacing of her skirt while her hands explored his shoulders, chest, and then down to the buttons on his trousers. They fell to the floor with a plop. Kate reached around and cupped his buttocks, still delightfully firm for man of his age.

He smiled in response and took her face in his hands. They kissed again, more passionately as the heat flared between them. He finished undressing her, undoing her corset lacing and letting his hands fall to her breasts. They were everything he'd imagined. Their delicious fullness tickled his fingertips. His hands came round to her backside and he pulled her fully against him. Words of love cascaded between them as they explored each other.

"Come, Kate." He helped her to the floor, their bodies still wet with the warm water that misted from the ceiling. His lips electrified her skin, covering almost every inch of her as she wept with desire.

Kate shuddered under his touch. She had wanted this for so long, to be loved and to love someone else equally. "Christopher." She cried under him as they passionately made love.

"I love you Kate." He breathed into her as the gentle streams of water poured over them. All the waiting, the danger, and the agony were forgotten in their moment of coital bliss.

But again for Kate, their intimacy was witnessed through the eyes of someone with cruel intentions.

Once Kate and Lord Wilson had finished, they slipped into their undergarments and went into the Manor to dry off. Outside Cecil Ellis double checked the knobs of an intricate camera. Despite the dim lighting and mist of the greenhouse, there were at least two clear images. His short tenure in infiltrating the Society had paid off handsomely.

Kate awoke in the arms of the man she'd always dreamed of finding, one that was not afraid of her spirited nature, yet treated her as a lady of distinction.

"You're awake." Lord Wilson brushed aside her hair to see more of her face.

"Did I dream this?" she questioned sleepily.

"I hope not." He gave a quiet laugh while reclining on his back. "Are you alright?"

"Hmm, yes." Kate purred while on her side with her leg draped over him. She nestled her head on his chest and kissed over his heart.

When they had returned to the warm comforts of the Manor in the late evening before, wearing just their soaked undergarments and coats, Leeds only smiled. "I'll take those wet things, Sir."

"We will be down for dinner at eight. Please, send Mrs. Leeds up to attend to Miss Church in a few moments" Lord Wilson instructed in a pleasant tone.

"Yes Sir."

Lord Wilson led Kate upstairs to the Lady's quarters and opened the door. "I've always meant for this room to be yours. Your haven for when you need time alone. But tonight after dinner, I'd like for you to reside in my room. Yes?"

"Yes." Kate replied in a dreamy state as she floated into her bedroom. Like all other rooms in the Manor, it was trimmed with exquisite paintings, tapestries, and furniture.

"Very well, my Kate. Mrs. Leeds will be up shortly. I will see you at dinner." He gave her a tender kiss and parted, closing the door behind him.

Kate slipped out of her wet things and opened a wardrobe. Inside, she found a lovely silken dusty pink robe. When she touched the soft fabric, her mind returned to Iris and the gown Ming had given her.

How much has changed in just a few months. As she prepared to remove her damp clothes, Mrs. Leeds knocked.

"Please come in." Kate smiled.

"Ah, Miss Church." Mrs. Leeds entered quietly. "May I help you tidy up?"

"Yes please." Kate accepted the help with a demure tone as she sat at the ornate vanity.

"I am delighted that you are here at the Manor, Miss Church. Lord Wilson has been quite fond of you for some time. I assure you, you have the utmost of privacy here." Her new assistant began to tend to her.

"Thank you Mrs. Leeds." Kate looked at her reflection. She was absolutely radiant with glowing skin and sparking eyes.

"Now how would you like for me to fix your hair?"

"Do you like your things?" Lord Wilson questioned over his soup. *She looks absolutely stunning,* he thought as his eyes wandered over her soft teal gown. Her hair was neatly done up in a bun.

"Yes, very much."

"If you don't, please, tell me. We can get other things made for you. Whatever colors or fashion you like."

"I'm very happy." Kate smiled. It was true. She hadn't been this happy since she'd returned to St. Louis and reunited with Abby.

Strax whined under the table and Leeds fetched him a snack.

"It seems everyone is satisfied now." Lord Wilson grinned as Mrs. Leeds brought in a main course of beef with potatoes and rich gravy. The two dined and then retired for the evening around ten.

Lord Wilson's heart beat as if it would burst. He could not wait to share his bed with Kate. They separated briefly as Leeds turned down the bed. "Will that be all, Sir?"

"Yes, thank you."

Leeds leaned in towards his master and patted his shoulder. "Well done, Sir. Good evening." As he turned to leave, Mrs. Leeds entered with Kate close behind.

"Miss Church, Sir. Good evening." Mrs. Leeds beamed.

Lord Wilson again felt the sweet burn through his body. His lady was home at last.

They made love again through most of the night and slept late into the morning.

His hand grazed along her tattoo. "You are strong, Kate."

To hear the phrase that Ming and Chin had told her in a British accent pleased Kate. "You know the meaning."

"Yes. When you were first treated, I wanted to know what it was. You've certainly earned it."

"I was marked, for protection." Kate reminisced. "One of the few things I have left from Ming and Chin." She looked away from him as a scowl crossed her face.

"I'm sorry I could not help them, Kate." Lord Wilson sat up and let his fingertips graze her chin. "When I came to Iris, I didn't know that Drasco had amassed so much of a gang. I came to recruit you and secure one of the keys. I didn't realize how badly you were outnumbered. Things escalated far more quickly than we expected with disastrous results. Know this, I meant it when I said I loved you from the moment I first saw you. Like you, I've lost so many others. The things I cannot even begin to tell you. I have only this, this Society. All for the greater good. And without it, our paths wouldn't have crossed. Never in our lifetimes, I'm certain." He kissed her forehead and ran his hands along her back. "Please understand that I am sorry. Can you forgive me?"

"Yes." Kate lifted her head and looked into the eyes of her beloved. "I forgive you."

"Thank you." Lord Wilson paused. "Now, say my Christian name again. It arouses me to no end." He chuckled.

"Very well, Christopher." Kate pulled herself on top of her Senior with a naughty giggle, more than happy to oblige his order.

16 A SHORT WHILE WITH MR. COLE

"We have word that Miss Church spent last night at the Manor." Director Roth's face was twisted with pain as he delivered hideous news during an emergency Discussion with Lord Wilson and Miss Church. "And that there was, well, an impassioned moment in the greenhouse."

Kate was stunned, her heart falling to her feet and the Director's office seemed to spin around her. She wondered if her attendant had said something, but Miss Beatrice couldn't have known with certainty that Kate slept with Lord Wilson.

Lord Wilson was also jarred. He gripped the chair with such strength that it was a wonder he didn't break it in two. "So someone spied upon the Manor last night?"

Director Roth was not pleased. He grimaced as he spoke. "I assure you, this was not something of my doing. It was reported to a higher authority. I didn't hear of it until an hour ago. My superiors wired to let me know of their displeasure, especially since Miss Church has been selected for a particularly prickly future Engagement."

"How?" Kate asked in astonishment, her skin going white. She suddenly felt as if the earth under her feet was crumbling into an open chasm, with the petulant vacuum of destruction pulling her in.

"Miss Church, I'll ask you not to speak at the moment. Lord Wilson is your Senior. He is ultimately responsible for your actions."

"But-"

"Miss Kate, please." Lord Wilson glanced at his Member with a withered look. The admonishment was breaking him. His heart stilled as he wondered if the end for them would be now or later.

"I can tell you, that I believe that this is the work of another mole, most likely someone tied to the Ellis family. And unfortunately he was given a perfect opportunity to expose you both. There were at least a couple of distinct pictures. I'll save you the pain of seeing them. Apparently they've developed quite the machine for capturing images. Quite frankly I don't care if you're having relations, as long as you're completing your fucking Engagements without causing a stir. This is about as unpleasant as it gets for me." Director Roth took a long drag from his cigar before continuing. "Miss Church has been immediately reassigned to someone of their choosing, a Mr. Cole, an assassin. They believe if she is able to be so calculating in all things, that her talents would be better used elsewhere."

"What?" Kate cried out as if someone had stabbed her, pain echoing in her voice.

"I'm sorry Miss Church. That is what I'm ordered to do. I have no say in this matter. I empathize with your predicament, but you must obey. You will report to Mr. Cole tomorrow for retraining. During this time, your movements will be regulated. No outside visits on the grounds. And you are not to have any contact with Lord Wilson whatsoever. You are dismissed." Director Roth waved his hand toward the door as they all stood. "Take great care Miss Church. You will not be given another chance. Understood?"

"Yes Sir." Kate's face crashed into a mess of tears.

"A moment?" Lord Wilson begged of their Director. He nodded and pretended to look over some random paperwork on his desk. Inside Director Roth ached for his old friend. And behind that pain was another worry that someone had dared to interfere with his territory.

Lord Wilson drew Kate to him in a comforting hug and then caressed her face. He kissed her forehead and spoke tenderly. "We won't let the bastards get us down. Don't be too soft, Kate. Hold on for now. We will prevail, I promise you. I love you." He pulled back while staring directly into her eyes. "You are strong."

Kate could only nod in return as she walked out with as much composure as she could muster. Words would not come to her. They couldn't escape from her throat which was as dry as a desert as she closed the door behind her.

Director Roth turned his attention back to Lord Wilson as Miss Church left the room, then spoke solemnly, "As you know, I could have Terminated you both. Between you and me, I understand that some of this could not be helped. Our business is a precarious one, sometimes absurdly so. I wish that you'd been able to constrain your activities to inside the Manor. However, as your actions did not go unnoticed by the Superiors, I have done what would most appease them. They would not want to waste your talents. Besides, killing you and Miss Church wouldn't solve anything and only allows The Mass satisfaction."

Lord Wilson managed a "Hmm." Inside he was infuriated, longing to kill the interloper without mercy or care.

Director Roth's eyes softened. He spoke more eloquently and kindly. "Dear friend, I know that you have waited a lifetime for her. You were able to choose her. She is a spitfire with a kind heart. Without her actions, I would be without Miss Pratt, for that I am grateful. At least now she will have the opportunity to live. Although you won't see Miss Church, you will know she is here." His voice then lowered and he again became serious. "They will always be watching. They think that she is now prepared for a much more dangerous position. She will most likely be sent to England without you. Please know that I did everything in my power to reverse this current situation. You Sir, have always been like a brother to me. And without Miss Church, I would have lost another partner. I don't know if I could live without Miss Pratt. But tread carefully, Sir, for I am grateful that you are still here." Director Roth was angry. He didn't like taking such severe actions on someone who did not deserve the punishment.

"Thank you, Sir." Lord Wilson replied stiffly. "Should I watch behind me then?"

"From me? No. But we need to find that fucking mole as soon as possible." The Director sneered. The two men immediately started formulating a plan to uncover some most unpleasant business at the St. Louis Society.

Kate was devastated. She walked to her room, her feet dragging, as if pulled down by lead weights. She had been foolish and was now being punished. She was paired with a Member not liked very well at the Society, Mr. Cole. His tenure hadn't been long at the Society, but he was known to be a violent ass of a man. The Society always needed assassins, those who could kill at a moment's notice without a tinge of regret. They couldn't afford to be too particular in such matters.

Her attendant greeted her warmly at her door, but Kate was miserable. She managed to hide her pain until after her assistant had helped her undress. Within seconds of Miss Beatrice leaving, the tears came, gushing torrents of pain and sorrow.

Kate wept bitterly under the covers for over an hour. She loved Lord Wilson, she had pined for him secretly for so long and finally had her desires fulfilled. She closed her eyes and let herself go.

Her mind raced to him. She could feel the turn of his gloved hand in hers, the steely blue eyes peering into her soul, the magical British lilt tickling her ears, making her spirits rise.

She wandered further into fantasy. They would play chess; she would win and demand a prize of sitting in his lap. She'd slide pleasantly onto his legs and push their match aside.

I'm such a silly girl, Kate thought while trying to dry her face. But she continued to dream. Lord Wilson would let her hair down and pull her face towards his. His kisses would be gentle at first, then more insistent. He'd help her disrobe, untying her corset laces while nuzzling the tender spots on her neck. His hands would graze her shoulders, pull her blouse away and brush over her breasts. She would turn around to him, and help undo his trousers. Kate would at last be able to touch him without hindrance; she would be bold, unafraid. Passion would overcome their inhibitions. It would feel heavenly, Lord Christopher Wilson would always be an excellent lover, she was sure of it. *Oh Christopher,* she thought, how she'd longed to call him by his Christian name again. She felt rising warmth, the beginnings of a splendorous rapture to be released.

"Miss Church? Miss Church?" Her attendant gently shook Kate's shoulder as her pocket watch buzzed on the nightstand. "It's time to get up Miss. Your appointment is in less than an hour." Kate sat up. The attendant pushed back the curtains to reveal an incredibly sunny morning. She had fallen asleep crying. *Oh to go back to sleep and finish her dream,* she mused sadly. "Can I bring you breakfast, Miss?"

"Yes, biscuits and gravy. And tea of course. Thank you." Kate mumbled. The attendant slipped out and Kate peeked at herself at the vanity. She looked a fright, all red eyes and tangled hair. Her thoughts returned to Lord Wilson. Tears came again. *How am I going to live without him? How could this have happened?* Her heart was broken before he'd had a true chance to touch it. She was so grateful to him. He had healed her body. Kate wished wistfully that he'd had the opportunity to do the same for her soul.

That night at the Manor, Lord Wilson could not sleep. Not warm milk or chamomile tea comforted him. After his attendant had gone to his quarters, and long into the night, he cried silently while sitting on the edge of his bed. He already missed her, her lavender perfume, her curiosity, even her temper. How he would live there without her, with no more Discussions, no more adventurous Engagements, he knew not. Miraculously, he had fallen in love again–it had been a long, long while.

He fantasized about stealing away with her, forgoing the Society's protections and running to the far west or even another country to live out their days quietly. She was strong, they would survive, and they would be lovers. All these months he had tried to hide his emotions, and believed that Miss Kate had done the same. She smiled brilliantly when they were allowed to act as marrieds. She looked wonderful in whatever they asked her to wear. Maybe, just maybe, times would slowly change; perhaps they would be a team again. *Such silly thoughts,* he laughed at himself inconsolably. He would have plenty of time to dream on his Suspension before receiving a new Member to train. When he finally fell asleep, it was almost 4 a.m.

"So you want to kill people, eh? Sounds like you're a pretty heartless one, Miss Church." Mr. Cole leered at his new Member. After only a few weeks inside the Society, he'd gotten exactly what and who he wanted. He could murder with abandon, have help in doing so, and then a regular toy to play with. And then, after the New Year, all of this would be gone and he would return home to Mummy.

Mr. Cole was of a rare group at the Society–an Assassin, given weapons and violent Engagements freely. They answered only to their Director, and sometimes above them if an unfortunate internal event transpired. Assassins were prepared for Invitations or a buzz of the timepiece at any moment. The devil's work did not have a set schedule, for evil could interrupt whenever it chose.

Kate sat taller in her chair. "I was assigned to you as my Senior. I am to do as you wish." Gone for now were regular classes and instruction, replaced with unbridled chaos.

"Very well then. You've been here longer than I and fell into some kind of fuckery, perhaps even literally." He stared into her eyes as if he knew what had transpired between her and Lord Wilson. "That's how you're with me, one can assume. I won't hesitate to tell you, any sort of variance of what I order you to do won't be accepted. You'll be Terminated with a bullet to the head and I'll be pleased to do it. Don't cock it up darling." He lit a cigarette with steely precision and blew the smoke in her face.

"Yes Sir." Kate coughed.

"Toughen up sweetie. I know that this isn't your first ride." He drew more of the tobacco into his lungs with a wicked grin. "I don't have to be a gentleman with you."

He's had to have seen everything. Kate worried, but lifted her chin in retort. "With all due respect Sir, you do however, have to train me."

"Not much, by what I've heard. Maybe I could teach you a few lessons in the sack, eh?" He came forward, leaned closer, and grasped her chin. "You dolly, could learn a few things from a man like me, I'm certain."

"Get your paws off me, you bastard," Kate hissed.

He responded with a hasty slap to her cheek that rattled her teeth and spotted her mouth with bits of blood. "Bitch. Didn't you know that you're mine now? I do as I please, or quite simply, you die." Mr. Cole remained in her face, undaunted by his new charge.

Kate dabbed at her lip and tried to hold back the tears that welled in her eyes. "Perhaps I'll choose death."

"Oh no you won't, not as long as you know that Lord Wilson is alive." He spat in her face.

"Jealous?" Kate fought back with words aimed to distract her new Senior.

"Humph? Of an old man? Hardly." Mr. Cole backed away. "I'm sure you provided all the passion."

Kate desperately tried to remain calm in the wake of his verbal assault. "I assure you, this is none of your business. That was then and this is now." Kate rallied back.

"Yes, it is now. And this is my business. Today we go out to the firing range. You'll learn to use some different weapons and need to be prepared for any sort of demise. Tomorrow will be your first Engagement." He growled at her. "Get up. We head out now." Mr. Cole almost pulled the chair from under her and stalked through his office door. "Now, Miss Church. Now." He barked over his shoulder.

Kate hurried behind her new Senior. It took every ounce of courage for her not to bolt in the opposite direction. As they hurried through the halls Kate made solemn vows.

I am strong. I will not let him hurt me. I will have Christopher back.

"Now Miss Kate," Lord Wilson urged his lady. They had managed to run through the snow on the grounds, climb over the surrounding wall, and rush over to Lafayette Park. They stood at the edge of the lake under a thick grove of trees where a small boat awaited them. "Here into the skip. We'll row across. It'll make it harder for them to follow our trail."

"Thank you, Sir." She gave her hand as Lord Wilson helped her into the boat. She quickly moved to the front. He jumped in behind and started to row with all the force as he could muster.

They remained silent as the water lapped the wood and the oars plopped through. The moon cast a blue glow over them. Kate sat stock still, illuminated in the glow like a patient angel.

As they reached the halfway point, Lord Wilson finally began to speak. "Kate this is a most dangerous undertaking." He was interrupted by a large bubbling in the water directly ahead. His eyes widened in shock as a dragon-like serpent emerged from the water. Its thin iridescent green scales glistened in the moonlight. It grew larger and larger as it rose over thirty feet above them and soon eclipsed the small float. Its eyes burned a bold red while a warm mist eased from its horrific grey nostrils. The massive wake of his presence shook the two into a tremendous fear.

Kate turned to see the beast and gripped the edge of the boat in horror. "Oh my God!"

Lord Wilson was frozen. He could not move, not an inch, even after willing his body to do so.

The beast extended its hooked claws with a terrifying loud hiss, and pushed down hard on the bow. Lord Wilson felt himself fly backwards into the chilly waters as the beast crashed, the cold rushing through his veins like ice. He shook his head clear only to see the jaws of the great sea monster open. A horrific stench blasted over them as his forked tongue flicked at Kate.

She'd fallen forwards onto the floor of the skip and was scrambling to escape. The beast roared with such might it echoed through the park and buried Kate's screams. Its head came down to the boat to catch Kate in its drooling mouth. She grabbed furtively at his sharp teeth as it spliced her limbs.

"Kate!" Lord Wilson moaned while almost standing in his bed, gripping a sheet as the terror of his nightmare ended. He ran his fingers through his hair to calm himself and stepped gingerly to the floor.

"Are you alright Sir? I heard quite a disturbance." Leeds looked over his master with concern.

"Yes, yes. Just a disturbing dream. Night terror." He mumbled as he sat and poured himself some water.

"Perhaps a glass of warm milk, Sir?" His help offered.

"Yes, splendid. Thank you Leeds." Lord Wilson gazed out into the night, ever so grateful the serpent hadn't been real. But it was a sign that Kate was in danger. That he was sure of.

Downstairs Mrs. Leeds warmed the milk as her husband waited beside her at the stove. "Such a terrible shame. Miss Church is so lovely. I sometimes don't quite understand this world we're in." She poured the hot liquid into a cup that Leeds offered.

"Bloody mess, I'd say. Not right, not at all," he concurred. "But if I know anything about our Senior, he'll make it right, God bless his soul."

Kate sat in the carriage with her new Senior. She attempted to stifle a yawn, not out of boredom, but for the lack of sleep. After practicing with several different guns the day before, she was allowed to go directly to her room for an evening meal and rest. Despite a tasty repast, Kate barely ate half of it.

As soon as her attendant cleared her dishes, Kate listened to the music box, with Strax at her feet, for hours on end. Another night of crying left her wan and bereft. When her pocket watch buzzed for breakfast, she was no happier.

Kate was restricted to her quarters for the next two weeks at the very least. She would leave only for Discussions and Engagements with Mr. Cole. She would miss Christmas and New Year's celebrations. *Was this my lot in life? How was this to be?*

With no desire to eat, Kate pushed her untouched food away, and she crawled back into bed with Strax for a fitful morning nap. She was forced to dress for lunch, for afterwards was her Engagement. The Invitation had come right before the noon meal. Its stiff, beige paper dropped into her basket.

Gone was the brilliant seal and crisp parchment of Lord Wilson. Kate fought tears again as she picked up the Invitation.

"Dear Miss Church:

Discussion, 2:00 pm, my office, Engagement immediately afterwards. I will meet you in the drawing room near the foyer entrance. Dress like a commoner.

C."

Gone too was the polite script and pleasantries. Kate tried not to be bitter as she choose her most boring dress, dark navy with no ostentatious décor. Its matching hat was an equally plain bonnet. Her face lacked color except for the reddish purple bruise that had popped up on her cheek after yesterday's tussle with her new Senior.

It, partnered with a swollen lip, was barely hidden by the short veil on her bonnet. She squinted at her reflection at her vanity and made a vow. *Society or no Society, I will find his weakness and he will be exposed.*

Lord Wilson made his way through the Society Hall as inconspicuously as possible. No dandy hat or suit today. No flower or kerchief in his pocket. He was not to be in the Hall per orders from those above the Director, except for Discussions on the mole. Director Roth, in all his directorly wisdom, made certain that Discussions would be held daily, regardless of the ignorance of those who wished to manage his Members from afar.

Mr. Scott had been sent on the stake out that had failed for Lord Wilson and Kate a couple of nights earlier. There hadn't been any movement from the Ellis clan. He gathered that they were stepping up their resources in hiding somehow. He would be debriefing his Seniors at 2:00 p.m. daily until their movements had changed.

This latest Discussion had just finished as Lord Wilson prepared to exit the Main Hall. But a familiar lavender scent distracted him. He turned to see Miss Church, waiting for her new Senior. She sat demurely in a seat right by the doorway of the drawing room.

Fortunately for the both of them, Mr. Cole was more than late, nearly thirty minutes so, as it was almost 2:30 p.m. Kate secretly had hoped that he'd died, when she saw Lord Wilson pass the parlor. Her heart pattered with joy as she pursed her lips to refrain from smiling at the sight of him.

He discreetly paused at her chair and pretended to pick up a newspaper off the end table next to her. As he bent over for it, they both pretended to look elsewhere.

Lord Wilson stood in the doorway perusing the paper as Kate continued to check her timepiece behind him.

"Are you alright?" he whispered.

"Yes. Be careful. He's very late, could be here at any moment." Kate returned the quiet talk. "I miss you." Her voice cracked.

"Be strong. We are working to change this. Should he do the least bit of wrong, contact Director Roth," Lord Wilson advised.

"Is this enough?" She turned her chin up to him and lifted her veil. Lord Wilson peered over his shoulder to see the destruction Mr. Cole had already done to his lover. His fist crumpled the edge of the paper in disgust. "Yes." He hissed as a furious anger broiled inside him. He withheld the temptation to scoop Kate up and take her to see the Director immediately. "I will tell him. Today. Be strong Kate. We'll find this spy. And most likely dump this Mr. Cole in the process. I am here every day at 2:00 p.m. meeting with him." He pretended to drop the paper and knelt at her feet. He looked side to side for a split second before gazing up at her. "I love you Kate. I will not abandon you. Don't be too soft." He discreetly kissed her hand before he rose and walked away. Kate inhaled sharply as her heart seemed it would explode and wiped her tears beneath her veil. "Compose yourself, you are strong," she mumbled.

Finally her timepiece buzzed with the arrival of Mr. Cole. She needn't have worried about being caught with Lord Wilson, for her new Senior had been much delayed with wiring and explosives that had to be handled with great care. No matter how precise and meticulous his manner was, Mr. Cole had to cave to his equipment. He was running out of time to have it in place for a very special evening.

"Remember, act casually. And be quick about it. I am certain you can accomplish this. It's not the first time you've killed someone, is it?" Mr. Cole quipped to his charge.

"Of course." Kate adhered to her Senior's advice as they waited outside of a small dress shop in Lafayette Square. The mistress of the shop had been taking supplies and extra cash home with her, one small bundle at a time. These thefts were thought to be in preparation for an escape from the Society. The Fixture also had a child out of wedlock, a four-year-old girl. The Society's urging to give the child up for adoption or move to another city with a new identity, fell on deaf ears. This could no longer be tolerated. Years of insolence were done.

"Very well. It's 3:55. Miss Beal will be closing shop. Be on your way." Mr. Cole practically pushed Kate out of the carriage.

Kate adjusted herself and trotted to the door way. A small bell jingle announced her entrance.

"Well hello dear." A young redheaded Irish woman greeted her from the rear of the store. "I'm about ready to close, but if you'd wait just a moment, I'll be right back to help you."

"Oh thank you, I really don't want to be a bother." Kate feigned a smile as the target ran to the back. Kate discreetly locked the door behind her, drew the blinds and hit the lights before turning back to the direction of Miss Beal. There would be no escape for her; Mr. Cole had already locked the rear door from the outside.

Miss Beal quickly loaded the days' earnings into a small bag underneath a sewing table in the storage room. "It never fails," she groaned to herself. "A last minute customer." She adjusted her neat bun and quickly stepped back into the store, which was now dark. "Hello?"

From behind the shadows, Kate put a small kerchief laced with poison over the seamstress's mouth. "I'm so sorry dear." Kate whispered as the woman dropped to the floor with barely a struggle. A bit of froth eased from the dead woman's mouth. Kate squatted beside her, wiped it away with a second cloth and put both contaminated pieces into a petite grain sack. As she stood to gather the stolen money, a young girl stood in the doorway, her shadow cast over the newly deceased.

"Where's my mummy?" She had the same sweet Irish lilt as her mother.

Kate was sickened at what had happened. Her insides churned and gurgled. The child was supposed to have been with a relative that afternoon, one who would keep her indefinitely with help from the Society. *Shit.*

"Oh, I'm so sorry. Um, well dear, she just needs a bit of a nap. It was a long day. Shouldn't you be with your auntie?" Kate was at her kindest, this was no fault of the child's.

"My auntie was sick today. Mummy let me play here. I just had a little kip, see?" The child pointed to a small basket on the floor filled with soft blankets in the back room. The girl yawned and rubbed her eyes. "Can you wake her up? I'm hungry." *How did I miss that?* Kate ached.

Kate couldn't believe at how wrong this Engagement had gone. Her stomach continued to flop wildly. The child had no part in this. Kate made a quick decision as she reached for the stolen bag of money. "Well dear, she must rest. Come now, we'll get you to your auntie." Kate tried not to choke on her words as she filled with disgust. This was Mr. Cole's doing. He planned the assassination. He should've known that the child was there. Now they had a terrible issue.

"But-"

"No darling," Kate cooed. "Let's go, it's getting late. I'm sure your auntie is worried." Before the girl could protest further Kate picked her up, stepped over the dead woman, and carried the daughter out the front door.

Across the street, Mr. Cole grimaced and spat. "What the devil?"

Kate looked at her carriage, tipped her hat briefly and ignored her Senior. Fortunately she remembered the address of the relative, as the recovered money was supposed to be delivered to the auntie after the planned demise of Miss Beal. Kate ran to a darkened street corner, hailed a cab and hurriedly bribed the driver with some of the larger bills from the bag. "Don't ask questions. Take this child to 629 Park."

Kate shoved the girl into the carriage. "They will say her auntie is sick, but you must leave her there. Don't hesitate. Drop her in the street if you must, but don't bring her back here." Kate whispered in the darkness.

"But Miss-" The cabbie looked horrified.

"Go now. Or there will be trouble. Don't look back." Kate opened her coat and flourished her pistol at the shocked cabby.

"Yes Ma'am." The driver sped off as Kate stepped back into the shadows. She counted to thirty and made haste back to Mr. Cole.

"Sloppy. Very sloppy." He chastised her as she jumped in beside her. "You should've killed the child as well."

"She wasn't supposed to be there. And you knew she was." Kate was more than livid. She withdrew the urge to pull her pistol on him as her face burned a deep red.

"Humph. Of no matter. You were to dispense of her within five minutes. That was almost ten." Mr. Cole smirked coldly. "So much for the deadly reputation of Miss Kate Church."

Kate watched out the window as they rolled along. "I fixed your mess. The money is being delivered to where it was supposed to go anyway. And you may have forgotten Society rules. No involvement with children. Maybe Director Roth needs to know of your lapse in judgement."

He again grabbed Kate's chin and forced her to look at him. "You will do no such thing, you rotten bitch."

Kate winced at the pain that shot through her already tender jaw. "Let me go, bastard."

He laughed at her as she struggled to break free of his grip. Suddenly she realized the carriage was heading far away from the Society grounds. "So Miss Kate, with all your loyalty, do you think you're getting everything you deserve?" He hissed. "Money, fine food, gifts? A man that loves you? Answers to your every desire?" His free hand dropped in her lap to tease her thigh.

"Everything I have been promised, I've been given." She dug her nails into his hand. He released her chin, slapped her face, and then pinned both arms as he jumped into her lap.

"Oh, but patience is not your best virtue though, is it Kate? You couldn't wait to throw yourself at Lord Wilson, that old sod. But you did finally get that too, didn't you?"

Kate then realized it was Mr. Cole that had spied on their amorous evening in the greenhouse. And that Mr. Cole was not his real name. "Jealous then?" Kate taunted back.

"I am not my brother Julian, a man good with the sword, and perhaps more good in his heart than I realized. Although I find you incredibly attractive Kate, you're the thief that's stolen my father, my brother, and one of my companions. I have no intention of loving you. Fucking you maybe, that might be fun, even against your will. Then you'll die, that is, unless you feel like switching sides and help us return the keys. It's an offer I'll make only once."

"How dare you even ask!" Kate's words were like cold hard steel.

"Oh, they do have you quite programmed for their little Engagements, don't they? All the secrets and lies. I'm sure you've been told some good ones. Did Lord Wilson tell you about your family Kate?"

She tried not to be baited. "There is nothing to know."

"Then you are wrong. I killed them: your sister, Abby, your brother in law, Ferris, and their servants. They were in Boston. Quite a nice home. I am certain it's already been given up to someone else." Mr. Cole's lilt dripped with evil.

Kate couldn't hide her surprise, her face paled. "I don't believe you," she stuttered.

"I almost killed Miss Pratt too. She's a lot like you. Spirited and likes to fuck old men."

"You're lying." Kate tried to wiggle out from beneath him.

"I think you know that I'm not. So then, a last chance for you. You join our cause or you die? Either way, you will leave with me tonight. When you choose to die is up to you."

"Never!" Kate spat at him for emphasis.

He wiped her sputum from his face with disgust. "Now that was wicked. Time to shut that mouth." Taking the same cloth, he sprinkled it with liquid from a vial he'd hidden in his glove. In a flash, he returned her phlegm to her by banding it over her face. The interior of the carriage soon went dark as Kate slipped under the influence of one of the weaker Ellis poisons.

"She should've been back by now. We all know it doesn't take four hours to assassinate someone only six blocks away," Lord Wilson grumbled to Director Roth. "And he beat her. A visible bruise. She had it covered, but that draws undue attention."

A rap on the door interrupted their Discussion. Mr. Scott burst into the room. "The young Miss Beal was disposed of as ordered. Her child was dropped off with the money by a driver at 4:15 p.m. He was not one of ours, but we were able to track him down. Said a woman paid him to take the child and that she brandished an odd pistol. He's agreed to be recruited, so any leak will end there. Unfortunately, he didn't see which direction they went. I think we can agree that Mr. Cole is our mole. And the Ellis family left during the hit. They're already on their way out."

"They have connections to Boston. I'm gathering that's where they might be headed. Alright, tear Mr. Cole's room apart!" the Director shouted. "I'll send for Miss Pratt to join you."

"Yes Sir." Mr. Scott left as quickly as he'd entered.

Lord Wilson sprung from his chair to join them. "I'm going to find her. And when I do, I'm keeping her."

Only an hour later, Miss Pratt winced at Mr. Cole's dossier. "I wish I had seen this. This is the man I shot in Boston, the killer of Kate's family." She pulled the drawing and description that their research team had put together after that fateful night from a different file. "There's no doubt in my mind."

"He was approved by those above me." Director Roth floundered at his desk. "We must be extremely careful moving forward. There's corruption at the highest level from the Mass. We're all in danger. I'm certain he wants the keys. Lord Wilson and Mr. Scott are preparing a search." His hand covered Miss Pratt's. "The weather is continuing to worsen, I'm afraid."

"But this is one storm we can weather. He has Miss Church. I would gather by now that he would've returned if he thought he could procure them," Miss Pratt comforted. An odd smile crossed her face. "I think I know where he might be going."

Kate awoke in the smoky haze of a basement bar. Her eyes slowly adjusted to the dim light. The last thing she remembered was sniping at Mr. Cole, when all went dark.

He'd put her under with one of his poisons that his mother had gladly supplied. When Kate refused to cooperate, she was dead weight. Like his cohorts, Mr. Cole was no closer to the keys than when he'd arrived at the Society. He needed to be rid of her, but was certain he could get something in exchange.

That led him to The Heavy Anchor, a dark burlesque theatre he'd recently visited. He'd killed a Member in the side alley after they'd participated in some tawdry acts.

The wayward Society gentleman had become quite smitten with one of the "ladies of entertainment". When she repelled his overtly rough advances outside of the whorehouse on the grounds, he kidnapped her under the guise of an urgent Engagement. He led her into the Bloody Third District locale, where there was a rich secret black market slave trade.

Before he could step inside to sell the voluptuous beauty, Mr. Cole approached him outside with an offer of his own, a bullet to the forehead. The Society girl was returned home without incident and she gladly serviced Mr. Cole later that evening. He made a mental note of this bawdy location especially for this sort of situation. Tonight he was prepared to dump Kate Church. The Mass had not been pleased and funds to procure the keys had run low.

Mr. Cole needed cash to get out of town and the Heavy Anchor was just the place to get it. Despite its worn appearance, the rundown palace drew the wealthy with a taste for the seedy side of life. Gilded carriages quickly dropped off their charges in the dead of night to procure their wanton desires.

The glass double doors, one of which was broken, had been painted over to hide the action of the interior. The foyer was done up in dark shades of navy wallpaper and burgundy curtains that covered chipping paint and brick. The wooden stairs to the balcony were falling apart, with chips of wood falling away from those with even the lightest of steps.

The showroom had long lost its bedazzled glory from the Civil War days when troops, steamship crews, and rail men had come to be entertained. The once radiant chandelier was missing gems and reflective pieces. Only three of the dozen lights still worked, which gave the room plenty of shadows for dirty deals in the dark. Everything was sold or bartered here: weapons, stolen goods, elixirs, spirits, and even people that had fallen to their most desperate state of being.

Mismatched chairs lined the threadbare poker and gaming tables. The seats were filled with beings from all walks of life, from the desperate hotel porter down on his luck, to the wealthy banker with far too much money to spend. There were even the occasional visits by dirty politicians looking to strike deals to lengthen their terms in office.

It was here that Mr. Gotham originally met the corrupt Member contact that led him to Madeline Fahey to secure plans for the Society grounds. The pleasingly plump older lady seemed to know all kinds of information and was happy to lead The Mass to the now dead Member.

Above the crowd was a small stage barely lit with dying gaslights. It was here that Kate Church had been precariously perched for all to see.

As Kate came round, she tried to move, but her limbs were bound to an overly large wagon wheel much higher up than the forms of people she saw through the fog of cigars. Each tug of the straps sent waves of pain through her arms and legs. The wheel was mounted on a large plank on the entertainment stage, which was probably the sturdiest structure in the place. The sounds of glasses, poker chips, and piano music sharpened in her ears. A voice rose above the din in the Clabber Lane dive.

"Ah ladies and gentlemen, we have a very special auction tonight. Something you'll quite enjoy I'm certain." A man in a tall black top hat and tails waved in her direction. His face was powdered white which made his greasy black handlebar mustache stick out like a cartoon. "It's not every day we get something quite like this."

Kate looked down at her body and was mortified that she was only wearing bloomers and a decorative red and black laced corset that barely held in her breasts. It was as if she inhabited the body of someone else. She'd been painted up like a tart, with deep red lipstick and rouge and topped off with smoldering dark eyes, her hair wildly teased into a high pompadour.

"Yes siree, she'll go to the highest bidder tonight. Who might want to take this lady for a spin?" The host grabbed the edge of the wheel, gave it a tug, and started it in motion. Kate moaned as the room began to turn. Her head burned and bile gathered in her throat.

Off stage, Cecil Ellis grinned wickedly and rubbed his hands together. A glee arose in him that was much more satisfying than death. Miss Church would be sold and continue to suffer. She'd bring in a pretty penny, that he was sure of. Revenge for his family would be eternally sweet.

Dizziness continued to cloud Kate's mind as the auctioneer began to prattle. "Let's start at one hundred should we? Yes, we have a hundred. Can we make it two? Ah, so quick gentlemen, two hundred." Hands flew up around the room from an assortment of vile characters.

"Two-fifty!" A rusty voice hollered from the back.

"Three hundred." An elegantly dressed man with two painted ladies already at his poker table chimed in.

"Three-fifty, but that's all I got." The raspy voice yelled again.

"Oh, but isn't she special?" The auctioneer stopped the wheel and wickedly cupped one of Kate's breasts that had popped over the top of the corset during her turn on the wheel. "Lovely. So plump." He playfully flicked her nipple. Kate could barely wiggle in disgust due to her confinement. Her skin flushed in embarrassment.

"Three seventy-five!" A new bidder joined in from the bar.

The man at the poker table had won another round and upped his bid. "Four hundred!" The girls next to him pouted. They were hoping to have more of his generosity later.

The room went silent for a bit. The auctioneer sneered. He'd only promised the stranger two hundred and had already doubled his take. There was no need to get greedy. "Going once. Going twice."

"I'll take her for nothing." A familiar lilting accent from above awoke Kate's senses.

From the wings of the burlesque stage, Cecil Ellis froze. He peeked out to see that Lord Wilson and Mr. Scott had entered the balcony. He ran out the stage door without a sound, but crashed down the icy stairs into the back alley. He determined that there was no way to salvage this mission, as pain pierced through his arm and shoulder yet again.

The crowd turned to the two men, and then they all scattered like crows. The Society Members held some of the largest weapons they'd ever seen. One could almost hear in their minds that no whore was worth getting shot over.

"Well that was easy enough." Lord Wilson quipped as the room emptied. "Good thinking Mr. Scott."

"You're most welcome Sir. He was just here last week, according to his log that Miss Pratt had access to. It appeared the most likely choice." They ran down the rickety balcony stairs. Their ambush had been a success. "How'd you know about it?"

"I'd been here once, a long time ago. But that tale is for another time." Lord Wilson grinned. "I'm coming Kate, darling," he yelled as he handed off his weapon to Mr. Scott and entered the main floor. He stumbled around over-turned chairs and broken glass, jumped onto the stage and removed his coat with a grand flourish.

Kate opened her eyes and gave a weary, "Hello."

Mr. Scott politely turned around to guard the entrance. It appeared that the former Mr. Cole was long gone. He just wanted to make sure no one else came back while allowing the two Members a private reunion.

"Hello, love." Lord Wilson untied her arms first. Her hands flew to her chest in embarrassment. He freed her feet with haste. "Hmm, not something you'd wear every day." He helped Kate down, covered her with his coat and whispered in her ear. "But I wouldn't mind seeing this lovely ensemble again sometime."

Kate leaned against him while at last coming to her senses. "Thank you, I think."

A clock behind the bar chimed midnight. Its deep gongs echoed around the empty show palace and announced the first hour of Christmas Eve.

"Merry Christmas Eve, Kate." He leaned in for a slow sweet kiss. "And sip." He proffered some serum.

"Oh, Merry Christmas." She'd totally forgotten about the holiday in this sordid mess. Her mind still reeled as the medicine warmed her.

"And to all a good night," Mr. Scott smirked. "And let's get the hell out of here and find that bastard." Even with the holiday, he was bent on revenge.

The midnight train heading east blew its whistle. Just as the train started to move, Cecil Ellis ran along the train tracks and leapt to the backside of the caboose. He clambered onto the railing and held onto the overhang, while waiting for the train to be further up the line before going inside. His reinjured shoulder was hurting yet again. The pain growing worse with every vibration and bump of the train.

"Nights like these are fantastic are they not?" Cecil was startled by of an approaching shadow of a woman. "Cold, crisp, with a million stars in the sky."

He hadn't noticed that the back door had been left completely open and hoped that she was speaking to someone else.

This thought was shattered as Miss Pratt stepped out with a closed parasol in hand.

"We meet again, Mr. Ellis." Her voice was as cold as the temperature outside. The train had gathered speed and a chill whipped through Cecil's clothing.

"Yes, and yet again, you've managed to surprise me. Although this time, I know exactly who you are Miss Pratt." He wanted to keep her talking, to distract her somehow. He needed to get off the railing. He couldn't hold on much longer. They'd be going over the Eads Bridge soon, and the air over the river would be absolutely freezing.

"As do I." She smiled back at him; the gaslights of the coming bridge illuminated her face. "But back to the skyline. The city is gorgeous isn't it?" St. Louis was starting to fall behind them as the train entered the bridge. "Ah, and it reminds me of one of my favorite Shakespearean quotes, 'It is not in the stars to hold our destiny, but in ourselves.' Funny thing about destiny and our choices. I think you made a poor one in killing the Tomley family."

"Oh, really? Not even after Kate Church had killed two of mine? What do you expect? For me to die like my father?"

"Precisely." Miss Pratt opened her umbrella and, with a quick flash, it blew a hole through the very center of Cecil. She popped it closed in time to see the horror on his face as he fell to his death into the mighty Mississippi. "That was for Miss Church and her family." She whispered.

Miss Pratt admired her new weapon that Kate had created. "Well done, Miss Church." With a quick shut of the parasol she hurried back into the caboose. She would return to the Society later that evening on a very positive note.

"I want her back. They can fucking Terminate me if they want, but I won't allow her in the hands of another while I'm alive." Lord Wilson roared at his Director.

Director Roth waved his hand furiously. "Sit, Lord Wilson. Good God man, it's one in the morning." His friend had every right to be angry. "It was obvious that Cecil Ellis, our temporary Mr. Cole, was the third mole to penetrate our Society. We found the film plates in his room. Like his brother, he seems to have planned on having quite the stay here. This has been no fault of yours or Miss Church. After some rest and an exam from Dr. Finch, she can return to your tutelage and the Manor tomorrow, on one condition."

Lord Wilson raised a brow.

"She will be allowed to choose her eventual permanent Senior. Those above me feel that she has served, for the most part, in an honorable manner. They no doubt want her in London this summer. You will still attend with her, but the final choice of partner will be hers. But I'm sure you're up to the challenge, Christopher?"

"I've never been more certain in my life."

"Godspeed my friend. And Merry Christmas." He put his head in his hands. "Do not be too soft." Director Roth murmured after his friend's exit.

Lord Wilson hurried through the empty Society halls to Miss Church's quarters. Her attendant was just leaving. "She's prepared for bed, Sir."

"Thank you." Lord Wilson gently rapped on the door and stepped inside. Kate sat on the bed with an exhausted look, but brightened at the appearance of her Senior.

"Are you better Kate, darling?" He sat beside her and put a warm arm around her shoulders.

"Yes. Very sleepy though." Kate was relieved that the evening was over, but in the back of her mind, some of Cecil Ellis' words haunted her. She would bury them there for tonight.

"The serum helped then. The bruise is almost gone." His hand stroked her face with a tenderness that warmed her to the core.

"Yes. Thank you." Kate was grateful but recent events overtook her strength. Lord Wilson could see her need for rest.

"Very good. Let me tuck you in. We'll Discuss tomorrow. I love you Kate." He pulled the covers aside and helped her in. "Good night darling."

"Good night Lord Wilson." Kate, in her exhaustion, fell into the old habit of addressing her Senior formally.

The expected rendezvous didn't happen for the Ellis family. When Cecil Ellis wasn't on his iron horse that arrived for a short stop a few hours after midnight in Springfield, Illinois, Mrs. Ellis angrily stamped out her cigarette.

"Bastards!" She hissed as a wisp of smoke died in the cold winter eve at the train station.

"Mother, I-" Atticus Ellis tried to soothe.

"Don't try to comfort me. I'm certain he's gone. We'll stay here overnight, just in case. Perhaps he missed the train. But we should be prepared to leave for Boston without him. We'll notify Mr. Crisp that we're on the move. There is no reason for us to stay. He can finish the job."

She turned away from her remaining son so he wouldn't see the single tear roll down her cheek.

17 A LOST MOMENT IN TIME

"So it's true then? He murdered Abby and Ferris. Cyrus and Martha too." Kate was more than upset. She clenched her fists so tightly that her forearms burned. She stood with Lord Wilson in the library the day after she'd been rescued from Mr. Cole, the eldest Ellis son. One of their most serious Discussions had begun on a Christmas Eve afternoon that was starting off rather horribly. The bliss of a successful rescue was long gone. Kate confronted her Senior about the nasty words Cecil Ellis had thrown at her.

Lord Wilson glanced at Leeds who quickly set down their tea and vacated the room. "Yes, I'm afraid it's true." He had so looked forward to today, not only to review the previous day's events, but to ensure Kate's happiness. He was incredibly off the mark.

"Everyone who is close to me has died, and it's because of you. Your selfishness. Your Society grandeur." Kate spat. "Worst of all, Tobias. I thought the Society wasn't supposed to involve children?" Her words poured out in angry bitter sobs as her face blotched over in redness.

"I had no choice. Sister Theresa was already suspected of having secured one of the keys from Drasco's men. The boy was my only safe link between you, her, and me."

"She knew? You're lying." Kate pouted as her trust in him eroded.

"No Kate. She was a Society Member. As is Sister Rosa." His

voice deadened. "All Fixtures, they knew the risks. But they all worked for the greater good. Tobias was supposed to leave with Sister Theresa, but Drasco got to them before I could intervene. But what I am most sorry about is the loss of your family." Lord Wilson's eyes softened.

"There was a lapse in one of our Members in Boston. Unfortunately his error caused their deaths. He paid for it with his life. I know that this is of little comfort to you. But we all take that risk when we join." His face narrowed with sincerity. "Kate, you must know, I did all of this to save our world. Not just the Society, the planet. There are those who wish to release a hell on earth. And it starts with the three keys. From the moment the Society discovered a unique machine in London, we knew it needed protection. I selected you to do this."

"It isn't true then. You don't love me. You've made me a mercenary for some crackpot mission." She was broiling on the inside as her jaw locked in pain.

"No. I was allowed to find someone with a dual purpose." Her Senior was cool in his defense.

"I'm going back to the Hall." Kate reached for her coat.

"No, I want you to stay here." He blocked her from the door by grabbing her arm.

Kate was aghast. She paled as her eyes widened in fear. Lord Wilson immediately let go of her, but then let his fingertips run over her cheek which was almost healed from the nasty smack of Cecil Ellis. "I-I won't hurt you Kate. Never, ever will I strike you. Please, please, sit down." He walked her to the lounger with a delicate touch.

Kate felt her anger dissipate. *Why does he have this control over me?* She wondered.

He sat next to her, then fully enveloped her in his embrace. Her head fell onto his chest as hot tears trickled down and moistened his shirt. "I am so sorry Kate. I had never dreamed I would find someone like you. Someone so kind, compassionate." He whispered. "I don't want you to go. Not ever. Please."

Kate lifted her face to him. "What about now? What happens?"

"You stay. If you were to leave, they'd find you. You'd be assassinated, if not by the Society, the Ellis clan or The Mass. I want you here, with me. I've already given Director Roth an ultimatum. I've issued a challenge to those above him that I must have you. The Society needs you here. I have been grooming and training you for this Engagement in London all along. You are my present and, I hope, my future, Kate. But you and my past have collided with this upcoming mission. You are the missing link for what must happen. You've earned their trust." He looked at her with tenderness. "And you've captured my heart." His hand grasped hers. "I will not lie to you about my love for you. I meant what I said. I've waited a lifetime for you. I've made mistakes in my treatment of you, yes. But know that I adore you, my darling Kate. There are no others. Will you be mine?"

Kate's head spun. She was overwhelmed by tragedy. *How much more can I take?* Her heart had been broken so many times. "I need time. Just, some time to clear my head."

Lord Wilson released her. His heart ached. He had so wanted a definitive yes. Without it, she could be assigned to someone else. His life's work could be for naught. "Alright then, I should be fair. Please think, I'll just need your answer tomorrow. May I pour you some tea?"

"Yes, please."

He poured a cup while slipping in a couple drops of serum and brought it to her. She needed to be well. "Here."

Kate sipped the warm tea. It calmed her and her eyes grew heavy. The room was still. Outside the cold brushed fresh snowflakes against the window.

"Let me take that, why don't you rest?" Lord Wilson took Kate's cup, helped her recline, and pulled a throw over her. "May I hold you Miss Kate?"

"Yes Sir."

Inside Lord Wilson's heart ached as they stumbled back to formalities. Kate was soon fast asleep as she clung to him on the settee.

The ballroom was magnificent. Chandeliers illuminated the luxurious tapestries and furnishings. Joyous couples waltzed around the splendorous room. Laughter echoed among the participants of a high society masquerade ball. The rustling of fine gowns, the aromas of delicious eats and happy toasts filled the air. It was a simple Engagement, one perfect for the troubled time that Kate and Lord Wilson were having. The only mission was to observe. Rumors had abounded that Mrs. Ellis was to attend. But it was late in the evening, and no one even remotely resembling her description had arrived.

"Shall we?" Lord Wilson offered his hand. She was dressed as a French courtesan, in a light blue and gold gown with a high white pompadour. Lord Wilson wore a matching frock coat. Each had Venetian papier mache masks that concealed their identities. They spun around the room in dizzy delight, until the musicians finished.

"No sight of them, Miss Kate?"

"None."

"Let us go upstairs."

The two ascended the long set of stairs to the second floor. The center of the upper level was completely open to the floor below. The perimeter consisted of an elegant wide balcony, surrounded by smaller rooms, historical paintings, and fancy furniture. Above was a stained glass dome. It's kaleidoscope of colors danced from the light of the chandeliers below. The lights hung from long golden chains that reached up far past the second floor and to the framework of the ceiling. Once at the top, they walked along the railings of the dais and peered down at the crowd.

Kate removed her mask to use her opera glasses. "No one with her description. No ring."

"Hmm." Lord Wilson checked his timepiece. It was almost 10:30 p.m. The ball would be ending at 11. "I'm afraid she isn't coming. Either she was apprised of our presence or her plans changed." Lord Wilson's eyes lingered over Kate's bare shoulders.

Kate could feel the heat from his gaze. She tucked her glasses away and returned his stare.

"Here, come now." Lord Wilson ushered her up against one of the building's marble pillars. He pressed her with passionate deep kisses.

Kate returned his love, letting her hands wander over his chest.

They moved across the wide hallway to an oversized ornate chair with a stunning floor to ceiling mirror behind it. Lord Wilson turned her round to face it. "Brace yourself, darling." He naughtily hiked up the skirt of her dress. Kate bent over the chair, grasping on the arms for what was to come. Her insides burned with desire. The verbal sparring of earlier times was forgotten.

He took her from behind, suckling her neck, while watching their faces in the mirror. He cupped her breasts from behind, coaxing them from over the topside of her gown. Her nipples prodded stiffly through his fingertips.

A familiar warmth began to pulse through her loins. Kate moaned in ecstasy as he pushed himself inside her. But as she climaxed, her eyes popped open to a frightening sight.

Mrs. Ellis had come up directly behind them with a coldness in her eye that made Kate shudder. She screamed as their adversary pointed a long pistol at the backside of Lord Wilson's head.

A loud bang echoed through the hall as Lord Wilson's brain matter and blood splattered the reflective glass in front of her. The warm blood trickled down on her backside as she jumped.

"Miss Kate? Kate?" Lord Wilson shook his charge awake.

"Oh, oh, my God." Kate mumbled as he helped her sit up.

"I think you've had quite the nightmare." Lord Wilson rubbed her back. "A particularly nasty one, as you screamed aloud a moment ago."

Strax was barking harshly. "Come here boy, it's alright." Lord Wilson cooed to their canine and let him onto the lounger with them.

Kate looked around the room in fear. "How long have I been asleep?"

"A few hours." There was a muted flash of lightning and the library rumbled with thunder. Frozen pellets pecked at the library's windows. "We're having a thunder snow. It started just a while ago. Why don't you lie back for a bit longer? And stay, at least for dinner? For the night, for safety, in your own room? And it's Christmas

Eve."

Kate nodded and ran her hands over Strax. She was grateful to have him at her side.

"It was just a dream Kate. It will be alright." Lord Wilson left to give dinner plans to the Leeds.

A pit in Kate's stomach told her differently.

The dining room in Wilson Manor was lit only with candles. Their subtle hue gave the room a comfort that relaxed Kate. A small Christmas tree held ripe pears, plums, walnuts, and popcorn strings, surrounded by ribbons and paper ornaments. The pine from the tree and cinnamon tea gave the room a delicious aroma.

"Merry Christmas, Kate." Lord Wilson helped her into her chair with a broad smile.

"And to you too." Kate tried to grin. She hadn't had a real Christmas in years. In Iris, they usually decorated the church, and sometimes the Saloon, but there hadn't been a lot to celebrate, especially in the end when the town was falling apart. Kate was overcome with emotion, tears misted her eyes. Everyone she'd spent the holidays with was gone; Riley, Ming and Chin, Ferris, Abby, and her father.

"Are you alright?" A wrinkle of concern came over Lord Wilson's face.

"I-I just miss everyone." Kate was visibly shaken, her face reddened with overwhelming sorrow.

"Oh Miss Church." Mrs. Leeds paused as she prepared to serve soup.

"I am so sorry." Lord Wilson stood, waved their help away for a moment, and came behind her chair. "It's alright darling. I know it's rough. Take a deep breath now." He whispered. He was very, very tempted to put her under, but didn't want to rely on his subversive methods all the time. He continued as he knelt beside her, "it will be alright. Perhaps we can make new memories tonight?"

"Yes, yes. Alright then." Kate inhaled and tried to relax.

"There is no need to hurry. We have plenty of time to enjoy the eve." Lord Wilson smiled and returned to his seat as Kate's pallor improved. He called Mr. and Mrs. Leeds back in.

"Perhaps grace is in order Sir?" Leeds prompted.

"Of course." Lord Wilson, although raised Anglican, had never been a spiritual man. But there was something special about Kate and her beliefs that sometimes made him wonder. He gave a brief blessing. "Father in heaven, we are grateful for this bounty upon the Manor. May it continue to be blessed forever more. Amen." He stole a glance at Leeds who nodded his approval. Strax gave a pleasant bark under the table.

They feasted on pheasant; potatoes drizzled with herbs and butter, cranberry tarts, breads and puddings. Kate ate to her heart's content and started to fight off subtle yawns as the Leeds cleared the table.

"Don't be too sleepy, I have a gift for you, Miss Kate." Lord Wilson grinned at his charge.

"But I didn't get you anything." She protested mildly.

"Did you have any time though, really?" He laughed. "No mind." Lord Wilson reached behind the tree and pulled out a package about the size of a large breadbox. "For you." He carefully set the gift down in front her.

Kate wondered what he could possibly give her that she didn't already have. She tugged the soft silk red ribbon to release the lid. After a rustling of the fine tissue paper, Kate could see the gleam of glass in the candle light.

"You might need to stand to lift it out," Lord Wilson urged.

Kate gently pulled a magnificent snow globe from the box. White flurries mimicked the snow outside. In the center was a small ceramic cabin with heart shaped windows surrounded by miniature pines.

"I hope it reminds you of the night we spent in Lafayette Park," Lord Wilson teased with a twinkle in his eye.

Kate flushed red and giggled. "Thank you, it's lovely." With a gentle grasp, she shook it and watched the snow swirl around the petite wonder-world.

"I'm glad you like it."

"Sir, would you like to retire for the evening?" Leeds inquired of his master.

"Miss Kate?" Lord Wilson asked softly.

"Yes, I'm still tired." She fought to keep her eyelids open.

"I will take her upstairs, if you would finish down here." The Senior nodded to his staff. "Come." He helped Kate to her room. They paused at the doorway with a bit of discomfort between them. "I won't force myself on you. I promised you that. But would you like to stay in your room or mine?"

Kate could barely resist his warm British lilt, but needed to think. "I want to be alone."

Lord Wilson couldn't hide his disappointment and conceded

with a wounded smile. "May I kiss you goodnight then?"

"Yes please."

With a tender caress of his fingers, he brushed her hair aside and gave her a smooth soft peck. "Goodnight Kate."

"Good night. Christopher." She fumbled on his name as if it were an afterthought as she stumbled into the room. A few moments later there was a knock at the door. Kate's heart pounced, thinking he would not be denied, but Mrs. Leeds strolled in to turn down her bed and help her undress.

"I am so glad you had a wonderful eve Miss Church." The rustle of her satin dress was almost loud in the stillness of the night as she helped Kate into her night clothes.

"Thank you so much Mrs. Leeds."

"Be sure to ring if you need anything. Anything at all." Mrs. Leeds eased out.

Kate quickly succumbed to slumber. But howling winds and ratting windows awoke her. She checked her timepiece, 2:30 a.m. and tossed about, trying to calm her mind. She could not empty it of the painful memories of the past. The bed was cold and lonely. Strax whined and she invited him in with her, but she still could not sleep. Kate checked her timepiece again, 3:00 a.m. She craved comfort that only Lord Wilson could bring.

Kate climbed out of the bed, slipped on her robe, tiptoed across the hall to Lord Wilson's bedroom and knocked gently on the door. When there was no answer, she felt foolish. Strax whimpered at her feet. "Shhh." She tried again, wincing as her knuckles met the wood, just a bit louder. She listened, heard a stirring, and as the knob turned, stepped back while almost falling over her canine.

Lord Wilson looked worried. "Are you alright Kate?" His hair was mussed and his eyes fluttered in the dark.

"I-I need to be held." She burst into tears, and immediately felt like a complete idiot for doing so. Her emotional walls tumbled down again.

"Come in, come in, then." He smiled at Strax. "You too." The dog happily followed his master. "Here a sip of water." He poured a glass from the pitcher at his bed stand and offered her the refreshment.

Like a child, Kate held the drink with two hands.

"Better?" He stifled a laugh.

"Yes. What's so funny?" She pouted.

"You astound me. So strong, yet so tender. Perfect in every way." *Not too hard, not too soft,* he thought. "Come on to bed then." He crawled in, and then patted the space next to him.

Kate climbed in after him, and they blissfully spooned. "You too," he again welcomed Strax who leapt onto the bed and made them both laugh.

"Let's try this again, shall we? Good night Kate." He cooed and kissed her cheek.

"Good night Christopher." Kate fell fast asleep in his arms, safe at last.

Lord Wilson treasured this moment as his heart slowed with her like their timepieces which sat next to each other on the night stand.

Kate awoke to the fine smells of a robust breakfast. She sat up with a yawn as her stomach growled. The curtains had been opened and sunlight poured into the room, the storms of last night long gone. She looked over at the other side of the bed for Lord Wilson, but he'd vacated the bedroom. Her pocket watch was silent at almost 10 a.m.

"Ah Miss Church, good morning." Mrs. Leeds strolled in and pre-emptively answered Kate's question. "Lord Wilson is already downstairs. He thought you needed more rest. Are you ready to get up then?"

"Yes, yes." Kate piped up happily. Mrs. Leeds helped with her robe and they strode across the hallway to dress.

"How about something red? For Christmas?"

Kate grinned. *Yes, it's Christmas.* "That would be lovely." Mrs. Leeds prepared a red silk gown for her lady. "Has he been waiting long?"

"Oh, Miss Church, if you only knew." Mrs. Leeds giggled. They hurried and rushed downstairs.

Lord Wilson rose from the dining table as Kate made quite the entrance. He could barely contain himself. *Could I handle having this vision of loveliness every day?*

His thoughts turned to Kate's decision as Leeds seated her. He'd asked for one today. After almost losing her again, he didn't want to wait much longer. And he damn well wasn't going to let some corrupt individual at the top stop him. "You look lovely Miss Kate. Merry Christmas."

"Thank you Sir. And a Merry Christmas to you as well." Kate blushed. The table was filled with fat sausages, piles of eggs, bacon, breads, and a sumptuous array of butters and jams.

"A quick grace then my Lord?" Leeds prompted.

"Ah yes." Lord Wilson nodded. "On this day of our Lord's birth, let us be grateful for our bounty and most certainly the company we keep. Of our loved ones, our staff, and yes, even our animal friends." Strax yipped in delight at Kate's feet. "Merry Christmas."

"Here, here." Leeds chimed in. And they raised their glasses in delight.

"I have no present for you Sir, and for this I am incredibly sorry. For I am much impressed with the snow globe." Kate moved a pawn on the board. It was mid-afternoon as the two Society Members enjoyed an afternoon game of chess.

"I only want your heart. You know that. That's all that matters." Lord Wilson's bishop took a threatening position.

Kate sighed and looked up from the table. "I need more time."

"We all need more time darling." Gone were the formalities, but there was still a wall between them. It was up to Kate to remove it. He tried a change of tactic. "Would you like to go to five o'clock services today? Perhaps it'll help you think?"

Unlike during her time in Iris, Kate had only made sporadic visits to the chapel on the Society grounds. "I think that might be wise." Suddenly Kate didn't feel like playing games. She was still exhausted. The days before had worn her thin. She'd begun to feel as wooden as the chess pieces before them. Conflict stirred in her, making her heart ache. Kate craved some solitude despite the cheery holiday. Yet she felt guilty for not giving him a definitive answer. Something still wasn't quite right.

"Will you tell me tonight then? I'll come for you for the

winter festival at eight?" Her Senior asked in a pensive tone.

"Yes, tonight then." Kate faked a smile and whistled to Strax. He looked up from his blanket but only whimpered. *This is a first,* Kate marveled. The canine truly now had two masters and he clearly felt the division between them. She gave him a gentle pat. "You can stay, I'll be back." Kate comforted more than her furry friend with that statement as she turned to go.

Lord Wilson stood and helped her on with her coat. As he buttoned up the front, he swallowed and finally spoke. "Kate, I know that you may be angry with me still for well, many things. But I want you to know, no matter what you decide, you are always welcome here. I love you." He gave her a polite kiss.

"Thank you." Kate hurried out to hide the tears she couldn't hold back. *Why should I leave to think when I can't even stand being alone with my thoughts?*

Kate headed out towards the chapel into the crisp snow white world, wishing it could always be this peaceful.

"Lord Wilson, Sir. Miss Church left her present upstairs. Her snow globe is still on her bureau." Mrs. Leeds hurried in as Lord Wilson watched her leave.

"Ah, no mind Mrs. Leeds. She'll be back." Lord Wilson put a finger to his chin. *Yes, she will be. I will make it so.* He vowed to win her over completely as the scarlet red of her dress and coat sparkled like a ruby against the snow.

It was 7:45 p.m. and Kate's timepiece buzzed with a reminder. Her insides churned. The Christmas service had been joyful and uplifting, but she still felt confused. She'd tried to nap, and to read, but to no avail. It was a relief when her attendant knocked to prepare her for the winter festival.

"Miss Church, which one would you like? You can continue to wear the red? No one downstairs has seen it. Or I have a stunning green velvet?" Her help had pressed the red and it indeed looked radiant. She'd seen it in Lord Wilson's eyes.

"I'll redress in the red then. It is lovely." Kate agreed.

The preparation didn't seem to last long enough. After the buzz on the nightstand, all was blissfully quiet except inside. Kate's soul was telling her something different. She was right, for in a few short moments her life would again change drastically.

Kate had just walked through what looked like a war zone. The cries of those she cared for ran a dull ache through her ears, muffled as if someone had filled them with cotton. Her limbs pained her as she noted gratefully that they were all still attached. She walked slowly, like through thickened mud that clung to her shoes. Time had frozen in misery at the Society. Smoke dissipated around Kate as she stepped out on the promenade, dotted with body parts, blood, glass, pieces of the Hall, and dirtied snow. The sharpness of the cold caused her to cough up filthy bits of phlegm. *What the hell happened to peace on earth?*

She wasn't more than ten feet from the blasted building when another bomb went off in the distance on the grounds. A flash of light and its accompanying boom sent a shiver through Kate. *That's the Manor,* her heart screamed.

"Oh no, no. No!" Suddenly all her senses sharpened into hyper-focus. Her ears filled with sounds of shouts and alarms sounding. Her skin crawled with the freezing air. She licked her lips and swallowed the taste of the acrid remains of explosives and fire. Her eyes focused on the Manor, almost seemingly too far to reach as she broke into an all-out run towards Lord Wilson's home.

Trees, snow-capped sculptures and shrubbery blurred past Kate. Tears froze on her cheeks. Her hair unfurled behind her while all she could think about was how selfish she'd been earlier that day. As she approached the Manor, Kate was almost inconsolable. "Christopher!" she rasped.

The precious genie lamp of the Manor was broken. Metal from the library twisted outward and the spiral staircase leaned precariously sideways. Kate climbed it anyway and made a small leap into what was once Lord Wilson's favorite space. All had gone silent.

The force of the blast had shattered the windows of Lord Wilson's library. Shards of glass crunched under Kate's boots as she gingerly crossed the room. She could not believe her eyes. Lord Wilson was slumped up against the demolished bookshelves, his eyes closed. If it weren't for a small trickle of blood from one of his nostrils, it would've appeared to the casual observer that he'd fallen into a deep sleep.

Kate bent over his broken body and felt for breath. When then was none, she knelt, then listened at his chest for a heartbeat. "No, oh no." She cried. *How could he be dead when all the love I feel for him is still alive?*

Their intimate moments together ran through Kate's mind as she sobbed into his chest. "Noooo!" Kate pounded her fists on her thighs while her head flew back in anguish. Her screams echoed through the empty Manor and over the grounds. She rested her head back on his terminally wounded body and prayed for any miracle.

No one was coming. It was eerily quiet. No barking or whining from Strax either. God knows where her beloved canine was.

Kate then raised her head to try and make sense of it all. How life had yet again taken another chance at love away from her. She wiped the small scarlet drops from his nose with her kerchief. Her timepiece buzzed and she quickly checked it. The time had stopped; the face was red, and then faded to black. Lord Wilson was truly dead.

Don't wait. Jilly's and Mr. Scott's words echoed. *I fucked up. I waited. I had the opportunity.*

Regretful tears rolled down her face as Kate gently brushed her fingertips over his lips. "I love you. I always did." She whispered and slowly kissed him. "For a last time."

Time, Kate remembered Dr. Harrison's time machine. She dashed down the spiral stairs to his lab. *Maybe he and the equipment hadn't been affected by the blast?*

As Kate burst through the door, she was shocked to see a stranger standing over Dr. Harrison's dead body. A thick line of vermillion oozed from a fatal bullet wound to the doctor's forehead. The aggressor was wiping his pistol clean. He looked at Kate with a wicked grin as he tucked it into his waistcoat. His face had been ravaged by some sort of blaze, the skin far too taught over his cheeks and thickened with scars.

"Oh Miss Church, I think you're just a bit too late to help anyone." He snarled which made his burned face even more repulsive.

"You bastard." Kate spat at her new adversary, a traitor to The Society.

"Bastard? Hmm, hardly. In fact, you killed a friend of mine in Chicago just a few short months ago. A mentor, father figure if you will. You managed to kill his son as well. And you insult me by calling me such a vile name?" He clasped his gloved hands in front of him and eyed her warily.

"Hmm, and what is your name then?" It suddenly occurred to Kate that The Mass had done a serious job in penetrating the Society. They had known that there was one more son and a mother left alive in the wicked Ellis family. It had been presumed he'd returned with her to England. Apparently they left another mole behind to finish the job.

"Mr. Crisp. But you won't need to remember that because you won't be alive much longer."

"Like the Ellis'? They got what they deserved." Kate replied calmly. She wanted to keep him distracted. Only he stood in the way of the machine that may or may not change everything.

"But you must question, are we really that awful? The Society gives you everything but the one thing most people are willing to die for, their freedom. Our side, well, we offer so many freedoms. Are you sure we couldn't yet persuade you to join us?" His eyes raked over her. "You have so many talents."

"Never." Kate continued to remain in control as she measured the room for possible weapons. Suddenly, being in the lab reminded her of one of her new inventions. Kate had worn her safety corset that had special pockets in the cleavage. The low cut red silk dress gave her perfect access. Kate did not let this realization show on her face. She feigned a haughty air as her gloved hand grazed her neckline.

"Well Miss Church, I'm a bit different from the Ellis clan that had taken me in. I don't fall so easily for the ladies. My stepmother always said I had the coldest heart of all her boys, but then again she adopted me. I was made to hunt; to capture and kill without recompense. My younger step-siblings, well, they were good men. But they enjoyed women. I suspect each of them fancied you in some way and hoped that perhaps they could turn your heart to them a bit. But I know better. You loved the man that's now dead upstairs.

Ironically, that same gentlemen ruined romantic notions for me long ago.

For me, it doesn't matter anyway. I like to kill as much as I like to make love. And right now, I need to kill you. I won't make the same mistake as Drasco or my adoptive brothers. I like to be efficient. I like to save time. And that is why you won't be able to use this lovely machine." He reached in for his pistol.

In a flash, Kate pulled two of her handcrafted gear moon stars from her décolletage. In quick succession, she knocked the gun from his hand with one and spliced open his throat with the other. They whipped through the air with the speed of a hummingbird's wings. Crispy fell to the floor as blood spewed from the gash in his neck. Kate quickly jumped over him and collected her weapons. He tried to speak as he was dying. Kate leaned in closely as she wiped the bloodied sharpened gears on his ascot.

"Now that, that was efficiency." She winked crisply at him as he perished.

Kate turned her attention to Dr. Harrison's invention. Their previous conversation had been brief, but the details came to her as if she'd heard them only minutes earlier. Kate hopped into the box's platform and fixed her eyes on the control board. She was relieved to see that the clock on the machine was still working.

Kate prayed as she estimated how much time had passed since the blast at the Main Hall at 8pm, right as the winter festival started. According to Dr. Harrison, she would only have fifteen minutes for changes to take place. She set the time back to 7:50 p.m. The blasts had been about two minutes apart.

So little time to save everyone, she worried. The time was now. *Don't wait.* Kate inhaled deeply, grasped the support bar of the machine's framework and popped her timepiece into the opening.

After her pocket watch was sucked into the divot with a sturdy click, she pulled the red handle. There was a bright flash and a jolt. Kate blinked as wooziness settled over her.

Dr. Harrison looked up at her in astonishment. He'd been cleaning up to prepare to attend the holiday festivities.

Kate jumped up without missing a beat. "Doctor, I am glad to say your machine works." Her excited tone changed to one of urgency. "Get out, now. Don't wait, someone is coming to kill you. Trust me, run to the garden, it's safe there."

And with that, Kate ran up to Lord Wilson's study. But he wasn't there. She called out briefly, but no one answered, not Strax, not even the Leeds'.

There was no time to search for them. Kate bolted to the Main Hall. When she arrived, it was packed with revelers. She'd hoped the bomb they'd set was like the one Drasco had fashioned; water had stopped it. Kate went to the nearest fire alarm in the foyer of the Main Hall and gave it a good yank. Horns immediately sounded as water seemingly sprayed from everywhere. Weaponed Members ushered everyone outside. She called for Lord Wilson, but remembered he hadn't wanted to be at the gala without her. It was already 7:55 p.m.

One more to save, Kate thought, *surely he would be in his library by now.*

She tore back through the grounds in the wet snow using every ounce of speed she could muster. As she approached the Manor, a light went on in the library. It looked so peaceful, but the stunning library would soon be a trap.

Kate's boot heels clanged on the spiral stairs as she charged upward. *I must save him.* She burst into the room with a tremendous clatter and completely out of breath, while grabbing the doorway for support.

"Miss Church, I was just coming to get you, the Leeds have already left for the party. I-" Lord Wilson squinted over his spectacles in amazement.

"We, have to go, now." Her chest heaved in fear as Kate attempted to run across the room and tripped on the carpeting with a nasty flop on the floor.

"What the devil?" Lord Wilson chortled. He came round to his charge to help Kate from the ground while trying to hide his amusement.

Kate scrambled as her heels caught in her dress and pain shot through her left leg. She'd twisted her ankle in the fall. "Now, we need to go. There's a bomb. For God's sake, pick me up. If you love me, we need to get out. Outside. Now!" She cried in her hysteria.

Lord Wilson's heart began to pace in panic. Kate's folly was not a show. "How long?"

"Four minutes." She reached for him with a fear in her eyes he'd never seen before.

He rushed to her side, scooped her up and in one fell swoop was out the door. He held Kate tightly as if she would die should he release her. The icy cold rail of the stairs chilled Lord Wilson's bottom as they slid down. He popped off the end with aplomb and took off headlong into the Manor's garden. He hoped they could reach a group of sturdy pines before the blast. The terror in Kate's eyes made him believe that a serious explosion was eminent. They needed as much protection as possible.

Kate buried her face into his chest and clung to his neck as he panted through the snow. She could no longer imagine life without him. *Don't wait.* Mr. Scott's and Jilly's words echoed in her head as they fell to a bed of prickly pine needles. "I love you." Kate whimpered as he shielded her with his body.

"Oh my Kate, I love you too." He kissed her as the library exploded in a hell of flames and shattering glass. Their bodies were pushed forward several feet in the wet snow as the roar and heat reached them. With loud snaps, errant pine cones and dead branches fell about them.

Lord Wilson inhaled deeply and gazed at the devastation behind him. A smoldering wreckage of twisted steel, papers and books belched grey smoke into the chilly December night. He turned back to Kate. "How did you know?"

"I lived through it the first time. You didn't." Kate gasped as she tried to sit up. Her heart finally slowed as she realized she'd succeeded in saving him.

Insistent barking from Strax startled them both. A dark figure was running from the Manor and heading for one of the Society's walls. The canine tore after the bomber, quickly closing in on the criminal, but only managed to bite off a snippet of his coat as he cleared the top of the sturdy brick.

"Strax! Here boy." Lord Wilson's call echoed on the snowy grounds.

The dog bounded through the drifts with sweet abandon to come lick the faces of his masters. "Good boy, good boy." Kate stroked his fur.

"Do you know who it was?" Lord Wilson spat as he assisted Kate. Never had the Society suffered so much loss on their grounds.

"He said he was a Mr. Crisp. He's part of the Ellis family. Do you know him?" Kate grumbled.

An anxious look furrowed Lord Wilson's brow. "Are you

certain?"

"Yes, why?"

"I'll explain later." Lord Wilson worried. His former friend had been rumored to be part of the Mass after his near death in London. *So long ago and he's still out for revenge,* he mustered. Their conversation was interrupted by a familiar band of friends.

"Are you alright?" Dr. Harrington yelled as he approached with Mr. and Mrs. Leeds not far behind.

"Other than a few banged up limbs, I'll think we'll be okay." Lord Wilson stood.

"Good God man, that was quite a blast. Miss Church, you're a life saver," Dr. Harrington gushed.

"Are you alright dear?" Mrs. Leeds cooed and knelt next to her mistress.

"Just a bit of a sprain." Kate grimaced as Mrs. Leeds unlaced her boot.

"How did you ever know?" Her assistant inquired as she prodded Kate's leg.

"Just a hunch." Kate gave a sidelong glance at her Senior. Very few Members would know the truth of what happened that night. Any more possible moles would be kept at bay.

"Well, the Hall fared much better. Sprinklers went off, perhaps at the first sign of smoke. A hell of a mess, water everywhere. Someone intended to do quite a bit of harm." Mr. Leeds gazed back at the Society's stalwart building.

"Dr. Harrington, can you assess any damage to the lab? Leeds, if you and the Mrs. would be so kind as to check on the remainder of the Manor and attend to Strax? Don't touch anything in the library. It'll need a full examination. Miss Church and I will need a few moments in the greenhouse."

"Yes Sir." The Leeds left round to the front of the Manor.

Once out of earshot, Lord Wilson leaned into his lab assistant. "Give me a full report of stats. I want to know any effects of the change."

"You're reading my mind, Sir." Dr. Harrington hurried to the blackened door of the lab. He shuddered as he turned the knob knowing that if Kate hadn't acted so quickly, he'd be dead. "Thank God Miss Church, thank God for you," He whispered to himself as he set about collecting various bits of data.

"And you, young lady, need a good dose of serum." Lord Wilson winked at his Member and carried her off to the cozy warmth of the greenhouse.

Once inside, he set Kate down on the pruning table and plucked a few fresh leaves from the serum plant. "Open." He gently commanded.

"Oh yes Sir." Kate grinned and stuck her tongue out at her Senior in jest.

He squeezed the purple gel in, with a tender hand closed her jaw and topped it off with a sweet quick kiss.

"Ummm." Kate murmured.

"Delicious, yes?"

"Tart, yet sweet." She smiled coquettishly.

"Just like you." He teased as he pulled a cloth from a drawer in the table, and then bent to inspect the damage. He snipped open her tights and let his fingers softly graze over the swollen skin. He carefully smoothed the serum over her bruised ankle while a mischievous grin emerged on his face. "Miss troublemaker." He chided as he wove the strands of cloth over the wounded limb. "Remember what happened when we were last here?"

"I don't think I'll ever forget." Kate ran her fingers through his hair.

Lord Wilson's eyes sparkled as he kissed over the cloth and made his way up her leg. He pushed up her torn stocking while easing his lips to the inside of her knee.

Kate shuddered and closed her eyes as a tingle grew inside her.

A small crash outside startled them, as a loose piece of metal fell from the damaged library. "Well, I take that as a sign that we need to check on the others." Lord Wilson laughed. He stood and pulled himself betwixt her legs and kissed her deeply before Kate could respond.

"And I'm the tease?" Kate guffawed as he pulled away.

"So much more than that." Lord Wilson's smile suddenly erased and his eyes dropped down while he absently rearranged her skirt. "You mean the world to me."

Kate felt pangs of guilt. "None of this would've happened had I said yes." She stumbled.

"No Kate, all of this and much worse would have transpired." He paused as his fingers interlocked with hers. "You said I died. And who else?"

Kate cleared her throat. "Dr. Harrington. And many others from the Hall."

"How did you know?" He pried while feeling the smoothness of her fingers in his hands.

"I couldn't wait. Something wasn't quite right." She inhaled as the pain of what she'd seen returned. "I thought I heard something in the quiet of my room. My attendant had just left. I went down the hall and a Member slipped away from the men's wing. I hadn't seen him before, so I went to follow but he'd already gone down the lift. I was curious to see where he'd come from. I noticed Mr. Cole's door was slightly opened and I could hear the ticking." Kate's eyes welled with tears. "I didn't even look, I knew what it was. Eight was a perfect time. The party downstairs would be starting. The Hall would be filled with Members." She began to hiccup her words. "I ran for the stairwell. I was almost at the bottom when the bomb went off." Kate was shaking now as she fully recalled the devastation.

"Go on love. Tell me what happened. Tell me so you can forget later." He stared deeply into her eyes as he continued to rub her hands softly.

"There were horrifying bangs. I don't think that was the only bomb. I'm almost certain. I could feel an intense hot rush of air and I stumbled back onto the last stair landing before the bottom. The window behind me shattered, like all the others. I shook my head to try and clear it. I couldn't quite hear for a moment. I'd almost forgotten where I was. I checked myself. Other than a few cuts, I was fine. I stumbled down the last flight to the door. It was blown from the hinge. I hurried down the hall to the party and, and-" Kate paused as sobs racked her body.

"Shhh, darling. Tell me. It will be alright." He continued to lock his gaze into hers.

"And there were bodies everywhere. Blood and limbs. Glass, lots of glass. Bits of furniture and, oh my God, people aflame. Oh

Jesus Christ, Members were on fire. They were melting. Some climbing into the fountains and snow to put themselves out. And screaming. Like hell had been released in the Hall." The horror on Kate's face stunned even the most steely part of her Senior.

"So then?" He moved a hand to her cheek and rubbed it with great care.

"I couldn't take it, I almost fell to the ground, but I went outside to try to clear my head. Make some kind of sense of it all, you know?" Kate's voice had grown small and wooden. "I saw a flash and heard another loud bang only seconds later, from across the grounds from the direction of the Manor. I-I ran as fast as I could." Kate stuttered. "And, and you were dead." Her voice cracked into a hush whisper. "Oh God, oh my God." Her head rolled forward into Lord Wilson's chest as she again wept hysterically.

Lord Wilson wrapped his arms around her. He wanted to pull her out of this memory, but he needed just a tad bit more information. "Shhh, shhh." He doted. "Come now; tell me how you rescued everyone, my brave strong lady."

"I-I thought about the time machine, so I ran down. And Mr. Crisp was there."

"Yes, dear. And tell me. What did he look like?" He pried ever so gently. It was a delicate task to bridge her minds of hysteria and sanity.

"I was confused. He was burnt, but it didn't look fresh. Oh God, he'd shot Dr. Harrington. Somehow he knew about the time machine. I would suppose Cecil, Mr. Cole, I mean, Ellis, had alluded to it. I guess he was waiting to see if anyone survived to claim it or perhaps steal it? I have no idea." A perplexed look crossed her face as Kate calmed. "I fought him and I hit him with the shuriken."

"The what?" Lord Wilson tried to hide his surprise. He didn't want to break the state of conscience he brought Kate to. He made a mental note to question her about this new weaponry later.

"Moon stars. I'd made them from gears and slipped them into my corset. They slashed his throat. It bled horribly." Kate winced.

Lord Wilson hid his shock at his charge's violent defense. "Oh, I see. And then?"

"I changed the time. Dr. Harrington was there. I told him to run. Then, then, I couldn't find you." Kate began to bluster again. "I had to run back to the Hall. I hoped they'd used the same bombs like the ones in Iris. Ones affected by water. I pulled the fire alarm and ran all the way back again, because, I-I" Kate's words fell out in a flurry of sadness. "I could not bear to lose you. Not again, never again. I should've, should have. Should have said yes. No more waiting. I was wrong. I was an utter ass of a human being." Kate whined as she nearly collapsed backwards onto the table.

"Shhh. Wake, Kate. Wake." Lord Wilson brushed a hand over her face with a wry smile. She'd uttered the words he'd longed to hear.

With a mighty heave, Kate inhaled sharply and grasped Lord Wilson. "Oh God. It was horrid."

"I see, I see." He calmed as Kate came around to the present. "It's going to be alright."

"But, but, I wanted to tell you that, I'm sorry. And I say yes. I promised. I mean, I meant to say yes to everything. I promised that I wouldn't wait anymore." Kate stuttered as her eyes widened.

"To what darling?" Lord Wilson grinned, selfishly wanting her to repeat herself.

"To you, to here. I want to stay. Here. With you, forever."

She threw her arms around his neck. "I know I'm being silly. But I mean it." She looked down as she flushed.

"I know you do, my darling Kate." He wiped her tears as he somehow managed to halt his own. "You've made me unbelievably happy." He paused for a moment to bury the sudden desire that rose within him. "But now we must check on the others."

"Blimey, what a mess." A cockney accented janitor mopped away at the mini lakes that filled the Society hallways. "Are all the buildings like this?" he whined. Others around him nodded. The water system on the Society grounds was most advanced for its time. All major spaces were equally protected once the alarm was sounded. Only the individual homes held by loftier Seniors were different.

There had been three large explosives in the Hall which was almost over-kill. Two would have taken out enough Members to halt works at the St. Louis Society for a very long time. A fourth, from Miss Church's estimates, had been planted directly under the library of Wilson Manor. It was a very personalized statement directed at him. Without Kate's intervention, the casualties would have been insurmountable.

After the foiled bombing, cleaners, Members and staff were everywhere in a flurry of tidiness. Mr. Roth gazed at the flood of people and water. He shuddered at what might have been. He met Miss Pratt at the lift.

"Miss Pratt." He tipped his hat.

"Director Roth." She smiled.

He closed the gate as the elevator took them upstairs. "Glad they've got this up and running. The third floor should be dry soon. The others by morning," the Director mused aloud.

"Yes, those massive heating units from Development are quite amazing. And your office?"

"Dry as a bone, I'd say. Very lucky." He looked at his lady and for a moment, wished that he'd had more backbone to say what he wanted. After what happened with Lord Wilson and Miss Church, he didn't want to stir up a hornet's nest. There was a disease at the top level of the Society. It had managed to infiltrate them and was looking for any signs of weakness. His relationship with Miss Pratt would remain a secret for now. He grasped her hand and turned to her. "I am just as lucky to have you."

"And I am as well." They shared a pleasant smooch as the lift stopped. Miss Pratt tossed him a sweet look over her shoulder as she headed for her private quarters. Mr. Roth hurried to his office with anticipation brewing. He couldn't wait to hear exactly what the hell had happened.

"So we now know for certain that Crispy is alive?" Director Roth took another deep inhale of a rare cigar. According to Kate, a hole ripped all the way through the building from floor to the roof where Mr. Roth's office had been before she corrected time. He would never again save cigars for special occasions.

"Yes. Miss Church described him to a tee, burn scars and all." Lord Wilson poured a deep glass of expensive alcohol. It was more than time to bring out the good stuff.

"And he implied that the Ellis clan adopted him. In his twenties no less, how quaint," the Director sniveled. "And just how did infiltrate us?"

"Much more simply than the others, as a Gardener. He didn't say much, just pretended to hang decorations. It gave him opportunities to set the bombs that Cecil Ellis had created. The bastard had stowed them in an airtight copper box in the toilet." Lord Wilson stifled a laugh with a swig of whiskey.

"Shame his ass didn't blow up when he took a shit." Director Roth took another drag of his rare tobacco. "Tomorrow we vet everyone. Again. No stone unturned. Each room scanned for any possible deterrents, even fucking broom closets. Any possible clue for where he's headed, plans, etcetera. Today is the last time, I swear to God. And I will personally extend my apologies and congratulations to Miss Church tomorrow. I am proud to have a woman like her as a Senior Member." He winked. "And how is she?"

"Collecting the rest of her things to bring to the Manor." Lord Wilson grinned. "She didn't want to wait."

"Good show, Sir. Well done. We'll expect a wedding then?"

"Yes, New Year's Day. Again, she didn't want to wait."

"My dear old friend, I know you didn't either. We all owe our lives to her and that miraculous machine."

"Did you feel the movement, the change?" Lord Wilson inquired with a curious look.

"Good God man, I was fucking Miss Pratt on my desk. I thought I imagined that I could keep it up for so long. And she climaxed twice. Or so we thought." The Director gave a deep belly laugh.

"Can't say fairer than that." Lord Wilson grinned wickedly as the two raised their glasses and downed their drinks in the early hours of a new day.

"Alright then, no more of these middle of the night Discussions. I am going to spend the rest of this Christmas with Miss Pratt. I do believe she was heated again just as the alarms sounded. I intend to, ahem, finish the job." Director Roth stood and shook Lord

Wilson's hand solidly. "Godspeed my friend and Merry Christmas."

Kate tucked the music box into its packaging one last time. At the Manor she'd be allowed to openly display it. It was the last item packed. Miss Beatrice locked the last steamer trunk with a wry smile. "That will be all then Miss Church."

"Yes. Thank you for serving me so well. I'm sure you'll be assigned to someone just as lovely."

"Oh indeed Miss. I received an Engagement of a different sort today." Her help extended her hand. A lovely yellow stone was perched atop a golden band. *Rewards, rewards,* Kate smiled to herself.

"Congratulations then." She gave the attendant a warm hug as a knock on the door interrupted their good-byes. A phantom buzz tickled her waist. Suddenly Kate realized she'd left her pocket watch with the Traveler.

Lord Wilson stepped in with two male attendants that briskly took away Kate's belongings to be whisked away to the Manor. Miss Beatrice exited with them. "You are ready then?" Lord Wilson held her coat.

She looked around the room briefly and then turned to face her fiancé. "As I will ever be."

Fenton Crisp discreetly rewrapped his wounded hand in the luxury car of a train bound for Boston. "Damn dog," he muttered angrily, pulling the bandage slightly tighter than it should've been. Strax's teeth had locked onto him just as he'd finished placing the bomb under the elegant framework of Wilson Manor's library. "After all that preparation, Cecil didn't mention the fucking dog."

After the Leeds had left for the Winter Festival, Lord Wilson had run to the greenhouse for a moment. He'd wanted a fresh red rose in his lapel, for he was certain Kate would accept his proposal. Once he'd plucked the sumptuous beauty, he'd remembered to pull the ring from his desk in the library. He'd intended to leave Strax napping in the warm comforts of the greenhouse, but in his haste hadn't closed the door completely. With a gentle breeze of night air, the door pushed open just enough that the canine smelled an intruder on the grounds. It was only a minute before he dug his jaws into the unsuspecting Mr. Crisp.

The bomber bit his tongue in order not to scream. Lord Wilson had just gone back upstairs. His timing couldn't have been more perfect. The earth seemed to move beneath him for a moment. Mr. Crisp hit Strax flat on the nose with the butt of his pistol with enough force to escape. He fell to the ground from underneath the steel architecture with a painful thud and ran for his life. There would be no time to see the Traveler, a machine that could be just as important as the three keys.

He ran through the snow with Strax close behind when the library exploded with tremendous force. Mr. Crisp wondered why the bombs in the Hall hadn't blown.

The Ellis clan knew their explosives. Miss Avery had helped devise the trap that night long ago in London. Once Crispy overcame his anger of near death and the loss of Elizabeth, he was more than happy to join in the revenge against Lord Wilson. His old friend had become his nemesis in an instant. The people he'd thought were his enemies, were now family to him. Miss Avery soon became Mrs. Ellis. She and Mr. Ellis treated him with the kindness of parents even though Fenton Crisp was already well into adulthood.

He dreaded telling Mother of the foiled plan. Mr. Crisp had used a wireless he'd stolen from the Hall to contact Mrs. Ellis. "And so they all live and you weren't able to secure any information on the

Traveler?" Her voice clipped at him through the new-fangled phone.

"I'm so sorry. I was prepared to take it when, well a dog-"

"A canine? What? You were stopped by a fucking dog?" Mrs. Ellis hissed into the receiver. "Well, there is no way to salvage this. Come to Boston. We'll leave for London to set new plans in motion there." On the other side of the line, Mrs. Ellis lit a fresh cigarette in frustration.

"Yes Mum. But I don't think that the time machine worked." Mr. Crisp whispered as he tossed the wireless into the Mississippi and boarded the train to reunite with those who intended to inflict the worst of evil. Fortunately for the Society, the Traveler had erased all memory of that lost moment in time. Further attempts at revenge would have to wait.

The diamond sparkled brilliantly in the early morning light. Kate took another long look at her left hand, almost not believing that even her fingers existed. *I'm really married. How did this happen?*

At that moment, the only thing that Kate wore was the ring the beheld the shimmering rock, thick blankets and the arm and leg of her husband wrapped around her. Lord Wilson's face was buried in the pillow above her head. The reflection of sunlight sent patches of extraordinary hues across Kate's face. She closed her eyes and smiled.

It had been a blissful week. After the night of the foiled bombing, there were a few Discussions to clear up old business, but Kate and Lord Wilson were quickly married. They decided not to wait until New Year's, and married the day after Christmas. The Manor was a bustle with temporary repairs when Kate moved in. There were no Engagements planned, no work to be done for the next week. They enjoyed a small honeymoon at home with horse rides around the grounds, tea and chess in the short afternoons, and long evenings of dinners and love making.

On New Year's Day, Lord and Lady Wilson had finished a most satisfying breakfast. Plates were being removed when a most handsome grin spread across Lord Wilson's face.

"And what is this shenanigan about?" Kate shot a suspicious look at her new husband. Christopher had given her many surprises that week. New jewelry, clothing, and more love than she realized that another human being could possess.

Maybe too much, Kate wondered, for when she awoke the day before, the sheets had been spotted with a bit of blood. Mrs. Leeds had been able to change the soiled bed before Lord Wilson had noticed. It had continued on a bit during the day and finally stopped. Kate made a mental note to speak to Dr. Finch as Christopher strode to the Christmas tree a last time. She turned her attention back to her husband.

"Another gift?"

"Yes." Lord Wilson handed her a small black box.

"You shouldn't have." Kate replied sweetly.

"Well, I had to my Lady Kate. Go on, open it."

Kate gently pried open the velvet box to reveal a shiny new pocket watch, with an equally elegant chain. Her fingers ran over the exquisite image of a magnificent rose on the front. As expected *"For the greater good. L.K.W."* was on the backside. She popped open the inside to a pleasant surprise engraved in the tiniest of script:

"I envy the felicity of it,

That it should be so near your side,

And so often enjoy your eye,

But have a care for it,

For I have put such a spell into it;

That every beating of the balance

Will tell you 'tis the pulse of my heart,

Which labors as much to serve you,

And more truly than the watch;

For the watch I believe will sometimes lie,

And sometimes be idle and unwilling,

But as for me, you may be confident,

I shall never."

"Now close your hand over it for a moment," Lord Wilson whispered. It stirred with a familiar buzz just as he checked his own time-piece. "Now then, we are reconnected." He put a gentle hand over hers.

"As we ever should be." Kate smiled. "That is lovely. What is the inscription from?"

"A love letter that Sir Christopher Wren wrote to his wife after he'd fixed her timepiece. He was an architect that rebuilt a large portion of London after the Great Fire, including St. Paul's Cathedral."

"How beautiful. That's amazing. Incredible, really."

"And practical of course," Lord Wilson mused. "Your old one melted into the Traveler. It had to be replaced."

"So time really was lost?" Kate punned as he pulled her close.

"Yes, gratefully so." Lord Wilson paused. "I hope to show you the Cathedral when we go to London this summer. It's quite astonishing."

"Oh that would be lovely, I can't wait to see it." Kate gushed with a gleam in her eye.

Little did Lady Kate Wilson know that she would soon see far more of the Cathedral than most.

The End

End Book Two of The Society Trilogy

The Society Trilogy:

Book 1- Strax and the Widow

Book 2- Revenge and Machinery

Book 3- From Lafayette to London

ABOUT THE AUTHOR

Victoria L. Szulc is a multi-media artist currently using Steampunk as one of her themes. She "lives" her art and has explored various hobbies and passions including: drawing, writing, volunteering, karate, yoga, singing, voice-over work, belly dancing and weather spotting.

Made in the USA
Charleston, SC
25 August 2016